WORTH

Jon Canter is the author of two previous novels, *Seeds of Greatness* and *A Short Gentleman*, both of them adapted for BBC Radio 4. He has also written stand-up comedy, television and radio scripts for many of Britain's most prominent comedians, and comment pieces for the *Guardian*.

Praise for *Worth*

'Hilarious... Smart, confident and, in places, eye wateringly upfront'
Elizabeth Buchan, *Sunday Times*

'As an advertisement for either urban or rural living among self-satisfied characters, *Worth* is a toe-curling horror story; as a cheeky and well-directed poke in said characters' eyes, it's a winner'
Independent on Sunday

's a sympathetic writer and one with a keen eye and ear for the absurd. There are sentences on almost every page which raise a smile'
Scotsman

'A consistently funny skewering of middle-class clichés with memorable characters and a dark twist'
Shortlist

ALSO BY JON CANTER

Seeds of Greatness
A Short Gentleman

JON CANTER

Worth

VINTAGE BOOKS
London

With thanks to Janette Canlin

Published by Vintage 2012

2 4 6 8 10 9 7 5 3 1

First published in Great Britain in 2011 by
Jonathan Cape

Vintage
Random House, 20 Vauxhall Bridge Road,
London SW1V 2SA

www.vintage-books.co.uk

Addresses for companies within The Random House Group
Limited can be found at:
www.randomhouse.co.uk/offices.htm

The Random House Group Limited Reg. No. 954009

A CIP catalogue record for this book
is available from the British Library

ISBN 9780099546825

The Ra   wardship
Council (ganisation.
Our boo   ied paper.
FSC i   leading
e   )ur

Prir   PLC

For Helen Napper

PART ONE

I used to be pretty. The night I met Renate, I was pretty but newly bald. What little hair I had, at the sides and back, I'd taken to Maurice, the owner of a West End barbershop. Maurice charged little but talked a lot. He had photos of boxers on his walls, boxers whose hair he'd cut. Judging from the photos, a boxer with a Maurice haircut always won, at the cost of that haircut getting sprayed with his opponent's blood. Maurice, whose style was itself pugilistic, razored and erased my remaining hair, acknowledging defensively that it was my head to have done to it what I wished, then adding, offensively: 'Why would a nice-looking boy like you want to look older?'

I was twenty-nine, no age to be thought a 'nice-looking boy'. I wanted to say to Maurice that my nice looks – by which he meant, surely, not my scant hair but my full set of eyes, eyelashes, cheekbones and lips, all those things which can't be shaved – were problematic. A nice-looking boy, like a nice-looking girl, can be wanted for his looks alone. You can easily assume that's all he has to offer. He can be mistaken, by women of strong will, for some kind of doll, and presumed to be lightweight. He'll revel in that light weight, for a lightweight man has less of a burden to carry, and indulge his tendency – his inclination – to be superficial and passive and lazy, which, let's face it, are enjoyable things to be. He'll be immature, since these strong women, who in turn

3

enjoy being strong, will want to be mature on his behalf, which is to say, control him. Such a man – such a *boy* – might well want to be bald, precisely because that will make him look older. Once he looks older, he reasons, he'll act older.

The look comes first, you see. That's the trouble with his (my) reasoning. That's your proof that I wasn't yet ready, at twenty-nine, to be a mature man. My new baldness didn't make me older. It didn't even, as I well knew, make me *look* older, whatever Maurice thought. A shaved head, when he gave me one, was a fashionable thing, as was a visit to a barbershop with a red-and-white pole, when you could afford to go to a salon. If anything, a barbershop-shaved head made me look younger. This was something Maurice, a seventy-year-old barber, wouldn't understand.

To be older, I had to get over Renate. But first, I had to meet her.

I'd been a copywriter for seven years, at an ad agency in Hanover Square, having graduated with a degree in art history. Why did I, as an art historian, want to be a copywriter? At my interview, that was Stone's first question – Stone who had his name on the door, Stone of Hammond Law Stone Fisk, Stone who, in his signature gesture, ran both his hands (both!) through his lustrous black hair. In what way was studying art history preparation for writing press copy, radio commercials and TV commercials about cars or pet food or fax machines? (It was 1994.) He asked this in his overemphatic, too loud voice, as if there were several of me, then leaned back in his chair, cocked his right leg and planted the sole of his right deck shoe on the edge of his desk, the better to seat himself and unseat me. Then – in a gesture I'd soon learn to loathe – he pushed with his foot and sent his chair rolling back on its wheels, till he bumped into the radiator; then, a minute or two later, he extended his arms backwards, like a man about to dive into a pool, and pushed off from the radiator to return to his desk. This was meant to make him look and sound – wheee! – like a free spirit, a corporate maverick. He rolled backwards, he rolled forwards. He *rolled*. I gave him an unsatisfactory answer, softly and coolly, knowing he'd respond to the softness and the coolness, not the answer. I could tell he'd schooled himself in management – he took pride in his ability to see below the surface of my answer, to the ninety per cent of my personality that lay, iceberg-style, beneath.

I ached to work for myself, if only to avoid questions such as Stone's. Myself would demand of me no bogus explanations. Myself wouldn't ask me, in the mirror, where I saw myself in five years' time. Myself would understand there was no pattern to the things I'd done in my life, in the order I'd done them. A curriculum vitae was an attempt to make sense of a life that had none, a life that was one damn thing after another. Butcher, baker, candlestick-maker, rich man, poor man, beggar man, thief. In what way was a degree in meat studies preparation for working with bread?

Stone, I learned, had taken up mountaineering since his second marriage had ended.

'Why mountaineering?' I asked Geoff, my art director, a giant Northerner. Geoff was a very Northern Northerner, with a dread of saying anything that might be thought pretentious. Stone, Geoff said, took up mountaineering because he was a 'twat'. He thought this the reason for all Stone's actions. He longed to be Stone's therapist, so he could tell Stone, for money, once a week, for an hour, that Stone was a twat – and when was he going to do something about it?

Geoff and Stone won seventeen awards for their 'Romeo and Juliet' TV spots for Fiat Punto, in which Romeo, a blue Punto, falls in love with Juliet, a pink. Everyone remembers the pink Punto driving onto the balcony, its headlights flashing as Juliet 'speaks'. I saw the commercial the other night, when I couldn't sleep. It was featured on *100 Greatest Car Commercials*. It came in at 39th, though it didn't seem any better or worse than the ones that came in 99th or 9th. Watching it made me sad. The false enthusiasm that prompted its writing and making had long since gone. That false enthusiasm was, in any event, paid for by Hammond Law Stone Fisk; it was bought false enthusiasm, which made it doubly melancholic. I was not only sad but annoyed. Romeo and Juliet are star-crossed lovers from warring families. It's a nonsense to make them different-coloured members of the same automotive clan. Why didn't I think that at the time? Oh yes, the idea was mine (and Geoff's). But somehow Stone, who was, as he would be, in the room when we presented it to him, believed the idea was his. It was Stone who was on *100 Greatest Car Commercials*, talking about what made it Greatest. (Shakespeare transcended boundaries. Shakespeare was upmarket and down-market too. Shakespeare was – wait for it, wait for it! – 'one helluva car salesman', followed by a grin of expectation that viewers would clap their hands and say, out loud: 'I *like* this man.')

Stone took the credit but I was indifferent, which infuriated Geoff. But indifference was my style, my credo. Indifference *worked*.

The receptionist at HLSF sat behind a desk wide and deep enough for six newsreaders and their shuffled scripts. This acreage was an advertisement for the agency's success: it made itself look successful by wasting its own space. No receptionist, though, sat behind that desk for long. How many times can a person say: 'Hammond Law Stone Fisk how can I help you can you hold please he /she's in a meeting can he/she call you back?' In the years I worked there, a dozen receptionists came in, sat down and, a few months later, got up and left. The fourth or fifth, Bonnie, was fired for answering the phone thus: 'Hammond Law Stone Fisk. Why don't you fuck off?' The caller, a client, insisted this was a personal attack, which was nonsense, since Bonnie didn't stop to find out who he/she was before telling him/her to fuck off. Bonnie had been to drama school. She had a strong if metallic voice and sang at the office Christmas party. She wanted to be in musicals, not trapped behind a reception desk in a verbal telephonic dance. It was Fate, not the client, that she was telling to fuck off.

I made a point of ignoring Bonnie, as I ignored all the receptionists. Their position on the social and sexual front line embarrassed me. Every lecher, every time-waster, every sad man, every messenger and monger of gossip stopped to talk and laugh and flirt or – Stone – show her the photos of his latest mountain. I simply walked to and from the lift without giving the receptionist a second glance. I made a show of my indifference.

A month before she was fired, Bonnie came up to me on a Friday night, after work, in the Bunch of Grapes. She asked me why I was a mystery man – what made me so special? She was both hurt and intrigued. A few days later, Geoff demanded to know why I hadn't told him about my going to bed with Bonnie, which he'd been forced to hear from Oz in TV Production, the only receptionist who graduated to a better job within the agency. I shrugged, which angered him even more. I didn't believe I owed it to Geoff to tell him about my sexual activities. He thought otherwise. He thought I was being superior by not sharing the information.

'You think you're so bloody clever, with your mystery act. It's all a big technique.'

Geoff was right. Every time I passed the receptionist, I gave her no second glance; but I gave her a first, oh yes, intending her to register it and wonder why it wasn't followed by a second. Geoff, of course, had no mystery and no technique. Instead, he had a wife. He and Sonia had been together since they were fifteen. She was his first girlfriend and his first and last wife. The notion of 'technique', where Sonia was concerned, was ridiculous, implying a gap between Geoff and Sonia, in which Geoff could operate and somehow 'work' her as a driver works a gearstick. Geoff raged against the articles in Sonia's magazines, which often told him to buy her a negligee.

'What the fuck's a negligee?' he'd ask. 'Is it something transparent, cos I tell you what, she's transparent enough already.' I was cool, which he wasn't, and never had been or would be. No husband-and-father is cool. In that very reception, I had seen him holding a twin girl in each arm, and then Hannah – or was it Emily? – deposited a slick of vomit in the gap between his collar and his neck.

Why else did I smoke, except to be cool? At Bristol University in 1993, there was a Smoker of the Year Award, which I was too cool to enter but, despite or because of that, won. It was the paucity of drags that caught the eye, said the chairman of the judges, in the pub where I was given my prize: a dozen packets of Gauloises Disque Bleu. I just waited and waited, he remarked, between drags, letting my cigarette burn down, allowing the red heat to march on my fingers, till the viewer was mesmerised by the long and precarious snout of ash; I'd flick that off, drag briefly and hard, then take the thing out of my mouth and leave it out, for ages. It was the non-smoking, that's what won the award.

Bonnie was the second of the two receptionists drawn to my 'technique'. The first was the aforementioned Oz, born Ros but nicknamed Oz, because she was Australian. I played no part in her nicknaming, though I benefited from it. Ros was frank, cheerful and loud, sometimes so loud she seemed desperate, which frankness, cheerfulness, loudness and desperation were magnified once she became Oz. Her Australian-style femininity: that was the thing for which she was known and liked, so she marketed it. She over-Australianised herself. And so it was that, one day when I was walking through the empty reception, she remarked to me that we must 'do it sometime'. I didn't demur. I sort of shrugged, which was the cool equivalent of bursting through a plate-glass window, on a horse, to rescue her from a burning building.

At seven the next morning, the phone rang in the flat Oz shared in Mile End, just as we were having sex. I say 'just as', though the sex had been going on for some time, with no sign of an end. So, when the phone rang and Oz said, 'That's Mum,' I took this as my cue to withdraw.

'No,' said Oz, pressing me on the buttocks with both hands

– I was lying on top of her – to indicate I should stay inside her. Then she reached over, took the bedside phone off its cradle, wished her mum a good evening and told her to hang on. At that point, she flipped us like a couple of contiguous burgers, putting herself on top of me; then she sat up, placed a hand on the wall above the headboard, for balance, while she held the receiver in the other, and returned to the call.

'How are you?' She bounced. 'How's Dad?' She bounced. 'Judith? Robbie? How's Gran? How's Peg?' She stopped bouncing. 'Oh no! Is she going to be all right?' I gathered that Peg was a dog who'd been hit by a car, which Judith, a learner, was reversing. Now Peg had her front leg in plaster. Her left. Then Oz – 'Is it OK if I do my exercises while I talk to you, Mum?' – began to bounce again, asking after various friends and the Melbourne weather, then proffering the bounce-worthy details of her faraway English life, with its work and its shopping and its flat and its films and its weekend in Brighton – 'Just a fun thing, Mum!' – with a male colleague, who turned out to be Stone. This was news to me, as Oz acknowledged, by briefly taking her hand off the wall and putting a shushing finger to her lips. I lay there, maintaining my penile stance, as she went on to itemise the items she'd bought at the Dickins & Jones sale. Then she put the phone down and said, in lieu of an orgasm: 'Shit, it's ten past, you'd better go,' signalling that we should travel separately to work. As she eased herself off me, she added, in her branded Oz way: 'You can come on the tube!'

A month later, the phone rang again in Oz's bedroom, just after seven in the morning. It was on my side of the bed, so there was time enough for me to say: 'That's your mum, isn't it? Sex?'

'Hold on, Mum,' said Oz. Then she got out of bed and opened the window, as if she wanted her mum to hear the noises from the street, in the way that a radio reporter wants to broadcast the local atmosphere. Then she picked up my shoes and threw them out, singly, in different directions. Why had I assumed there'd be sex, just because there'd been sex before?

I never found the shoes. I crossed and recrossed the Mile End Road, in my socks. I walked up and down on either side, but I couldn't see the shoes, only cars, buses, bikes, motorbikes and people. The shoes must have landed on or near people. But those people didn't want to get involved with those flying, landing shoes. They weren't interested in the shoes' story, with its anger and loneliness. Maybe no people saw my shoes. Who sees two shoes on the Mile End Road? Had they landed in the countryside – had they landed in The Lane, Worth, Suffolk – everyone would have seen them. All the nine or ten folk who walked The Lane of a morning, walking for walking's sake, as opposed to the money-seeking walk of morning Londoners, would have gazed on them in wonderment and looked around, to see whence they had come. Cars, in Worth, would have stopped.

Before I descended into Mile End station, for the long L-shaped underground journey that would take me to the Archway flat I shared with Sam Davey, I took off my socks, even though they were my only protection against the shit, gum and burger juice that are shoe-massaged into the skin of the city. In socks, I looked like a man who'd failed to put on shoes, because he was mentally incompetent. In bare feet, I looked like a man who had chosen to walk barefoot. My bare feet were a *style*.

When I got back and told Sam Davey the story, he remarked that I never, in my sexual life, 'got beyond Reception'. I didn't argue. Arguments are not laconic and I shared Sam Davey's laconic way. He and I had been best friends since we were sixteen, not that we'd ever use the smiley phrase 'best friends'. My few words, Sam's fewer: we were drawn together by that lack, wanting only to express our cynicism with maximum drollness, maximum cool, maximum minimalism. We found our place on the sidelines and stopped there, scoffing, choosing to arrest our own development. His father was a caretaker, his mother a nurse; my father an antiques dealer with worn-out shoes, my mother dead. We were not born to money but could be cool without it, in our south

10

London state school. And we drew. That was the coolest thing. We drew dogs, we drew people, we drew Alice Taylor, the most beautiful girl in our year.

Drawing was the one thing Sam Davey wasn't cool about. He drew with an intensity I found alarming (and hoped Alice Taylor would find alarming too). He lost himself in the detail of her windowpane-check skirt. He had the talent and the technique to lose himself. I didn't. As an artist, I was never not self-conscious. I decided, early on, that the drawing was not 'about' the windowpane-check. It was about looking at Alice Taylor's face, for as long as I could, without the obligation to speak to it. The quality of a drawing, I decided – for, though I didn't say much, I thought a great deal, I had Radio Self on all the time, with its sixteen daily hours of speech – was not in the detail but in the capturing of a mood. This, in its vagueness, was a very convenient thought. I couldn't compete with Sam Davey, so I didn't. Sometimes I think I would have tried for art school, not a history of art course at a university, if I hadn't sat next to him in Alice Taylor's bedroom and seen him drawing that skirt.

I got Alice Taylor, because I was prettier than Sam, but couldn't keep her, because she needed to know what I thought and felt.

I met Renate at the private view of Sam Davey's *Crowd Paintings* at the Bethnal Green Gallery. I own his first *Crowd Painting*, which he did when he was sixteen. It's a painting of our 1989 school photo, an astonishing feat of painterly endurance. I paid him five pounds for it. Sam Davey reckons, with his droll bitterness, that it's now worth five pounds. He thinks he'd be famous if he were autistic and painted his crowds from memory. But he's not and he remains 'on the cusp of being fairly well known', a phrase he puts into every description of his own work, knowing the gallery will remove it and replace it with something like 'his work explores ideas of individuality within a societal context' or some such value-adding blah.

11

When Renate came over, I was standing with him and Dad. Dad was looking from painting to painting, counting out loud the red dots which indicate a painting has been sold. Dad is the same age as Sam Davey and me; he was at school with us. Dad, whose real name is Paul Baker, passed his driving test on the day of his seventeenth birthday. He used to drive the three of us to parties in the suburbs of south London. Once, he drove Sam Davey and me home from a party to which he hadn't been invited. He came to the house, at one in the morning, to collect us. We knew nothing of this till the hostess brought us to him. He was standing on the doormat, refusing to come any further, for fear of being thought a gatecrasher. We were astonished that anyone would do such an *old* thing. So, as we got in his Austin Metro, cruelly sitting together in the back, we gave him the nickname 'Dad'. It was the sign of our gratitude and ever-so-slight contempt, which was unworthy, because Dad was a good and kind man, even at seventeen, who (excessively) valued our friendship, thinking us 'interesting' and himself dull.

I felt Renate before I saw her. She came up behind me and placed her palms on top of my now-bald head, then slid them down slowly over my ears, till I heard two whooshes – as if my head were a rock between two seas.

'I'm Renate,' she said, in her German-American-accented English. (The German because she was German – her father was BMW's European Marketing Director – the American because she loved America.)

'Richard,' I replied, offering her my hand, countering her extravagant gesture with a calm how-d'you-do. I was asserting that she wouldn't unnerve me – I'd match her every overstatement with an under. (This was my notion of 'asserting myself' as opposed to, say, pushing her over and running for the door.) I felt queasy with excitement. This was love at first sight, as it always is, the love defined in those first moments, terminally. Sure enough, for the next four years, Renate and I had a queasy and exciting love, with Renate dominating me, because I let her, pretending that if I knew she was dominant, that made me wise to it and somehow strong.

'What do you love to do?' That was her first question. Not 'What do you do?' but 'What do you love to do?' It didn't sound like spoken English. But it had to be answered. I told her I loved drawing animals. She said that if I blew them up to 'ten metres tall', I could exhibit them in the gallery where she worked. I didn't think this was a good idea – my animal drawings, mostly of my father's Labrador, painted over the thirteen years of its life, designed to give me something to do when I spent the day with my father, weren't good enough to be magnified to 'ten metres tall'. No, it was a terrifying idea, but it had the ruthlessness and clarity of a successful one. Renate was just a young woman working in a gallery for hardly any money. But she was so famous and unavoidable in those few square feet – the ones occupied by her and me and my friends – that it was easy to foresee those square feet would become a square mile, a county, a country, and so on. And so it proved. In the years I was with her (which is to say next to her or near her or behind her), Renate became more and more successful. The last time I saw her, in a dentist's waiting room in Suffolk, half an hour's drive from The Lane, Worth, she was in a photo in the *Sunday Times Magazine*, one of the Fifty People To Watch Out For in 2006. She was smiling as she stood on the bonnet of an open-topped car on Mulholland Drive. Of course, this being a rural dentist, to whom news travels slowly, it was already 2009. But there was nothing faded about Renate. She looked like a rocket about to take off.

Renate didn't want me to be as successful as her, no more than a gangster wants his moll to be as good as him with a gun. I was expected to be at ease with successful people and their sidekicks (of whom, of course, I was now one). Successful people were the only people Renate knew, or wanted to know. That was why, the night we met, she never addressed a word to Dad, who looked neither like a successful person nor an attractive sidekick. He looked like a dull person in his own right, so she didn't waste an instant unearthing his qualities, even though she was a ferocious unearther. I didn't protest on Dad's behalf; I never protested on anyone's behalf, not even my own. I simply went with Renate's flow, which took me to Berlin and Paris and Rio and the cocaine-lined bathrooms of models and singers and actors and artists, much to my colleague Geoff's disdain. He accused me of being too 'interesting' for the beer-and-fags after-work camaraderie of the Bunch of Grapes pub, off Hanover Square. He loved, though he pretended he didn't, to hear my tales of a club called the Where House. There, at four in the morning, Renate and I and her friends (for our friends were always her friends) checked in our clothes at the cloakroom and danced naked till it was light and time to go home. Geoff was nauseated. He didn't want to be 'hit in the face by tits at five in the morning', instinctively picturing a scene that was farcical and wearisome, spitting that 'five in the morning' as if the tits were conspiring to keep him awake. For the scenesters, though, it was thrilling, but not in a sexual way, no, we were running on narcissism, we were dancing with ourselves. 'Firestarter' by the Prodigy: that's my naked song, the song they played at the Where House every naked hour. I cannot hear 'Firestarter' without thinking about myself.

Renate thought the Where House 'amazing'. But then Renate drew on a bottomless, self-filling well of amazement. Everything connected with fashion or fame astonished her. I was with her the day she moved into her flat in Belsize Park. (Six months later, when she told me it was time, I moved in there myself.) I opened the door to the plumber, who'd come to plumb her washing machine. He was a big man, maybe six foot six, with a gold chain round his neck. I can't remember his name. I can only remember what she told me about him, in his presence, as he put his metal briefcase of tools on her marble counter: 'He is the plumber of Noel Gallagher!'

'Amazing,' I said. In deference to her, the word was now my default utterance; it was what I said when she offered me a cup of coffee. 'The plumber of Noel Gallagher': it was an unfortunate phrase, as if he had inserted his hand inside the blocked Gallagher and watched with satisfaction, on withdrawing it, as a tide of anthemic songs poured out of the great man. How was it that we shared a plumber with the architect of Britpop (who always seemed to me, an instinctive Blur man, to be more of a builder)? This was what Renate wanted me to ask. But I didn't give her the satisfaction. I didn't care or, to be accurate, I cared but I didn't *want* to care. Later, while Renate was on the phone to her best friend Ingrid, I watched my clothes tumble over each other, shirt-sleeves flailing. The washing machine's gdug-gdug became, in my head, the fearsome wail of 'Wonderwall', Liam Gallagher's voice going round and round, round and round, as if there were a dog trapped in the washing machine, its head stuck to its tail, howling Britpop up its own hole.

When I saw the plumber out, he confided in me: he hoped the machine didn't leak, or she'd be down on him like a ton of bricks. Women like her 'turned'. They were nice to you then something went wrong and they 'turned'. Why was he telling me this? Because he didn't think that 'she' and I were a couple. He thought I was some kind of servant, like him, and/or some kind of gay. I should have said: 'Don't talk about my girlfriend like that!' But I could never say of Renate that she was 'my girlfriend'; I was her boyfriend. And she did. She did 'turn'. I had seen her, not an hour before, in the baker's, 'turn' on the woman who'd earlier sold her an organic rye loaf. In Renate's opinion, it didn't have enough seeds.

Renate always called her 'my best friend' so Ingrid would feel explicitly obliged to call Renate *her* best friend. As the best friend and boyfriend, we had much in common. We understood the attraction and repulsion, though Ingrid was healthier – more feminine – in the way she argued with Renate, then got over it, whereas I did nothing and waited for Renate's mood to change of its own accord.

Ingrid had done a year's architecture at the Royal Institute of Technology in Stockholm before succumbing to modelling, since she couldn't walk down a street without being 'spotted'. (She regarded modelling, like I regarded advertising, as something you did which didn't define you.) Ingrid was beautiful, where Renate was sexy, but she couldn't understand the expectations her beauty aroused in men. Men became besotted with her and expected to have sex with her. That she understood. 'But why do they expect me to help them choose a birthday present for their sister?' I shook my head. I could understand, but I couldn't explain.

One morning, as I breakfasted and Renate rowed nowhere, fast, on her rowing machine, she asked me if I'd like to have sex with Ingrid. Since they were best friends, I assumed they'd discussed the matter. I gave one of my accepting shrugs.

I had been with Renate for four years, as far less than one half of a couple. I wanted to leave her but didn't know how, or did know how but didn't have the courage so to do. Now I found myself in a state of sublime mental ease. I wanted to split up from Renate; and here was Renate, splitting up from herself on my behalf and, what's more, telling me that Ingrid would be my next girlfriend. It was as if I were standing on a dotted line, which I didn't even have to sign.

'She is my best friend. Of course you love her,' said Renate. 'We'll have big sex together.'

My head flopped forward as if I'd been shot. Renate wasn't handing me over. She was retaining me and adding Ingrid, thereby doubling the number of those she controlled. Three is a crowd and she loved a crowd, did Renate. I can't think of her without a crowd, having met her in a crowd standing with its back to paintings of crowds, 'private view' a misnomer for that collective unseeing of an artist's work, in favour of drink-fuelled gossip. Sam

Davey paints crowds but is isolated from them, in his studio, painting them from photographs or his crowded imagination. He's compelled by but wary of crowds, which (ironically) take him away from his place of work. But Renate has no such ambivalence. She lives for them. If there's no crowd, she wills one into being, as I discovered that first night I was with her, when she shouted: 'I love your cock!' What did she mean, she loved my cock? She barely knew it. But there she was, shouting at it, literally shouting at it as if my cock were deaf, which naturally it is. But I'm not and I was on the end of it, my ears no more than three feet away. Here was Renate, with her magnificent body, which seemed to be composed of outsize fruits, a body which I was later told had 'the best tits in the art world', by that expert source, Renate herself; here she was, with her hands on my cock, growing it, and yet my queasiness outdid my excitement, because the shout could only have been for the benefit of the crowd, which wasn't there. Like Sam Davey, Renate has a crowd in her head, but she plays to it. The crowd in her head goes 'Renate!' and she in her head goes 'Whoo!' Renate is a performer, so you, as her partner, are her fellow performer, whether you want this or not. What's more, her performance doesn't vary, from the public to the private space. There's no stillness, as for the camera. It's always an arena perform-ance, of Bono-like self-regard and scale. To be close to Renate, as she performs, makes a man feel alone.

Renate formed Renate Management in 2003. Traditionally, artists had been represented by gallery owners, who took forty or fifty per cent. Renate took twenty-five, for which she not only sold your work but arranged for your washing machine to be mended or called your baker to bawl him out. She sold your work despite not having a gallery herself. She hired places in which to exhibit your work – clubrooms, warehouses, the Where House. For the art-seeker, these places were often hard to find, which only added to their allure. Of course, as an artist, you might graduate to a conventional gallery. But you'd take Renate with you, on a fee basis, because you knew you couldn't do without her. Who'd confront the gallery if you felt they were doing you wrong? It was your job to make art, it was not your job to confront. Confrontation was Renate's job. Job, pleasure and compulsion. What's more, Renate knew everyone, which was always to your benefit. Renate knew everyone as God knows everyone – she knew what they were doing, even when they were on their own, and she believed they felt bad if they weren't paying some kind of obeisance to her. So she'd call them and tell them they should write an article, for the *New York Times*, about John Smith.

John Smith was her first client. I never liked Smith, a skinny man of almost violent ambition, with a fat blond moustache which was wider than his mouth and more than covered his upper lip. If you put your face under John Smith's and blew upwards, the moustache would flap. I wanted to do this the first time I saw him; and then I never wanted to do it, ever.

Did Renate like John Smith or only pretend to do so because of her job? All I know is, she told me I'd like him if I tried harder. But I didn't want to try to like him, and I hated the notion of catching myself, or being caught, in that act. So I found a way to be or not to be with Smith, which involved no trying. I absented myself and hoped he wouldn't notice my absence. I never agreed with a word he said, of which there were thousands. But neither did I disagree. My body was there in the room with him but not my personality. In all this, I made a terrible mistake.

Renate made no mistakes with John Smith. She took pride in him, had faith in him, mothered and fathered him. She gave birth to him, in fact. When she met him, his name was Angus Campbell-Brown, which he didn't think was right. He wanted a neutral name that made you think of nothing. Renate came up with John Smith, the first English name she'd ever heard. Angus clapped his bony hands and smiled at me, telling me, in his Edinburgh burr, how lucky I was to be with a gorgeous genius. I blanked him with my best Warhol stare. I warholed him, or so I told myself. Then he puckered up and gave Renate a dry kiss on the lips, in his pseudo-flirtatious style. Angus was only interested in men and John Smith would be no different.

Renate told me John Smith would win the Turner Prize. She was right. John Smith won the Turner Prize for *Something/Light*, which was exhibited in Berlin, Tokyo and Rome before coming to London to be shown with the work of the other shortlisted artists. You entered four rooms with walls and a floor and a ceiling and an attendant. In each room, the lighting changed from blue to red to green to yellow, over a two-minute period. That was it. A lot of people were angry with John Smith. They thought he was a con man laughing at them. They were wrong. He was the opposite. He was a non-con man not laughing at himself. Smith was completely sincere, if that's what matters, and devoted his life – and therefore Renate's and mine – to talking and writing about the ideas behind his ideas. The idea of *Something/Light* was, I thought, tiny; you could pop that idea in your top pocket and forget it was even there. But the booklet he wrote to accompany his exhibit was forty-eight pages long. He was like a painter who paints a dot then puts it in a sixty-foot by sixty-foot frame. There were at least four pages about the attendants, whom Smith described as 'components'. I hope they never read that booklet. They thought their job was to sit there and attend, making sure nothing was touched. (What could be touched? The ever-changing light?) But John Smith had decreed they were part of the play they thought they were watching. And if John Smith decreed it, it became true. That was the genius, if not the art, of John Smith.

The night after he won the Prize, John Smith celebrated with a party in his loft. His loft was, technically, not a loft, being on the third floor of a four-floor building overlooking the Thames. But this was the end of the Loft Age, when what was once pure was now mainstream. Loftiness had spread to lower floors. You could have the loft aesthetic – the openness, the wood, the sense of a unified life – on a third floor, a second floor or even a ground floor. Dammit, you could have a bungaloft.

We were all there, 'we' being Renate and Ingrid and Sam Davey and I. The longer I was with Renate, the more time I spent with Sam Davey, to Renate's irritation. He was not an artist she wanted to manage. That didn't trouble Sam Davey, who knew he was never going to win the Turner Prize; he was, in his own estimation, a 'blunting edge' artist. But Renate couldn't believe he didn't want something from her – management – which she didn't want to give. What he wanted, of course, was to amuse, and be amused, and unsettle the powerful with his jibes and his irony, verbally tunnelling under them then attacking from behind. He wanted what he'd always wanted, since he and I were teenagers. But we were thirty-three now. We were meant to *be* the powerful, or speeding down the highway to the houses where the powerful lived, in order to evict them and take their places. Instead, we were in John Smith's loft, thinking sneering teenage-style thoughts about the Turner Prize winner and his manager. What kind of man sits with his old friend and sneers at his own 'girlfriend'? It could not end well.

At ten, John Smith was still talking about where he went from here, by which he meant from *Something/Light*. Sam Davey and I, who didn't care where he went, were doing coke in the kitchen, which, sadly, was separated from the living space merely by space. There was no place, in John Smith's loft space, where you could get away from John Smith's space. Where we wanted to go from there was a John Smith-free space, a restaurant – preferably with John Smith paying. How could he talk for so long without eating?

'To the centre of the world!' said Renate, without warning, standing up and raising her glass. Everyone except John Smith stood up and raised their glasses. (Renate, who'd given up drinking, had nothing in her glass but raised it, nevertheless, and knocked back the air.) Why didn't John Smith stand? It can only be that he thought he was the centre of the world. Like a bride at a wedding, he couldn't stand for the toast to the bride.

'I can't take this any more,' I said to Sam Davey quietly. With that, I went to the coat hooks opposite the front door where, surprisingly, there was a wall. It was December. John Smith, a fastidious man, had hung his winter coat on a hanger and put the hanger on a hook. I touched the right-hand breast of his coat and felt its wallety heart. Then I took the wallet out of the coat.

My heart was going boom-diddy-boom; but that was cocaine, not conscience. From the wallet, I took out a wad. I'd never seen a wad like it. There seemed to be about two thousand quid in the wad. I divided it in two and stuffed it into my pockets. The wad chafed my thighs. The money *hurt*. I gestured to Sam Davey, from my concealed position, and we left, without telling anyone.

I counted it out, in a restaurant in Knightsbridge. We'd decided that John Smith would buy us dinner, with whatever money was in his wad. It was a matter of honour that we wouldn't spend his money on anything else. But we'd spend *all* his money. I wasn't going back to his coat, to stuff his change in his pocket.

When the waiter came over, I indicated the freshly counted pile, which I'd placed totemically in the centre of the table. I told the waiter we wanted food and drink to the value of nine hundred and sixty pounds.

'Does that include service?' he asked. We liked him for that. He was cool. We said it didn't. We thought we owed it to John Smith to pay for the tip ourselves.

The waiter took us, I guess, for famously obscure T-shirted people, possibly the bass player and drummer for a massively successful band, whose rhythm section waiters could not be expected to recognise. Certainly, our order had a rock'n'roll stupidity: one Duck Liver Pâté, at eight pounds twenty-five, one Smoked Salmon and Scrambled Eggs, at nine seventy-five, and two bottles of Château Lafite Rothschild, at four hundred and seventy-one pounds each.

We asked him to repeat our order. He told us, with professional pride, that this would not be necessary.

'We'd just like to savour our order,' I said. He nodded and repeated it.

I smiled at the woman at the next table. She was sitting opposite a bullfrog of a man, much older than her. While he was slurping his oysters, she was looking at anything that wasn't his face; hence her alighting on mine. I hoped, for her sake, the man was her father, not her lover. Sam Davey reckoned she was an escort. He fantasised the bullfrog was paying her 'a John Smith', as if the unit of currency in this restaurant were nine hundred and sixty pounds.

At three in the morning, I was in the bedroom of Renate's flat, weeping from everything: John Smith's space, the coke, the theft, the Turner Prize. I was weeping because I couldn't remember the taste of my bottle of Château Lafite. Surely I was owed that memory, after spending four hundred and seventy-one pounds. But no, I remembered only the price. Then Renate came in, with Ingrid, and asked me where I'd been and why I'd disappeared without telling her. I said I'd gone for a meal with Sam Davey, which ended her interest. She went off with Ingrid to rummage through a pile of CDs, giggling. Why didn't they notice I'd been crying? Even men would have noticed.

I went to the bathroom and did something I've never done before or since: I used vomit as a weapon. I vomited with malice aforethought, attacking the water in the toilet bowl. I was sick of – sick *against* – my life.

I stared at my sick: my share of the food and the wine and the tip, my five hundred and thirty pounds' worth of puke. It looked so average, so mediocre. It looked like any old used food that stinks at you from a gutter. I flushed.

John Smith was in the living room with Renate and Ingrid, who was dancing. Renate spoke for John Smith, as managers do. 'John's money was stolen from his coat in his place.' Ingrid carried on dancing.

'Did you see anyone go to his coat? Some of those people we didn't know so well.'

I shook my head.

John Smith smiled at me. 'It's only money,' he said.

'You'll make more,' said Renate. 'Clothes off!'

Renate turned up 'Firestarter', to a volume fit for those who live at the centre of the world, and don't care who knows or hears.

Wherever John Smith went, I avoided him, using the medium of dance. I'd lost myself in 'Firestarter' a hundred times. It wasn't hard, with twirls and head-snaps, carpet-gaze and ceiling-gaze, to lose John Smith too. Much of the time, I simply shut my eyes and shook my head, as if responding to the mania of the song, but of course I was saying no-no-no to myself, over and over.

I heard Renate shout: 'Where are you going?' Then John Smith shouted back: 'You'll see!' Ten seconds later, I felt it was safe to open my eyes.

Ingrid and Renate were dancing together. I couldn't see Smith. Then Ingrid and Renate stopped. Ingrid had her back to me, obscuring my view of Renate. On Ingrid's right buttock was a tattoo of a black cat with green eyes. The eyes were disproportionately big.

'Oh yes!' said Renate, clapping her hands with approval as John Smith – so that's where he went – returned from the CD player, having put on Spandau Ballet's 'True'.

Renate, a woman of strong opinions, had always hated that song; now it was John Smith's choice, she applauded it.

Was that a lie, a change of heart, or management? She spun Ingrid round and, from behind, cupped Ingrid's breasts with her hands and squeezed; and now I couldn't count the ways I felt nauseated and re-nauseated, as Ingrid, facing me, yawned. Of all the things she could have done or said, she yawned, as if bored by having her breasts squeezed by Renate, as a boss might squeeze them, a sweaty nylon-shirted boss in his nineteen-sixties heyday, all brute and Brut, squeezing his secretary's breasts from behind as she made his tea.

Then the women danced around me. I felt Ingrid's nipples on my shoulder blades and her hands on my buttocks, which was all good, but then Renate turned her back to me and reversed, thrusting her bottom into my groin, and wiggling it. This was, theoretically, very exciting, but the furious pendulum motion of Renate's buttocks was too much like the action of a dog. Renate was like a dog drying itself on its back on a carpet, which made me the carpet. I was a fucking carpet, that's what I was. I was as sexual and aroused as a carpet.

I turned away. *I know this much is true*, said the song, as I found myself lip to lip with John Smith's big blond moustache.

'Let it happen,' said Smith. After drooling this cliché, his mouth stopped moving. His face descended. He knelt in front of me and placed my shocked cock in his mouth. But why was it shocked? John Smith was a Turner Prize winner. He had the egotism and ambition to make the world accord with his vision. He'd decided that my indifference to him – the blanking, the silence, the absence – was a come-on, which was fair, given that this had often been my 'technique'. But I didn't want to be fair to John Smith, that triumph of certainty over talent. I was outraged. Then the outrage passed and I felt the justice. I'd brought John Smith upon myself, by taking nine hundred and sixty pounds from his wallet. John Smith knew I'd taken his money and was exacting justice. He was the police, the prosecution counsel, the jury. He was the judge who'd sentenced my cock and the jailer who'd locked it in his mouth. And then the outrage returned. This was no justice. This was torture, which no one deserves. John Smith's mustachioed mouth was no soft O. It

24

was more like a dustpan and brush. His lower lip was the pan and his fat moustache was the brush, feverishly sweeping my cock clean, hurting it, giving it brush-burn. My cock had never felt more disturbed. It flopped and stubbed about. Frustrated, Smith withdrew. He got to his feet and placed his hands on my shoulders.

'Make yourself hard and come back,' he whispered. Whispered! This was John Smith's lovey-dovey-speak, his erotic manner. I nodded. I turned and walked, as slowly as I could, past his and my and Renate's and Ingrid's clothes, which would doubtless stay on the carpet till the cleaner, later in the morning, bent down and picked them up.

When I got to Renate's bedroom, I sat down on a corner of the bed, which she owned but I shared. This was the beginning of the end. Of that I was sure. But I'd been at the beginning of the end for a long time. When she put her hands on top of my head and slid them down over my ears – that was the beginning of the end. I'd grown accustomed to it.

I put on a new set of clothes and walked down the corridor. Happily, I was able to pass the living room without being seen, since Renate's flat was composed, in the old-fashioned way, of doored rooms.

It was five in the morning when I set off to walk to Sam Davey's flat, the one I'd shared with him before I moved in with Renate. I walked the hard way, via Hampstead and Highgate – the uphill, along and downhill way – to prolong the journey. Every time a light went on, I felt sad. How many of those lights were switched on by a woman without a man? What was a man in a city supposed to do? Was he meant to stop, whenever a light went on, and offer himself up, knowing there was every chance he was not the man for this woman and she was not the woman for him? Such were the infinite possibilities/impossibilities of the city. Every time a woman moved out of her place, or paired up, another one moved

25

into another place, or separated or – God help us all – was born, then grew up, then was twenty when I was fifty-three. Would I walk these streets at fifty-three? Which of these women would I look at, when I wanted to look at women? Did I have the choice not to look at the twenty-year-old women? I mean, would I look at them whether I wanted to look at them or not? I ached to live in a place where there were no women, or one woman.

Sam Davey, who painted till two in the morning, would be angry when I woke him up. I saw that with a sun-rising clarity as I walked down Highgate Hill to Archway. But when I rang his bell, I didn't wake him. Renate had already called him. When he said he didn't know where I was, she accused him of lying, of siding with me against her. And then she accused me, in my absence, of preferring him to her.

I stayed at his flat for the next two nights, making plans to call Renate and tell her that our relationship was over. That's right: I spent two nights planning a phone call – the dialling, the waiting, the 'it's me', then the saying and the fear of the response. The fear was that Renate would want me back, because I was the only one who didn't want something from her. She had told me this, many times. I was the only one she could be with, when she was depressed, because I didn't demand anything. That, as she saw it, was a beautiful truth, whereas I saw it as an ugly one: why didn't I want something from Renate, in exchange for giving something? Why did I feel all right with her, when she was depressed and asleep? Why, though I demanded nothing, did I take so much – all my food, all my lodgings, all my instructions?

On the second night, a removal van drew up outside Sam Davey's flat, ready to disgorge its contents: my clothes and a leather chair that smelt like an old horse. It was my only contribution to Renate's furnishings. She'd always loathed it and now she'd returned it to the flat whence it had come.

For those two mights, I reverted, for comfort, to my past life with Sam Davey in our Archway flat, with this difference: that though the food was just as bad as it had always been, and the conversation just as sporadic, the music was new. He introduced me to the Strokes, whom he loved. I loved them too. I felt, as I listened to them, that music was more important than life.

'This is incredible,' I told him. 'These people are younger than me but I love them. They're the first band that's younger than me that I've really loved. That proves I haven't lost my touch.'

He looked at me, as he'd never done before, with pity. I knew I shouldn't stay there any longer.

Geoff gave me a room in his and Sonia's house. He gave me the back room on the first floor, where they kept the suitcases and the tent. On the first night, I went to bed at half past eight. I listened to him, in the next room, singing a lullaby to the twins. And then he came into my room and, between grins, sang Spandau Ballet's 'True'. (Oh yes, I'd told him everything. I wanted to tell the story, out loud in the air, where it's not so frightening.) And then he kissed me – on the forehead – and left.

I lay awake, listening to the twins talking. A week later, I rented a one-bedroom flat in south London. That was decisive. But the decisiveness is misleading. I knew I didn't want to live in a one-bedroom flat in south London, so deciding to live in one was, perversely, an attempt to spur myself to get out of it. I needed to find out exactly where I did want to live, and with whom, and who exactly I'd be when I was living there.

A year later, I went to Sam Davey's exhibition of his latest *Crowd Paintings* at the Bethnal Green Gallery. Renate was only there in painted form. She was dancing naked in *Naked Dancing Crowd*, next to a woman with a tattoo of a cat on her buttock. Sweetly, Sam had painted me circumcised, which I'm not, so I could deny that the figure next to Renate was me. I stared at the me-figure.

27

He was a lost-and-gone man. But then a painting does that to a person. You're not immortalised by an artist but embalmed.

I turned away from it and, finding myself on my own, glanced at the suited man nearest to me, to see if he was conversation-worthy. He didn't look as if he'd welcome my verbal advance, which only provoked me. At this time in my life, I was trying harder, just as Renate always said I should. The hard-trying often left me on the edge of tearfulness or, as here, aggression.

'Hi,' I said, 'I'm Richard.' He nodded but didn't offer his name, exuding the energy-saving that comes from great wealth. (Later, I'd learn he was shy; but then he could afford to be, couldn't he?) He wore wire-rimmed glasses and looked distracted.

'What d'you do then, to earn a crust?' I asked, in a mock-matey way, already prepared to dislike him – looking forward to it, in fact. He told me he had an investment portfolio. But that wasn't what I'd asked. I'd asked what he did, not what he had. If he'd said he had some apples and pears and bananas and a stall and some fingerless gloves, I'd have understood the connection between what he had and what he did (sold fruit from a stall). I wanted to know what he *did* with his investment portfolio but, fighting vagueness with vagueness, I refused to be bothered to ask. Nevertheless, I pictured it. I pictured him entering a building at seven in the morning, then ascending to his office on the thirty-third floor, to gaze at his portfolio in the light of the morning sun.

He fell indifferently silent and I fell piquedly so. We looked at the woman to his right. She was small with brown eyes, a lovely little mammal of a woman: soft, sad and warm. She was looking at *Naked Dancing Crowd*. I hoped that, if she looked at us, she wouldn't recognise me from the painting. But she showed no sign of turning her head. She looked and looked at that painting. As guests at a private view sometimes do, she was using a painting as a way of avoiding anything and anyone else, just as the woman in the restaurant had looked at me as a way of avoiding the bull-frog. Then the portfolio man said to her: 'Are you ready to go?'

She turned her head. He told her he'd go and get their coats, which undermined her, since she hadn't agreed to their going. Immediately, I knew he was wrong for her and I was right.

'Hello,' I said, 'I'm Richard.' She told me her name was Sarah. I had only a coat-getting time to make sure I saw her again. When she asked me if I was a painter too, I said no. Then I asked her, speedily, who her favourite painter was. She said Vermeer. I offered to show her the Vermeers at the Wallace Collection.

'That sounds nice,' she said, factually but not flirtatiously. Why would she say that if she didn't think it sounded nice? Why would she agree, given we'd known each other thirty seconds, unless she had a sense that she liked me and I liked her, and that the liking was not flirtatious but a fact?

I asked where she worked. She looked embarrassed as she named a law firm in the City. (It was striking how embarrassed she was; Portfolio & Coats Man clearly worked in the City too, but had shown no embarrassment.) She told me she often worked fourteen hours a day but didn't know why she was telling me this as she earned a lot of money and she couldn't expect me to feel sorry for her. But I knew why she was telling me this: she was letting me know she was unhappy. I asked her full name and memorised it, along with the name of her firm. Here was the romantic dividend of an advertising job: it trained you to remember multiple surnames.

He arrived with their coats. She smiled but didn't say she looked forward to seeing me again, which I took as a sign that she did look forward to seeing me again, but would keep our seeing each other again from him. They left.

I wanted to call her the next morning, but waited three days, cursing myself for still clinging to 'technique'. When I called, she told me she wasn't sure our meeting was such a good idea. She felt she'd been too forward. I told her it would be worth it, if only for the Vermeers. She said that, in any case, she couldn't see me for the next four weeks. I took that as a further sign: she knew our meeting would be momentous. It deserved – and she'd give it – a build-up.

'You know I live with Mark,' she said. I took that as a third sign. Why would she tell me she lived with Mark, unless to fore-warn me of the difficulties we faced?

When she arrived outside the Wallace Collection at two o'clock, four Saturdays later, I was frightened I wouldn't recognise her. I don't mean I wouldn't recognise her face. I'm referring to her soft and warm mammalian aura. If she arrived without that, I'd feel she wasn't the person I'd met. But the aura was there, all right, it was everywhere, it arrived fractionally before she did, as good auras should. She was just as I'd remembered her, but shorter. You had to lean – if not exactly down, then in – you had to travel towards her to communicate, for she didn't have a short person's over-loud voice, not like Renate, who boomed, even though she was tall.

I felt so pleased to see her that I didn't say a thing. Nor did she. As we walked up the steps, I wanted the steps to go on for ever. I wanted the entrance to the Wallace Collection never to arrive, because I was gripped by this sudden and certain know-ledge: the Wallace Collection contained no Vermeers. Why had I said that it did?

'I'm afraid all the Vermeers are being cleaned,' I said, as we entered the building.

'Oh,' she said. And then she stopped. 'What Vermeers do they have, then?' she asked.

'Dirty ones.'

She laughed. It was the first time I'd heard her laugh. Thrillingly, she laughed with her whole torso: belly, head, shoulders, hair. She got the lot in.

'Have you had lunch?' she asked.

'No,' I said. That was my second lie to her, the dirty Vermeers being my first. I wanted my second lie to be my last.

At the restaurant, she told me she had been to a state school, as I had. Her father had been a tax inspector, but was now dead, as mine was (my mother, I mean – the point is, we were each minus a parent); and then, when a short man walked past the window, wearing wrap-around dark glasses, looking like Bono, she told me she didn't like Bono, as I didn't. These were all signs. Everything was a sign, an augury, a *hope*. Had she punched me, I'd have taken that as a sign that she was angry with me for not finding her earlier, for not saving her from the years with Mark. (Mark! What a shit name.)

'How long have you been with Mark?' I asked, pausing before the name, as if to insert the first of a pair of inverted and distancing commas.

'Eight years.'

'Eight years,' I repeated. I didn't want to damn the eight years and I didn't want to praise them. I just wanted to lay the eight years on the table, where she could see them for herself. But I didn't achieve that. When I heard my voice, I knew I was telling her that the eight years on the table stank. She was quiet for a little while. I waited for her to change the subject but she kept to it. She told me she didn't feel disloyal to Mark, eating in this restaurant, because Mark would never eat here. He only liked a restaurant called Le Petit Soldat, where he always ate the same thing (Confit of Duck). He found Le Petit Soldat perfect. There was no reason not to go to Le Petit Soldat.

Mark, she said, had a brilliant mind but found it hard to talk to people. That shouldn't be held against him. He had a first-class degree in mathematics and was an investment analyst because he responded to the intellectual challenge. He didn't pursue money for its own sake. He used it to travel and buy paintings and first editions. He loved to sing and was in a choir which would soon perform Bach's *St Matthew Passion*. He was diabetic, which accentuated his natural caution. The previous evening, he'd flown to Granada for a long weekend with his mother. At last there was something I liked about Mark: he was hundreds of miles away.

Then she told me that, before we'd spoken at the gallery, she'd seen me and thought I looked unhappy. And now, having met me and seen how little I ate – she didn't know this was my second lunch – she was convinced. I was only too eager to agree to this unhappiness, because I believed unhappiness was yet another thing we had in common. The dominant, rich and successful Renate had made me unhappy, just as the dominant, rich and successful Mark had made her similarly so. I described Renate. I told her Renate prevented me from being the person I wanted to be. Did she understand what I meant?

In the event, she kept her own counsel. We left the restaurant in silence, just as we'd entered the Wallace Collection two hours earlier. I had a plan to extend our time together – I'd suggest we go to the cinema, to give each other a rest from talking. But after we'd walked about twenty yards, she looked up at a Marylebone mansion block and said: 'Well, that's where I live.' I loved that apologetic 'well'. It told me that she didn't own the place and could envisage a life beyond it, that she hadn't been born in a mansion flat and was not expecting to die in one, that she craved the ordinary, as I did.

'Oh, right,' I said, then I stared at the flat, with an expression that was multiple-choice and therefore conveyed nothing. My expression was unhappy, yearning, determined, fawning, hopeful, despairing, loving; it was like those winter stews Sam Davey and I made in the Archway flat. We'd put a chicken in a pot and add thyme and garlic and bay leaves and a bouquet garni and red wine and a stock cube and black pepper and a pint of water, then bring it to the boil and let it simmer for a couple of hours, till all the flavours merged, to make what? Brown. The taste of brown.

The taste of brown nothing and brown everything. I looked at Sarah's flat with a brown expression.

'That was lovely,' said Sarah. 'Thank you.'

'No, thank *you*,' I said, but it came out wrong. It sounded sneering and adolescent.

'Maybe we shouldn't see each other for a while,' said Sarah, and because I had too many things to say, I said none of them. I nodded. I nodded and was cool, which I no longer wanted to be.

'Well, bye then, look after yourself, don't be unhappy,' she said. I said bye and turned on my heels. The sooner we started not seeing each other, the sooner the not-seeing would be over. That was my version of hope.

I walked towards Oxford Circus station, intending to go home to my flat and read a good book. Or a bad book. It would make no difference. I would not be able to take in the words.

What did she mean by saying we shouldn't see each other for 'a while'? How long was a short while and how long a long? And wasn't that 'we' a sign? Sarah and I were 'we'.

I didn't go down into the station.

Ten minutes later, I was back beneath her balcony, not that I knew which her balcony was, given that her section of the mansion block was divided into sixteen flats. So I rang each of the bells in turn, asking everyone kind enough to answer: 'Sarah?' It felt religious, intoning that name over and over. The final bell-answerer was a woman. I didn't recognise her voice but she recognised her name. She asked: 'Who is this?' I told her it was Richard. She paused, for me to give my surname. But I knew she didn't know my surname, so I said: 'Richard from earlier,' which she said back to me, uncertainly.

Then she sounded flustered and told me to wait, she'd come down.

She opened the door then shut it behind her, which was not what I hoped she'd do. She was calm and, thankfully, took control, suggesting that we go for a drink. I apologised, archly, for my unwarranted intrusion, actually saying: 'I apologise for my unwarranted intrusion.'

'Why did you come back?'

'I wanted to see you again.'

'Well, you're seeing me.'

She stopped. It was quarter to five, according to the shoe-repair shop outside which she'd stopped, which had a big clock in the window, because what can you put in the window of a shoe-repair shop? No one wants to look at repaired shoes. The shoe-repair shop was shut, as they always are. I pictured the madman inside, at the back, for such shops are always run by madmen, made mad by the stench of leather and polish and the days, weeks, months and years in the company of the ghosts of feet.

She stopped to indicate she was going nowhere until something was decided. I understood that so I stopped too. But I didn't stop as suddenly – as *much* – as she did. I slowed down, stopped, ahead of her, then returned to where she was standing.

She looked up at me with her stopped face, neither encouraging nor discouraging me, assuming nothing. I would have thought, given I'd come back, she could safely assume everything.

The door of the shut shop was set back from the road. I shepherded her onto the doorstep, but stayed on the pavement, so we could be the same height. I put my arms around her and she looked at me and we kissed. I couldn't remember when last I'd kissed and been kissed. It was certainly not in my thirties. The kisses – there were several – obliterated the shop, the pavement, the passers-by, the road and the traffic. Then it got to work on the other side of the street, obliterating the buildings. Then it ate up our identities, our histories, until we were as innocent, powerful and strange as two kissing babies. Missing the point, which was that each of us was giving the other everything, a man shouted: 'Give her one!' We felt each other hear him but we didn't look at him. A man in a van? A man leaning out of an open window? A black man in a white shirt? A white man in a black shirt? A man who, when he wasn't shouting at kissers, shouted on the floor of the Stock Exchange? Sarah stopped kissing me.

'Nothing can happen while I'm with Mark.' I nodded then, keen to put a question to which her answer would be yes, asked her for her mobile number. She gave it to me then asked for mine.

'Me next, darling!' shouted the man. I looked over my right shoulder. He was outside the pub, on the other side of the road: a fat, off-white man in blue jeans and trainers, in a cluster of grinning men.

The readiness is all. The readiness to get off and stay off at the right stop. Sarah was my stop. She was my terminus.

Such were my crass thoughts, made crasser by my presence on an escalator at Oxford Circus station. I'd left Sarah, for the second time, and was heading back to my flat.

As I neared the bottom rung of the down escalator, a woman stepped onto the first rung of the up. She was a big, curvaceous woman of the kind that had always been my type. Now I had no type. Sarah, the individual, had ended type. I wanted the individual Sarah. The woman smiled at me, then ran down the up escalator and met me at the bottom. It was Oz.

After she threw my shoes out of the window, Oz apologised, blaming Stone for her unbalanced state, and told me I'd 'always been there' for her. I didn't understand this. I'd been there for her twice and both times I'd been vaguely absent, which I thought was what made me attractive. Nevertheless, we had sex again and, the next morning, she took me out and bought me a pair of shoes, telling me I wasn't her type, and asking me why she always had her best sex with men who weren't her type.

While I was with Renate, I was consistently unfaithful with Oz. The key thing is the consistency. Oz and I had sex once a year, on the eighth of August. This was her idea. Stone was a difficult and mercurial character who often made her unhappy. (He insisted on keeping their relationship 'secret', though everyone in the building knew about it.) She needed to know she'd always have a man on the eighth of August, the night before her birthday, so she could begin the new year of her life feeling wanted. 'A man': that was me. I made her feel wanted, even though she told me when to want her. I made up a lie for Renate and repeated it once a year: the ninth of August was my father's birthday. His immediate family – his son and his sister, my Aunt Mary – spent the night before his birthday at his house, so they could have a birthday breakfast with him. For the first two years, I felt guilty about this lie, then angry. Why did Renate never want to meet my father? What kind of 'girlfriend', after four years together, doesn't send your father a birthday card? All she had to do was send him a card, then he could have told her his birthday was in December; at which point she could have exposed my lie. Why did Renate make it easy for me to lie to her? Why did she never remark on my Aunt Mary's devotion to her brother, given that she lived in Boston? Did Renate not remember where my aunt lived? No, she neither remembered nor cared.

Oz led me out of Oxford Circus station to the nearest pub, then told me to buy her a Campari and orange juice, a drink pink as a strawberry milkshake. Then she asked me, with great urgency, whether I'd heard about Stone.

'It's a catastrophe,' said Oz.

This was the perfect Stone-related word. His life was a series of catastrophes that didn't wait to happen but just went ahead, without telling Stone, who gave the impression he was the last to know: two divorces, a mountaineering fall, the suicide of his alcoholic brother, all of which disasters confirmed Stone in his view that he was a 'survivor'; the man mythologised himself as the central character in the song 'My Way'. And now, in his forties, he'd got in touch with his first girlfriend, the one he'd had when he was sixteen. With the mountaineering curtailed by his damaged back, Stone had taken up time-travelling, had gone back instead of up. He'd gone back to the Stone of sixteen, feeling, apparently, that this Stone was the best version of himself. Oz had told him she would wait for him to get over it. And, while she waited, she was going, on her own, to see the Abba musical, *Mamma Mia!* – the fourth time she'd done so since Stone had gone back and back and back and back to his first girlfriend.

'It cheers me up,' she said. 'But *you* can cheer me up now.' She went up to the bar and shouted: 'Anyone want a ticket for *Mamma Mia!*? Forty-two pounds fifty but I'll let you have it for twenty.' I admired her.

We drank for an hour in the pub. She talked and I listened, which is all she wanted me to do. But then I drifted, speaking but not listening to what I was saying, re-running the events of the afternoon in my head, freeze-framing and inserting deleted – no, that's the wrong word – *unmade* scenes, scenes of love-making in Mark's flat, in the living room and the bedroom, which took a deal of effort to visualise, since I'd never seen his living room or bedroom. I had to furnish Mark's flat from the shops of my imagination.

And then Oz told me I had to come home with her because she didn't want to be alone.

I said: 'But it's not the eighth of August.'

'Fuck you,' she said, then was silent, to make me fester in my own cruelty.

We left the pub. A drunk walked towards me with intent, holding an unlit cigarette. It was the fat, blue-jeaned man who'd shouted 'Give her one!' He was now three hours drunker and in another part of town, apparently on his own. He leaned into my cigarette lighter, missed a couple of times, then connected.

'Thank you very much,' he said softly. 'You're a gentleman.' Now he was alone, he was polite and vulnerable.

At Oz's flat, drinking supermarket brandy in her bedroom, I told her we couldn't have sex because I was in love with someone else.

'Are you back with the lesbian Nazi? I thought you'd broken up.'

This was toilet, photocopier and Reception talk – the nuance-free talk of the office, where everything was black and white and shorthand. How many people in that office, people I didn't even know, knew *me* enough to 'know' I'd lived with a 'lesbian Nazi'? I didn't want to be known by anyone but Sarah. I wanted a private life.

There were no curtains in Oz's bedroom, so she'd pinned dark sheets over the windows. How long had she been, temporarily, in this flat, waiting for Stone to realise she was the one, the third one, the third wife? How long would it take him to get over his first girlfriend? How long would it take Sarah to leave Mark? I didn't know Stone's first girlfriend, or Mark. I didn't know Sarah. I was a fool.

'Get your knickers off,' said Oz, who'd already done that herself. Was it mateyness or contempt or self-loathing that made her call my pants 'knickers'? I took my shirt off instead, with extraordinary fastidiousness.

'You don't need to fucking *fold* it!' said Oz.

I got into bed. I did nothing.

'Who are you in love with?' she asked.

I told her the name, though the name didn't coincide with the person I was in love with. The name was public but the person was private.

'You love screwing her, right?' asked Oz.

I took a long time to answer then said: 'I've only kissed her.'

'Wow,' said Oz. 'Everyone's going back to being a teenager. What would you like to do to her?'

'It's private,' I said.

'Fine,' she said, 'think about her privately while you're doing it to me.'

Above us, in the roof space, we heard a scuttling.

'Don't worry about him,' she said.

'What is he?' I asked.

'A rat. Or a pigeon. I'm not sure.'

She threw off the duvet cover and told me to get on with it, not in words but by pointing at the spot. She raised her legs, in a giant V-sign, and pointed at her own spot.

I wasn't to blame. The city was. It was a public encounter in an Underground station that had brought me here, an encounter which wouldn't have occurred had I been returning home, across a field, to some cottage in a country, near which no musical played.

The day and night had been a series of incidents, a fractured and unsettling metropolitan thing. Nothing had succeeded as planned, which meant everything had failed unplanned, spontaneously, bringing me to this bedroom. Sex with Sarah, which I would never have (and did not deserve), would have been a labour of love, while this was unmistakably a labour of sex, with puffings and gruntings. The urgings of Oz made her sound like a trainer, railing at a boxer. Then I shivered and she cried out, in frustration – 'What?' I'd shivered from an attack of sound, the huge angry sound of an American man on a passing car stereo, shouting at me about bitches and guns, which were nothing to do with me; consequently, I didn't hear the first few rings of my mobile. I got out of the bed and rushed to my trousers. 'Is that Richard?'

When I heard her voice, I took the phone out of the bedroom and into the kitchen and opened the window, though it was December, then leaned out, the further to distance myself from that bed, where I'd betrayed her – it wasn't a betrayal at the time, for at the time I didn't believe I'd see her again, but now I knew

I'd committed retrospective adultery, which made me feel more wretched and ecstatic, because she was calling me in the middle of the night, which must mean she wanted me.

She'd rung Mark in Granada with his mother. She'd told him she didn't want to be with him any more. He was preventing her from being the person she wanted to be.

'Something wrong?' shouted Oz, concerned, from the kitchen doorway. She had a right to be in her own kitchen doorway, a right to roam her own place, a right to be concerned, because a phone call in the middle of the night is concerning. But why the shouting? She was not at the bar of the pub now, shouting about her ticket. Why the fucking shouting? Was it born of growing up in Australia, where people lived hundreds of miles apart?

'I'm fine!' I shouted back, with an aggression she didn't deserve; and then she increased the volume by slamming the kitchen door.

'Sorry, that's the woman who lives in this flat,' I said, which was true. I wanted to say something that was true, though of course there was something of the lie in it, something of the lie in the night. 'The woman who lives in this flat' – a curious way to describe the woman, as if the woman were nothing to do with me and I had nothing to do with this flat.

I didn't say anything and neither did Sarah. The silence went on for a long time, far beyond the point at which you ask the other person if they're still there. We knew we were still there. And then the silence, which was at least shared, was terminated, at my end, by more booming 'motherfuckers', because the driver of the car with the motherfucking music, instead of driving away from this neighbourhood, was lapping it. And now I said, because I was fearful: 'You still there?'

'I'm not leaving Mark because of you,' she replied. 'I don't even know you. It's nothing to do with me who you're with.'

She sounded tearful.

'I don't even know you either,' I said. And I stood there and she, at the other end of the line, stood or sat or lay there (I couldn't say), but I could say she was feeling as angry as I was. Surely, this was how love felt. The loved one infected you with her own mood, or she absorbed your mood and shared it, but not in the sense that she halved it – what would half-anger be? – no, she felt your anger and your loneliness and your despair with you, to the same degree. You went down together.

'So when can I see you?' I asked.

She told me she didn't know if she wanted to see me. I told her she did. She said she'd made a fool of herself and I told her she hadn't. She told me she'd see me in a few weeks, which I negotiated down, with crying and silences and pleading, to forty-five minutes or so.

An hour later, I got out of a minicab and entered Mark's flat, talking. I didn't stop talking for a further hour, keeping one hand on the arm of the sofa and the other on my knee. I told her everything that had happened to me since I'd last seen her, and then I went back to 1973, the year of my birth, and proceeded, with gaps, to the night she and I had met. The windowpane-check skirt of Alice Taylor. My mother's death. My smoking prize. Stone's mountains. Renate's under-seeded loaf. Ingrid's yawn. John Smith's mouth. The stolen meal.

'Now tell me about you,' I said awkwardly, but then I wanted to be awkward. Awkwardness was a sentence I knew I had to serve. I had to live through awkward time.

She told me she had a competitive elder sister, whom she didn't like. She told me Mark was the son of a refuse collector and a Co-op cashier (his adored mother). He was the only pupil at his school who'd ever won a place at Oxford. He felt himself, at Oxford and in the City, to have the intellectual but not the social apparatus of his peers, who were privately educated, with a queue-ignoring sense of entitlement. He thought himself inferior, which expressed itself – as it had when I met him – in a chilly manner. He felt inferior so he acted superior. He hadn't eaten an avocado till he was twenty-four. And then he didn't like it.

'You can laugh, if you want,' she said. I wanted to, but I couldn't.

She asked me why I hadn't taken my hand off the sofa. I looked like I was guarding it from thieves.

'Go and wash your hands,' she said.

Three months later, in the shock of love, we were living together.

I was we. I was two people – no, *more*, there was more of me. After six months of living with Sarah, I'd gained a stone and a half. I'd swollen with happiness. And I liked broccoli now.

It was Sam Davey who spotted this. He invited Sarah and me and Dad round for a brown dinner, which he'd greened with a side dish of broccoli.

'Delicious broccoli,' said Sarah, who was kind, but had integrity, failing to praise the brown which gave her no pleasure.

'That's right,' I said. 'We love broccoli.'

Sam Davey, smirking, claimed it was his duty to tell Sarah he'd never seen me eat broccoli. He was sure I didn't love it. I either hated it or was indifferent. Sarah smiled, knowing he was mocking me but complimenting her, on her power. She had made me a broccoliphile.

I didn't smile. There was a principle here, which I wanted to defend. 'I didn't say I loved broccoli. I said *we* love it. You can love something together you don't love on your own.'

I knew as I said it – how could I not? – that this sounded like nonsense. But love gave me a licence to talk like this. I shouldn't be afraid to use that licence and I wasn't. I was fearless, emboldened, released. I'd said too little for too many years. Now I owed it to myself and my loved one to say too much.

'Why don't you just give your broccoli to Sarah?' he asked. 'Then she'd get more. Wouldn't that be better than pretending to like it cos she does?'

'It's lovely to see two people so much in love,' said Dad, sounding even older than usual and, strangely, like an old woman, perhaps a grandmother who hasn't been listening, on account of

42

her deafness, but has spent her time at the table marvelling at the young couple's faces.

Four months later, we got married in London. Then we made our decision.

Stone took it personally. Many Londoners did. He saw my quitting the agency to move to the country as an attack on him. And not just him. He told me his house was a walk away from Chinese, Japanese, Korean, Indian, Thai, Italian, Spanish, French and Mexican restaurants, as if by leaving the city I was not only betraying him but the restaurateurs of many nations.

'And what about the Geffrye Museum?' The Geffrye Museum, I learned, was also a walk away: it housed a brilliant re-creation of period living rooms, from 1600 to now. Then he paused before adding: 'Apparently.' Stone had never been to the Geffrye Museum. But it was there.

'I can go to it any fucking time I like,' he said, with alarming self-loathing. (It was well known, throughout the building, that since the breakdown of his re-relationship with his first girlfriend, Stone had started drinking heavily. How else would he drink? The man had no lightness in him.) Didn't I see that the presence of the museum, and the presence in the capital of a thousand places like it, amounted not just to a quality of life but a *quantity* of life? He allowed himself a little smile of self-satisfaction. Then he wrote down 'quantity of life' on the pad in front of him. He was Creative Director, after all, and he'd just created.

'What are you going to do in the country?'

I told him I was going to be a freelance illustrator. I was going to draw animals. This was what I'd always wanted to do and now we'd decided – my wife and I had decided – it was time for me to do it. That word – 'wife' – got to him. He had no wife. He envied me mine and resented her influence.

'You'll come crawling back in here within the year,' he said.

43

'You'll be begging me for a job. How old are you now? Thirty-five? That's too old to be doing what you've always wanted to do.'

At my leaving party, they gave me a milk churn, a cider press and a framed map of the London Underground, to remind me of all I'd lost.

PART TWO

W e'd let our lives be run by others. I was the mighty Renate's appendage, Sarah the nurse and social representative of the awkward, diabetic, brilliant, life-sucking Mark. Now we were on the same side, for and against: for a move to the country, against Renate and Mark. I had never been to the country with Renate, except for the occasional weekend, which she always shortened, by leaving on Saturday morning to avoid the traffic then returning on Sunday morning to avoid the traffic, making it clear that what she wanted to avoid was the country. The country, as she saw it, was where you went to remember how much you loved the city. But she didn't need to remember, because she never forgot. She was a woman devoted to objects and buildings and people, men and women and the things they made and bought. Nature didn't concern her. She had no garden; the one window box she owned was an artwork, containing plastic babies in soil.

And then there was the money. Our flight from London was a quest to earn less money. This was not as perverse as it sounds. The quest was to exchange lots of bad money – gained from advertising and working in the mergers and acquisitions department of a large law firm – for less money that was always and only good. In Sarah's case, this meant working four days a week as a solicitor for a homeless charity in Ipswich, the other three days to be spent gardening, walking, fruit-picking, practising yoga, singing in the local choir. We'd bought a cottage, outright, in Worth, Suffolk, with the excess money Sarah had earned, plus a lesser contribution from me.

The cottage, which was only forty minutes' drive from Ipswich, was only two hundred thousand pounds. Everything, at this optimistic time, was *only*. Sarah was my saviour, though she denied it, saying she was simply the person who'd galvanised me into doing what I'd always wanted to do. (In other words, she was my saviour.) She spurred me to make a portfolio of my drawings and then write ninety-seven emails in pursuit of an illustrating career. I saw a dozen illustrators' agents, all of whom told me it was a bad time and I stood very little chance of making any money, and one of whom took me on; and then I had meetings in the offices of art editors and picture editors and advertising agency art directors and children's book publishers. I watched them turn the pages of my portfolio. Sometimes they stopped and looked and sometimes they stopped, for a long time, but didn't look, because they were thinking of something else, at which point I was in a meeting with them but they weren't in a meeting with me.

They too told me it was a bad time. My old-fashioned, pencil-drawn style was not what people were looking for these days. Nevertheless, there were many that promised to bear me in mind if anything came up, which amounted to a promise to forget me, which promise they kept when I stood up to leave and was thanked for coming in, the thanks preceded by a deadly 'but', as in: 'But thanks for coming in.' But followed but followed but; but then there was the editor of children's books who said she had a little book about pig detectives for which I might be right, her hunch being that my old-fashioned style was (like my bald head) 'fashionable'. Was this a paradox or a nonsense? I didn't care. Renate had told me to make my drawings ten-metre-tall art. This woman was commissioning me to draw little pig detectives standing over dead bodies, with magnifying glasses in their trotters. This was nothing to do with art. I would be a craftsman, drawing pig detectives to make sufficient money to live in a cottage. Renate and Mark didn't make 'sufficient' money. Mark was an investment analyst for a private bank. He was not pursuing sufficient money, any more than Renate was pursuing sufficient fashion and fame.

Our cottage in The Lane, Worth, about three miles from the coast, was called Hay Cottage. It was one of a pair of brick/flint farm workers' cottages. The other was called Myrtle Cottage.

Mr Hargreaves, a businessman, now widowed and retired, had bought the pair in the sixties, letting out Hay Cottage and keeping Myrtle Cottage as a holiday home for himself and his wife and his two daughters. Hay Cottage was perfect for us. We only needed a two-bedroom cottage, with the second as a study where I could work. We liked the fact, the small but telling fact, that Hay Cottage was the last cottage as you headed east out of Worth. Beyond it there was nothing but farmland, then the sea. This was the nothing we wanted.

As I stood for the first time in the low-beamed kitchen, I felt elated. I'd married a woman who was short enough, as I was, not to knock her head on the beam; and I could say, over a phone, to anyone I knew in London: 'You can't miss it. It's the last cottage on the right as you drive through Worth.'

I could even say it from the middle of the road. Oh yes, my mobile worked in the middle of the road. I'd checked, not just for the thrill of knowing, but for the thrill of standing in the middle of the road, talking. You could see – or hear – the nearest car long before it arrived, as The Lane was almost Roman in its straightness. I stood talking to Sam Davey for ten minutes. How long could you stand in the middle of a road in London without being killed or sectioned?

We walked up the stairs. We looked in Bedroom One and

Bedroom Two. We glanced at the bathroom and toilet. Then we came downstairs, admired the fireplace in the living room again and returned to the kitchen. It was all over, bar the conveyancing. We would buy Hay Cottage.

'It's lovely,' said Sarah to Mr Tully, the estate agent. 'Why's he selling?' In this way she suggested, with velvet and steel, that we were keen but suspicious.

'I believe Old Man Hargreaves – ' he started. I wanted to stop him there. Who wouldn't want to buy their cottage from an 'Old Man Hargreaves'? He sounded as trustworthy, wise and old as a king in a fairy tale.

'I believe Old Man Hargreaves wants to cash in for his retirement. He's still got next door, of course, but he's getting a bit old to make the journey. So he's hardly ever here.'

'Do the daughters use it much?'

'No. One lives in Brussels and the other finds it a bit too small.'

Mr Tully was a bearded man of fifty, with a peculiar dry smell. He wore a tweed jacket, a wine-red cardigan and shiny grey trousers. In all my time in London, in all the flats I'd seen, I'd never met an estate agent so badly dressed. He could have stood in the field outside, spread his arms and scared away birds. How could you disbelieve a word this man said, when he was so blatantly uninterested in material things – in *materials*?

It was all true. Old Man Hargreaves never came to Myrtle Cottage again. We lived in Hay Cottage for months before anyone turned up next door.

Worth had a population of a hundred and fifty, which didn't include second-home owners. On the first morning we woke up there, seared by damp, we were warmed by our superiority to those glorified visitors. We lived in Worth. We lived nowhere but Worth. What, though, was Worth? Without a pub (the Bell had closed down, though the sign remained), a shop (converted and sold, as a modest third home, to a man who worked for Goldman Sachs), a church or a school, Worth was a place that existed more in the minds of its inhabitants than on a map. When asked where I lived, I never said Worth. To foreigners, I'd say I lived about eighty miles from London; to Londoners, I'd say I lived about forty minutes from Ipswich; in Ipswich, I'd say I lived near Orford, famous for its castle and church and quay and lighthouse and shingle spit and general shop. Famous to *me* for its general shop, which was the nearest to our cottage. There, on day three, I had my first conversation with a Worthian. She was at the till, ahead of me, a mannish woman in her late sixties. To judge from her basket, she lived on chocolate cake and budget, sub-drinkable red wine. She told me I'd just moved into Hay Cottage. I agreed. Hers was the cottage 'next to Keith and Margaret'. I looked blank, which was fair enough. I couldn't be expected, after three days, to know Keith and Margaret. She said hers was the pink cottage with the quince tree. That only made me look, if it were possible, blanker. She stared at me as if I didn't know what 'pink' meant whereas, of course, I was trying to remember what a quince tree looked like. I was fooling myself. I had never known.

'Where's your cottage in relation to the?' I asked. And then I ran out of words. What were the landmarks of Worth, in relation to which she could place her cottage? In London, I could have said 'station' or 'bank' or 'Tesco Metro' or 'Pizza Hut' – there were so many easily remembered, man-made marks on the land. Here, the landmarks were natural: were bushes, were trees, were fields. I couldn't name any of them, not yet. I was still in a rural daze. No matter, though. Something else was now on her mind.

She'd paid for her goods, so our time together at the till, as two shoppers, had passed. At this point, she was asking a question in her own time.

'Where will you pray? I go to Sudbourne, but there's Iken. And Orford. If you want to go to Sudbourne, we can share a car. What do you think?'

She had a reddish face, the colour of a cherry boiled sweet. We had nothing in common but Worth, yet that meant everything to me now. It was my new home, a place of love and goodness and marriage. Had I met this woman in a shop in London, round the corner from some new flat we'd bought, I'd have said we weren't believers or, to lessen the blow, we weren't churchgoers. Either way, I'd have delivered a blow, with the London subtext: *Don't talk to me ever again because you are mad.* But here I felt a duty to her, because of our shared landscape. I wanted to make her happy, or not unhappy, as a tribute to our countryside.

'Nineteen pounds eighty-five,' said the shopkeeper, who was our witness. Where did he pray, this Orford shopkeeper? I couldn't choose Orford as my pretend-church, for fear he'd expect to see me there on Sunday.

'I'll discuss it with my wife,' I told her. I'd been married no more than a few months. 'My wife' still felt like a bogus claim, much as a con man might refer to 'my three-hundred-acre estate', the faster to induce you to give him your trust and your money. 'My wife' didn't belong to me, as the estate didn't belong to him. But this woman heard the opposite: she understood immediately that I belonged to my wife. Without my wife I couldn't make the churchgoing decision, though my wife could make that decision, and many more, without me. This was marriage at its most protective. She, my wife, was the shield – was the marriage – and all I had to do was hide behind her, even when she was absent. 'My wife' terminated the conversation. It repelled the outsider, who told me to drop in the next time I was passing. Then she left the shop.

'She should mind her own business,' said the woman rearranging the meat in the freezer. I thought she must be the wife of the man behind the till, which he confirmed, in his embarrassment, by trying and failing to look as if he'd never met her.

You might think this was what I wanted to hear; you might think I'd find it liberating to hear someone say it. But I didn't. I thought it was mean to talk about a person as soon as they left a shop. Leaving a shop, or any kind of room, was a social death. Those who were left behind should observe a decent silence, before they spoke ill of the departed. Was it pious of me to think like that? Was I trying to be a better person? Yes. What was wrong with that? It was a worthwhile aspiration. (This was what Sam Davey couldn't understand: who would try, in his mid-thirties, to like broccoli? He dismissed the attempt and refused to accept that the attempt could be successful.)

I left the shop, without comment. Fifteen minutes later, I saw, up ahead, a pink cottage with what had to be a quince tree, for there was the boiled-sweet-faced woman getting out of her freshly parked car, with her shopping. This was it: this was the next time I was passing. I had no intention of dropping in. Nevertheless, I braked, as if a slow drive-by were an excellent compromise between dropping in and not.

I pulled up, about twenty feet beyond her cottage. I sat there for a minute, to give her time to enter her cottage and put down her shopping. I imagined a cat. Then, to give both of us more time, I imagined a dog. The set of her features strongly resembled a bulldog's, which made it more likely she'd choose one as a pet. I carried on sitting. This dropping-in: it was like the putting-in of the garden fence posts we'd bought to replace the ones that had rotted. I didn't want to do it. I wanted to *have done it*.

I looked over my shoulder. I saw a man come out of the cottage next to hers, then go to a blue MGB sports car in his drive. He started loving it, with his hands, in ways I couldn't see, though I could sense his devotion. I guessed this man was the Keith she'd mentioned, the Keith of Keith and Margaret. I would talk to Keith. I would not, despite my earlier and best intentions, talk to that woman again. I'd never tell her we didn't go to church. She'd learn it, from my avoiding her. Then, if she wanted, she could pray for me.

I got out of the car and walked down The Lane, pseudo-casually, stopping when I drew level with the MGB, as if my attention had been diverted, mid-saunter.

'How old is she?' I called to Keith.

'She's a GT V8. 1973. They stopped making them in '76.'

My question – my connoisseur's 'she' – had loosened his tongue. For the next few minutes, he told me about his car, showing me round it, inside it and even under it, before I said goodbye, got back in my own car and drove the hundred yards home. I was delighted to have met him, though I couldn't remember anything about his car.

Weeks later, on a Sunday morning, the latest of many spent in each other's company, I carried a mug of coffee into our garden, where Keith was putting in the fence posts. In the kitchen, Margaret was giving Sarah a free manicure while Sarah, in exchange, read the lease of the beauty salon Margaret was about to rent in Leiston, a small town about ten miles away.

Keith was apologetic: he'd promised to put in the posts weeks earlier. There was no need for him to apologise. I'd merely asked him if he could recommend a handyman and he'd pointed his thumb at himself. This was characteristic, in many ways. First, he preferred a gesture to words. (Only cars made him verbose.) Second, it was kind. Third, he was a man of action, however delayed. So many of my own actions, in those first few weeks in Worth, were attributable to Keith. He took me fishing, he took me sailing, he jogged with me, I joined his five-a-side football team, I cycled with him, I picked strawberries and raspberries and blackberries with him, never able to keep pace with his fingers-to-fruit, fruit-to-container rhythms. When I cycled and jogged with him, I made a quasi-rural virtue of my slowness: I was relishing Nature, as opposed to whizzing past it. I hoped he'd think this deliberate. Being deliberate, I thought, was in itself rural. Urbans were neurotic, never deliberating before deciding to be paranoid, or alienated, or bored. So I genuflected before every raspberry and picked it with care.

'You're meant to pick 'em faster than they grow,' he said slowly. Only when we fished did I keep up with him. You can't hurry fish.

I engaged in these activities because I thought they were good for me and because Keith asked me. (It was always me. There was no question of his asking Sarah or Margaret. Wives had their own activities.) Sometimes, he carried out an activity on his own, while I nodded, or admired him, or gave him money for materials. Who was I to deny him the pleasure of installing an LED floodlight with a built-in sensor in our back garden? We didn't even know we wanted it, till Keith told us we did.

Keith had grown up in Sudbourne. He was a postman, the son of a nurseryman and the grandson of a farmhand; down the generations, the men's hands were getting less smelly. Nevertheless, Keith was at home with soil. I watched as he attacked it with 'my' new spade, which I'd bought with him in mind.

'Nice coffee,' he said. I'd offered him freshly ground coffee from Javanese beans but he wanted Nescafé, with milk and two sugars, insisting that the Javanese was too good for him. In matters of taste, he deferred to me. He acknowledged my coffee would taste better than his. But he wanted, and felt at home with, worse.

There we stood, Keith drinking the coffee, me watching him. He raised his mug in my direction. In his kind-to-be-cruel way, Keith constantly showed me I was a man of inaction, a coffee-maker. In my London-bred way, these were the actions I was trained to take: hailing taxis, hailing waiters, going to parties, going to gigs, going to clubs, galleries and films. Everyone I knew in London loved films. What did it mean, to 'love' films, as opposed to loving fishing or sailing? It meant ruminating, opining, list-making, nodding, shrugging, smirking, forming a downturned mouth. These weren't actions. Scorsese, yes, was a man of action, a man of 'Action!', who expressed his love of films by making them. I expressed mine by watching them, a human being where Keith was a human doing. That was why I never suggested we went to a film together. I could have given Keith my opinions, literally. I could have said: '*Toy Story* is one of the greatest works of art in the history of cinema. Now take that opinion and spread it.' But Keith wouldn't have valued those opinions, not as I valued his actions. What is an opinion worth, compared to a fence post?

'Look at you boys! You're like an old married couple!' shouted Margaret, as she and Sarah came out into the garden to find us standing silently together. Margaret was a frankly enormous woman, who revelled in her size, making jokes about it, as she made jokes about everything else. Far from putting women off her beauty salon, she claimed they came in, took one look at her and instantly felt more beautiful.

She had all the local authority we lacked: like Keith, she'd grown up in Suffolk and had never lived anywhere else. (Keith, as she celebrated – and comically regretted – was her only ever boyfriend, the one she'd had since they were sixteen and he'd been brave enough to put his arm around her at a school fire drill.) Margaret had an excess of opinions, which we were only too happy to adopt, about the stuck-up bitches and angry wives who came into her salon. We didn't know them but, listening to and laughing with Margaret, we felt as if we did. Margaret's views became our prejudices. We followed a small-mouthed stranger round the Co-op, hating her for her meanness, convinced this was the Elspeth whom Margaret called 'Arse-Mouth', the woman who'd given Margaret a Christmas present of a bar of soap with a hair in it.

Margaret was generally thrilled with us, because we weren't what she expected. She'd been to London a few times, as a teenager, and hated it. She was convinced that all Londoners were self-important snobs, who thought themselves too good for the likes of Keith and her. Sarah had told her that, as we saw it, there were no 'likes of' Keith and her. But she insisted. They were two people from a working-class background who lived in the country. That we didn't look down on them proved we weren't typical Londoners.

One Sunday night, in bed, we admitted it. We admitted to each other we were proud of our friendship with Keith and Margaret. Margaret was right. Many people we knew – Londoners, all – wouldn't have formed this friendship. Sarah's sister would have dismissed Keith and Margaret as 'common'; Renate would have found them ugly and unfashionable. Mark would have recoiled from Margaret's overtness.

'It's great to meet new kinds of people,' said Sarah. To say Keith and Margaret were 'kinds' of people was akin to their describing themselves as the 'likes of'. But the fact was the fact: we'd never, collectively or singly, made friends in London with a taciturn postman and the funny owner of a beauty salon.

'She's so entertaining,' said Sarah. 'And it's great the way Keith gets you out of the cottage.' This was one of Sarah's gifts: the neatness to find two thoughts – Margaret's entertainingness, Keith's getting-me-out-of-the-cottageness – tie them up neatly and put them in a box, a box labelled 'Keith and Margaret', a box you could look inside any time you liked, to see the advantages of Keith and Margaret.

My job was to draw sixty-four illustrations to accompany the text of *Crackling and Lard: Pig Detectives* by Lucy Carter, the first book in a (proposed) new series. Lucy Carter's real name was Ziggy Kinski. This unsettled me, on a daily basis. Some ten books earlier, he'd reneged on his name, thinking it too scary, dark and hairy for little kids. Ziggy Kinski thought 'Ziggy Kinski' was holding him back. But now he loathed Lucy Carter, with her bland blonde name, so redolent of Agas and English entitlement, and him the son of Polish immigrants. Carter had stolen the tiny shard of limelight that was Kinski's due for (just about) making a living from writing children's books.

The work was not as I'd imagined it. I was an animal illustrator living in the country. That evokes an outdoor life of observing and drawing animals. But this was not appropriate in the case of Crackling and Lard.

Crackling (female pig detective) and Lard (male) had a varied working life. In the morning, they might be visited by a vicar's wife, who needed them to talk her cat down from a tree. In the afternoon, they might be asked by a woodchopper to track down the fox that killed his chickens. If I headed off from the cottage, carrying my sketchbook, it was conceivable I might find a tree with a cat up it, but not, beneath it, two mixed-gender pigs, furrowing their porcine brows. Pigs, in their natural state, did no detective work. They didn't cordon off chicken coops with yellow gaffer tape. They didn't interview foxes, one soft on the fox, the other hard; nor, in their piggy eyes, was there anything of the beadi-ness of cops' expressions. They didn't even stand up. There was nothing, therefore, for me to observe. I was stuck indoors, with my imagination.

I was working by myself and for myself, though. This was wonderful. And, every so often, in those first few weeks, there was a perfect moment, one you could point to and say: *There it is. Look at it. That's why we're here.*

'Job done,' said Keith, on a morning of unsurpassable beauty. The four of us looked at the new fence posts.

At my insistence, we'd never cooked for Keith and Margaret, nor they for us. We had a tacit agreement, or so I thought, not to share food. On too many occasions, Margaret had recommended pubs for meals and, on too many non-occasions, we'd not taken her advice. Margaret's recommendations always started with a price: 'For ten pounds ninety-five . . .' she'd say. 'For nine pounds seventy-five . . .' 'For twelve pounds fifty, for two courses, if you go on a Monday night . . .' And then she'd list what you got for your money, which was, time after time after time: roast pork, apple sauce, gravy, Yorkshire pudding, roast potatoes, peas, carrots and cauliflower. Sarah had a moral attitude to food – it should be good, good for you and cooked by good people, who were made better people by the process of buying and cooking it, or growing or rearing and cooking it. She couldn't even summon up enough hypocrisy to respond to Margaret's listings with an 'Mm'. To her, roast pub-pork and its mushy crew were cooked by bad people. It was me who had to mutter 'That's fantastic value' or the more evasive 'Is-that-the-pub-on-your-right-as-you-go-down-the-hill?' As a restaurant man, though, I came by a different route to the same conclusion as Sarah. Margaret's recommended food had to be bad: there was too much of it for the money. If I paid twelve pounds fifty in a restaurant, I expected little food for my money. In effect, I *demanded* little: three anchovies, say, folded in on themselves in an anchovy star, secreting a solitary spit of celeriac, lark-heart and fennel foam. A larger food amount was unacceptable; a smaller commanded even more of my restaurant-respect. For twelve pounds fifty, I expected to see a lot of white plate.

The previous Sunday, despite all this, Sarah had unilaterally invited Keith and Margaret to lunch, even saying what she'd cook: Pasta With Beetroot. Margaret made an approving noise, Keith said nothing; but, as Sarah pointed out, when we argued about it later, Keith often said nothing. I told her the Pasta With Beetroot was a mistake. Keith would hate everything about it, even the With. Why, Sarah countered, was I protecting Keith from new experiences, when the converse didn't apply? The previous weekend, I'd spent a night with Keith on a beach, fishing, never having spent a night on a beach before, so why couldn't Keith eat purple pasta for the first time? We had to assert ourselves, if we wanted to advance the relationship. We had to say: this is what we like, this is who we are.

I wasn't convinced. I wanted to stick with the Keith I knew, even though I'd only known him for a matter of weeks. This was cautious and conservative of me. But I felt that caution and conservatism were native – native to the countryside, native to Keith.

The advance came shortly after Sarah served Keith his Pasta. Even though he knew the Pasta was coming, it surprised him. He looked at his meal. Then he looked inside it. He peered inside his Pasta in the hope of seeing breasts, legs, wings, livers, kidneys, a heart. Anything he thought of as food.

'Why d'you leave London, then?' he asked. Already I was worried. Never before had Keith initiated a conversation. The Pasta With Beetroot had angered him into speech. What's more, his question was puzzlingly redundant, since we'd gone over this the first time we were together. Sarah had been a City solicitor for eleven years. Fearing burn-out, she needed a change of life and a change of scenery. She wanted to work for a charity and devote the rest of her time to yoga and gardening and having a healthier lifestyle. I'd had enough of working in advertising. Now I wanted to follow my dream of being an animal illustrator. We'd told this story many times. Too many times. We'd simplified it to the point where cliché followed cliché. 'Change of life', 'healthier lifestyle', 'follow my dream'. It was verbal fast food, made for easy digestion. We served it up and then were keen to move on. Now here was Keith, sicking it up for further inspection.

'This is lovely, Sarah,' said Margaret of the food; but it sounded less like a compliment to Sarah than a warning to Keith to change the subject. He took it as such. He acknowledged the warning but didn't let it divert him.

'I'm just asking,' he said to Margaret. Then he turned on us. 'Is it cos there's far less blacks round here?'

'Far fewer blacks,' said Sarah. She reddened, angry at herself for seizing on his grammar, not his offence.

'You can't say that, Keith,' said Margaret.

'It's true, though,' said Keith.

'Course. But you can't say it.'

Now I too looked at my Pasta, not that it mattered where I looked. Sarah's thoughts were in my mind and mine were in hers. She was thinking we had to say something. *I* had to say something. I had to say something to show Sarah I was not the man she met – the man who'd left Renate's flat, early one morning, never to return, but hadn't said (as Sarah had said to Mark) that I was leaving because she was preventing me from being the person I wanted to be. Sarah had confronted Mark, whereas I had merely absented myself from Renate, because I was weak. But I was no longer weak. Sarah had made me strong. Or had she? This was what she was wondering, as was I. This was our joint thought.

I was weak on account of the fence posts. Keith had put in our fence posts, out of the kindness of his racist heart. If I could disagree with Keith in a civilised manner (which was another way of saying 'If I could carry on being weak'), then Keith would carry on putting in future fence posts for as long as I asked him; 'future fence posts' standing for everything that required skilled manual labour, something to which I could only aspire, but no longer did, not now I'd met Keith.

'I told him not to drink,' said Margaret, wanting us to feel for her, letting us know this had happened before. But it wasn't the drink talking. It was Keith. What did Keith have against black people? Nothing. He didn't know any. He feared what he didn't know. Over time, I could persuade him his view was misguided. Wasn't that better than confronting him now and repelling him, terminally? Shouldn't I, in a year's time, as I followed him up a ladder to give him his coffee, while he replaced a rotting window frame, explain that once you met a person, any person, you no longer saw them as a type of person but a – I abandoned this fantasy because Sarah was looking at me. I no longer knew what

61

she was thinking. Then she told me, she told all of us: 'Richard used to live with a black woman.'

Margaret flushed. Keith looked worried. He'd been wrong-footed, all right. My living with a black woman: this was not what he'd expected. Of course, this was not what I'd expected either. But I was thrilled. I'd never heard Sarah lie before. It delighted me, it gave me a sexual thrill that she did it so well. I was lassoed by her lie.

'I did,' I said, surprised how strong my voice was. 'I lived with a black woman for four years. Renate.' I called her Renate to make her a person, not an ethnic definition. I called her Renate so I could answer questions. If Margaret, trying to keep the peace, asked me what Renate did, I could say she managed artists, one of whom had won the Turner Prize. And then – as who wouldn't? – I pictured Renate, naked and black. I'd never had sexual fantasies about Renate. But this Renate was different. The black Renate didn't have the white Renate's personality. She had Renate's superb body, without the Renate. I needed to give her a different head, though. A woman with Renate's head, blacked up, was not a black Renate. What a perverted pleasure it was, to remove Renate's head and replace it with the head of a black woman. She looked like – once again, I had to stop, because Sarah wanted me to say something more. I looked at Keith and I said: 'It's over.' He didn't understand, as I knew he wouldn't. But Margaret did.

'Come on then,' she said to Keith, scraping her chair backwards as she got to her feet. Keith got up too, but not before advancing his food bowl to the centre of the table. Margaret said: 'Thank you for the drink.' I liked her for that. She was a quick-witted woman who knew not to thank us for the food.

Sarah and I remained at the table while they walked to the front door, opened it and slammed it. It was a mark of the size of our cottage that this took so little time.

'That was brave.'

'You've made me brave,' I said. It was true, wasn't it? She'd made me brave, at least when I was with her. I took Keith's bowl and ate his pasta, even though I still had pasta of my own. I felt like an ancient warrior, eating a body part of the enemy he'd killed.

'I was bluffing,' said Sarah. 'I had no idea Renate was black. You never told me. I mean, why would you? She ruined your life. The colour of her skin's irrelevant.'

I felt weird and lonely. She'd never met Renate, with whom I'd spent four years of my life, nor even seen a photo. She thought I was the kind of person – oh yes, we were back to that – who claims that a woman has ruined his life but never, for fear of being misunderstood, mentions the colour of her skin. What kind of person is that?

We'd known each other two years, which was nothing. We were alone in our country cottage and had just lost the only friends in Worth we had. What happened now?

We couldn't import our London friends. Our cottage was too small. So we drove to London every weekend. Sarah called it 'reverse commuting'.

If we went back to the city at the weekend, we'd enjoy it at its best. The worst of the city was, simply, that the city went on and on and on and on and on and on. But not if you were there from Friday night to early Sunday evening. It went on and on, which was exciting and manageable; and then you left. You left, what's more, just as those city people with houses in the country were inching back to London, nose to tail with the BMW, Audi or Merc in front. This contraflow made for jam-free driving and a certain self-satisfaction. We hated self-satisfaction in others but we revelled in our own.

The London people, like the traffic, were also at their best. It was the weekend. They were at home, not worsening their characters getting from their bedrooms to their places of work, with all that journey's frustration and pain as a driver, say, turned left and knocked them off their bike and they lay there, on the pavement, bloody and dazed, with four good people crouched around and a thousand walking past; a thousand London Bad Samaritans, forced to circumvent the ring of Good, telling themselves they were in the majority and therefore no worse than most people and, besides, they couldn't stop as they were already late for work and, anyway, what mad flying and landing fool would cycle down a London street in rush hour? At least, as a pedestrian, you could walk round the body; as an Underground passenger, you could not walk round a person under a train. You didn't even see that person. The station announcer gave you the bad news: your train was delayed because of a person under a train. That person could be under a train twenty stations hence and still mess up your journey. Twenty minutes, half an hour, thirty-five minutes – how long did it take to de-person an undertrain? It was a person. It wasn't a crowd. Why had the person done it, if not to hurt you, hurt *you*?

Our London weekends started with a list, which I concocted. The list might include a restaurant, a film, an exhibition, another film, a cafe, a walk, another restaurant (preferably at lunchtime, when the food was cheaper), a market, a department store, a play above a pub, a comedy gig, a music gig, et cetera. Et cetera: I'd never understood the meaning of the phrase till we started our reverse commuting. In London, there was always another thing. Stone was right. It was the quantity that was unique.

We stayed in the Kennington house of Sarah's younger sister Jane and her husband Patrick, a barrister. Jane had told Sarah, when Sarah was fourteen and Jane was twelve, that Jane was going to have four kids and marry a rich man. This she'd almost achieved. Patrick, exuding contentment, made out that the house and the three children were nothing to do with him. 'Not my department!'

was his answer to any request for information about his own life.

Jane had, in her words, 'a problem buying clothes', though the truth was she had a problem not buying clothes. She claimed that, if she had her way, she'd always wear the same sloppy T-shirt and jeans. It was society's fault that she didn't. Society, according to Jane, forced thinner and younger women to work in the clothes shops which society made Jane enter. They made her feel she wasn't thin or young enough – she was thirty – for the clothes near which they stood. She felt they were putting pressure on her to prove herself. So she tried on clothes and bought them; then tried them on again in her bedroom, where there was no pressure, not from Patrick, who thought her clothes weren't his department. In her bedroom, she hated her newly bought clothes. Now she was pregnant, she hated more of them than ever. That was why, when we arrived at eight o'clock on a Friday night, a choice of Jane's rejected purchases would be hanging on the hook of our bedroom door, for Sarah to help herself. To denote a rejected item, Jane inked a black cross on the label.

One Friday, we arrived to find a red dress with silver studs. Sarah was insulted. How could her sister think she'd wear a dress like that? Keen not to be like Patrick, I told Sarah to try it on. It hung loosely on her, reaching her knees, because there was more of Jane than Sarah. More bust, more hips, more height, more aggression, more need. When you saw them together, you thought Sarah had made herself smaller than her sister, by a lifetime's recoiling from her.

'I like it,' I said.

'It's not me,' she said uncertainly, confused by my approval, not sure if she should let herself be altered by the dress. 'When am I going to wear it? It's so loud and stupid. What a waste of money.'

I agreed. It was loud, stupid and wasteful. That was what made it so supremely metropolitan, perfect for wearing now. Sarah could never wear it at her homeless charity, nor at her yoga lessons, nor on a footpath.

'OK, then I'll wear it for the restaurant.' Sarah rang Jane to say we'd arrived and how much she loved the red studded dress. We were in Jane and Patrick's house in London, while they were in their country house in Dorset. Every weekend, they lent us their empty London house. That was the beauty of the arrangement.

We set off, at ten at night, for a Korean restaurant not far from Leicester Square.

Sam Davey entered the restaurant. Every Friday night, we met him in a different restaurant and talked about the events of our week, even though our week in Worth often contained no events, or merely events repeated from the previous week. Sarah found this embarrassing but I reassured her. We went to London to talk to our friends and not be forgotten. We didn't need them to remember what we said.

Sarah stood up and kissed him and his companion Rachel, decisively. These kisses, though planted on them, were directed at me: she was showing me she'd be friendly to them. She was showing me she'd made the decision to *try*.

'Wow!' said Sam Davey. 'Amazing dress. I love the studs.'

'Thank you. It's a cast-off from my sister,' replied Sarah, sitting down hastily, as if to deny him any more full-length views of the dress. She grabbed the pepper off the table – a curious, tense gesture – as if it were a bishop that she'd just taken with the castle of the salt. Sam Davey made her feel nervous and inadequate. She felt he was art school in his need to be mysterious and unsettling. Even when he said a straightforward thing, such as 'I love the studs', she felt you were foolish if you didn't realise he was thinking something else, such as 'Christ, look at those studs!' You couldn't see into him. He had that remote and ironic skin which – unlike me – he didn't want to shake off.

It saddened me that my wife didn't love my oldest friend. But I couldn't say she was wrong about his remoteness. Nothing in his life was straightforward, except his paintings, which were clear in their intentions and execution. He was a father now, but only saw his two-year-old daughter every other weekend, because she lived with her mother, Liv, who wasn't quite his girlfriend but wasn't quite not, which meant that Rachel, this woman he lately took to restaurants, was in turn not quite his girlfriend and not quite not. Sarah regarded this as an attack on conventional marriages such as our own, which it wasn't. Sam Davey didn't have a social or political purpose to his private life. He just had a mess.

Dad entered the restaurant and waved.

'Hi, everyone. Hi, Sarah, how was your week?' It was exactly the question he'd asked the previous week, in a Japanese restaurant in Bloomsbury.

'The same,' replied Sarah, but there was no sarcasm or melancholy, just a teasing welcome as she pulled back the chair next to her. I couldn't increase her enthusiasm for Sam Davey or reduce her enthusiasm for Dad. When Dad asked you a question, she felt, he wanted to know the answer. He cared. He cared about me and now he cared about us. He *was* a straightforward man. He was a dentist, which everyone could understand, as opposed to an artist. He met a girl, fell in love with her and married her. It made no difference to Sarah – didn't make Dad more suspect or complicated – that he'd done this twice and both times the wives had left him. He was a decent man and his wives were a pair of idiots.

We ate quickly as there was a late-night film – Asif Kapadia's *The Warrior* – at the Ritzy Cinema in Brixton. At two in the morning, on the pavement outside the cinema, we all hugged each other and agreed it was a brilliant film and then Sarah and I caught the night bus back to her sister's house. On the upper deck, she asked me how I knew it was brilliant, as I'd fallen asleep. I told her that I'd fallen asleep out of happiness, with my wife and my two oldest friends beside me, which was brilliance personified. She asked me if this was sarcasm, which it was, to this limited extent: her hug of Dad was twice as long as her hug of Sam Davey, which was as soulless and technical as the hug of a security guard checking for weapons.

On the Saturday morning, we took the dress with the red studs to the charity shop, en route to Tate Modern, then, via the cheese shop in Covent Garden, my favourite Italian cafe on Charing Cross Road and the fabric shops in Berwick and Broadwick Street in Soho – Sarah resolving, from now on, to make her own clothes – we ran to a Brazilian restaurant in Percy Street, off Tottenham Court Road, for lunch. We were late, by about half an hour, as we were due to meet Hattie and Charles at the Serpentine Gallery at two. We ordered, quickly, then waited. I suggested we ring Hattie and Charles to say we'd be late but Sarah pointed out that they had a little girl who slept between two and four. They'd planned our meeting so they could leave her, asleep, with the woman who helped them. 'The woman who helped them' stuck in my throat – why didn't they call her a nanny? Sarah explained that she wasn't a nanny, but a PhD student who helped them in return for a room at the top of their house. That shut me up. We sat in silence for a time. It became a restaurant silence, a prayer for food. I suggested we leave but Sarah demurred. We'd ordered and we had an obligation to eat what we'd ordered. The food didn't come and didn't come. She stood and had a long conversation with the waiter, out of my earshot. Ten minutes later, we were walking towards Oxford Street carrying a carrier bag full of foil containers, Sarah having converted our meal into a takeaway. She sat on the bus to Marble Arch, with this bag on her lap like a big hot baby with shrimp and coconut breath.

We knew we had to get rid of the food, as Charles wouldn't like it. Hattie wouldn't mind – Hattie would enjoy the spontaneity – but Charles – never Charlie – wouldn't want to sit on a bench in Hyde Park with us, watching us eat Brazilian food with our fingers, as we didn't have any cutlery. He was too important to see such a thing.

We got off the bus at the stop opposite Lancaster Gate station and looked for a poor person to whom we could give the food. But we couldn't find one. I told Sarah to wait at the entrance to Hyde Park. I ran, hazardously, across Bayswater Road and offered the bag to a *Big Issue* seller outside the station. He was a guy in his twenties with a dazed expression. He explained that he was selling a magazine for homeless people and wasn't begging for food. I told him that I knew he wasn't begging but I really wanted to give him the food, which he thought was an insult. He said it smelt 'weird'. I asked him if he'd accept the food if I bought a *Big Issue*. He agreed. I bought a copy, walked away, then saw him put the food in a bin.

'Hey!' I shouted. 'That's food!'

I took the bag from the bin and tried to force it into his hands, which was hopeless, as they were full of *Big Issue*s.

And then, from behind, an arm gripped my neck. The arm had a tattoo of a spider. My eyes were flush with the black yolk of its head.

'It ain't worth it, mate. Let it go.'

I obeyed the arm. I literally let the bag go, dropping our Brazilian food onto the pavement. Then I walked at a calm and even pace, as if the arm had ordered it, without looking back. And then I ran back across Bayswater Road.

Hattie was Sarah's best friend. She taught geography at a secondary school in west London, as well as coaching the hockey team, having played the game for Surrey. I'd taken to her the moment

I met her, because she kissed me and said she was thrilled Sarah had found me. It couldn't have been clearer that she preferred me to Sarah's desiccated ex.

'Why did you tell me he's losing his looks?' she asked Sarah. 'I think he's *finding* them!'

'Fuck off!'

I couldn't have been happier with this exchange. It meant that Sarah, unlike Renate, had been drawn to me not because of my looks but because of their loss, which boded better. Then there was the joy of hearing Sarah tell her best friend to fuck off – Sarah, who didn't swear enough. All this pleasure was compounded by its marital safety: despite her vibrancy and appetite, I didn't find Hattie sexually attractive, not having Betjemaniacal loins that were stirred by 'hockey' or 'Surrey'.

As a student at University College London, Hattie had fallen for Charles, a geography lecturer, twenty years older. Now a professor, Charles was a world authority on climate change, renewable resources and the survival of our planet. He was a man of phenomenal intellect and remarkable persuasive powers, a man known to presidents and prime ministers and – let it not go unsaid – an egomaniac who made everyone feel that their lives were less worthwhile than his own. That, of course, was precisely what went unsaid, every time I met him, every time he shook my hand as if it were the first time we'd met, so little impression had I made the previous first time we'd met. I was his wife's best friend's husband: surely he had a duty to remember me. The first first time we met, he asked what I did, his patrician gaze disconcertingly directed at the gap between my eyebrows; when I told him I was illustrating a children's book, he said: 'Very good.' That was it. He had no supplementary questions. My life, like a child's homework, had been marked. There was nothing more to be said. So, the second first time I met him and he asked me what I did, I was reluctant to tell him again, for fear of hearing the 'Very good' again. But I was sitting with him in his living room, beneath a photo of him with Clinton and Bono. I had to say something. So I told him I was illustrating a children's book, to which he responded: 'Hattie! Have you seen my reading glasses?' During my answer, short as it was, Charles had had a thought; that thought had relegated all other thoughts, had gone straight to number one on his thought chart. Hattie, far too quickly, came into their living room, found his glasses on the mantelpiece and brought them to him. Why did she put up with him? After we left their house, I got as far as 'Why does she' before Sarah stopped me. She explained they'd been together fifteen years and had a strong understanding, which begged the question: what did each of them strongly understand? Charles understood Hattie would find his glasses; what did Hattie understand he'd do for her? Sarah said he'd told Hattie she made him 'complete'. That was her life's work: completing Charles.

Now, in the Serpentine Gallery, where we'd been for about two minutes, Hattie glanced at him. He was in the middle of the room, studying the lenses of those very glasses, cleaning them with a cloth. Expertly divining his thought, to save him the trouble of expressing it, Hattie said: 'I think we're going.' That was it, then. Charles had silently decreed that the art in the Serpentine Gallery had detained us long enough. Hattie, as his wife, was obliged to go along with this, so we were too. I wasn't enjoying the art either. But the art was on the list. The art had to be looked at, before we could get to the next item, which was to walk to that golden spot in Hyde Park, where you could look east towards the Serpentine, north towards the Italian Gardens, west towards the Round Pond. This was, according to Sarah, the loveliest point in London, which was why it was on the list. What's more, it was insulting to us to leave the gallery early, when we'd gone through all kinds of struggle and embarrassment to get there on time.

As we walked through the park, Sarah's mobile rang. She said 'Hi' then walked away, wanting privacy. I followed her, keeping my distance. I found myself halfway between her and Charles and Hattie, unable to hear any of them. I was thinking about our forthcoming journey to Geoff and Sonia's, for early-evening drinks. We were now, thanks to Charles's premature departure from the gallery, ahead of ourselves. We were not due at Geoff and Sonia's till half past five but it was only quarter past two. If this item ended early, what would we do before the beginning of the next? I didn't want to be in London, on a Saturday afternoon, choosing what to do. I'd made my choice – our choice – before we came. I didn't want a thousand possibilities. I wanted certainty, of which there is only ever one.

Hattie approached, to see what was wrong with Sarah, who was heading for me, looking distraught. Charles hung back. Whatever was wrong, it was too parochial to be worth his attention.

Jane and Patrick had returned to London early, Patrick having left behind the bundle of papers he needed to read at the weekend. While he read and the children played, Jane went shopping. In an effort to deal with her shopping problem – not solve it, but make it a better class of problem – she decided to go to her local charity shops. If she wasted her money, at least she'd waste it on a good cause. What's more, there'd be bargains. She lived in a smart neighbourhood. The Arthritis Shop had designer dresses, not just cardigans worn by old people on the day of their death. It was in the Arthritis Shop that she came across her red dress with studs and a black cross on the label. Why had Sarah lied about loving it? Why was she deceitful and ungrateful?

Hattie was furious on Sarah's behalf, more furious than Sarah herself, who looked defeated. I withdrew. I was the husband, but I was still new. I wasn't sure I was ready or willing to attack my wife's sister, as Hattie was entitled to do, having been Sarah's best friend since they were nine.

Charles and I – the husbands – found ourselves together on the short sideline, like the last two boys waiting to be picked for a team. We appeared to have something in common, which must have pained him.

According to Hattie, Sarah had done nothing wrong: she'd worn the dress, then given it away to charity.

'I was just trying to please everyone,' said Sarah. She looked like she didn't have the strength to stay upright. Now I understood. She was hungry. She was shaky with hunger, like me. She'd taken her lunch on a bus, in a bag, then given it to me. She'd never even *seen* her lunch.

Charles put a hand on my shoulder, to stop me shaking. It was extraordinary to be touched by him. Then he addressed us, not about the dress, which was (as he saw it) the superficial cause of our upset. No, he spoke to us about our lives in general. The guru looked down from the mountain top and saw our lives.

'You're trying to do too much. This whole reverse-commuting thing's unworkable. Humans aren't designed to be everywhere and nowhere. I'm a citizen of the world but I have one home. In Ealing. With Hattie. You need one community. One emotional and physical landscape. Then you're nourished. Otherwise you don't know where or who you are.'

Having broadcast, Charles fell silent. I was stunned. Where had he heard of 'reverse-commuting'? Hattie must have told him this was what we did and he must have listened and remembered. Charles had remembered something about us. And now he'd spoken, he'd pronounced, he'd devoted thirty seconds of his sought-after time to saving our two-person planet. He'd presumed to comment on our little life and found it wanting. But he was right. That was the thing. He was absolutely right. We couldn't carry on doing what we'd been doing. It was driving us mad.

PART THREE

The first we heard of her was the thunder of her removal van pulling up outside her cottage, early on Monday morning. (She herself had, presumably, arrived in the night, while we were sleeping.) The men got out and opened the back. From our living-room window, we saw her furniture before we saw her. That was how we got the news that a woman had moved in next door. We had no local intelligence, no foreknowledge. We got the news as cavemen would have got it: directly, with our eyes. Then we saw her come out of the next-door cave to greet the men bringing her possessions.

'Old Man Hargreaves must have died,' said Sarah.

'She's probably one of his daughters,' I said. It was a truly rural conversation, containing only eternal verities – death, fathers, daughters, the bequest of property – expressed in banal words.

The woman turned, to instruct the men where in the cottage to take a chaise longue upholstered in yellow velvet. We got our first frontal view: a tall, pale-skinned woman with red hair and an air of easy command.

'She looks nice,' Sarah said.

I nodded. I was glad it was Sarah who said this. It wouldn't have been right for me, as the husband, to be the first to volunteer that this woman looked nice. It would have sounded as if I found her sexually attractive, whereas, when Sarah said it, 'nice' had a multiplicity of meanings. It could mean any or all of: friendly, well dressed, well-meaning, forgiving, optimistic, kind. It could even mean sexually attractive.

'Bright,' Sarah added. And now I could agree, loudly. 'Bright' was something I could say of a woman without sounding as if I fancied her.

'Yes, she looks very bright, doesn't she?' It was true. The woman had bright eyes. She looked highly intelligent, almost scarily so.

'That's an amazingly beautiful shirt,' said Sarah, 'to wear when you're moving stuff around.'

I said nothing to this. I was too busy working it out. Was it a compliment or an insult, flattery or bitchery, bitchery *as* flattery? It was a tailored white shirt and, yes, it was impressively white and probably expensive. Was she meant to wear a dirty shirt for moving her stuff? Her stuff, in fact, as it disgorged from the van – a pink sofa, multicoloured plastic kitchen chairs – looked clean. And hadn't she hired dirty men to move it?

'She's stylish,' said Sarah unambiguously, fearing she'd sounded sharp. She wanted to hit – ping! – a note of pure admiration.

The woman followed the men and the sofa into her cottage. As she walked back down her path, Sarah withdrew from the window, worried she'd see us looking. I did likewise. We'd had a friendship – Keith and Margaret – which had gone wrong. We didn't want to repeat our mistake, which was to be too friendly, too soon. We should take our time.

'OK, I'm off,' said Sarah. 'Don't talk to her till I get back.' I understood. We'd been together when we saw her for the first time. We should be together when we first spoke to her. Sarah didn't want me getting ahead of *us*. If this woman were to be a new friend, she had to be our new friend. My old friends could never be Sarah's old friends, just as hers could not be mine. Even when an old friend of mine became a new friend of hers – Dad, for example, though he was, as yet, the *only* example – I ached for her to travel with me to the time when Dad was sixteen and a new friend to me. I thought she could only understand him if she'd known him as long as I had. That Dad was the same at thirty-six as sixteen was not the point; you had to live through those years, to know and feel how much he wasn't changing. You couldn't cheat that time, couldn't jump the history queue. Similarly, when I met Hattie (without Charles) and she said or did something amusing, Sarah would always be overly amused, as if to say, look, you can see what I saw in this girl, when I was nine and she was nine: I was cautious and she was bold. You can see what she was like before she married Charles and became his facilitator.

With Keith and Margaret, I'd spoken to Keith first, which was already divisive; he then assumed he had nothing to say to Sarah, who would be his wife's friend. But then Keith didn't have female friends. There was no mixed doubles about Keith, no couples whacking the conversational ball from man to woman, woman to woman, woman to man, man to man. With Keith, there was a men's doubles pair and a women's doubles pair, standing on opposite sides of the net, with their backs to each other.

I kept my promise not to speak to her. Sarah, arriving home about six, found a pot of parsley and an envelope on our doorstep. The woman had written 'The Occupiers, Hay Cottage'. Sarah studied it, becalmed. She was in an envelope trance.

'Aren't we going to open it?' I asked.

'Sorry, yes.'

The letter was signed 'Catherine Hargreaves': it was like a signature on a letter in a televised production of a Jane Austen novel: such calligraphy, such clarity, such an artful 'g'. To look at it was to feel improved. As for the pot of parsley, it was perfect. She'd had the courage and style to give us something of little financial worth. It was the parsleyness of the parsley that mattered, not its price.

She told us she'd moved in next door and, supplying her number, invited us to knock or call.

'Why don't I just call her now?' I asked, taking the phone off its cradle.

'No,' said Sarah.

'No, you're right,' said I. It was too crude and precipitate, even though she'd asked us to do it.

Sarah suggested we write her a letter, since she'd written one to us. I agreed and volunteered to post it, meaning she'd get it on Wednesday. Thirty-six hours or so: that seemed an appropriate interval between her letter and our response, neither too eager nor too casual. Sarah, puzzled, asked why I was going to post the letter. She lived next door. Why didn't I just go next door and put it through her letter box? I couldn't admit to my mental lapse, which I felt was due to my incarcerating myself in our cottage for ten hours, from the time Sarah left for work to the time she returned, so as not to bump into the woman next door. All I could do was bluff. I explained that if I went next door and put it through her letter box, she might hear me and come to the door and open it and talk to me, which wasn't what we wanted – we wanted to meet her together.

From the next-door cottage came the rumble of a sofa, on castors, being repositioned. Sarah instinctively moved towards the sink, to distance herself from the sofa and its owner, Catherine Hargreaves. We sensed she knew we were in here, talking about her. For the first time, we thought our adjoining cottages told a single story – if you sliced off the upper halves of the cottages and looked at them from the sky, you'd see a cross-sectional narrative, with Catherine moving the sofa, and Sarah and me crossing to the sink. Before she moved that sofa, Catherine had (probably) gone upstairs and looked out of a window to see that the parsley pot and the envelope had been taken inside by her neighbours. The sofa noise was Catherine clearing her throat, a-hemming to signal that we owed her an answer.

'OK,' I said. 'Here's the plan.' I didn't, when I said this, have a plan. But it didn't matter what the plan was, as long as I volunteered one with confidence, in a voice not so loud as to suggest irritation. A minute later, Sarah and I were knocking on Catherine Hargreaves's door or, rather, Sarah was knocking and I was taking a step back. Having knocked, Sarah stepped back too – for the plan was not to enter Catherine Hargreaves's cottage but to invite her to ours, to give her some respite from moving her furniture around.

She opened the door. Sarah and I, overlapping, introduced ourselves and each other. I shut up, to avoid further repetition. Sarah thanked Catherine for the parsley pot and the letter. Catherine invited us inside. Sarah refused, duly counter-inviting her to ours. Catherine accepted and we set off for our cottage. Her territory was divided from ours by a wall no more than two feet high – we'd walked out of our front door and stepped over it to get to hers. But so keen was Sarah to do the right thing, as opposed to the natural thing, that she walked up the path to Catherine's gate, then turned right and proceeded through our gate and down our path to our front door, making the journey about sixty-seven times longer than it needed to be. We followed, Catherine and I. Catherine said we must have been living in our cottage about three months. I agreed. Then Sarah observed that Catherine had moved in this morning, we'd heard the removal van arrive around half past eight. I couldn't imagine how our talk could get any smaller. By this point, we were only halfway through our absurdly long, if short, journey.

Yes, Old Man Hargreaves had died. He'd left the family home in Norfolk, where Catherine had grown up, to her sister, who had a husband and a couple of kids, and therefore needed more space; he'd left the Suffolk cottage near the sea to his daughter Catherine, because there was only one of her. We'd never doubted it. When we first saw her, we knew, instinctively, that she was single. No child or partner would come out of her cottage and follow her up that path, to support or berate her, tell her there was someone on the phone, offer the removal men some tea, tug at her shirt – all the stuff that partners and children do. There could have been a dog, but we'd have heard or seen it when she opened her door. That left a cat; but, after an hour of being in our cottage, she'd not referred to a cat. Single women, whether supermodels or hundred-year-old virgins, always referred to their cats; as a single man, I'd got used to that. Albert, Roger, Geoffrey, Rod – Oz's cat was Rod – they sounded at first like boyfriends, then they came into the room and scratched you. No, there was no cat, there was only Catherine Hargreaves, who reminded me of another woman I knew. Who, though? As I found the second bottle in the pantry and brought it to the kitchen table, I thought back on the women I'd known. But I couldn't find her, the Catherine lookalike. I flattered myself that she reminded me of someone I could no longer place, so many had been my sexual partners. (I assumed, in my vanity, that she reminded me of a sexual partner, as opposed to a work colleague, or someone I'd once sat opposite on a train journey protracted by delays.) Then I looked at her again and knew: it was Elizabeth the First. Catherine had the pale and singular authority of Elizabeth the First.

She'd been living in Brussels as a translator for the European Commission but had now decided to settle in Myrtle Cottage, the holiday home she'd loved since she was a girl. She'd take translating jobs as and when she could. Italian and Spanish were her main languages. She'd studied them at University College London.

'I bet you got a first,' said Sarah, sure she was right, excited that our new neighbour was clever.

'It was a long time ago,' said Catherine, which, in its elegant way, was a Yes. I asked if she knew Charles Maidment, explaining that Sarah's best friend had married him. She told me that everyone

82

knew the brilliant Charles Maidment – she'd even gone to one of his lectures, despite not being on his course.

She paused. 'He took me out to dinner once.'

She paused again. 'Nothing happened.'

It was the pauses I loved. She produced these two little holes and filled them perfectly. From what she put into them – the smiles, the delicate eyebrow moves – we knew it was she, not he, who'd decided that nothing would happen. Our new neighbour had turned down Charles. She'd punctured his big head. This was blissful. I refilled her glass.

Twenty years earlier (she was, we thought, forty or so, about five years older than us), Catherine had dined, once, with the man Sarah's best friend later married. It was not much but it was huge, given that three doors down was a woman who called us to prayer and two doors down were Keith and Margaret, with whom we had so little in common that we'd made that the foundation of our friend-ship. *Look, everyone, we've made friends with people with whom we've got nothing in common! Aren't we tolerant!* I knew if we kept talking, we'd find more in common with Catherine. I was right. Her own best friend Victoria, unlike Hattie, hadn't married a famous man. She'd married a book dealer called Duncan, whose brother was a famous man. His real name was Angus Campbell-Brown but he was better known as – 'John Smith!' I shouted.

Catherine had spent the previous weekend at Victoria and Duncan's house, with John Smith.

'Isn't he terrible?!' I shouted and Sarah, under the table, put a restraining hand on my knee to stop me shouting again, or leaping to my feet. She was embarrassed by my overexcitement, but my overexcitement was justified. Catherine felt as I did. She found John Smith 'creepily ambitious'. His brother Duncan, a gentle man, went quiet in John Smith's presence. He was obviously wary of his brother's power, which had oppressed him all his life. Now, suddenly, Sarah and Catherine left me behind, because their subject was the oppressive power of siblings which I, as an only child, was presumed to know nothing about. Sarah, sensing Catherine would understand, told the story of the red studded dress. Catherine responded as if the red-dress events had happened to her. She was, like Sarah, the sister in the hand-me-down dress. Her elder sister Mel – she who'd been left the big house – was the one who did the handing-down, the manipulating.

There we were, the three of us, on a Monday night at our kitchen table in Worth. On a Monday night in Worth, there were no activities. The activity, the pastime: it was *us*. There was no sound in Worth, not that we heard, apart from our talk and the neck of the wine bottle donking the rims of our glasses, then glugging. There was certainly no noise from the neighbouring cottage. The neighbour was here, with us.

It was half past eight. We'd been talking for an hour and a half. Sarah asked Catherine to stay for supper. She declined, not wanting to stay too long, which only made us want her to stay longer. We had pasta, we had cheese, we had vegetables. What did she fancy? Behind us, in Catherine's line of vision, was a free-standing vegetable rack. Sarah directed her to study it. I understood. Sarah wanted (needed?) Catherine to love the vegetable Keith hated, the one that had unleashed his dark tongue. Sarah was shooting for a small happiness, no bigger than a root vegetable. Say it, Catherine, say it. Name the purple beauties. Hail the roundheads.

'I like pasta with courgettes,' said Catherine. 'Or beetroot. Beetroot's very good. Have you tried it?'

I smiled at her. I didn't look at Sarah to check she was smiling too. We weren't members of a beetroot cult. We weren't looking to exclude Catherine if she didn't conform to our food beliefs. But I know we both smiled because Catherine looked from Sarah to me and said: 'I obviously passed the test.'

We listened to Catherine as Sarah silently weighed the pasta, I filled the pan with water, Sarah stepped back to let me past,

I put the pan on the gas ring. We'd done all this hundreds of times. We didn't need words. We'd have done it in silence even if Catherine had not been there, talking. When we first cooked together, we gave instructions/requests to each other – could you pass me the, can you go to the, can you get me the, get the, I'll get the, give me the, could you weigh the – but now, by the thousandth performance, these instructions had been internalised; now we boiled and filled and tossed and reached and fetched and roasted without them. We were a fully choreographed kitchen couple. We'd been together two years.

I'd never felt more of a husband than I did that night. A husband isn't a man, not in the way that a warrior's a man, or a caveman's a man. 'Man' denotes aggression. Replace 'men' with 'husbands' and what you lose in aggression you gain in kindness and domesticity. *The Grand Old Duke of York, he had ten thousand husbands.* In our kitchen, that evening with Catherine, I knew how it felt to love and be loved. I knew what it meant to be both more and less than a single person; more, because there were – duh! – more of us; more, because of the currents that ran between us, the energy supplies; more, because the one could confirm, with or without words, the rightness of what the other was saying; less, because Catherine was uninhibited. There were things one of us might not say for fear of upsetting the other, in front of a third party; whereas Catherine, the third party, had no 'other' to upset. She was singular in her opinions and, what's more, she was unique. She was the only single person in the room. The eye went to her. I (we) noticed and was (were) flattered that, as the evening went on, she felt she could ask us anything. She wasn't careful to present a self we'd find endearing. She wanted to speak the truth and have the truth spoken back to her.

How, she asked, did we know John Smith? I told her. Then, because a *man* attacks what he fears (his ex) but a *husband* has nothing to fear, secure as he is in his love for his wife and hers for him, I went on to describe my ex, Renate, as a dynamic and exciting person. That, in turn, led me to praise the phenomenal intellect, determination and success of Sarah's ex, Mark. Sarah and Catherine, increasingly, looked at me as if I were *on* something, which I was – I was high on loving and drinking and living in the country. Then I drained the pasta, Sarah grated the beetroot and Parmesan and the three of us slurped the purple.

At 10 p.m. – London early but country late – Catherine kissed our four cheeks and told us how pleased she was to have met us and how nice it was to think we were only next door. Then she walked out of our cottage and over the wall and was home.

In bed, there was only one topic. We spoke of her in a hush, which you could attribute to her proximity. But the hush was pleasurable and intimate, like a conversation in a provocative corset.

Sarah whispered that Catherine was beautiful. I whispered that, no, she was striking. 'Striking' isn't an easy word to whisper; but I wasn't going to lie there and accept that Catherine was beautiful. Sarah wondered what I meant by 'striking', so I told her: Elizabeth the First. The bed creaked. (It was months before we realised that the bed didn't creak at all; it was the floorboards.) Sarah insisted that Elizabeth the First was beautiful, as Catherine was. But it turned out she didn't mean Elizabeth the First; she meant Helen Mirren, who'd played her on television. Helen Mirren, I opined, was not beautiful or striking – she was strong and sexual, as opposed to sexy. Sarah asked me to define the distinction. (I suspected there was none.) But we were now two removes – Elizabeth the First, Helen Mirren – from Catherine. I was safe now. I could relax. I blathered, till Sarah fell asleep.

To step out of our front door and see her in her cottage – no, not even that – to be in our cottage and know she lived next door, that was enough. It was at once comforting and exciting, exciting because we didn't yet know her, comforting because we did, or felt we did, or sort of did. She was a familiar stranger.

From that tiny pot of parsley, everything grew. The next weekend, Sarah knocked at her door to say she was driving to the nursery at Wenhaston and did Catherine want to come? I was excluded (and happy to be), on account of my horticultural ignorance, but included when they came back to ours, thirsty for coffee and laden with mulberry trees, one for each garden. The two women made a joint statement. The trees, Sarah said, were four years old and wouldn't, Catherine said, fruit for another five years. I felt as if it were me they were planting. They were telling me I was going nowhere. In five years, simply by staying where I was, I'd eat mulberries from our garden.

'Sarah says you've never been to Staverton Thicks,' said Catherine.

'We thought we'd go now,' said Sarah.

'Then you're coming back to mine for supper,' said Catherine.

She took us to the places she loved. She was not like Keith. Keith went everywhere with a purpose. When he took me to the beach, it was to catch fish. When he took me cycling, it was to pick fruit. When he took me sailing from Aldeburgh to Orford, it was to get to Orford. (When we got there, I asked him what we did now; he told me we waited for the right time and tide to return. There it was, then – the purpose of our going was, in fact, to come back.) Catherine, by contrast, understood that we hadn't moved to the country to get anywhere or do anything, not to hunt, not to shoot, not to fish, sail or farm. We'd moved to the country for the largest purpose and the most nebulous: to live.

Catherine, unlike Keith, hadn't grown up in Suffolk, gone to school there, worked there. She'd come to live where she used to holiday, and that was the spirit in which she took us to places – the living holiday spirit. Sarah knew all about this. She too had always holidayed, as a child, in the English countryside. She'd camped and caravanned in Dorset, Devon and Cornwall. She'd even grown up in a North Downs village (Tandridge), whereas I'd never breathed the open air. I'd grown up in a London suburb, which was like living in a box inside a box. There was the box (Acton) and there was the bigger box (London).

The medieval forest at Staverton Thicks was the first place Catherine took us, before the sand dunes and reed beds of Covehithe and the church in Blythburgh known as the 'Cathedral of Suffolk'.

'You get these wonderful yellow flag lilies round the edge of the lake,' said Catherine, as we walked towards the forest. 'Where all those pollarded oaks are, that's Old Staverton Woods.' I could tell that Sarah was memorising; she'd disseminate this information at a later date, probably to her mother, who'd in turn memorise and disseminate, believing that knowledge was something you shouldn't keep to yourself. As for me, I looked into the distance, vaguely. I knew, just, what an oak was, but had no idea what it looked like pollarded. I was hoping to see a pollarder pollarding as we spoke; preferably, for ease of identification, he or she would be wearing a jacket with a 'P' on the back.

'I've seen foxes here. Badgers. There's a World War II bomber buried in the bracken. But I've never found it.' She smirked. 'I love your shoes.'

'Oh yes!' said Sarah, smirking with her.

I loved my shoes too. They were green suede Chelsea boots, with pointed toes, from Shelly's Shoes in Oxford Street. I'd owned them since I was a teenager and had had them re-heeled and -soled many times. They were my clubbing shoes, the ones I'd taken off when I'd danced naked at the Where House. And now here they were, near a forest, toeing leaves.

As a single man, mocked for his footwear by a single woman,

I'd have been irritated by the insult, or coolly disregarded it, which comes to the same thing. In my vanity, I might have wondered if the woman was provoking me to get my attention, in which case I'd have given her what she wanted, though not to the degree she wanted. A small smile, maybe. Some not-ignoring. But here, as a bald teddy bear of a husband, I knew to be a good self-deprecating sport. It was my role to join with them in laughing at myself.

'I suppose they're a tad inappropriate,' I said.

'I can't believe I let you out of the house in them,' said Sarah. And now, for the first time, Catherine joined *me*. She defended me against my oppressor, my footwear monitor, this wife who wouldn't allow me out unless I was correctly dressed, like a bouncer-in-reverse.

'Actually, they're rather nice. You don't want to be one of those people who has all the right gear. Then you're just a person out of a catalogue.'

As we got ready to go out to Catherine's, for supper, I asked Sarah if I should put on the shoes again. I was teasing her but she thought I was mocking her. She thought she deserved to be mocked. She couldn't understand why she'd made that remark about letting me out of the house. She didn't want to control me. We should be equal partners, each with rights and obligations, neither with the power to tell the other what to wear. There should be a 'negative equality' in a marriage. I was fresh out of the shower, towelling my crotch, wondering how we'd got from my green suede shoes to negative equality, though Sarah, in her concern to be a good person, sometimes confused goodness with humourlessness.

'What do you think I should wear?' asked Sarah. I asked her why she couldn't wear what she wore on the walk. She told me we should make an effort. We should dress to go out, even if we were going next door. Why did I equate lack of distance with lack of effort?

'Tell me what to wear,' she said, without irony.

For the forty years before he sold it to us, Old Man Hargreaves had rented out Hay Cottage. For forty years, he'd given it a landlord's love. There was nothing structurally wrong with it but nothing aesthetically right. It was a temple to Artex, the Greek god of shit.

Myrtle Cottage, which he owned but occupied every summer, most weekends and occasional Christmases, was where he brought his wife and their two daughters, Mel and Catherine. Catherine, as she showed us round, kept apologising for how nice it was. And how big. How *bigger*.

From the front, our cottages looked like twins. But they were big and little sisters. Myrtle Cottage had a third bedroom, which Catherine now occupied, in the roof. He'd also built an extension at the back, where we dined, a glass construction, an outdoor indoors, a place where you went to be fed and watered, while you expanded; a human greenhouse.

'I don't know if you're planning an extension. But I wouldn't object. How could I?' Thus, in her crisp way, Catherine told us that our friendship wouldn't be ended by planning objections which were, after all, why most friendships with neighbours didn't even begin. Everyone knows the neighbour 'journey', which starts with a smile and ends in court. A neighbour, as any cynic will tell you, isn't someone who lives next door but a random malefactor, geography's revenge. And they breed, oh yes. The only thing worse than a neighbour is a neighbour's child, who grows up to be a drummer; but it's not so bad, you don't notice the drums, or so you shout at the people to whom you're desperate to sell your house.

'Thank you,' we said to Catherine, in unison. It was one of

many exquisite moments that summer. (I shouldn't write 'that summer', in that faux-elegiac way, as if it were our Last Summer; we didn't *die*.) It was one of many moments in which Catherine brought us together, making us say or think the same things, at the same time. Yes, that's exactly what we'd do. We'd put an extension at the back and we'd put a bedroom in the roof. We'd clone Catherine's cottage, thereby doubling our internal landscape. And in that extra space we'd put a baby. We were, after all, a young couple, even if we weren't, in our mid-thirties, all that young. As half of a young couple, I felt sexual, but not sexy – yes, that was it, that was the distinction – I felt that my purpose was to breed. Just as an old man could die at any time, I could breed at any time. I had thought, on moving to the country, that this breeding instinct would be heightened by proximity to animals. But that wasn't it. I'd found myself, when first driving down The Lane, diverted by two pigs piggybacking in a field. They did it with a mechanical vacancy that didn't make me feel like breeding. Those fucking pigs, thinking nothing, keeping their eyes on the field in front of them, made me feel like driving. They might as well have been sucking mints from a circular tin. No, it was warmth and wine and the company of my wife that made me feel like breeding; and the presence of a single woman, encouraging us to extend our cottage.

Catherine poured us both more wine, from one of the bottles of red burgundy she'd inherited from her father along, of course, with the cottage.

'Delicious,' I said.

'Lovely,' said Sarah but, unlike me, she was referring to the Thai chicken curry, which must have taken far longer to prepare than our pasta. What's more, Catherine had taken the trouble to bring it to us in fullyformed portions, as in a restaurant. There was no wondering if you'd given yourself too much. She'd given it already, in perfectly judged amounts.

I was woozy with benevolence. 'Soma' by the Strokes was

playing – cool music, from my single days – but it turned out to be playing in my head. I felt the flesh on my face thickening. This next-door dining was a treat. You could drink and drink some more and your partner could do likewise.

'We'll have to get a cab home,' I said. This time, it was Catherine and Sarah who reacted in unison, with a synchronised silence. I winced, remembering I'd made this joke an hour earlier, when it was new.

'If you ever want a cab, John from Middleton, the retired policeman, he's delightful, he talks if you want and not if you don't. And his stories are all about crime, so they're interesting.' With this, she got up, in the middle of the meal, and fetched an ancient alphabetised black book with a white label – Useful Numbers – opened it, turned to C for cabs, then copied John's number onto the sheet of lined paper she was, for our benefit, filling with Useful Numbers. John the cab driver sat happily on his line, below Jumbo the logman, Doug the joiner and the all-purpose Rosie, a yoga teacher and bookkeeper who also upholstered chairs. I tried to decipher what was written in the black book next to 'Andy', in the handwriting of her mother. It was: 'Ipswich, fifteen shillings'. Andy was a pre-decimal driver, a sixties man, whose name had been written in a now-dead hand – Catherine's mother, we learned, had died of cancer some years earlier. There'd never been an Old Woman Hargreaves.

'You must give me the recipe,' said Sarah, then corrected herself. 'Give *us* the recipe. I don't really know what makes Thai food Thai.'

'There's a spice stall at the farmers' market, first Saturday of the month.' ('Spice Stall/Farmers' Market/1st Sat', she wrote, below John the cabbie.) 'I don't cook much,' she added. 'There's no incentive to cook when you're on your own.' Sarah went quiet. Catherine had somehow 'outed' herself as a person who lived on her own. It was a statement, albeit a statement of something we all already knew. How should we respond? If she'd outed herself as gay or Christian, we'd know. We'd respect and tolerate her path and know not to feel pity. But this living-on-your-own: was that a path? A chosen path? Or a condition from which she'd recover? We were on the point of saying something kind when, thankfully, Catherine stopped us.

'Least I didn't take to you to the Hat and Feathers. I hope you haven't eaten there. It's where Keith and Margaret go. Have you met them?' I thought I couldn't get happier, but she'd proved me wrong.

'Keith and Margaret!' I replied, making her (suppressed) exclamation mark explicit. I had no doubt: she felt what we felt. I'd been right about John Smith and would be right again.

'He's a nightmare, isn't he, he's the prince of darkness, and she's just this lovely funny fat person, let's face it.'

Over the next few minutes of anecdote-trading, Keith got darker and darker and Margaret lovelier, funnier and fatter until, through the glass ceiling of the extension, we might have seen her sail over our heads, that lovely, funny, luminous fat balloon. Catherine had known them for twenty years. We'd known – and then de-known – them for a couple of months. So Catherine more than shared our opinion. She validated it. She was our senior partner in Worth, with a lifetime of local knowledge. We wanted her plumber and her joiner and her bookkeeper, yes, but most of all we wanted her opinions which, like those phone numbers, were facts. Facts aren't necessarily truths, as you'll know if you've ever been in a pub and heard a loudmouth shout: 'That's a fact!' But Catherine's opinions, to us, were true.

'There are so many couples like Keith and Margaret. Where you can't understand it.'

We were tense and excited, waiting to learn what we couldn't understand.

'One of them completely manipulates the other. It's Keith, isn't it? You don't think so when you first meet them, but he's in charge.'

'It's always the quiet ones,' I said. But this was pub cliché and wrong.

'No, with my sister and her husband, it's the loud one, believe me.'

'I believe you,' said Sarah.

'So many people are weak. Or disloyal. Or manipulative. You're lucky to have found each other.'

Downstairs, in our fridge, were the foiled remains of the Thai Chicken Curry and the subsequent Apricot and Almond Tart, bequeathed to us by Catherine because she was off to Rome the next day, to visit friends. Upstairs, in our bedroom, we cuddled each other, like babes in a cottage, warmed by each other's bodies and her words, their sentiment and their unsentimentality. We were lucky to have found each other, not because Sarah was gorgeous and I was nice – no, she hadn't larded us with romcom goo. She'd praised us for our negatives: not weak, not disloyal, not manipulative.

'She's got no one,' said Sarah, into the dark, stating an injustice. We embodied that injustice. Why should we have each other when Catherine had no one? We lay there, contemplating the cruelty of our luck. Sarah unclasped herself from me, as if to make for parity with Catherine, lying alone in bed on the other side of the wall, but on a higher plane, in her bedroom in the roof.

'She wants a man, doesn't she?' asked Sarah. She didn't mean that Catherine wanted a man, as opposed to being on her own. She meant Catherine wanted a man as opposed to a woman.

'What do you think?' I asked.

'Definitely. From the way she touched your head.'

At the end of the evening, the three of us had walked from her glass room to her front door. Near the doormat, Catherine kissed Sarah, then me. I then kissed Sarah, which was weird, since I wasn't saying goodbye to her.

'What did you do that for?' Sarah demanded, embarrassed. Catherine laughed. Then she asked Sarah if she might touch the bald top of my head, as it was something she'd wanted to do since she'd met us. Sarah told Catherine to be her guest. Catherine stroked my crown. It was nothing like the two-handed stroking of my head and ears with which Renate introduced herself, all those years before. It was more like a person stroking a dog, in front of its owner, to show the owner that the person likes dogs. I had the sense, at the time, that she touched my head for Sarah's benefit. She was saying, manually, to Sarah: 'I like these. But I don't want this one. I want one of these for myself.'

In exchange for her food and wine and company, her local numbers, her validation of our opinions – her validation of *us* – we decided to provide Catherine with a man.

For years and years, I was an advertising copywriter in a building in Hanover Square. Now I struggled to remember anything I'd produced, apart from the Fiat commercials. That's because an office is not a factory but a theatre. An eight-to-ten-hour play's produced, every day, by the characters in the office. It's their relationships with each other that stoke the drama. Customers, clients and members of the public are offstage. That is why, famously, leaving cards are the best things that come out of offices – after, that is, they've been opened in the office, so all can enjoy the look on the leaver's face. Geoff and I spent weeks on Stone's leaving cards. We wanted to give him several, to show much we thought about him and *what* we thought about him. There was satire, too, in offering him a selection, since this is what we did every time he, as our boss, asked us to present him with an idea. We would never go into his office with a single idea and the conviction it was right. We went in there with several, for him to reduce to two or three, while wheeling his chair away from his desk and (deliberately) knocking the wall with the back of his head, in a parody of tortured creativity. (As Geoff remarked, 'What's creative about choosing?') Then the two or three ideas became one; and Stone presented the chosen one to the client, with an intense belief I found embarrassing – I found Stone's belief literally unbelievable, as if he'd drunk from a bottle called Belief, whose effects would last only the hour and a half of the meeting.

Geoff and I reckoned we'd present him with six leaving cards. He could then play his game of sending us away to work up two or three of the cards into better-achieved versions of themselves, from which he'd choose The One. Of course, he might miss that joke and simply thank us for giving him six leaving cards. But the joke was on us. For all the time and love we put into his leaving cards, Stone never saw them, because he never left. I left, instead, leaving the leaving cards, which Geoff swore would have their desired effect. It was his belief that if we made the cards, they'd somehow curse Stone into leaving, like a coffin you build secretly in the shed to make your mad, bad dad die in his bedroom. But just as dads are bound to die, so Stone was bound to leave, whether we made those cards or not. Geoff's belief was illogical. Our cause had no effect. Then again, it was a belief, so it didn't have to be logical. Geoff was inspired by his hatred for our boss to produce his finest work: a drawing of Stone on the cross, captioned 'Thank Christ you're leaving', the crudity of the joke offset by the delicacy of the drawing. Geoff had no doubt this was 'work', since he did it, over many, many hours, in that building, while being paid, albeit to do something else.

If Hammond Law Stone Fisk was a multi-storey theatre, what was the study/second bedroom of Hay Cottage, Worth? I felt, on the first day I sat down to work there, like the hero of a late Beckett play, a very late Beckett play, the kind he might have written the day he died, in which the lights go down then up again and you see nothing, because there's nothing to see. The hero is humming at the bottom of a well but you can't see the well because the well has been paved over and you can't hear the hero because he's humming to himself. How much theatre can one man generate? I had no hate, lust, love, resentment, comradeship, humour or envy, other than that I felt for myself.

Now, a few months later, I loved everything about that room. I knew what was wonderful about working on your own in a room in the country. There was quiet, there was calm, there was light, there was time, which was nothing like the time in a London office. I don't mean there was a 'lack of distractions'. Time didn't present itself to me as a 'lack'. Time was a gift. Each minute of the working day was delivered to that room, having been buffed, measured and weighed, inspected and quality-controlled. Every minute was sixty seconds long and Swissly perfect. In an office in London, as everyone knows, other people literally take your time, stealing about forty minutes from every hour, with their jokes and their questions and their complaints and their gossip and their insistence that you watch a thirty-four-second clip of otters holding hands, because nine million, four hundred and twelve thousand, eight hundred and ninety-six other people have watched it, the first of them voluntarily and the rest under instruction.

Then there was the view. I could see no pigs from the cottage, only cattle, sheep, a farmhouse, land and sky. But the view was my friend. *Crackling knocked at the door of Lard's pigloo. 'One of Mrs Hen's chicks is missing!' he cried. Lard quickly pulled on his trousers.* I couldn't illustrate this without dreaming. The purpose of the dream was not to hallucinate a pig's trousers. It was to dream that the pig's trousers mattered and, while I was drawing them, nothing else did. The cattle, sheep, farmhouse, land, sky and birds helped me reach that desired dream state. At worst, they exuded indifference. My aim was to be lost to the world, and they couldn't care if I was lost or not, which was fine. At best, over time, they made me feel I too had a place in their landscape. They were a cow or a barn or an avocet and I was a man at a cottage window, illustrating a children's book about pig detectives. I was one of the all things bright and beautiful, a creature somewhere between great and small.

As soon as I sat at that window, I could delude myself that my work was important, without which delusion I couldn't do the work. When I sat at the (non-opening) seventh-floor window of that building in Hanover Square, I didn't have to delude myself that my copywriting was important. When I worked for Hammond Law Stone Fisk, they did the deluding for me. It started as soon as I approached the building and saw those four names, big and black on the smoked glass of the double doors. Already, four people thought the building mattered. And then I entered and saw the receptionist on the phone, the motorcycle messenger hovering before her, carrying a package; the people-with-appointments waiting on the red leather sofas, not reading the magazines on the low tables but watching HLSF's latest commercials playing and replaying, silently, on the screen on the wall, while smart people, doing-well people, headed for the lifts, studying the winking numbers on the panel above the lift doors. Receiving, phoning, hovering, carrying, waiting, watching, playing, replaying, doing well, heading, studying, winking: something was happening here. Surely. Surely. And then there was the salary. They wouldn't have paid me that much if my work hadn't been important.

The boiled-sweet-faced woman had died. There was already a For Sale sign outside her pink cottage. When new owners moved in, we'd knock on their door and patronise them. We'd tell them where the nearest petrol station was, and where to find a takeaway Thai. The woman's death was a rite of passage for all three of us. She had passed on to the afterlife, while we'd progressed to our next stage as residents of Worth. We were villagers who'd outlived another villager.

In this second stage, we were more wary, less inclined to talk to strangers. Sarah stopped going to the Worth Yoga Class, on account of a fellow pupil who'd never even talked to her, which was why Sarah left – to deny her that opportunity. This woman's mat was always in the front row, nearest the teacher. Her name was Emma-Kate and everything about her spoke of domination and greed, even her name, which had two components to all the other women's one. She weighed, she told the frizzy-haired woman on the neighbouring mat, what she'd weighed when she was twelve. The frizzy woman looked puzzled. She didn't know what she'd done to provoke this revelation. (She'd done nothing; she was just there, next to Emma-Kate, who spoke through her to all the women.) A great deal of this adult-child body was on display. Her leotard rode up her buttocks, as if it wanted to be a thong. There was worse. She'd lived in Marylebone and run a public relations consultancy in the City. Now she'd moved to Suffolk to start a new consultancy, with clients from the charity and environmental sectors.

This was why Sarah withdrew: not because they had nothing in common but because they had too much. Sarah had lived in Marylebone, worked in the City and come to Suffolk to be a lawyer for a charity (and practise yoga). She wasn't even sure that she didn't weigh the same as she did when she was twelve. I told her she was naturally slight and, anyway, it wasn't a goal she'd set out to achieve, nor did she boast about it. But Sarah refused to be convinced. Looking at Emma-Kate was like looking at that most terrifying thing, a mirror. I tried again.

'But this woman's a rich controlling bitch. You're not controlling or a bitch. And you're not rich, not now anyway.'

What she feared more than anything was that Emma-Kate would seize on these similarities and make Sarah her friend.

That last lesson, as they'd put away the mats, Emma-Kate had looked at her, with friendly intent. Sarah uttered 'Sorry', then left. (Why had she even said 'Sorry'?) She contacted Rosie, the bookkeeping, upholstering yoga teacher Catherine had recommended, and arranged to go to her house for individual tuition. It was more expensive but more rewarding. The not-seeing of Emma-Kate was itself a reward.

What a pleasure it was to know Catherine but not Emma-Kate. Catherine did not demand you knew her, whether you wanted to or not. As if to prove the point, the phone rang as we said this. Catherine never knocked on our door without phoning in advance. (In the country, I discovered, you never use the doorbell. Country people knock.) She always made an appointment-to-knock, in deference to the demands of my work and the chores and pleasures of coupledom, such as the two of you being together and doing nothing at all, which is neither a pleasure nor a chore. She understood that an unexpected phone call's nothing like an unexpected knock. You can agree not to answer the phone but you have to go to the door. The knocker knows. The knocker knows you're there. Your car's outside.

It was a Saturday morning. Catherine was wondering if we wanted to go to the beach at Dunwich. There was a particular patch of sea off Dunwich beach from which you could look back at the land and not see a single man-made structure. Sarah listened to Catherine's voice on the phone, while I just about heard it, live, coming from the other side of our living-room wall. A minute later, I heard her front door slam, and so began the latest of our Saturday expeditions. This was what we did on Saturdays. Who could, or needed to, remember what we used to do? That first Saturday we spent at Staverton Thicks was Saturday Zero.

The three of us apart. The three of us together. Sarah with me, Catherine apart. Sarah with Catherine, me apart. Catherine with me, Sarah apart. Those were the permutations, of which the most common were the three of us together and Sarah with Catherine, walking ahead of me, talking about sisters.

'Does she have to live with us?' This was what Mel, aged two, asked her parents, when she visited her newborn sister in hospital. That quickly became of one of their parents' 'amusing' family stories. Catherine had heard it so often she believed she remembered it. She knew she remembered Mel, when Catherine was two, standing on their father's lap, with her back to Catherine, preventing Catherine from seeing her daddy's face.

We drove to Dunwich in our car. Catherine sat in the back and told us her history with men. Men in London. Men in Brussels. Beautiful men. Married men. Unfaithful men. Weak men. Men who couldn't face the truth. Married unfaithful weak men who couldn't face the truth. Why were men like this?

This question – 'Why are men like this?' – was not directed to me but to us. We were a husband and wife. I was not, as I've already said, a man, which meant Catherine could say what she liked about men without offending me. I was, in effect, an ex-man. Of course I had opinions, but when I expressed them, the women went quiet and waited for me to stop talking so they could start again, as if they knew more about men than I did, which in a sense they did, since I'd never lived with or loved or been betrayed by a man. Nevertheless, I'd been a man, which was more than they had; there were times in that driving seat when I wanted them to defer to my knowledge. But they didn't. They just wanted me to drive. At such times it was me, not Catherine, who was outnumbered. She was a single woman outnumbered by a couple. But I was a lone man in a car with two women.

Michael, the love of her early twenties, was a lecturer in philosophy at Birkbeck. He was a beautiful man with a beautiful mind who was unfaithful with many other women, 'serially but not seriously', according to him. But that wasn't true, not for the student who took him so seriously that she committed suicide. Gilberto, who worked at the Italian Embassy in London, was only ever unfaithful to Catherine with one woman. But she, it transpired, was his wife: a wife he kept secret from Catherine for the first six months that Catherine and Gilberto were 'together'. Then there was Charlie, who was a gardener (and a poet. I knew, as soon as she said he was a gardener, that Charlie wasn't just a gardener. And so it proved. He was not even just a poet, but a poet whose debut collection had won two prizes). She loved Charlie and Charlie loved her but he would not commit to her, claiming he was not 'worthy' of her. What, asked Catherine, did that mean? Did it mean he found her too demanding and, if it did, why didn't he say so, truthfully, to her, instead of making obscure allusions to her in his opaque prize-winning poems? Did the prizes make him feel she was not worthy of him, which he couldn't say, so he said the opposite, thinking that if one of them wasn't worthy of the other, it could never work out, no matter which of them was unworthy?

She was not frightened to explore these difficulties with a Jungian analyst. After working with him for five years, she fell in love with an older man, who was sensitive and brilliant but (once again) married. His name was Simon and he was the analyst. (That was the order in which she gave us the information, not for dramatic effect but so we'd think of him, primarily, as sensitive and brilliant.) Simon was truly in love with her and wasn't the first analyst to have a relationship with a patient. We shouldn't think of it as an abuse of trust, when it felt like the quintessence of trust. He talked about leaving his wife for her. He even asked her to consider converting to Judaism, in order that they could be together. (There was no question of his converting to the Church of England, not that Catherine would have wanted him to.) But still we weren't to think badly of him. We were to think badly of her sister Mel who, having winkled all this information out of Catherine, wrote, without asking Catherine's permission, to Simon's professional association demanding they send her 'his balls on a silver salver'. They declined but the consequences for Simon were severe. His wife divorced him.

'A silver salver,' repeated Sarah. 'That's typical, isn't it? Why did she have to have them on that? What's wrong with a plastic tray?' I wasn't even sure Sarah was joking but the car, which had been a torture box for half an hour, became a place of laughter. Catherine was thrilled. She leaned forward and put both hands on Sarah's shoulders.

I parked the car at the Dunwich beach car park, near the cafe with the wooden refectory tables outside.

'There's someone for everyone,' I said. The women went quiet again. Catherine, I'm sure, didn't believe me, while Sarah was embarrassed. It sounded like something I'd been told by a greetings card. But I was convinced. After all, there'd been someone for me.

Men didn't tell the truth about their thoughts or actions or feelings: that was Catherine's theme. This was why truth mattered so much to her. She prided herself that she dealt in it – not just factually accurate information but integrity, truth to oneself. She knew her opinions and stuck to them. She didn't change her opinions if she found they weren't modish or acceptable. As Catherine and I walked down the beach together – for we'd got to the point in our friendship where we could talk to each other as we entered the sea – she told me it was wonderful that I'd said that thing about 'someone for everyone'. The coming and staying together of two people was a secular miracle.

'I can see you love Sarah. You're faithful. That's wonderful.'

She dived in and was off. She was a powerful swimmer. Sarah and I couldn't keep up. I lay on my back and made like a starfish. The starfish was my favourite stroke. It was an anti-stroke, which got you nowhere. But anyone who's lain on his back on a carpet, in a flat with Sam Davey, for years, listening to Radiohead and looking up at the damp patch – *We must do something about the damp patch* – will naturally, in water, opt for the starfish. I looked at the sky and thought of myself as faithful. I was a faithful husband. I was proud that Catherine had identified me as such. It was a shame, though, that she hadn't referred to my unfaithful past. Did she even know about it? I hadn't always been faithful, which made my faithfulness, now, more remarkable. I wasn't, by nature, faithful. 'Faithful' – that was the adjective Catherine had pinned to me, the adjective you pin to a servant or a West Highland terrier.

Sarah swam to me and pressed my belly with her hand, collapsing my starfish.

'Have you told Catherine about my past?'

'How d'you mean?'

'I mean, have you told her about my past?'

'You mean John Smith sucking your willy? Why don't you tell her? It's your willy.'

'No, no. It's all right.'

We swam back to the shore.

Half an hour later, I brought three portions of fish and chips out to the refectory table.

'I'm ravenous,' said Catherine. We agreed that food was never more needed or deserved than after a swim.

'I love your crawl,' I said, knowing that Sarah loved Catherine's crawl too. This was the kind of thing a faithful husband can say. 'I love your crawl': sycophantic and lecherous, as spoken by a single man.

'We've found you a man,' said Sarah.

'Really?' said Catherine. 'That's very kind. Terrifying, though.'

'There's nothing terrifying about him,' said Sarah. 'He's a good man and true.'

'What's his name?'

Sarah gazed down at her chips, in search of his name. She could never remember his real name, since we always called him 'Dad'.

We'd had the idea as we sat on the beach together, watching Catherine swim. Dad was the man for Catherine. He was a decent and kind and straightforward man, the antidote to those torturing and complicated lecturers, poets and analysts.

As for the truth, on which Catherine insisted, I told it straight away. I told her that Dad was married – calling him, obviously, Paul. I told her Paul lived on his own and had been separated from his (second) wife for over a year. She asked why his marriages ended and Sarah, who'd never met either wife, came straight back with: 'They were stupid women who didn't deserve him.'

'What else should I know about him?' asked Catherine. Now, at last, I could assert myself. Catherine knew all about men, but nothing about Dad. I told her how, aged seventeen, he'd driven Sam Davey and me home from that party to which he hadn't been invited; how, a few years later, a paranoid Sam Davey had called him to the flat we shared off the Holloway Road after we'd taken magic mushrooms with the two French-language students who lived in the upstairs flat, and I'd climbed a tree in the garden and was unable to come down; how Dad had arrived, with his own ladder, and gently coaxed me onto it, from my awkward angle, his branch-side manner gentle and encouraging, his hands firm and decisive, one hand manoeuvring my feet onto the rungs of the ladder, while the other gripped the belt of my jeans then hoicked me into the perpendicular; how, instead of judging us, he left us the ladder, in case it happened again; how we couldn't get the ladder out of its fully upright position, so were forced to leave it on the floor of our kitchen, where it stretched diagonally through to the living room; how he was the only dentist I'd ever known who properly explained to his patients what the hell he was doing in there; how, before I went to him, I'd had a non-speaking dentist, a music-less dentist and a country-and-western dentist, whereas Dad had amassed the largest UK dental surgery collection of piano sonata CDs. To sit in his chair was to learn to appreciate classical music. Every six months I listened to Beethoven, Chopin, Ravel, Liszt, Schubert,

Mozart, Haydn or that Russian composer – here I faltered – the Wolfman, the Peter and the Wolfman, while he said, 'Cavity, lower left six.'

'Prokofiev,' said Catherine. The sun was shining on the Dunwich cafe and the little children at the next-door table were giggling as their dog put its paws on the table, in an effort to reach their chips. I felt good. I'd told Catherine about Dad and, just as important, I'd mentioned drugs and the French-language students who lived upstairs, so she'd get a sense of the badness of my past; she'd surely assume, from the language students' proximity, that we'd all had *sexe*; whereas the truth was, Sam Davey slept with Isabelle but I slept with Isabelle *and* Mathilde. (Just by thinking that sentence, I knew I could never say it, out loud, to Catherine. 'I slept with Isabelle *and* Mathilde' – it sounds like something a six-year-old would say to his friend in the back of the car, prompting his mummy to say: 'Don't boast.') I told her that Dad's first wife, whom he'd married when he was twenty-one and she was nearly thirty, was a neurotic woman who thought Dad was the only man who could deal with her neuroses. She'd manipulated him into marriage and then got bored with him. His second wife was an actress and singer. She was insecure, as all actresses and singers are, and had left him for the leading man of the musical she was in. After the musical ended, the leading man shocked her by asking her to return the key to his flat.

None of this, I stressed, made Dad a victim. Dad was strong. He'd declined to have his second wife back after her affair was over. Every morning at seven, I told her proudly – as if it reflected well on me – Dad went to his local pool and swam seventy lengths, a mixture of crawl and butterfly.

'He has a wonderful upper body,' said Sarah, which sounded celebratory and truthful as, when said by a man of a woman, 'She's got big tits' does not.

Catherine's tongue made a little clucking sound. She swallowed her last mouthful of cod and asked when she was going to meet him.

We rang Dad later that day. Is it possible for 'we' to ring? Yes: Sarah picked up the phone, punched the digits, pressed Speaker, then stood the phone on the table, allowing us to speak to Dad together. Now we told Dad how wonderful Catherine was, with her poise and clarity and sophistication, her accomplishments, her love of outdoors, her swimming.

'Breast or crawl?' asked Dad.

'Crawl,' said Sarah. 'She's brilliant. We've just been swimming with her on Dunwich beach. She's amazingly fast.' She paused, worried she'd overdone it. 'I mean, she doesn't do it professionally.'

I laughed. Dad laughed. Sarah laughed. I don't think any of us exactly knew why. The laughter signalled that the overture was over and the opera now had to begin. We agreed a Saturday in early August, for Dad to come up and stay.

Dad would be the first overnight visitor to our cottage. We bought pillows, pillowcases, fitted sheet, duvet and duvet cover for our as yet unused sofa bed, so our living room could convert into his bedroom. We took all this white stuff out of its wrapping, hauled and unfolded the bed from the bowel of the sofa, then took the pillows, the pillowcases, the fitted sheet and duvet and duvet cover for a brief test-nap. Sarah was disconsolate. She found the bed hard. She wished we'd already converted our roof space into a bedroom, so we had a spare bedroom with a decent bed. I told her Dad wasn't coming for the bed. He was coming for Catherine.

Sarah thought we shouldn't try too hard. We should just introduce them, then stand back. I asked her how we were going to

107

stand back, when Dad would be staying with us and Catherine lived next door. We'd be their chaperones, their host and hostess, Dad's landlord and landlady, their friends and, anyway, there was no room in our cottage for us to stand back. Besides, why shouldn't we try too hard? Sarah was good at trying too hard. She applied herself industriously to the causes in which she believed, as and when she believed in them: the study of law, the practice of law, mergers and acquisitions, the diabetic Mark, the homeless, me, moving to the country, yoga, Catherine.

'OK then,' said Sarah, pleased I'd called her bluff, and then she thought of everything. What would he like to eat? Where would he like to go? We thought he'd like to go to Blythburgh Church, Orford Church, Orford Ness, Orford Castle, the beaches at Covehithe, Southwold, Walberswick, Dunwich, Thorpeness, Aldeburgh and Shingle Street, Framlingham Castle, Snape Maltings, Staverton Thicks, Butley Priory and Butley Creek. We thought he'd like to go to a pub, maybe the King's Head in Woodbridge or the Low House at Laxfield or the Ramsholt Arms at Ramsholt. We thought he'd like to stroll through the towns of Halesworth and Beccles and Saxmundham and Bungay and the villages of Yoxford and Peasenhall and Westleton and Middleton and Wenhaston and Great Glemham and Sweffling and Bramfield, just to relax. And as we made this list we understood what we wanted from him, maybe because he was a Londoner: we wanted him to know our life was good. We had quantity of life.

It was Catherine who said that, after driving from London, he'd probably just like to laze around on Aldeburgh beach. We agreed. She hadn't yet met him and already she was sensing his wishes. This was what we wanted to encourage. So, as soon as Dad arrived, we got him out of his car, into the cottage, gave him a glass of water and then put him in our car, in the back, with Catherine.

We put a cold bag of foodstuffs in the boot for our picnic and then we headed off.

It was immediately apparent that Dad expected Catherine to talk and Catherine expected Dad to talk. But Dad was not a talker. He was a talkee. That's what had drawn him to me and Sam Davey in the first place, the teenage place; he liked to listen to our cynical banter, which wasn't a stream but a series of spurts, punctuated by a cool and mocking silence, which teachers should have called 'smart insolence'. We didn't only mock, though; without warning, we'd lurch into praise. Praise as dogma. Sam Davey would suddenly and terminally opine that Joy Division was the only band that mattered, or I'd say that Parmesan/Isabelle Huppert/Chet Baker/squid was the only cheese/actress/trumpeter/fish that mattered. But Dad wasn't bantering, insolent or dogmatic and never pretended to be, which lack of pretence was what made him seem older, made him seem Dad.

What did Dad think of Catherine? Since she was quiet, there was nothing to go on but her looks. She wore a blue linen shirt. She had a sun hat out of a Renoir painting. There wasn't enough sun in the back of our car to necessitate a hat, which meant she was wearing it for style not protection, though it partly obscured her face – in that sense, she was wearing it to protect herself from the rays of Dad, his potentially burning gaze. With her pale skin, she didn't look like someone who would go to a beach for the sun. She was a bather not a sunbather. Her skin, in fact, looked unusually pale because Catherine had hennaed her hair. I wanted to say to Dad: Listen, you've never seen this woman before but I'm telling you, she's got new hair. It's a sign. She's renewing herself. In her mind and on her head, it's spring. She is ready and willing to embrace the new. You are the new. But Catherine's expression and hat conveyed the opposite: she was wary of the new and wasn't going to make it easy for the new to get near her.

There we sat, the four of us, with Sarah at the wheel, each with an invisible airbag of silence inflating in front of our faces. Soon we wouldn't be able to speak. Our noses and mouths would be stymied and contorted, as if painted by Francis Bacon.

'Have you had a good week?' asked Dad.

'That's an onion field,' I said. I had to say it, as the smell was in all our nostrils. Then Sarah took over, as is the driver's right. She told Dad – and indeed Catherine – that I'd had a great week. I was nearly at the end of my work on Crackling and Lard and had fixed up a date to take the finished drawings to the editor. She said this with such pride that I reciprocated, telling them Sarah had had a great week too – by threatening court proceedings, she'd forced a local authority to accommodate a pregnant sixteen-year-old living on the street and give her a basic allowance. I felt good saying this. I'd listened, that week, to what she'd told me about her work. Listened and remembered. Maybe, a thousand weeks hence, I'd neither listen nor remember. In this way, *by threatening court proceedings* became the language of love.

Sarah glanced in her rear-view mirror. Evidently, she saw the eyes of Dad, because she said: 'Sam's got us tickets to see the Strokes,' which would mean little to Catherine.

'Sam Davey?' asked Dad. (After two years, Sarah was still too new to know he was always known as 'Sam Davey', except on the phone, where he was called 'Mr S'.)

'Yes,' said Sarah and then she asked Catherine if she knew the Strokes. She didn't.

'They're really fun,' said Sarah and told me to put on the CD.

Dad, we knew, had no interest in popular music, unless it had been popular in 1710 or 1849. Catherine liked World Music, as did Sarah, especially music from Africa. So why was Sarah calling the Strokes 'really fun'? She was applying herself to loving the Strokes, as I had to broccoli. I should have been thankful as she tapped the wheel in time, whereas I was thankful only that she didn't sing along.

'Turn it up!' she said. So I did, though I knew it wasn't to enhance her pleasure. She wanted to divert attention from the silence in the back.

The sea was in sight now. I hoped that, when they got out of the car, Dad and Catherine would be brave enough to say to each other that they were relieved, finding in their mutual dislike of the Strokes a similar bond to the one that united Sarah and me in our aversion to Bono. In the event, as Sarah opened the boot to get the cold bag, Dad addressed his first remark to Catherine.

'I hear you're a keen swimmer.'

'Yes,' she said. He waited for her to add to her answer. But no extension was forthcoming.

'Well,' said Dad, gesturing towards the sea. 'We've come to the right place.'

Catherine said nothing. What was there to say? She was silenced by his nervous banality.

Ten minutes later, with the towels laid out, Catherine sat clutching her knees to her chin, while Dad looked out to sea, I read the paper and Sarah lay on her front, reading a book.

'Anyone coming for a dip?' asked Dad.

I demurred.

Sarah rolled over. 'You two go,' she said to Catherine and Dad. 'I want to finish my book.' She rolled back over onto her front. There was nothing subtle in any of this. I could even see – as I'm sure could the others – that she had about two hundred pages left.

'OK,' said Catherine briskly. She took her shirt, shorts and plimsolls off, stood up, hoicked the straps of her black swimsuit with her thumbs, Olympic-competitor-style, then walked towards the water alongside, but not with, Dad.

Sarah, of course, rolled over again and sat up. I put my paper down. We watched and wondered. We knew they both loved to swim and here they were, swimming.

'Maybe they'll have a race,' I said.

'She's got to give him a bit of encouragement.'

'That's right.'

Catherine and Dad entered the water and swam in different directions.

In the early evening, back at our cottage, Sarah and Catherine announced they were going next door, in a way that suggested they were going next door to do and say female things. They left. Alone with Dad, I hoped we wouldn't discuss the non-events of the day so far. Thankfully, I could tell he hoped likewise. This was one of the benefits of meeting when we were immature. As sixteen-year-olds, we wouldn't have discussed his chances with this girl next door. So that's what we did. We stood there, not discussing it, both aware that Catherine and Sarah were probably doing the opposite, in their fearless female way, on the other side of the wall.

Dad said he'd like to drive to the nearest off-licence, to buy a bottle of wine. I pointed out he'd already brought a bottle but he said he wanted to add to it.

'OK then,' I said. He needed to get away, needed to replace this situation with another, even briefly. And I wanted him to go away, so I didn't have to stand there, thinking up subjects unrelated to Catherine. He went. I told him to leave the door on a latch, in a parody of practical man talk – men, speaking of latches but not of the heart.

I took advantage of the time alone to make a Velvet Underground Salad, a dish Sam Davey and I had invented in our early twenties. It consisted of spring onions, tomatoes, avocados and cucumber. You got spring onions, tomatoes, avocados and cucumber and you chopped the fuckers to the Velvet Underground's 'I'm Waiting for the Man', the greatest cucumber-chopping track in the history of recorded salad, four and a half minutes of unrelenting riff that chopped its way through three or four cucumbers, then chopped them again. It was a male salad – no, an unmarried salad. I could never make a VU Salad with Sarah.

When I heard the door open, I stopped chopping and turned off the music. I shouted that Dad had gone off to get a bottle. Sarah, alone, entered the kitchen and asked: 'Why are those spring onion bits so small? They look like dandruff.' I shrugged. Her mood was businesslike. She told me Catherine had given her the number of the Hargreaves family architect who'd done the loft conversion and kitchen extension. Then she asked what Dad had said about Catherine. I shook my head to indicate: nothing.

'She likes his body but she doesn't think he's very interesting. I told her we thought he needed a bit of encouragement.' I nodded. I was taken aback that we hadn't just thought it but said it. Things, on the other side of that wall, had indeed been said. But the said things were not just the manifestation of Sarah's emotional (female) competence. They spoke of her lawyerly steeliness. In the gentlest way, she'd threatened Catherine with court proceedings if she didn't encourage Dad. And then I heard the front door open and shut again. A few seconds later, the scent of Catherine entered the kitchen, just before she did.

Catherine, lipsticked and perfumed, was wearing a black dress cinched at the waist with a full skirt that stopped a few inches above her knees. I didn't understand it. Nobody did or does or can understand it. Why was this display of fabric and flesh so provocative, when more flesh and less fabric, earlier, on the beach, was sexlessly healthy? Was it that I'd never seen Catherine dressed like this before? Her neck and arms and shoulders and black-strapped area were positively creamy, while her legs had never been so long or beautiful. I was astonished by her shoes. I'd never seen shoes so delicate and flimsy, so pale-toned, so ethereal and transparent, until I realised, a millisecond later, that her feet were bare. What did I want from her? Nothing. I was faithful. I didn't want to have sex with Catherine, except in theory. I wanted to have theoretical sex with Catherine. What did that mean?

'Wow!' said Sarah and, finding that we were side by side with our backs to the cooker, looking at Catherine, she put her arm round my waist. Was she checking me for excitement or expressing her own? She was clearly delighted with, and for, her friend.

'You look gorgeous,' she said. And then to me: 'Doesn't she?'

'Absolutely,' I said, in a dry, deep voice, as measured as a knighted civil servant's. Sarah took her arm away, pissed off by my lack of enthusiasm. I was behaving like a single man, under the influence of salad. A woman looked gorgeous and so I feigned instant indifference, to stand out from the slavering crowd even when, as here, there was no crowd. I was treating Catherine like a Hammond Law Stone Fisk receptionist, which did us both, and Sarah, a disservice. I was never going to seduce Catherine, with my provocative indifference to her sexual allure. Nor was that my purpose. *Our* purpose. I knew that, yet I behaved as if I didn't. Why couldn't I say I loved her dress, as I'd said I loved her crawl? Could you not love a woman's dress without loving its contents?

There she stood, unsure of her own attractiveness, as somehow all women are. Our job was to assure her of her desirability.

'You don't think it's too much?' she asked.

'No. It's lovely,' said Sarah. 'It brings out your curves. Doesn't it? You're a man.'

'You look nice,' I said. But this blandness didn't satisfy either woman, so I added: 'It brings out your ladyshape.' They laughed.

'We've never heard that,' said Sarah. It was the first time I'd heard her refer to Catherine and herself as *we*.

'Ladyshape!' said Catherine. There was no need to repeat it. Its moment had passed. Then, happily, I was released. Catherine apologised – not to me – for her shoelessness, saying she'd got fed up trying on pairs and, anyway, it was summer and she thought if she'd overdressed her top half, she'd underdress her feet; and then the door opened and shut again and we all went quiet, to acknowledge the return of Dad, with his bottle of sweet wine.

114

'Hi,' he said, generally, and then to Catherine: 'What a beautiful dress.'

The beauty of Catherine's dress was, as he saw it, a fact. He stated a fact. Catherine thanked him and smiled. He said it in a straightforward way, from the centre of himself to the centre of her. There was no vanity in it, no lechery, no adornment, no pose. Dad never posed. He hadn't, over the last twenty years, adopted a series of poses, prior to saying *this pose, the one I'm adopting now, this is the real me*.

At two in the morning, we were still in our back garden, sitting round a table laid with (dying) candles. I couldn't see what I was doing as I upturned the sweet-wine bottle and shook the last drops into my glass, then lifted it to my lips to find that no drops had landed inside it. The evening had been elongated, then elongated further, to give time and more time and more time and more time for Dad and Catherine to find each other attractive. All hope, it seemed to us, was gone. Whoever stood up first, to bid the others goodnight, would confirm it. He or she would put the sheet over Cupid and pronounce that capricious little curlyhead dead.

Catherine was discoursing on the failure of the Italians to achieve a workable political system, a subject on which she had every right to speak, having spent so much time in Rome. As I tried to understand the difference between the Chamber and the Senate, I debated, with myself, whether her discourse meant she wasn't sexually interested in Dad. Of course it didn't. She was a creature of intellect and appetite, as was Dad. She could pontificate and desire. Dad had, an hour earlier – two or three hours earlier? – discoursed on plaque, a word the rest of us had bandied since childhood, without understanding what it was, or became. (It became tartar.) The plaque speech didn't mean that he didn't desire Catherine.

She got to the end. We were all silent. I was thinking of drumming my fingers on the table, in the hope that one of my fingertips would land on a drop of sweet wine. Then Dad said it was amazing to see me here. Wasn't it only three or four years since I'd been living with a colleague from work, in the spare bedroom of his house in Finchley? I agreed it was, it was three years.

'That's what love does for you,' said Dad. 'Now the two of you are living happily ever after in the country.' At this point a barn owl hooted, as if to confirm we were living in a rural idyll. That seemed corny to me but Dad was delighted.

'*I'm* certainly happy you're here,' said Catherine. Irritatingly, this had been the pattern: one of them would say something nice about us, then the other would add something just as nice. This was probably because we were what they had in common.

'When I was little,' said Catherine, 'we always ignored the people in this garden. My dad called them "the rental people". "Don't bother the rental people! Don't upset them!" So I didn't. Course, my sister always looked over the fence and smiled at them. I used to duck down and try to pull her away.'

'What was that like?' asked Dad. 'I'm an only child.'

'I thought you might be an only,' said Catherine. 'I can imagine you contented with your own company.'

Dad thought about this for a moment, as did we, all of us unsure if Catherine were paying him a compliment.

Sarah, who hadn't spoken for a while, seized on the silence to say she was tired and she thought she'd had too much sun and if nobody minded she had to go to bed and I wasn't to do any washing-up, we'd do it in the morning. Then, decisively, she kissed Catherine and Dad in turn, on the cheeks, before telling Dad she hoped the sofa bed would be all right, nobody had slept on it yet, she hoped it wouldn't be too short or too hard. Dad protested – he was sure it would be OK – but Sarah told him not to be too nice, he should complain if it was too short or too hard. These were her goodnight gifts to the company: fears that the unused sofa bed would be too short and too hard and that Dad would be too nice to complain. Finally, she kissed me. As she did so, I felt she was smuggling something into my mouth, like a woman tonguing a junkie prisoner his heroin wrap. What she passed me were three little syllables, a *so* and a *fa* and a *bed*. She wanted me, after she left, to go on about the sofa bed. And so, soon as she left, I apologised to Dad that our cottage was small and my using the second bedroom as a study meant that the only spare bed was the sofa bed. I hit the three syllables hard. And then I stood up too. Dad thanked me, then Catherine thanked me, then Dad said he would do the washing-up and Catherine said she would help him. This was the best we could hope for, then: the man and the woman we'd introduced would do the washing-up together.

I left them in the garden and went up to our bedroom, knowing instantly, as I opened the door to that darkened room, that Sarah was awake and would shortly speak. Nevertheless, I soft-shoed it to the bed, took off my clothes and sidled in.

'Oh well,' she said. I switched on the light on my side of the bed. I couldn't sleep, with the sound of the table being cleared and two people walking to and from the garden into the kitchen below our bedroom.

'I don't mind if you read,' she said.

'No, it's OK,' I said and switched off my light.

'Are you asleep?' I asked, after a minute or so.

'Yes,' she said. But a few minutes later, she turned on her light and sat up.

News travels fast in the country. There are fewer buildings, vehicles and people in its way. There is also less news, so each news item stands out, like a headline. Consider the news that Dad was arriving from London. That broke a couple of minutes before he pulled up outside our house. The news travelled first to my upstairs study window, from which I saw his car, nearly a mile away, turning left onto The Lane, Worth, off the road that leads from Snape to Orford. Some fifteen hours later, at 02.47 on Sunday morning – I looked at my digital alarm clock, as if expecting the police to ask what time the 'incident' occurred – there was more and bigger news.

I heard footsteps, four footsteps, not one person taking four steps but two taking two, one with shoes, one without, down our brief corridor. The four feet went out of our front door, which, softly but unmistakably, opened and shut. It was at this point Sarah turned on her light and sat up.

'Did you hear that?' she asked, shushing me before I had time to reply. We heard Catherine's door open and shut. And then we heard nothing

'You see?' she said triumphantly, as if she'd been doubted. 'They just needed time on their own.'

I was unconvinced. They'd gone next door. That was all.

'Maybe she's just showing him her cottage,' I said.

'She'd do that in daylight,' said Sarah witheringly. 'This is wonderful.'

'You think so?'

'Shhh!'

We lay there and listened, with feeling. Sarah's feeling was one of uncomplicated excitement. She even held my hand. Mine was a more complicated feeling. Dad, good old Dad, my old friend, our friend, was in the house of our new friend Catherine. Well might Sarah and I hold each other's hands. This could not have happened without us. I was certain of that, which certainty made me proud but sad. I had never, till now, felt older than good old Dad. Sarah and I were ancients, who had blessed Catherine and Dad; not like parents, no, more ancient, more like gods, a couple of gods brought out of retirement. What exactly were we doing now, side by side in our bed? We were listening out for the sex of others. We were voyeurs, in sound. We were auditeurs.

That was what we were reduced to, or had grown into. As we listened, hearing nothing, I felt a presence in our bedroom, the presence of the past, a ghostliness. With my unclasped hand, I reached for the newspaper on my bedside table. And there, at the top of every page, I found the ghost. The paper was dated the eighth of August. It was the night when, as an unmarried man, I'd had four successive years of sex with Oz. Sex with Oz was haunting me, but now I knew what it was that was haunting me, it lost its power to hurt me. This journey, from guaranteed unmarried sex to married lying there, listening out for the sex of others – this was not a journey from happiness to unhappiness. On the contrary. Those nights had been demeaning, weird and misanthropic: my arrival at her flat, our shared refusal to acknowledge why we were there, my distance, her crap studenty food – tuna, rice, tinned tomatoes, cigarettes for dessert – my sitting on her red sofa reading *Hello!*, reading the carpet, anything not to look at her; then her checking her watch, like a bad actress signalling it was 'getting late', and asking me if we were going to do it or what. Then the sex, sadly unforgettable, that digging-for-victory war-effort sex, accompanied and followed by her abuse, born of self-loathing. Soon as it was over, she'd tell me I could piss off now I'd got what I'd come for, as if she hadn't got what I'd come for too. So why did we both look forward to this, for four years in a row? Why did we get excited about it, when we knew it would disappoint? No, wait – we didn't know it would disappoint, for then it wouldn't have disappointed, it would have fulfilled our low expectations.

'Shhh!' said Sarah again, though I hadn't spoken. From above us, one room east – the roof space of Catherine's cottage – we heard something. We heard *doof*.

A male *doof*. And because we heard it and had been waiting for it, had been listening out for it, it seemed not like an utterance but a broadcast. We were tuned into Radio Doof and then, as if someone had turned the dial on a big old radiogram, a few seconds later we were tuned in to another station, except we hadn't quite left Doof behind, we were on the cusp of that and the next station, with its female presenter. We were listening to the overlapping signals of Radio Doof and Radio Aaaah. Then the signal from Aaaah got stronger than Doof's. But, as when a radio alarm comes on in the night, and you're shocked, you're viscerally alarmed, the volume of Doof reached a frightening pitch, the one at which you think, Jesus, that will wake the neighbours, especially when, as here, you are the neighbours. And then all the stations shut down for the night and there was radio silence.

'We've done it,' said Sarah. 'Amazing!' She sighed and switched off her light. But we hadn't done it. Catherine and Dad had done it. Why was Sarah sighing? She didn't even sigh when she and I had sex. To what other post-coital cliché would Sarah resort, in celebration of someone else's sex? Would she tell me 'That was wonderful'? No, not that but this: she fell asleep, in moments. Just before she did so, she whispered, 'Well done,' then sweetly and gently, from six o'clock to four o'clock, adjusted the position of my dormant cock.

We woke up excited. We hugged each other.

When they knocked, at eleven on that Sunday morning, we were ready. We'd contrived the coffee-and-bread aroma which bespeaks a happy and sellable home, as any estate agent will tell you. But the happiness had not been uninterrupted.

'Don't do anything to put them off,' Sarah had told me in the bathroom, an hour earlier. I thought she was telling me not to put them off each other but no, she was telling me not to put them off us. We must be the perfect embodiment of the coupledom state, so they too would aspire to being a couple, like us. Here was Dad, bruised by marriage, living apart from his wife; there was Catherine, man-wary. In their presence, I was told, I had to be a good partner to Sarah. I wasn't to belittle her, ignore her, patronise her or shout at her.

I was nonplussed by these instructions. She polished the bathroom mirror, furiously, with a page of the *East Anglian Daily Times* – a newspaper, even a local one, worked better than a cloth. She had no reason to polish the mirror so hard, unless she were trying to get to the other side. I asked her when I'd shouted at her. She admitted I never had, but even this withdrawal of an accusation sounded like an attack – a man who felt passionate about her, she implied, would shout at her. She went on to tell me I could be 'withdrawn and involved with myself'. I could be 'self-centred, remote and emotionally lazy', which seemed like the same accusation, differently worded. And then she put it into yet more words: I didn't try as hard as I did when we met. But, she said, bracing me for the good news, that was normal. 'I mean, I love you and everything and I know I've got faults of my own.'

Whence had this dissatisfaction come? It wasn't my fault we were an old couple, as compared to the new couple next door. Anyway, I wasn't going to stand in the bathroom and listen to that stuff. And so I hoovered. I'd never hoovered except when asked and now, in a parody of a perfect partner, I got out the Hoover on a Sunday morning, unsolicited, and hoovered the rugs and the floorboards and the sofa and the sofa cushions, with great clumpings and exaggerated movements. There was no difference between this sulky, parodic hoovering and the real thing. To the dust, it was all the same; the Hoover's asthmatic wheeze was terminal, whether it was applied with love or, as here, with bitterness.

Not to be outcleansed, Sarah went for the wooden and tiled surfaces with a duster, attacking them as she had the bathroom mirror. As I rammed the corners of the room with the Hoover, she tornadoed crumbs off the table, the little bastards hurtling into her cupped hand. I quit the Hoover and grabbed an aerosol can from the cupboard under the sink. I fssssted foam onto the windows, macing their transparent faces. Now I understood why cleaning products had those names: *Vim*, *Cillit Bang*. These were not references to their own strength. These were tributes to the caustic power of those who used them in anger. The window cleaner, which was called *Mr Muscle*, might as well have been called *Fuck!*

Sarah whooshed water into the electric kettle, then crash-landed it onto its base and tortured some coffee beans. Then she looked for cups but couldn't find them.

'Do you know where they put the cups?' she asked. I helped her look for the cups which Catherine and Dad had put away after they'd done the washing-up.

'They should have used the machine,' said Sarah. It was a nothing remark but it mattered because it was said in a peaceable tone.

'Yes, they probably did it by hand so they could have more time to talk to each other, and put everything away,' I burbled, not even listening to what I was saying. I just wanted to say something.

'Yes,' she replied, 'all they needed was time on their own.' Then she added, needlessly: 'Without us being there to keep them company.'

'That's right,' I said. Now the mood was OK. In a few seconds, it would be good. Our mood had gone, in half an hour, from good to bad then back again. It seemed we didn't control the mood. The mood changed, of its own accord. We just had to live through it.

Ten minutes later came the knock. We imagined this as their knock, the sound of synchronised knuckles on wood. It was all we could do not to run to the door.

Sarah opened it. There they were.

'Hi,' said Sarah. 'How are you' – a fractional pause – 'both?'

They came into our kitchen and didn't leave. Nobody left till late afternoon, when Dad drove back to London. The churches and forests and beaches and pubs and walks did not apply. Neither

Dad nor Catherine wanted to 'do' anything, which of course Sarah and I took as a sign, not of their exhaustion but the pleasure they took in each other's company. They'd rather sit in our kitchen, looking at us and each other, than stare at pollarded oaks or naves and apses and altars – all those churchy interior design features which leave you speechless, not from awe but from a simple absence of anything to say.

Sarah and I didn't address them as a couple. Of course we didn't. That how-are-you-both was an aberration. We didn't want them to feel like 'both', for fear of embarrassing or intimidating them. What we wanted, though we couldn't say it, was acceleration. We wanted them to have been together for weeks and months and years. We had an ego, a couple's ego – we wanted them to be an instant version of us.

In that kitchen, as coffee was followed by lunch, they had no chance to be a couple, because Sarah and Catherine were inseparable. They had a way of being together in which each was in charge of the other. 'Olive oil!' Sarah would shout at her, then, a few seconds later, Catherine would shout back: 'Garlic!' They shouted because they were projecting their voices over a World CD called *Best of Ethiopia*. From time to time, Catherine shimmied, which was utterly and unselfconsciously endearing. She even, at one point, sang along, which defied belief. I studied the CD booklet, which displayed the lyrics. All of them were variants on a celebratory theme. Basically, unless otherwise stated, the lyrics of a *Best of Ethiopia* song were goat-related, as in:

> *I bought a goat from the market*
> *The goat fed my family for many days*
> *Soon I will buy another goat*
> *A goat makes us happy*

When the CD was – finally, finally – finished, the women brought the salad to the table.

'So how did you and Richard meet? I've forgotten,' Dad asked Sarah.

I suspected he remembered but wanted to hear the story from us. I was only too keen. Here was the advertisement for ourselves of which Sarah had spoken. I stressed the struggle we'd had, the fraught beginning without which no happy ending is earned. Overriding Sarah's objections, I progressed quickly from the night we met at the gallery to the night Sarah called me when I was in 'another woman's' flat. I talked of my despair that I'd put Sarah off, which allowed her to say she was not put off so easily, which allowed me to return to the despair. I told Catherine and Dad it was a time in my life when I was a fool and 'sexually all over the place'. I knew this was the boastfulness against which I'd warned myself, boastfulness clad in the short skirt of regret, and I expected Catherine to chide me for it, which she did – 'I don't think we want to hear that,' she said, speaking on behalf of herself and her comrade Sarah – but I felt I was entitled to boast, invited to boast, having been asked by Dad to describe our meeting. I felt that I'd been found by Sarah, and couldn't convey that without rehearsing the ways in which I'd been lost.

'I just meant, there are always problems at the beginning. You know? It's always labyrinthine.'

This went down far better. Catherine nodded. Dad nodded. They, of course, were at that beginning. The kitchen went quiet, as they thought about problems ahead and, for that matter, problems present, problems now in the room.

'But you always know, don't you?' said Sarah. Her words were vague but her meaning was specific and optimistic. She was celebrating, no question, the goat of new love on which Catherine and Dad were feasting. They knew they wanted each other.

'So what do you think of Worth?' she asked Dad. It was a question expecting the answer 'It's lovely', which he duly gave. So she told him of the cottage for sale three doors down, with the quince tree in the front garden. And then Catherine told him more, for she, unlike us, had been in that cottage when the boiled-sweet-faced woman was alive. Catherine knew what needed to be done: it was a question of repositioning the kitchen so you got the morning sun, which the architect who'd done her cottage – and would shortly do ours – could help him achieve. Dad said nothing. There was nothing he needed to say. A future was being built for him and everything was under control. He looked pleased but uncertain, unused to being the focus of the attention he normally focused on others. I saw his future and I liked it: we lived here, Catherine lived next door, two cottages away lived Dad. Why not? I'd moved here. Now it was his turn. We'd moved to Worth as strangers and now we were filling The Lane with friends, we were colonising it with our warmth and affection, we were leading the way, which is what a couple can do.

Dad went back to London, Catherine went back next door. Later that night, more news arrived. Catherine phoned it to Sarah, who passed it to me: they'd arranged to spend the weekend in London in a couple of weeks' time.

'I'll tell you everything, you'll be the first to know,' said Catherine. 'That's the least I can do. After all you've done for me.'

'We haven't done anything,' said Sarah. 'We just introduced you.' Catherine thought this false modesty. The truth was, we'd done a good deed and we knew it. We had a right to be the first to know everything. That knowledge was not a gift, to show her gratitude for what we'd done. It was a debt. She owed it to us to tell us everything.

We were already looking forward to that weekend. We were looking forward to an event at which we wouldn't be present. We were impatient for the weekend when Catherine and Dad would be together without us. That was the next stage in their relationship. And, let's not pretend, we were looking forward to being the absent friends, the ones they talked about, the ones they'd call first, with the news.

That next weekend, we were due to go to London ourselves. We hadn't been there since the end of our reverse-commuting fever. London couldn't hurt us now. We were happy in the country, happy in our working lives, happy that our new friend was involved with our old friend. We were no longer desperate for the metropolis. To prove it, we'd decided to go there, do one thing, then come back. We would go to the city where there were ten million things to do; and do one. To us, this was exhilaratingly arrogant, like breaking into a bank vault to steal a one-pound coin.

The plan was to leave at five and drive halfway – to Manningtree station, where we'd park the car – then catch the train to London and meet Sam Davey at the gig, returning to Manningtree at the end of the night or the early hours of the following morning, allowing for encores. Sarah had been rehearsing for the gig all week. I'd downloaded all my favourite tracks by the Strokes onto an iPod, so she could listen to them without my being aware. But still she made me aware. If, when wearing the iPod, she saw me enter a room, she'd start to nod.

I appreciated she was making a social as well as musical effort. This would be the first time Sam Davey, Sarah and I had spent an evening on our own, not counting the several thousand other fans in the Hammersmith Apollo and the members of the Strokes onstage. Sarah never said a bad word about my oldest friend. She couldn't, because her problem with him, as I'd grown to under-stand it, was his resemblance to me. If you married me, you didn't need a friendship with Sam Davey, since you already had me. Now the waters get murky, though, and the people in the waters murkier, their faces and characters hard to discern. What do I mean by 'me'? I'd married and moved to the country. I'd grown less like the 'me' that resembled Sam Davey.

The morning of the concert, Catherine set off for Norfolk to spend the day with her sister Mel. This was not Dad-related knowledge, so she wasn't obliged to tell us. This was one of the many facts about each other which we freely dispensed, out of friendship. We were no longer neighbours but friends who lived next door.

We were in our garden, at four in the afternoon, when we heard the knock at the door, preceded by a boy running into Catherine's garden and shouting, in disappointment, that there still wasn't a swing. That was followed by a girl, more sophisticated, telling him this was good, as he couldn't fall off it. She sounded about eight or nine or ten or eleven or twelve – I was too far from being a child myself to age her and too intimidated to look at her. I wanted to keep a fence between us, because she sounded like a girl who could only be appeased by a parent waving a credit card, like a plastic white flag.

Sarah followed me to the front door. As I opened it, Catherine squeezed through the first available human-sized space, not waiting for me to open it fully. She looked distraught. She said, in a quiet voice, that she was sorry to bother us. In my normal voice, I said there was no problem. Sarah immediately shushed me, realising Catherine didn't want to be heard by the neighbours – the people, in other words, in her own cottage. We went into the living room. Sarah closed the naff French windows put in by Catherine's father. (We'd get the Hargreaves family architect to suggest a replacement.) Now she felt free to speak freely.

Her story was swiftly told: she'd gone to Mel's house in Norfolk, Mel's children were bored, Mel suggested they all go to Catherine's cottage instead, which excited the children, since it was by the sea, so they agreed to do that, despite her husband

Gordon's protest. Gordon felt it was unfair on Catherine to make her drive back to Worth, whence she'd only just come, but Mel thought Catherine would do whatever would make her niece and nephew happy, though Catherine could always, if she preferred, stay in the house in Norfolk while the rest of them went to her cottage by the sea. Of course Catherine didn't prefer this sarcastic alternative. That was that, then, with this gloss: Mel didn't want to drive all that way and then return a few hours later, with her tired children in the back of her car (the children and the car, evidently, were always 'hers'), so they'd decided to stay overnight.

The story made us angry. We understood that this was not the story of a Saturday but the story of a life, two lives, the lives of Catherine and Mel, the one the victim of the other's manipulation. Catherine, so often regal with us, was not the Queen sister. Mel was.

Already sorry for bothering us, Catherine now apologised for lying about us. She'd told her sister, falsely, that we'd invited her for tea on Saturday, which she'd declined on the grounds that she'd be in Norfolk at the time. But she wasn't in Norfolk at the time – which was now – she was back in her cottage. We'd hear her and wonder why she'd lied to us about being away. Hence her presence in our cottage to explain the truth – which wasn't, of course, the truth.

I tensed with the effort of following this. I feared she'd ask me to say it back to her, to prove I'd understood. But Sarah remained unmuddled: 'Then we'll make it all true. You're invited for tea!' So saying, she shooed me towards the kitchen. When I returned, plus tea, the women were piling grievance on grievance. Catherine was telling Sarah that Mel's very presence in her cottage made Catherine feel her life was smaller and less significant than Mel's, who lived in a bigger place and had a bigger life.

'Does she move your things?' asked Sarah.

Here was a grievance she didn't even know she had, till Sarah supplied it from the cupboard of grievances she had with her own sister, Jane.

'She walked into my kitchen just now and she saw a lemon and she put it in the fridge, when I wanted it out and I don't even keep my lemons in the fridge.'

'She's no right to do that,' said Sarah. 'Stay here as long as you like.'

A few minutes later, I took the tea tray back into the kitchen. It was just before five o'clock. Sarah appeared. She told me she couldn't come to the concert as she didn't want to leave Catherine.

'Course not,' I said.

'You go,' said Sarah. 'You and Sam go. Sell my ticket.'

Then Catherine appeared. She told me she the last thing she wanted to do was to make us change our plans. We should both go to the concert. She'd shelter in our cottage a while longer, then return next door. Sarah demurred. She wasn't going to leave Catherine here on her own. Hadn't Mel suggested Catherine stay on her own in Mel's house? The idea was appalling. No, Sarah would stay and I would go.

'You must absolutely go,' said Catherine. 'Go. Go now. You're probably late already.'

'Mr R!' said Sam Davey, when he heard my voice.

'Mr S!' I replied.

This was our standard phone greeting, spoken in ironically overexcited voices. Mr S and Mr R were the monikers we were given by a young, tieless English teacher keen to be 'in' with the cool kids, curiously unaware that keen is the enemy of cool. Twenty years on, the greeting made me tense. It was unsuited to what I had to say. It preserved us at the age when nothing mattered.

I told him we couldn't come to the concert tonight and were sorry. He heard the tension and asked what was wrong. So I told him.

'We have to look after our neighbour. Her sister's in her cottage. So she can't go home.' He said nothing. I carried on. 'She's got serious sister problems.'

Sam Davey laughed, not because he thought I was making this up but because he knew I wasn't. I used to go to clubs. I used to know people – artists, musicians, fashion designers – but now I knew neighbours, now my wife and I stayed at home on a Saturday night to look after our neighbour with the serious sister problems.

'Has she tried rubbing ointment on the sister? That might make her go away.' I said nothing, so he asked: 'Can't Sarah look after her?'

This I had been expecting: the implication, old as marriage itself, that a married man would rather be out with his mate than home with his wife, that marriage is duty and mateship pleasure, that a woman in crisis can only be looked after by another woman (the wife), for what would the husband do, other than exude discomfort and inadequacy, nod at everything his wife said and wear a 'concerned' expression, when his only true concern was how he could get away to join his mate?

'No,' I said.

'OK,' he said, 'I'll sell your tickets. Don't worry about it. I understand.'

What did he understand, though? He understood I was a compromised man who wasn't doing what he wanted to do.

'We introduced her to Dad. She's having a thing with him,' I said, in an effort to make him appreciate this neighbour's significance, to him as well as me.

'Wow! Is she mad?' He was referring to Dad's second wife, Suzy, the singer and actress. In fact, he was referring to all Dad's women. From the beginning, we'd always called his girlfriends 'mad', when what we meant was 'needy', but to call his girlfriends 'mad' was, backhandedly, to call Dad 'sane'. He was, as we saw it, a sane man to whom mad women were naturally attracted.

'No, she's sane,' I replied. 'And she doesn't sing.' This was a reference to Suzy's compulsive singing, for which Dad had often apologised, as if it were his fault that when his wife opened the fridge, she sang 'I Don't Know How To Love Him' to an audience of cheese.

'I have to go now,' I said. 'Our friend needs me. The Strokes don't need me.' I didn't even like saying the name. There was a time for saying 'The Strokes' and the time had passed, whereas the time hadn't passed – and never would – for Beethoven, Chopin, Ravel and Prokofiev. 'The Strokes' embarrassed me.

When I returned, Catherine and Sarah were talking about Mel's money. Mel had manipulated Old Man Hargreaves into leaving her the big expensive house, while Catherine got the cheap cottage. That was injustice enough, but it was compounded by Mel's gift for making money, which she'd also inherited from her father – cruelly, she'd inherited his money *and* his gift for making it. Mel 'grew' businesses and sold them. She was now on the point of selling her fitness clubs and was hungry – greedy – for the next moneymaking opportunity. Catherine was more like their mother, who wrote short stories and had worked as a civil servant, till their father married her and converted her into a mother and hostess, someone who made five-course meals for him and his golfing chums, because she was, in Catherine's word, 'weak'.

A generation later, in a gender reversal, Mel married a golf pro, Gordon, and converted him into a father and businessman, co-managing director of their various enterprises. But there was nothing 'co' about it. Gordon's business was being his wife's servant, an increasingly sullen, resentful and alcoholic servant, though apparently very good-looking, in a saturnine Scots way. Gordon didn't have the balls to leave Mel, but that was only because Mel had chopped them off. (It was disturbing, when she talked about Mel, how often she said 'balls'.) For example, when their daughter was born, it was Mel who named her, unilaterally telling Gordon that their daughter was called Phoebe. Unfortunately, she spelt it wrong. She sent out printed cards which announced, in that proper, official, curly black, my-life-is-important typeface, the birth of Pheobe. When Catherine pointed this out, Mel screamed at her. She could name her daughter what she fucking well liked and it was none of Catherine's fucking business and, anyway, the cards had gone out. Catherine told her Pheobe would be mocked at the best schools if her name was spelt incorrectly. Mel put the phone down and registered the name as Phoebe.

'You'd think she would have thanked me.' We told her we didn't think that. She didn't sound like the thanking type.

And so began a lifelong – Phoebe was ten now – war for the soul of the girl with the troublesome order of vowels. It was fought by her mother and her aunt and was futile, since there could only be one – Mel – winner. As the godmother (on which Old Man Hargreaves insisted), Catherine took it upon herself to counterbalance Mel's commercial and populist regime. Catherine took Phoebe to Verdi's *Simon Boccanegra*, when the child thought she was going – for the second time – to *Harry Potter and the Something Something*. Then, for her tenth birthday, Catherine bought her a thousand-piece jigsaw puzzle of Millais's *Ophelia*, Catherine's favourite painting when she herself was ten. In return, Catherine got a *thank u* text, which she thought insufficient. But worse was to come. When Catherine next went to Mel's house, she saw the jigsaw puzzle in the bin.

'That's terrible,' said Sarah and then, remembering the red studded dress, added: 'At least she could have given it to a charity shop.' This was a joke against herself, which Catherine would not allow.

'Oh no, it's nothing like what happened with you and your sister's dress. That was a dress your sister had rejected. This was a present I really loved. It wasn't a hand-me-down. I saw it in a

132

black plastic bin liner. I'm sure Mel put it in there. Ten-year-olds don't put jigsaw puzzles in black plastic bin liners. It's the mother who does that.'

'That's right,' said Sarah.

'That's right,' I agreed.

We invited her to stay for supper. She went back to her cottage, briefly, to tell her sister a further lie, which was that she'd been wrong about our invitation – we'd invited her to supper not tea.

After supper, Sarah suggested Catherine stay the night. She even had a battle plan: Catherine should tell Mel she was staying with us so Mel's kids could each have their own bedroom. It would seem like a sacrifice but be a victory, since she'd be escaping her sister's claws for the rest of the night. In fact, she needn't even go home. She could phone Mel from here. We'd give her a toothbrush.

Catherine agreed. The plan was foolproof. It was a hot night so she didn't even need her nightdress. Catherine agreed, on two conditions. First, we weren't to get up in the morning. She would make herself a cup of tea and then go. Second, if there were a knock at the door in the morning, we weren't to answer it. It would be Mel, wanting to meet Catherine's new friends. Mel would want to thank us for housing Catherine and giving her kids their own rooms. She'd want to thank us for something we hadn't done for her sake or the sake of her kids. And she'd be nice to us. That was the thing. Mel would be nice to us and make us like her, hoping that, in time, we'd like her more than we liked Catherine. We told Catherine that would never happen. We gave her our word.

We went to bed glad Catherine was downstairs on the sofa bed, sleeping the sleep for which Dad had been destined till she'd taken him away. We felt like her protectors. She had no husband to protect her against her sister. Except me. She had Sarah's husband and she had Sarah.

Sarah told me she was sorry we hadn't made it to the gig – a word which, in her discomfort, she got wrong, saying *jig*. She asked when the Strokes were playing in London again. I told her it wasn't necessary to go a Strokes gig to know what a Strokes gig was like. All gigs were the same, it was only the band and the venue that differed. Let's say the gig was at the Hammersmith Apollo. When the band came on, everyone stood and cheered and the vocalist said, 'Good evening, Hammersmith!', which was a nonsense, since even if you came from Hammersmith, which only a fraction of the audience did, 'Hammersmith' was not your name, any more than Jesus' name was 'Nazareth'. Then the vocalist swore – 'Let's fucking do this!' – to show he lived on the edge, when swearing had been, for many years now, unthreatening. Then the band played their opening number and you watched them play, not onstage, where they were too small to be seen; you watched them on the giant screen above their heads. You had paid hugely and travelled far to see a live band and now you were watching television with five thousand strangers, who all cheered the intro to the opening number, to prove they recognised the song, except the people sitting in front of you, who cheered when the vocalist got to the title, which proved they recognised the title. Then two hours later, after an interval that gave you too much time to drink a pint of beer, or urinate, but not enough to do both, everyone stood up for the last song, except the people in front of you, who'd been standing for the last four or five. But the last song wasn't the last song, because everyone stomped and bayed for an encore, regardless of how well or badly the band had played. The logic was simple and stupid: you had to have an encore because you had to have an encore and that encore had to have an encore, encores begetting encores until the band didn't return for thirty seconds, forty seconds, fifty seconds, a minute

– at which point the people in front of you stomped and bayed even louder – MORE! – even though they knew there'd be no more. Then the house lights came up and the people in front turned to go. For the first time, you saw, in profile, their faces. They looked bored. It was shocking how bored they looked. Five seconds earlier, they'd been stompers and bayers – MORE! Now they had car-park faces, tube eyes, bus frowns. It was over.

No, a man of my age didn't need to go to gigs. He needed only to have been.

Next morning, having heard Catherine leave, we got up. We decided, without even discussing it, the one of us suggesting it and the other agreeing, that we would stay indoors. We had bread, we had coffee and our frozen milk was thawing. We could read the Sunday papers online. If we went out in our garden, front or back, we'd present ourselves as targets for Mel. Did she not, as a child, peer over the fence, to look at the rental people?

At four, we heard Mel's family leave. We heard Mel, on the path outside Catherine's cottage, tell the children to thank Auntie Cathy (no, that wasn't right, she was Catherine). We heard nothing from Gordon, except for some angry ignition and revving. And then they were gone.

We rang Catherine. We told her we'd stayed in all day to protect ourselves and tantalise Mel. Catherine said she felt awful. She hadn't meant us to imprison ourselves on an August day. But we could tell she was delighted with us.

When I did go to London, a few days later, I went with the age-old rural purpose of taking my wares to market. I carried my portfolio to the publishing house, just off Long Acre in Covent Garden, and went through my sixty-four illustrations with the editor. Owing to rewrites and cuts, half a dozen of my illustrations were no longer needed. There were another ten to be revised according to Ziggy or the editor's wishes. I'd sent all these illustrations ahead, as JPEGs. Ziggy, who was unwell, had emailed his comments to the editor and me. The editor could have emailed Ziggy and me with her comments on his comments. But then she and I would not have had a meeting.

I hadn't had a meeting for a long time. I'd forgotten their unique rhythms and ritualised weirdness. I felt about meetings as I felt about gigs. I had no need, any more, for meetings. There was work and there were meetings, where you talked about the work you'd done and the work you were going to do, but didn't do any work. The only work was done by the Young Person, who came in at the beginning of the meeting to take orders for coffee from the nearest cafe, as their reward for getting through university and their training for running the company in twenty years' time, with their highly developed street-crossing and polystyrene-carrying skills. The first item on the agenda was small talk, which got smaller and smaller till the small talkers were embarrassed into moving on to the second item, which was the start of the meeting. The meeting was always dominated by the people who were good at meetings, which didn't mean they were good at their jobs. There was a dramatic confrontation twenty minutes in, between two people who hated each other and had deliberately sat as far away from each other as possible, thereby making it easier for them to raise their voices. The first hater shouted something like: 'Why don't you take responsibility for what you've done instead of passing the buck?' To which the second hater shouted: 'How dare you sit there and say that when I've been working on this thing day and night for the last six months and you've done nothing? Why don't you do your own fucking job instead of fucking accusing me of' – at which point the Young Person returned and said: 'They didn't have any blueberry muffins so I got almond and lemon,' cueing the Bathos Interlude, when all that fury had to be suppressed, while the haters tried to work out which polystyrene cup contained their coffee, and whether a 'W' written on the side meant With Sugar or Without.

As the editor was about to tell me which illustrations she didn't like – or 'liked less than the others' – her phone rang. She established who it was then told me she'd have to take the call. She took the call. I sat and watched and listened. Why was she so much more alive and excited than she'd been when talking to me? That was easily answered. I didn't matter to her. I was a freelancer, a supplier. I worked outside the building. I had neither gossip nor power. I drank my large cappuccino, though I'd ordered a regular one.

She hoped, at the end of our brief meeting, that I hadn't come to London 'just for this'. ('It must be a four-hour round trip,' she added when, in fact, it was five.) 'No, no,' I said. 'I've got a couple of other meetings.' That was the answer she wanted and the one I'd always give. She could invite me to a meeting at three in the morning – I'd still say I hadn't come to London just for that. Oh no, I was going on to a four-in-the-morning conference call with Australia, followed by a power dawn breakfast.

At six that evening, I was in a cafe near Leicester Square, which, however wrong that cappuccino had been, was a demotion from sitting in a meeting and having a cafe brought to me. I couldn't catch the train to Suffolk till seven thirty-eight, such were the restrictions of my Saver Return ticket; I'd been sitting with the same coffee for half an hour, keen not to spend the money I'd saved on the ticket. Then I made a mistake. I turned a page of the *Evening Standard*. There, in a double-page feature, was the face of John Smith. I'd not seen it for three years. It no longer had a moustache.

137

John Smith, said John Smith, had transformed himself into a different kind of artist. But he'd always thought of himself as an artist who transformed himself so, in that sense, he was exactly the same kind of artist as he'd always been. I sighed and read on. Two years earlier, he'd taken up photography. The results were now on show at the National Portrait Gallery in an exhibition called *Police and Thieves*, photographic portraits of policemen, policewomen and convicted criminals, with nothing to tell the viewer if the subject was on the right or wrong side of the law or, he implied provocatively, both. There was an audio element too: a ninety-minute loop of the subjects' thoughts, not just about crime but 'love and food and politicians and furniture and stuff'.

To gigs and meetings, I could now add newspapers. A man of my age shouldn't read newspapers, not if he isn't in the newspaper himself. Newspapers are clubs for the people in them. I abandoned the article, unfinished, left the paper on the table, and walked to the door of the cafe. Then, perversely, I returned to it and read to the end, looking to see if it mentioned John Smith's manager. His manager, Renate Schreiber, 35, was 'very, very excited' by the latest phase of John Smith's career. Seeing her name had the opposite effect from the one I feared. It made me feel I didn't know her. I had known her but I didn't now. I longed for the warmth of my wife and our cottage, the place where I knew and was known.

I walked out of the cafe. I turned right to go to Leicester Square station and begin my long journey home. A few yards in front of me, near the station entrance, was Dad, kissing a woman. I stood still. The kiss went on. Then it ended and the woman turned and walked in my direction. I ducked and carried on ducking, kneeling to tie my laces. Unfortunately, I was wearing my green suede Chelsea boots, which of course had no laces. I scrabbled on the green suede instep with my fingers, in a ratty motion. The woman walked past without seeing me but that didn't alter the fact.

I'd seen Dad kissing a woman and no longer wanted to go home, to our cottage and its neighbour.

The kiss astonished me with its intensity and location, its adolescent theatre – they were kissing outside an Underground station, like oblivious teenagers, and they were kissing as if the kiss weren't foreplay but the thing itself, the sex, the summit of ecstasy. The woman Dad was kissing was his wife Suzy. That was the most astonishing thing of all. I'd never seen a man and wife kiss like that. It just wasn't a marital kiss. Marriage was a civil contract, it was the civilisation of sexual desire. When the vicar said, 'You may now kiss the bride', he didn't mean tongues, wetness, gurning.

I stood with my back to the cafe entrance and watched Suzy, from a distance, enter a stage door. Evidently, she had got another job in a musical, one now in its 'nineteenth fantastic year'.

'Richard.'

I turned.

'Hi, Dad!' I said, with a faked surprise that embarrassed us both. He knew I'd seen him earlier.

'That was a lovely weekend,' he said.

'Thank you. It was great to see you. Sarah really enjoyed seeing you too.'

'It was great to see her,' he said. 'What are you doing here?'

'I'm on my way home on the seven thirty-eight, that's the first train you can take if you buy a Saver Return.' Now the small talk had to stop and the meeting had to start. It was nearly seven. Seven thirty-eight was a deadline.

'My life's very complicated,' said Dad. 'I've never been pursued. Not like you. Now they want me. I don't know why.'

This was too much for me. I didn't need to be told that I'd once been pursued. All I needed was to know who knew what. What did Catherine know? I didn't want to know anything that Catherine didn't know.

139

'Do they know about each other?'

'Yes,' said Dad. 'Yes and no. Suzy knows about Catherine.'

I'd never felt more beholden to him. Sarah and I were two little people whose happiness he held in his palm. By saying Catherine didn't know about Suzy, he'd clenched his fist. I now knew something Catherine didn't, which Sarah would soon know too and then, together, we'd have to decide what to do with this knowledge, the knowledge that couldn't be unlearned.

What exactly didn't Catherine know, though? I wanted to be clear. I felt like a pig detective, slow and regional, amateur.

'Are you back with Suzy then, Dad?'

He shrugged.

'I'm having an affair with my wife.' It was a droll and ironic sally, of the sort he expected from Sam Davey and me, but there was pride in it too: the women wanted him.

'There's my nurse, too. She cares about me.'

'Why d'you need a nurse?' I oinked. 'What's wrong with you?'

'My dental nurse!' Three girls passed, laughing and shouting. Everyone who passed laughed and shouted or was drunk or Japanese.

'She's a really interesting woman,' Dad went on. 'Strong. But vulnerable.' I nodded. I didn't know if he was speaking of his wife or Catherine or the nurse. I had taken this man for granted for twenty years and now I couldn't keep up with him.

'I'm not sure how interested she is in me. It's all so new.'

'Right.' (This, surely, was Catherine.)

'I think maybe she just wants a man. She seemed, you know –'

'I know,' I said, not knowing, just trying to cut him off. I didn't want him to tell me what Catherine seemed. I couldn't deal with the knowledge I had and didn't want any more.

He gripped my arm. 'You won't say anything, will you? She's coming to stay this weekend.'

This request not to say anything didn't apply to Sarah. Dad, twice married, surely understood that a husband and a wife have no secrets. They have their own secrets, yes, which they keep from each other. But if you tell one of them *your* secret, you know they will tell the other. They don't withhold *other people's* secrets.

I got home at ten. At midnight, we were still talking. Ours was the only light on in Worth.

At Roofspace, the homeless charity where she worked four days a week, Sarah gave advice about possession proceedings, antisocial behaviour injunctions, housing disrepair, unlawful eviction and harassment. She acted only for tenants and homeless people, never landlords. I knew all this not because she was my wife, but because I'd looked her up on the Internet. I googled Roofspace, found her name, and learned what my wife did. Of course, sometimes, she told me what she did – as when she threatened those legal proceedings so the sixteen-year-old could get somewhere to live. But mostly I had no idea. I didn't feel defensive, though. Most husbands don't know what their wives do all day, nor most wives their husbands. Most people don't know what most people do all day. But that night, when I came home with the knowledge of the kiss, I had a strong sense of who and what my wife was, professionally. I had thought her, on first sight, a small warm mammal, and so she was, but the mammal was a tiger. I gave my wife the facts and she gave me her opinion, fiercely expressed and partisan. There was no question whose side she was on. She was on our side. What's more, ours was the side of justice and decency, and anyone on the other side was oppressing us and in the wrong.

We shouldn't tell Catherine. It was a simple conclusion, easily understood, but she reached it from an extraordinary number of directions, criss-crossing and speeding all the way.

We'd introduced Catherine to Dad. These were people we liked, who liked each other. Our responsibility to each of them for the

141

behaviour of the other was nil. We weren't answerable for what either of them did to his or her self or the other. If one of them told us something in confidence, we had no obligation to tell the other. In fact, we had the opposite obligation – we were obliged *not* to tell the other. Dad had told me something in confidence. Dad and I were the two parties to that confidence, that contract, if you will. He had given me the confidence in exchange for my silence. All third parties were excluded and irrelevant and had no rights to that confidence. Sarah was only technically a third party, since a husband and wife were 'one flesh'. She was, in other words, me; or, as she put it, she was 'subsumed under the general heading of "me"'. (She said that – I did not and could not, not being a lawyer, make that up.)

Overwhelming as all this was, my instincts told me we were taking Dad's side against Catherine. She assured me this wasn't the case. Only if we betrayed Dad's confidence, and told Catherine what we knew, would we be taking a side. The side would be Catherine's.

'But doesn't Catherine need our protection?' I asked piggily. Sarah answered my question by asking another: didn't Dad need our protection? What had Catherine not told Dad? What secrets, comparable to Dad's affair with his wife, had she not revealed to him? We knew she went to Rome. What did she do in Rome? Did we know she didn't have a lover in Rome? I shook my head.

'Exactly!' said Sarah. 'We know what we know. But we have no idea what we *don't* know.'

I told her she was exhausting me. We went to bed.

In bed, she was different. In bed, it's not so easy to be a lawyer. She reminded me of Catherine's fury when her sister Mel interfered in her private life, demanding the analyst's balls.

'We don't want that, do we?' she said.

'No,' I replied. I liked this argument better than the others. We shouldn't tell Catherine what we knew because it would upset her. What's more, she might get angry.

We saw her the night before she went to London to spend her weekend with Dad. I presented her with a drawing I'd done that afternoon – a map of the route from Latimer Road Underground station to Dad's flat, complete with a line of short arrows, when one long arrow would have done. She was touched. She told me that, as it happened, Dad had volunteered to pick her up from the station.

'How's he going to know when you're getting there?' I asked. It was a reasonable question, since no one could predict what time they'd get to a tube station, as opposed to a mainline station, which was subject to timetables. She told me she'd text him when she reached the previous station, Westbourne Park; he'd then set off in his car to meet her. I was puzzled. How could she text him from an Underground train? She reminded me that Westbourne Park was overground. Then she thanked me, playfully, for my concern.

'You're more of a "Dad" than he is,' she said, duly embarrassing me.

We'd always been concerned for Catherine, because we liked her and she liked us. Concern came naturally. Now it didn't. Now what came naturally was a self-conscious, agitated concern. We were, in our anxious and guilty state, being nice. I could have told her how to get to Dad's flat but, being nice, I drew it. Similarly, when Sarah asked what Catherine was going to wear for the concert – he was taking her to a BBC Prom at the Albert Hall – Catherine said she wasn't sure. She thought she'd wear a dress.

'A dress sounds lovely,' said Sarah, which was a noise, a nice nothing noise. What dress?

When Catherine left for London next morning, our concern

didn't stop. On our way home from the supermarket, we stopped at a house in Sternfield, outside which was a table of home-grown fruit and veg for sale. I got out, went to the table, picked up a bunch of beetroot and put my money in the cash box, as I'd done most Saturday mornings, on our way home from the supermarket, since we'd lived in Worth. I got back in the car and Sarah drove on.

'Oh,' said Sarah, glancing at the bunch, 'you only got one then.'

'Yes,' I said. 'We only wanted one, didn't we?'

'Yes, no,' she said, which is always infuriating. I realised what she meant.

'Stop the car,' I said.

'No.'

'Stop the car!'

'No.'

'Stop the car and I'll go back and get a bunch of beetroot for Catherine.'

'I can't turn round here, it's too narrow.'

'I'm not asking you to turn round. Stop the car. I'll walk.'

Sarah pulled over in one of those 'passing places' gouged out of the edge of a country lane. We were now about five minutes, on foot, from the beetroot table.

'I'll go if you like,' said Sarah, who was now doubly guilty: guilty about Catherine and guilty about accusing me of my failing in my duty to her, by not buying her a bunch of beetroot which she hadn't even asked for.

'No. I'll go,' I replied, without moving.

'Don't bother. It was only a thought. We know how much she likes it.'

'What about lavatory paper?' I asked. 'We bought a load of lavatory paper but we didn't buy any for her. We know how much Catherine likes lavatory paper.'

Stung, Sarah turned the key in the ignition. I grabbed her key-hand and rotated it, turning the ignition off. Then I got out of the car, with our bunch of beetroot, and I hurled the bunch of beetroot by its leaves high and far into the landscape, the four roots flying like a cluster of purple grenades. I didn't see the bunch of beetroot land but I did see a bird take wing, suddenly. I recognised the bird as a magpie. I was pleased with that. I loved animals but was spooked by birds. When I lived in London, I knew nothing of them, beyond pigeons and sparrows, and now I knew something. I got back in the car.

'What did you do that for?' asked Sarah.

'We're equal. OK? Catherine doesn't have beetroot and we don't either.'

We drove home in silence, which continued for much of the day.

At seven that evening, I started a risotto, knowing the thing would keep me at the hob for at least forty-five minutes, stirring and staring, my risotto body language deterring Sarah from coming near. She switched on the radio and tuned it to Radio 3, hoping for incessant music. There was no music, though. There was only an announcer welcoming us to the Royal Albert Hall for that evening's live BBC Promenade Concert. As she spoke, we heard the burble of the concertgoers arriving in the auditorium. We were in our rural kitchen, listening to a BBC broadcast of Dad and Catherine, a hundred miles away, milling about and burbling. We had listened to them having sex and now we were listening to them burbling.

'For Christ's sake!' said Sarah and switched it off. This simple acknowledgement of absurdity was enough to bring us together, halfway between the hob and the table, where we hugged. The hug didn't bring the thing known as 'closure'. There was no 'closure' in this situation, only its ever-present opposite, *openure*, the sense that you're walking about with a door left ajar in your brain, through which the thought – of Catherine – can enter any time it likes.

We resumed, resumed talking about it, had a feast of it after the previous hours of famine. But now Sarah's argument was different. There was no *need* to tell Catherine what we knew. She'd find out anyway. She was a forthright and fearless person, committed to skewering the truth. She'd discover – maybe she already had – and that would be the end of it. Dad wasn't right for her anyway.

'No? Two weeks ago, we were telling him he had to buy a cottage down the road to be near her.'

'And us. Catherine and us. As a holiday cottage. It's a holiday romance.'

This is what she did, in her lawyer's mood. She stated things, too firmly, then dared you to find a flaw.

'How can it be that? Catherine lives here. She's not on holiday.'

'True. But Dad's on holiday when he comes here. And Catherine's on holiday when she goes to London. It only takes one of you to be on holiday for it to be a holiday romance.'

I told her she was talking nonsense. She didn't contradict me, which was as close as she got, in this mood, to agreeing with me.

'Dad's not complex enough for her. She likes analysts and poets. Dark people. Dad's too nice.'

'What's wrong with nice? Catherine wants him, his wife wants him, his nurse wants him, maybe "nice" is what women want. Catherine's had lots of complex men, now she wants a nice one. I mean, she's not "nice", she's complex. If one of you's nice and one of you's not, that's balanced, isn't it?'

'Which one of *us*,' asked Sarah, 'is the nice one?'

That was the worst of it. We could never talk about couples without talking about ourselves. I wooden-spooned some risotto into my mouth. It was overcooked. It had the texture of baby food.

Catherine came back from London late on the Sunday night, when we were in bed but not, of course, asleep. As soon as we heard her car pull up, Sarah said we should invite her round. We should get in touch with her before she got in touch with us. If we waited for her to contact us, she might construe that as a sign of guilt. We had to show her that we weren't afraid of her and had nothing to hide, even though we were afraid of her and had something to hide.

I got out of bed and and put on some pants and trousers.

'You're not going to invite her round now, are you?' asked Sarah. 'We're asleep.'

I told her I was going to put a note through Catherine's door, inviting her to come round for a drink before supper the following night. Sarah was worried that 'before supper' sounded hostile. Those words made it too clear that we weren't inviting her for supper. I should just put 'a drink', thereby accentuating the positive aspect of the invitation (the drink) rather than the negative (the supperlessness).

I opened the bottle an hour before she arrived. It was a supermarket bottle of Côtes du Rhône, which I'd bought because it was cheap. I decanted it to make it perform to its best. I was being nice, decanting nice. Sarah tasted it and wasn't impressed. Out of a decanter, the wine tasted fraudulent, as if it were trying to pass itself off as better than it was. And so, using a funnel, I poured it back into its humble bottle, where it was at home.

Catherine could not have been more breezy and charming.

We, in our collective tension, over-nodded and were too interested – 'Tell us more!' – as she described Dad's flat, their lunch in a Lebanese restaurant, their visit to the Lots Road auction house in Chelsea, where Dad was hunting for a painting or a piece of furniture to give to his parents for their fortieth wedding anniversary – 'Aaah, that's nice,' said Sarah.

We moved on to their early-evening drink in a bar near the Albert Hall, then to the concert itself, at which point we became part of the story, because Sarah said we'd switched on the radio.

'It was spellbinding, wasn't it?' asked Catherine. We agreed, though we'd switched off before the spell began.

'Did you have a drink in the interval?' How much longer could we delay the crux, the climax, the showdown, the outcome, the prognosis, the damage, the shit?

Catherine didn't answer the interval question. We had got there. This was it.

'He's a very nice man. He listens. He's attentive. He's concerned.'

Under the protective wooden screen of the table, Sarah took my hand.

'I'm sure he's a wonderful dentist.'

'He is,' I said. I've got the teeth to prove it.' Sarah gave my hand a preventative squeeze, not wanting me, in my anxiety, to show Catherine my teeth.

'You know when you said there are always problems at the beginning. I wondered what you meant. What did you think the problems would be?'

The 'you' was me. Catherine was looking at me when she asked the question. But it was Sarah who answered it, Sarah my hand-holder. She told Catherine we were worried that Dad wasn't ready for a relationship, given that he hadn't been apart from his wife for long. 'And,' she added, 'we weren't sure he was worthy of you. We thought he was. But we weren't sure.'

This was an answer of great skill. We hadn't been sure he was worthy of her; we had no doubt she was worthy of him. We thought he was worthy of her, though, we *thought* so, but now here we were, prepared to be disappointed. If it turned out she'd been disappointed, it would turn out we'd been disappointed too.

'But you knew,' said Catherine. She was calm. She was in command. She wore the white shirt she'd worn the first time we saw her, out in The Lane, directing the removal men. I thought about her at the European Commission, translating, in that shirt. I couldn't picture the European Commission – was that the building or the people in the building? But I could see her in a gathering of dark-suited Euro-men. They would all rate Catherine, with her poise. She'd give their arguments, in translation – arguments for allowances and subsidies, arguments against quotas – her own natural authority.

'But you knew.' There was no accusation more effective than 'you knew'. 'You knew' was the crime where the criminal wrote his own charge sheet, noting in excruciating, incriminating detail the time and place and nature of his crime, his knowledge. 'You knew': of course you did. Everybody knows. You knew, when you shouldn't have known, and you kept the knowledge from the people who needed it. And now you were going to be tried and found guilty, you lying, weak, knowing bastard.

'We knew what?' asked Sarah, which was a lawyerly, but not human, response. Catherine didn't have to tell us what we knew. We knew what we knew. Catherine was staring at me. My face was already – what else? – beetroot.

'We had sex and then he told me everything.' (You see? Dad was not that nice. He had sex and then he confessed. He didn't confess first, for fear there'd be no sex.) 'He was very honest,' she added, as if to say that Sarah and I were less honest than Dad. But then we'd never had sex with her. We'd never been in bed with her, after sex. A naked body could do that to you, it could make you tell it everything. Dad had sworn me to secrecy but he hadn't sworn himself. He had, perhaps, gone into that bed promising himself he wouldn't tell her anything. But who got out of a bed having kept the promises made on the way in?

'You didn't tell me he was still involved with his wife. You knew that when you introduced us, didn't you?' There it was then: the charge sheet. We were accused of knowing, when we introduced them, that Dad was still involved with his wife. But we weren't guilty. We hadn't known when we'd introduced them. I'd discovered it later, in an incident near Leicester Square station, of which Catherine was evidently unaware. We hadn't been charged with the crime of which we were guilty.

149

'I just want you to be as honest with me as he was. Promise me you'll always tell me the truth. I need that security. I'm a woman on my own.'

Where was my wife, the lawyer, now? She was holding Catherine's hand. That's right. She had taken her hand out of mine and placed it, across the tabletop, in Catherine's. She was holding our accuser's hand. She was not *threatening court proceedings* if Catherine didn't withdraw the slanderous charge that we'd known all along, and substitute the accurate charge that we'd known subsequently, but hadn't told her. Sarah was, in effect, pleading guilty to 'knowing', never mind when, that Dad was involved with his wife. She wasn't arguing about detail, though the detail was crucial. I was shocked.

I got up from the table, taking the bottle with me, intending to replace it, even though it was still a quarter full. I poured that quarter away, crudely, like a man urinating into a sink. I couldn't understand how Dad had got it right when we'd got it wrong, why Catherine was praising him for his honesty, contrasting it so favourably with our cruel dissimulation. Never mind his honesty, what about his actions? The man had sex with her while knowing he was involved with his wife. (And the nurse, don't forget the nurse.) Our 'crime' was the withholding of information. How could we hurt her more by withholding than he did by doing?

'We're so sorry he hurt you,' said Sarah. I was so glad she said that. 'We just want you to be happy.'

'I know you do,' said Catherine.

Then Sarah burst into tears.

I could have gone for her. I'd have got there first, as I was approaching her, carrying a new bottle, while Catherine was sitting on the other side of the table. Instead, I let Catherine get to her feet, turn right, left and left, negotiating the corners of the table, and put her arms round Sarah. I let Catherine touch my wife before I did, because she was the cause of my wife's tears.

Sarah was sitting and Catherine was crouching, the better to embrace her. I could have leaned in and embraced them both, my right hand on Sarah's right shoulder, my left hand on Catherine's left. Was that allowed? Helpful? Weird? What was the etiquette for a three-person embrace?

'Don't, don't, it's not your fault,' said Catherine to Sarah, making me think it was my fault, which it was, in a way, because I'd known Dad for twenty years. Dad was my friend, before he was our friend. And I was a man. A man, at a time like this, is a fault. He's a two-legged fault.

Next morning, there came a letter from Dad. We stood together, near the doormat, reading it. He told us Suzy had moved back in with him. He'd always be grateful to me and Sarah for introducing him to Catherine, a woman of great style and beauty and intelligence, whom he hoped he hadn't hurt too much. He was sorry if he'd landed us in it. If we ever felt like a weekend in London with Suzy and him, we were always welcome.

I told Sarah we'd done a good deed, which puzzled her. I explained that Dad's affair with Catherine had obviously made Suzy jealous. (Suzy, of course, had earlier had her own affair.) Without Dad's affair, Suzy might not have gone back to him. Sarah shook her head.

'That's a very legalistic argument,' she said. Apparently, she could make legalistic arguments but I couldn't. I didn't have the qualifications.

As we stood there, a letter (stampless) came through the letter box. We knew from the handwriting that it had travelled with its writer from next door. We stayed silent and immobile till we heard her shut her front door. Then Sarah, eccentrically, sat down with her back to the door to read it, out loud. I sat down next to her.

'Thank you for the drink last night. I'm so sorry I upset you both. That's the last thing I want to do.' At this point, she changed the subject, so I stopped Sarah and made her read those three sentences again. Catherine had a genius for this truth business, which we just didn't have. Every word was a truth-nail, which you felt as she hammered it in: she was truly thankful and truly sorry and truly didn't want to upset us (both, I appreciated that 'both'). But then there were the words she didn't write, which you felt too. Which were true too. She didn't forgive. She didn't withdraw anything she'd said, because she wasn't sorry for the content of what she'd said, only its hurtful effect.

That was that, for the Dad matter. Somehow, she made that the last word. And then she told us that she'd spoken to the Hargreaves family architect, a woman called Moth Fraser, and given her our number, with a view to her coming to see us this weekend, as she lived in London during the week but had a cottage in Suffolk. Evidently, after Sarah's tears, Catherine had gone home and immediately done something to help us.

At the end of the letter was a flourish. She hoped that last night would mark a new stage in our friendship, in which we'd feel more free to tell each other – wait for it, wait for it – the truth.

'Right then,' said Sarah. 'Here's a truth.' I knew what she was going to say: we'd been falsely accused of knowing about Dad, from the beginning, and now we were going to go next door and explain that to Catherine. But I was wrong. Instead, Sarah told me she was pregnant.

I put my arm round her and kissed her. We had never been so tiny, on the doormat together with our backs to our country-cottage door. We felt like two little gingerbread people, gone soft and bendy with age. This was wonderful and frightening news, so wonderful and so frightening that I didn't say anything, the fear shutting up the wonder and the wonder shutting up the fear. Sarah was the only one who spoke.

'We mustn't tell Catherine yet, or she'll think my bursting into tears was to do with the pregnancy. You know? Maybe it was. So let's just wait a few days. I don't want to upset her.' She paused. 'What is it about you and me?' she went on, and I knew she was going to tell me, because the truth, like a psychotic wasp, was stinging everyone. The truth was I'd been with a dominant partner (Renate) and she'd been with a dominant partner (Mark), who didn't appear to be dominant but was, so reliant was he on Sarah, on account of his illness and awkwardness. Mark was passive-aggressive and Renate was aggressive-aggressive. (All this was the worst kind of truth, the truth you know already, which doesn't need repeating, but is being repeated, by a woman you have to let speak, because she's just told you she's expecting your baby.)

Mark and Renate, she went on, needed people like us. That's what we were. We were people like us. There wasn't really a word for us. Secondary people? Junior people? Neither word was right. But we knew who we were, didn't we? And now, even though there were two of us and only one of her, it seemed we wanted or needed or were destined to be junior and secondary to Catherine.

'That's all going to change,' I said. 'Now we're going to be secondary to the dormouse.'

I'd given it a name. From then on, it was 'Dormouse', a punning and twee conflation of the door at which we were seated and a foetus the size of a mouse. I soon learned that lots of couples give their unborn a nickname. That's what people like us, who are not special, do.

PART FOUR

It was like no other doll's house I'd seen. They'd all been mock-Tudor or Georgian-style. This one, which dated from the thirties, had a flat roof and looked like the work of Le Corbusier or some such modernist architect. It was a doll's house with a flat roof. I couldn't imagine any dolls in it, only miniaturised European writers and painters, a tiny James Joyce with detachable spectacles and hat, an articulated Freud standing over an inch-long couch.

The doll's house had been among her mother's effects when she'd died of cancer. Catherine had found it in a cupboard in her mother's bedroom while Mel was preoccupied downstairs with Phoebe, who was having a tantrum because she said her grandparents' house stank of dead people and she didn't want to stay in it a moment longer. Gordon, to escape, had wandered upstairs and discovered Catherine carrying the doll's house along the corridor, hoping to sneak it out of the house without Mel noticing. If Mel noticed, she'd want it for herself. Much to Catherine's delight, Gordon offered to carry it downstairs for her, then take it out and put it in the boot of Catherine's car. If Mel saw him, she'd assume he was putting it in their car, not Catherine's. As it happened, he'd got it into Catherine's boot without Mel noticing. The doll's house became Catherine's; and now it was ours.

Sarah hugged Catherine. Then it was my turn. How long should our hug last? I'd be guided by Catherine. When she took her hands off me, I'd take my hands off her. The hug duly happened and was brief.

'But what if *you* have kids?' asked Sarah, in the spirit of the new, truthful regime, in which you said what you thought or knew as soon as you thought or knew it. Catherine felt sure she wouldn't have kids but, if she did, she'd reclaim the doll's house. She was clear and without self-pity. And then she surprised me by asking to see my drawings. The two of us went upstairs.

I'd never shown Catherine any of my drawings. All she knew was the authorised story of my work, as opposed to the thing itself: how I'd always loved drawing; how I'd met Sarah and she'd insisted it was time for me to do what I loved; how we'd moved to Worth and made our lives smaller and cheaper so we could follow our hearts.

I showed her a series of drawings of Lard. In the first, he was running after Ellie the Eagle, who had swooped on, and flown off with, a picnic hamper in Fudgley Wood, just as Firewoman Fran and her husband Stan were sitting down to enjoy it. Lard kept chasing, hopelessly, waving his trotters in the air. But, as it turned out, there was hope after all, because the hamper wasn't properly fastened. It opened and disgorged its contents all over the wood, at which point Ellie the Eagle let it go. Lard then made it his business to track down each egg sandwich and tomato and cucumber slice and apple and nut and chocolate finger, eating everything he found, Kinski having convinced the editor that this was a joke about porcine greed not police corruption. Lard didn't get away with it, though, because Ellie swooped again, while he had his snout in the mayonnaise, and swept him clean off his trotters by his right ear, subsequently dropping him in Fudgley Pond.

'They're charming,' said Catherine. 'Surprisingly old-fashioned.' I nodded and smiled. *Charming* was a compliment and you don't reply to a compliment, don't question the wording, don't negotiate a bigger compliment. *Old-fashioned* was a compliment too, implying craftsmanship and solidity. What she gave with *old-fashioned*, though, she took away, even before she gave it, with *surprisingly*. I was a fashionable man, then, pretending to be old-fashioned. I was superficial, speedy, shallow, urban, more at home with a shiny new leather jacket than its source, a cow. Surprisingly, I was a children's book illustrator, living in the country.

'What are you doing next?' she asked.

I shook my head, dumbly. I had no idea what I was going to do next.

'Can I ask you a question?' she went on, which is never itself a question, just a warning that what's about to be said will hurt. 'What's Suzy like?'

I didn't know who Suzy was. I looked at Fudgley Pond. Then it came to me. As soon as I knew who was meant by the name, my answer came out like bullets.

'Skinny. Mad. Manipulative. She walks around singing hit songs from shows.'

'Thank you,' said Catherine, as if she'd known what I was going to say. She was right, then. The truth was, Dad's wife was inferior to Catherine. The truth was on Catherine's side.

She looked, for once, girlish. She made a kind of *tee-hee* expression, which told me we'd had a tiff – a couple/single person's tiff – but now the three of us were all right again.

'You carry on,' she said, like a passing royal to a factory worker. With that, she left the room and went back downstairs.

I stayed at my desk, as instructed, even though – the drawings being finished – there was nothing for me to carry on doing.

Sarah was pregnant and craved grapefruits. That was her symptom. I was proxy-pregnant and suffered from name-failure. You said a name to me – 'Suzy' – and I failed at it. I heard it and repeated it to myself, but could still make no sense of it. If I distracted myself – chopped an onion, cut my nails, looked at a drawing – I'd discover who 'Suzy' was. I had to look away and look back.

After Catherine left the room, I checked for emails. Bold in my inbox was 'Andrew Stone'. When I clicked and read his opening words – *Dear Richard, As an Alcoholic* – I assumed Andrew Stone was a stranger and his email was generic. In a few lines' time, he'd tell me he'd drunkenly deposited twenty-five thousand pounds in my name in a safety deposit box in Nigeria, or ask me to write to the US president objecting to Israeli war crimes, on behalf of Alcoholic Friends of Palestine, or he'd invite me to a reunion for all pupils who joined my school in 1984 and were now alcoholics. It was only via these fantasies that I was able to reach Andrew Stone. He was Stone. Stone was now an Alcoholic, with a capital A. He felt stronger and happier and more positive as a result. Stone made it sound like a promotion – he'd been sought out by a headhunter, on behalf of a leading alcoholic organisation, whose name she couldn't reveal because, of course, it was anonymous.

Stone was writing to me as one of his Twelve Steps. He was making amends to all those he'd harmed when he'd been under the influence – the compulsion, the possession – of alcohol. He wanted and needed to tell me that he should never have claimed credit for the Romeo and Juliet commercials I'd created with Geoff Owen. If I gave him my address, he would send me all the awards he'd won for these commercials. In fact, the next time I was in London, why didn't I come and see him at his new office and he'd give me these awards, in person? At this point, the email became, explicitly, an advertisement for Andrew Stone.

Stone had left Hammond Law Stone Fisk, which shook me. When you move to the country and think back to the city, everything and everyone is fixed. It's just as you left it. Leaving the city is like leaving a house: nothing changes or moves when you've gone. It's *you* who changes and moves. Stone was part of my

London furniture, but now he'd checked himself into a removal van and moved on. He'd founded the Blue Catalogue, a mail-order company which sold blue clothes and sheets and curtains and crockery and cushions and bags and watches and shoes. It was, he wrote, 'a unique adventure in retailing', yet downstairs, on the little round table by the kitchen door where I put the things that I didn't know where to put – leaflets for yoga workshops, plastic bags in which to put clothes for charity – was the White Catalogue. What, beyond blueness, was the difference between his Blue Catalogue and our White one?

Stone, like Renate and John Smith, was one of the London monsters from whom Worth had made me safe. I sat there, mocking his newly Alcoholic, newly Blue phase. But I choked on my own mockery. Stone had a job, while I was a surprisingly old-fashioned children's illustrator who'd got to the end of a job and was short of another. What was I doing reading his email, if not as a displacement from my own joblessness?

Depressed, I found a new displacement inactivity. I put on my iPod and listened to all the blue music I could find – Miles Davis's 'All Blues' from *Kind of Blue*, New Order's 'Blue Monday', the White Stripes' 'Blue Orchid' – while I stared out of my window and pictured Sarah in our garden, with our baby, a generic baby. Then it struck me that the room in which I was sitting – my study, formerly the second bedroom of our two-bedroom cottage – would by then be a bedroom again. The baby would want my room for its bedroom, which would be fine, if we could put another bedroom in our roof and I could work in our new, as yet unbuilt, extension.

Moth Fraser was in her mid-seventies. She had short cropped grey hair and slightly scary, bulbous eyes – probably from a thyroid condition. She wore blue and white, the colours I now saw everywhere. On the bosom of her white blouse, suspended by a cord, her blue-framed glasses perched, lenses upturned, ready to break the fall if her eyes popped out.

Moth Fraser had an uncensored quality. Catherine had told her we were both quite pretty, with which she wanted us to know she agreed, and also that we were expecting a baby, so she'd brought a bottle of champagne. Sarah wasn't sure if you should drink champagne in the early stages of pregnancy but Moth was sure you should drink it when you were seventy-five and it was after ten on a Saturday morning and you didn't, in her phrase, 'give a fuck'. So Moth and I got stuck in. Glass in hand, she wandered up and down and through our cottage, then out into the back garden to look at it from afar, recalling it as 'tumbledown' in 1969, when the Hargreaves family had bought it and she'd done it up on their behalf.

'This is going to be an absolutely lovely job,' she said. 'I'm just going to use your loo. It's mine. I built it!' (What was she talking about? She was an architect. She built nothing.) She broke into a run, eccentrically dropping her glass on the grass. While she was gone, Sarah worried. How could we employ a drunken architect? We'd end up with S-shaped walls. But no. Thirty years earlier, Moth Fraser had drawn up plans for the conversion of Myrtle Cottage. She proposed to use these plans again, saving us hundreds of pounds. Why not? Myrtle Cottage and Hay Cottage were a pair. She had modified the one and now she'd modify the other, in precisely the same way. I looked up at the attic bedroom in Catherine's cottage, then down and sideways at Catherine's glass extension. What Catherine had, we would have.

'Coffee?' asked Moth. Traditionally, it's the hosts who ask the guest if she wants coffee.

How long had we known Catherine? Had we met her sister, Mel? How did we think they compared? What did we know of their parents?

162

Sarah and I said as little as we could, fearful she'd pass on everything to Catherine, with a gossip's distortions. Anyway, I wasn't finding speech easy, being woozy with champagne and buzzy with coffee. Everything I said sounded (to me) as if it were coming out in fast slow motion, from a mouth three inches further forward than my own. But no matter. Moth talked enough for three.

Catherine, she said, had the brains and the beauty, while Mel had the animal magnetism and the (there they were again) balls. Catherine was prone to unhappy love affairs, while Mel wouldn't know love if she found it in a handbag in the Harrods sale; she ruled her husband 'by sex and fear' and it was a wonder he hadn't hit her with a number nine iron. Mel had her father's forcefulness, energy and charm. (Charm? We doubted it.) Their father, we learned, was called Tony, which was a very different name from 'Old Man' Hargreaves. That name reeked of pipe tobacco and tweed. 'Old Man' would never – as Tony did – drive sports cars and crash them or, on a whim, buy a flat in Rome, from the proceeds of his business, which was manufacturing motor oil. Had we been invited to the flat in Rome? We shook our heads. Moth was sure we'd be invited, one day. It belonged to his daughters now. Tony had left it to Catherine and Mel, jointly.

I stopped listening to Moth Fraser. I nodded and smiled while I listened, in preference, to the voice in my head, which was asking me why Catherine hadn't told us she'd inherited, with her sister, a flat in Rome. Suddenly, she was half a flat in Rome richer, which made her a person we didn't know as well as we thought. She hadn't lied to us, but she'd omitted, she'd withheld this Roman flat information, as we'd withheld our information about Dad and Suzy. Perhaps she'd withheld it because she didn't want to make us feel like financial inferiors. Then the voice in my head got angry, as those head voices will. It felt cheated. She was, in the story she'd told us, the less-loved sister, the poor relation, but now the fairy-tale case had been altered. He'd left the big house to Mel and the cottage to Catherine. But he'd left the Roman flat to them both.

Sarah turned to me. 'I'm happy with that. Are you?' I didn't know what she was talking about, because I hadn't been listening, but I told her and Moth I was happy too, taking the happiness cue from my wife.

'Splendid!' Moth stood up and said we'd meet again in a few weeks, after she'd contacted the building firms she'd like to tender for the job. 'We've got till April to build a dream house for the Dormouse!'

I'd missed that bit too – the bit where Sarah told her our baby's nickname. Moth Fraser kissed us both. She was glad, she said, to be a part of our expanding family. Then she made her final remark, extra loudly, like an actress who wanted to be applauded as she left the stage: 'I'd go mad in a village like this if I didn't know Catherine.'

'Oh well. We're committed now,' said Sarah, after she left.

We had no idea how much the work would cost, because Moth had been canny enough not to guess. But the builders would guess, all right. They'd come in, look around, shake their heads, knock on walls as if they were doors, go outside and look up at the roof, tut, then tell us how much it would cost. But it wouldn't cost that, it never did. The budget was always exceeded, whether they were building you a kitchen or an airport. Why, then, did they give you a figure? They might as well quote you a fruit. They might as well say, it will cost you a grape, knowing that when your attic bedroom was finished, you'd lie in it, weeping, knowing you'd spent an orange or, more likely, a watermelon.

To claim we were poor was offensive to the truly poor. There was, though, an offensive truth here, which couldn't be denied, as we drove to the supermarket: we weren't comparing ourselves with African famine victims, stick people with flies around their eyes. We were poor as compared with our neighbour. What those African stick people had to do, if they wanted to make us rich, was to move to Worth and put up a hut next door.

Why did we have to turn our cottage into the twin of Catherine's? I was exasperated and took it out on the supermarket's products. (Why kitchen paper? What was its purpose, except to be sold? It was a popular room cynically attached to a much loved material.) We didn't have to have an extra bedroom and an extension. I could work in our existing bedroom. All I needed was a desk. That was what couples did, when their babies arrived. They sacrificed space, they accommodated, they literally accommodated. But Sarah was determined. We'd do the work, whatever it cost.

'The baby deserves it,' said Sarah. I couldn't accept this. The baby had done nothing, it hadn't even been born, it didn't *deserve*.

'*We* deserve it then,' countered Sarah, taking the cheaper of two organic chickens. Then she gave herself away: 'We certainly deserve it if Catherine does. There's only one of her.'

'She's rich,' I said, putting back the cheaper chicken and taking an even cheaper. But it was still organic and only cheaper because it weighed less. Bizarrely, though it was headless and dead, this organic chicken felt richer than me. It had roamed on more land, it was a landed chicken, not like the frozen paupers in the freezer below, who'd lived in shit, a thousand to a room.

Catherine was rich but, once upon a time, we'd been rich too. Sarah had worked in a City law firm and I'd worked in an ad agency, mediocre as it was. Was it possible to envy one's old self, as if one's old self were a neighbour in time?

We headed for the till. I walked in front of the trolley because the trolley, with its contents yet to be paid for, was now the source of my panic. Who could we ask for money? Our parents weren't rich. Sarah's mother was the widow of a tax inspector. My father was, unlike Tony Hargreaves, an unsuccessful businessman. He owned a two-bedroom flat in Wandsworth, along with a lease on an antique shop. As Sam Davey said, my father had a pot to piss in, but only because he hadn't sold it. When I'd called him to tell him about the baby, he'd asked if there was anything he could do. Now was the time to call him back and tell him: he could die. Wasn't that what your parents did for you? That, it seemed, was what Tony had done for Catherine.

'We can't afford to be poor,' said Sarah. 'So we'll manage it somehow.' I believed her, because she'd managed it before, she'd managed to buy our cottage for cash and she'd managed *me* – not in the Renate sense of telling me what to do, but of finding out what I wanted to do and helping me do it. She told me not to dream of being an illustrator, but to do it. And I'd done it. Not that I could now remember the dream, a word I'd come to loathe, now I had no work. I was meant, in that supermarket, to dream of walking downstairs from our attic bedroom, carrying our baby, and gliding together towards our extension, where I'd lift the baby high in the air and go: *Whee!* But dreams didn't function like that. They weren't conscious constructs of better worlds. You don't, whatever the man said, have a dream that one day all men will live together as one, regardless of race, colour or creed. That's a hope. That's a wish. But it isn't a dream. You have a dream that all men are walking into an exam room, in their pants.

We arrived at the till but I kept on moving. I walked over to the noticeboard on the supermarket wall. There was an ad for an in-store Customer Services Assistant. I read it, without understanding it, not sure if I could do it or be it.

When I looked back at our purchases, travelling along the till to their final reckoning, I saw Sarah had bought a supermarket orchid. I marched to the till and grabbed it, to save it from the cashier. I told Sarah we couldn't afford orchids. Sarah told me to calm down. The orchid wasn't for us.

Catherine identified it as a dendrobium. She was delighted but asked what she'd done to deserve it. It was to thank her for recommending Moth, said Sarah. Moth was going to use her old drawings, saving us hundreds of pounds. Catherine told us we needn't have got her anything.

'We wanted to,' said Sarah.

'No, really. A bar of chocolate would have been fine.'

'That's what *I* said!' I shouted, embarrassing Catherine and upsetting Sarah. But it was true. We were eating the very chocolate we should have bought her. We were sitting in her conservatory, eating Green & Black's Maya Gold, which was on special offer at three bars for the price of two. We could have given Catherine a bar – the third bar, the free bar – and kept the other two for ourselves. But Sarah was insistent. We had to spend money, we had to be generous, because of the money we were saving on the drawings. What about the (bigger) money we were spending?

I apologised to Catherine. I should have apologised to Sarah but I was still upset with her, so it wouldn't have been a truthful apology, simply a tactical one.

'No, no, I understand. It's difficult,' said Catherine. I took her to mean – since I'd shouted at my wife – that being in a couple was difficult. Now the business with Dad was over, she was spared that difficulty. She looked poised again, uncompromised, radiantly single, sitting in that conservatory uncluttered by a partner's stuff.

'Listen,' she said, as if we ever didn't listen. She was about to make a pronouncement, one that would remind us that she thought about us just as much as we thought about her and was, in fact, always one move ahead. 'Listen, I can lend you a few thousand pounds. If it helps. I'm sure she told you about the Aston Martin and the flat in Rome. It's not fair, is it? I've got this' – gesturing at her domain – 'and I'm a lady of leisure. And it's all an accident of birth.'

Sarah got to her feet, thereby making herself taller than Catherine, and said: 'That's kind of you but we'll be all right.'

Sarah asserted that, without a pause, while I was still thinking, holy shit, holy *grail*, she's just offered to lend us a few thousand pounds. What did she mean, though? What was her 'few'? Her few was not our few, was it? Her raisin was, surely, our pomegranate, but that was good, that worked in our favour. Catherine, whom we'd known a few months, was offering to lend us thousands of pounds.

Sarah, having asserted herself, was still on her feet. It was awkward for her, now, to sit down again. So she advanced to the edge of Catherine's rug, which was six feet long and about three and a half feet wide, and asked where it came from and when and where Catherine had bought it. Sarah looked at that rug with a covetousness that was Old Testament. She stood there, coveting her neighbour's rug.

Catherine and I stood up and joined her.

The rug had been left to Catherine by her father. It was an eighteenth-century prayer rug from Anatolia, which her parents had bought from Sotheby's – her mother having chosen, her father having paid – in the 1980s.

'It's extremely beautiful,' said Sarah.

'Isn't it!' said Catherine, who didn't have to thank Sarah for the compliment, since the compliment was owed to her parents. We all admired it, silently, till Catherine ended the reverie. 'You should see the one he left Mel.'

This had the rhythm of a punchline to a joke. But there was no joke. I caught Sarah's gaze, for the first time since I'd shouted at her. We had no Anatolian prayer rug, but at least we had each other, whereas Catherine had her sister. Her sister was the significant other to whom she'd always return.

'Your baby will be nothing like my sister,' she said. 'I've absolute faith in that.' Her eyes flared, in a little blaze of hatred, and then she asked if we'd like more coffee.

Dad, unlike me, was a dad, with an eight-year-old son and a six-year-old daughter. Sweetly, he'd sent me a compilation of his favourite Chopin nocturnes, to congratulate me on my impending fatherhood. I downloaded it onto my iPod immediately.

A few days later, on a Monday evening, when Sarah was at yoga, I ventured to the bottom of the garden to listen to it.

Chopin's nocturnes were mature and magnificent. They calmed and centred you and put you in touch with things – truths – to which you couldn't put a name. I knew all this without ever having heard them. Chopin was a master. He belonged to the classical canon. I didn't care whether I liked his nocturnes or not. I simply wanted to invest in that canon and get, in the form of truths, my dividend.

I stood there, looking at the sheep on the marshes, as the light faded. This was an experience I'd never had. I'd never once been still, for an hour, in nature, doing nothing other than being part of the landscape as day became night.

Who was I? That was the question nature was asking me, as I stood in its grip. In the city, the who-am-I question is easily answered: I'm the person who lives in this street, shops at that shop, has read the book of that film which is advertised on the side of that bus, which is carrying thirty men who are wearing my trainers. I'm validated. Now, with no people or neon or buildings to define me, who I was was up to me. I was a jobless husband whose wife was expecting a baby. I loved my wife and I'd love our baby and everything would be all right. Somehow.

When I ran out of nocturnes, I stood there, with my back to our cottage, in my own silence. I felt rooted. What did that mean, in the city? It mean 'stuck'. You were rooted because you were sitting in a stationary car or standing in a queue. To be rooted was to feel frustration that you weren't somewhere else, somewhere better, somewhere further forward.

From the bottom of our garden I heard our car pull up at the front of our cottage. That would be Sarah, returning from her yoga. I loved my wife and I wanted to get back to her. I turned round to walk up the garden and into our cottage. After two or three

169

paces, my eye was drawn to the only source of light, which was coming from the attic bedroom of Catherine's cottage. Catherine was at the window, looking at the night sky. She was lit from behind by an overhead light and from the side by some other light – a table lamp, presumably. I could see her but she couldn't see me. There was no reason to look into the dark of our garden, when the Plough and Orion's Belt were available in the sky. She was naked. Why would she not be? She lived in a cottage that overlooked nothing but marshland and sheep. And our garden.

I stopped. I played dead. I looked at her breasts. They were large, like Renate's. Renate was a woman proud of her breasts, in a place and at a time – the London of the early twenty-first century – when women were obsessed with reducing themselves to the skinniness of boys, as part of their calorie-controlled self-loathing and mutual competition. But Renate's breasts were weaponry – she used them to make herself outstanding – and therefore her breasts seemed hard, whereas Catherine's looked soft and beautiful.

What should I do? Should I carry on looking? Yes. Since she didn't know I was looking, there was no offence. Her ignorance was my bliss; no, not 'bliss', that's too strong. I had been strongly affected, yes, when I first saw her, but the longer I looked, the less was her power over me. Familiarity bred not contempt, nothing like it, but acceptance. There was Catherine, with her beautiful breasts, naked at her window, and here was I, and that was the end of it.

And then I was distracted by another light, this time from the first floor of our cottage. The light was on in our bathroom. Sarah was in our bathroom. Then I heard the lavatory flush and the banality of this, the sexlessness, the contrast between Catherine's fantastic breasts and the lavatory: this was cruel. There was sexuality in one cottage and lavatory in the other, so I knew to look back at the breasts, given that the more I looked at them, the more sexless and ordinary and quotidian – the more lavatory-like – they would be. Then the light went off in our bathroom. Sarah would shortly come downstairs and wonder where I was. It was time for me to stop playing dead. I had to go back into our cottage.

I walked, slowly and methodically, moving through the night unnoticed. Catherine didn't see me and didn't see me and didn't see me. I know, because I didn't take my eyes off her. And then, five metres from the cottage, I was floodlit, by the LED floodlight with a built-in sensor which that dextrous racist bastard Keith had installed, a million years earlier, when we were friends. The shock of it made me look away from her. She was now, surely, looking at me. How could she not be? I'd been illuminated, shockingly. Did she think I'd been looking at her? I didn't know. I had, in that absurd and self-defeating phrase, to 'act naturally'. There's nothing natural in acting naturally. It's a hundred per cent acting.

I knew not to make great play of looking everywhere but up at her window. The only way, I thought, of doing that – of not making great play of not looking up at her window – was to look up at her window. So I did. I looked up at her window. Miraculously, it felt natural. It felt like what a person would do, drawn by the light.

She didn't turn away or cover herself. She looked, but it was the look a driver gives, as they drive past, to a pedestrian of their acquaintance. Because she wasn't thinking of herself in a sexual way – she was probably thinking about her sister – she didn't think of me in a sexual way, nor did she think my look was lustful, which it wasn't, I was careful to look at her with as flat an expression as I could 'act', given that I was looking for the first time – *acting* looking for the first time – at the lit window of a neighbouring cottage, which I didn't know – pretended not to know – had a naked woman behind it.

Then she turned away, as if someone had called her. I stopped

171

looking. I carried on thinking, though: if I hadn't stopped looking, what would I have seen? Would I have seen her buttocks as she walked away from the window? It was a question of angles and relative heights. No, of course I wouldn't have seen her buttocks. A man sixty foot tall would have seen them. But, being a giant, he would not have been affected by them, belonging as they did to a creature of a different order. They would have aroused him no more than I was aroused by the buttocks of an ant.

These thoughts depressed me. I felt reduced. I was a procreator now, I practised the unerotic sex of a biological functionary. I was a pig. I was Catherine's pig neighbour.

I decided not to tell Sarah. I wanted to tell her, because that would be the best way to make nothing of it. I wanted to say *I just saw Catherine naked at the window* to which she might say *Oh. What was that like?* And I might reply truthfully *It was nice. She has lovely big breasts.* But you cannot say to a slight, slender, small-breasted woman – even when she's your wife – that you think your neighbour's bigger breasts are 'nice'. The married chalk doesn't want to hear that the single cheese is 'nice', much as you might protest there's no comparison. You've just said you like big-breasted cheese. How is that not a comparison with small-breasted chalk?

Sarah came down the stairs and told me she'd just phoned Catherine to ask her about local builders, not wanting to rely on Moth Fraser's opinions, or just go for the cheapest quote – she thought Catherine's local intelligence would be more up to date than Moth's.

I approached Sarah and hugged her.

'What's this for?' she asked.

'No reason.' She was unconvinced. She wasn't expecting a hug and felt she'd done nothing to earn or provoke it, and so it was something of an irritant. But I couldn't explain that I was hugging her because she'd phoned Catherine, which had caused Catherine to move away from that window. Sarah was there, at that window,

172

as I was. Our presence at the window wasn't physical, but we were there together nevertheless. I had just looked at the woman at the window but Sarah had phoned her. That was the difference. Sarah had done something.

She'd made a decision, which couldn't be unmade. She was going to go back to the world of money. She'd leave Roofspace and find a better paid job, a moneyed job, so we could do the building work on our cottage and have a nice life with our baby. We'd moved to the country and done what we wanted to do. Now we were expecting a baby, we had to do what we had to do. I had to find more illustrating work and she had to read the recruitment pages.

We'd borrow the money for the building work from the bank, as soon as we found out how much it would cost. Our earnings, recently, had been low. But we owned our cottage outright. And we were living at a time when banks would lend you money if you asked nicely, or just asked.

Every morning, Sarah turned the pages of the *East Anglian Daily Times*, while eating a grapefruit and spraying the local faces with juice. It was the paper of the community. To be pregnant was to join the community, with its antenatal classes, hospitals and health visitors, playgroups, playgrounds and schools. We were no longer living in isolation. Those days were gone.

'There!' she said, finding what she was looking for, though I don't believe she knew what that was.

The panic didn't leave me for the rest of the day. It manifested itself electronically, in the sending of emails to everyone who'd ever rejected my drawings, and many who hadn't yet had that chance. To each I sent a JPEG of the cover of *Crackling and Lard*, saying it was the first of a planned series, but not saying that no one was planning it yet, as they were waiting to see how the first one sold. The point was to tell the reader of the email that I, as the illustrator of the series, was in demand; I'd almost certainly be unavailable for any other work, unless they offered me any, in which case I could do it immediately. They'd know this: they were sophisticated people, who weren't easily fooled, but whose status demanded that all those who wanted their business had to make a big and bold fooling effort. What they didn't know – which made an email preferable to a letter – was my address: Hay Cottage, The Lane, Worth, Suffolk IP15 5NJ. That address suggested an artist in retreat, a famous and successful artist, who needed to escape from the world in order to do his work. A man of my non-fame and non-success couldn't justify an address like mine. The world wasn't pursuing me, so why the need to escape?

Two weeks later, those potential rejectors, by doing nothing or replying with killing kindness, had fulfilled their potential. It was Thursday evening and I was on my own. Sarah was heading to the Somerton Hall Hotel for the East Anglian Women in Business Conference, the thing that had made her exclaim 'There!' when she'd seen it advertised in the paper. Thursday night was Welcome, Induction, Drinks and Supper. Friday was Keynote Speech, Sessions, Lunch and Workshops, concluding with Afternoon Tea. 'It pays to network!' said the ad, at the bottom, just above the price, inflated to keep out the riff-raff. That was a bluff, surely. Only the riff-raff would attend, paying heavily to meet dynamic and important people, but meeting only each other.

An hour earlier, a corporate woman had come out of our bath-room, in her armour and warpaint. I saw my wife in her pre-me mode, her living-with-Mark look, dark-suited and serious, every hour of her working day chargeable and expensive. My wife, before she met me and brought us to the country, to be better people.

'Wish me luck,' she said. She looked determined, but sad, as if her life was about to take a turn that was necessary but wrong. Homeless people were a cause, East Anglian Women in Business were not.

'You won't say where I am, will you?'

'Course not!'

She didn't need to remind me.

We cared about Catherine. I admired her and wanted her to be all right, not least because she so clearly cared about us. Sarah's feelings were stronger than mine, though. She felt more concerned and, since the offer of the loan, she felt competitive. She wanted to show Catherine she didn't need her help to get what Catherine had, which was a cottage big enough for three, with a mulberry tree in the garden. (We already had the mulberry tree.) I didn't feel competitive. I didn't compare myself to Catherine, though I could see the advantages of having what she had, and I didn't feel a need to prove myself to her. Husbands, I thought, don't feel the need to prove themselves to female friends.

We never wanted to hurt her again as we'd hurt her over Dad. That was something we felt to precisely the same extent. We had to tell her everything, said Sarah, but then she went on to define that everything as 'everything that concerns her'. East Anglian Women in Business wasn't included.

'Catherine would never go to a thing like this,' said Sarah, putting the phone down, having read out the long number on the front of her card and paid for her EAWIB registration. This was the crux. This was why she mustn't be told. Sarah was grubbing around for work, which Catherine could afford not to do. Catherine, thanks to money, had a life without embarrassment. What did she actually do all day, this self-described 'lady of leisure'? In the time we'd known her, she'd only referred to one translating job, Spanish to English, for the *Journal of Eschatology*. She read books to, and played the piano for, old people in old people's homes. She was active in the Aldeburgh Sailing Club, a club for people with money, and in Suffolk Gardening 4 the Disabled, a club for people whom money couldn't save. She travelled and cooked and read and went to concerts of world and classical music. She was a member of the Worth Choral Society. As Sarah listed all this, with resentment, she suddenly stopped and found herself saying: 'Actually, it sounds fantastic.'

There was something ambassadorial about Catherine, from which we sought refuge. We could imagine her as an ambassador's mistress, though not an ambassador's, or anyone else's, wife. Some damage, some sibling damage for which she blamed her sibling, though surely the parents were at fault, some early sibling damage had been done to Catherine, which stopped her being a wife, not that she would have chosen to be a wife. (Why should she choose marriage, just because we had?) We pitied her, then told ourselves not to. She was not to be pitied. We couldn't picture her as the ambassador's wife, but we could picture her as the ambassador.

There's no conference for East Anglian Men in Business. What would East Anglian Men do, in a hotel, together, for twenty-four hours? Men don't network. They don't talk to each other in lavatories. They don't care what it is to be male, as females care what it is and what it costs to be female.

A hundred women sat down to eat. (I wasn't there, but I know. Sarah told me everything.) Those who knew each other sat next to each other. There'd been time, over Drinks, for everyone to get to know someone. But Sarah had hung back, hoping her reluctance would be taken for shyness not superiority, though at this point she felt both shy and superior. And so she found herself next to other shy/superior women, who'd similarly spoken to no one, and a talkative black woman from Norwich who refused to sit next to the two other black women at the table, because she hadn't come all that way to start a 'ghetto'. She had a printing business; the woman opposite ran a cleaning business; and the woman on Sarah's left, sitting at the end of the table, was in a wheelchair and had a business supplying wheelchairs. She gave Sarah her card and told her to get in touch if she ever needed a wheelchair. Sarah, intimidated by the woman's authenticity, kept apologising that she wasn't in the market for a wheelchair. But the woman told her not to be so sure – she might crash her car on the way home. That was fair enough. It was a conference. The woman was there to do business.

At the other end of Sarah's table were a couple of glamorous, loud-laughing, thin women, failing to eat their skimpy foodstuffs – lettuce, diced chicken breast no bigger than dice. One toyed with her noodles, twirling them like a teenage girl fiddling with her hair. Sarah recognised her as Emma-Kate, the woman in her yoga class from whom Sarah had fled. Next to Emma-Kate was a dumpy woman, eating meat and potatoes, which provoked Emma-Kate to offer her the forkful of noodles to 'try'. The dumpy woman ate it then recoiled when the second forkful was proffered. 'You're fattening me up for Christmas!'

When the coffee arrived, and these thin women passed their complimentary green-wrapped chocolate mints down the table, Sarah knew what she had to do. Wheelchairs, printing, cleaning: these were not for her. She had to go where the money and the ambition were. The scary Emma-Kate was a skinny missile, unstoppably in the ascendant. A few months ago, for a couple of weeks, she had laid her yoga mat behind Emma-Kate's. Now was the time to remind her of that. It was time to cash in.

Sarah excused herself and walked the length of the table. As she approached, Emma-Kate got up and moved away with her friend, a woman with blonde corkscrew curls, like a naughty girl in a children's story. They scurried off, giggling. Sarah took their departure as an insult, even though she was sure they hadn't seen her approach. An insult and an omen: Sarah was destined not to connect with the women who mattered. She'd come all this way and would go home with nothing, having met no one. She felt sick. Her chance had gone.

The next day, after *business models, global opportunities, start-ups* and *glass ceilings*, came Lunch. If the twenty-four hours of the conference were a school year, it was the end of the second term. You could walk past the girls you'd met on your first day – the printing girl, the cleaning girl, the wheelchair girl – without acknowledging them. They were your past, as you were theirs. 'A winner learns lessons from the past.' That was what the keynote speaker had said.

Sarah stalked Emma-Kate as she walked into the dining room and headed for the buffet. She took up a position three trays behind her, though Emma-Kate didn't need a tray. A saucer would have sufficed for her mouseworth, which she took to the nearest table, followed by Sarah, who sat down next to her and, after a few moments, said – to her profile – that she recognised her from a yoga class in Worth. Emma-Kate knew immediately that their sitting together was no stroke of luck. Sarah had targeted her. She turned her head but didn't look Sarah in the eyes, instead glancing at her left breast. This was acceptable, this is what everyone did, since that's where you wore your name tag. But she didn't recognise Sarah's name. A few seconds later, she didn't recognise her face either.

'Right,' she said, terminally. She was agreeing that Sarah had recognised her from the class, much as Madonna might agree, if you went up and said you recognised her from a concert at Wembley Stadium. It was a fact, to be acknowledged, which acknowledgement ended the conversation. Then the two women heard a ringtone and Sarah, pathetically, reached for her phone as if the synthesised strings of 'I Will Survive' weren't bound to be coming from Emma-Kate's.

'Hi,' said Emma-Kate and then, for the second time in eighteen hours, she got up from the table and moved away from Sarah.

While she was away, the woman with the corkscrew curls arrived and sat down. There was Sarah, the gap where Emma-Kate had been, and then this woman. She had evidently seen Sarah engaging Emma-Kate in (what looked like) conversation, because she introduced herself. 'Hi. I'm Mary.' That brief mouth movement of Emma-Kate's, that bored 'Right', seen from a distance, had worked for Sarah after all. She was accredited. She had access to Emma-Kate's friend, Mary.

Mary was familiar to Sarah, as I had been when Sarah first met me at Sam Davey's private view. It had taken her no more than a glance to know that I was like Hattie's brother's best friend from school, the one who'd dropped out of university to be a woodturner in Scotland, the one who played guitar and wrote songs, the one on whom she'd had a teenage crush so intense and unrequited that it had once made her cry in his presence. (When I heard all this, I loved him too, though I didn't think he sounded anything like me.) As for Mary, what was familiar to Sarah was her expression – sharp to the point of corrosive – and her energy. She was a 'player'. Sarah's clients, when she worked in mergers and acquisitions, were players, people of limitless energy and tireless focus, who loved to play and played to win and won.

Sarah, as a lawyer in a City firm, had always been thought a good listener. That was the principal reason she'd done well. She wasn't a good listener, though, not according to her. It was just that she found herself with good talkers. A good listener, most of the time, was someone who knew how to keep quiet, someone who'd been to Shut Up classes. She was no more than an average listener, but she had a very good listener's face: large brown eyes and a serious expression. These were genuine. In childhood photos, she already had that face, the thoughtful and sympathetic listener's face, in contrast to the aren't-I-pretty-look-at-me-face of her sister Jane.

Mary made some dismissive comments about the disappointing standard of the speeches. It was clear what she was trying to convey: I am worth more than this conference. I am not an East Anglian woman. I am a *national* woman. She then, without pause or invitation, told Sarah her business plan. She pitched to Sarah. Sarah was obliged to look at her, which made Sarah hungry, because she couldn't eat her food while she was looking at Mary. Cruelly, food was crucial to Mary's business plan. There was a Food Revolution happening and Mary wanted to be part of it. Sarah nodded, not knowing what the Revolution was, but keen to discover. Already, sensing that Mary might be her and our salvation, Sarah looked and listened hard, waiting for the capital letters. In every pitch, there were words that began with capital letters. 'Food Revolution' were two such words. Sure enough, a few moments later, Mary talked about a 'Pub Crisis'.

At this point, Sarah did something she knew would flatter and surprise. She got out a pen and pad. She became lawyer to Mary's client, journalist to Mary's celebrity, secretary to Mary's boss. Now she had the pad, Sarah was free not to look at Mary, who, instinctively, leaned towards her, the better to dictate those capital letters in 'Gastropub Explosion'. Mary, who had Money in Place, had her eye on seventeen pubs in the region, which were for sale because of the Crisis. They were in beautiful locations, had excellent parking and were close to tourist attractions.

'The whole of the region's a tourist attraction,' said Sarah. Mary looked surprised by Sarah's power of speech. Sarah hadn't spoken for minutes – now this! I'm proud to say this was a stratagem I'd taught Sarah myself, learned from my advertising agency meetings: if you said nothing for a long time, the something you eventually said took on the status of a revelation. Why do the silent speak, unless possessed by a truth they can no longer suppress?

'That's right,' said Mary.

'God, my husband's a moron!' said Emma-Kate as she headed back towards the space between Mary and Sarah.

'Right,' said Mary, irritated by the interruption, and then, with shocking speed, she pounced on that space and landed next to Sarah, who felt like an animal Mary was about to inseminate or kill. And so, while Emma-Kate swapped their plates and Mary ignored her, Sarah felt Mary's pushy breath in her ear. Her plan was to create a gastropub brand. The first. The First. It would be the McDonald's of gastropubs. Every Wild Rabbit – that was the brand – would serve the same basic menu. You would know what you'd be getting, with this key difference: every McDonald's looked similar, but every Wild Rabbit would look different, because country pubs were individual, which was their allure. You got the price promise and value guarantee of a McDonald's, in a uniquely beautiful building.

'It's an exciting idea,' said Sarah. You can criticise a player, you can question their numbers, but you cannot not be excited. The truth was, Sarah *was* excited. Mary had the exciter's gift.

'So what are you looking for?' asked Sarah, meaning not what, but who.

'I'm looking for someone to help me have fun.' Of course she was. Fun was what players played for. In her office, Mary would bounce up and down on the balls of her feet. She'd clap her hands when exciting things happened. Mary had no inner child. It was there on her face, it was outer. She was a forty-something child. Such people succeeded.

'Either as an employee or an equity partner. If they're brave enough. Or rich enough.'

She gave Sarah an unmistakable I'm-richer-than-you look. It was more like a scent, something that came from her skin.

'So, what do you do then, Sarah?' After twenty minutes of talking about herself, she'd asked a question about Sarah, which Sarah knew to be a question about herself: *what do you do then, Sarah, that flows out of all I've said about me then, via you, back into me?*

'Come on, we'll miss the next session,' said Emma-Kate,

181

standing up and tugging the collar of Mary's jacket, thereby revealing the label. She'd had enough of Mary talking to her new friend. Mary didn't need a new friend. She had her old friend Emma-Kate.

As she was led away, Mary gave Sarah a we'll-meet-again look.

Sarah paid no attention to the next session, or the one after. She thought only of the Wild Rabbit gastropub chain. Did the idea have any merit, now she was unexcited? It was new, which was alarming. Novelty, in an idea, was a ninety-nine per cent guarantee of worthlessness. New ideas, like new restaurants, were mostly disastrous, and Mary was planning a *chain* of disasters.

Sarah heard her internal legal voice, arguing this case against, but there was a case for the defence too, which was just as forceful, and far more exciting: a ninety-nine per cent guarantee was no guarantee at all, omitting as it did the one in a hundred – the Microsoft, the Coca-Cola, the McDonald's. She looked across at Mary, so pert and pretty next to her bored, texting friend Emma-Kate.

Sarah visualised, which was a revered technique in business, and not to be confused with dreaming. She saw the three of us – herself, myself and the baby – in the garden of the Bell, the disused Worth pub. In her visualisation, the Bell had been converted into a Wild Rabbit. Every table was occupied. Sarah looked up at the Wild Rabbit sign, with pride, as the drawing of the rabbit on the Wild Rabbit sign was by me.

There was tea, black as coffee, and there was coffee-flavoured coffee, paler than the tea. The conference was ending, with hundreds of adieux and a few au revoirs. Standing near the long table with the white tablecloth, drinking her un-coffee, trying to make her plastic-wrapped dwarf biscuit last, Sarah was given two business cards by two recruitment consultants, who separately apologised that they hadn't had the chance to talk to her.

'Your card should have a photo,' she said to the second, fearing she'd confuse her with the first. It was an excellent idea, Sarah felt. It was a Business Card Revolution.

'I hope I'm not that forgettable!' said the woman.

'Your name means nothing without your face,' said Sarah, which, like so much truth, sounded like an insult. The woman turned away and approached Mary, who gave her the gesture all beggars understand: *I will give you nothing*.

Mary looked round the room. When she saw Sarah, Mary mouthed 'Coffee'. Sarah, understanding that this was not an invitation but a command, nodded, got a second cup, then carried them both to Mary. The closer she got, the more she felt herself filling with hope, as a tank fills with petrol.

'Nice to see you again!' said Mary, who took neither cup. Instead, she offered up her cheek for Sarah to peck, Sarah who'd known her since lunch, Sarah whose multitasking abilities Mary was now testing. Sarah kissed both cheeks, while spilling no coffee.

'Let's sit down,' said Mary, leading her away from the crowd.

Now the hand that held her own cup started shaking, so she abandoned that cup on a table and clung to Mary's, with both hands. Mary was ahead of her and didn't see this. It would not have looked good. They sat at a table by the window.

'EK's driving me mad, as usual,' said Mary. Sarah surmised that EK was Emma-Kate. She nodded, not wanting to reveal that EK had only ever spoken – 'Right' – one word to her. She didn't want to bitch to Mary, an acquaintance, about Emma-Kate, who was barely even that. She hoped Mary would move on but was glad she didn't, because Mary explained that EK was the woman she'd wanted as her partner in the gastropub business. EK, however, was too preoccupied with her horses and her kids. Mary left a pause before 'and her kids'. It was a bitch-pause implying that EK saw her kids when – and because – her horses weren't available.

At this point, Sarah, remembering that EK had worked as a PR consultant in the City, lived in Marylebone and moved to the country, told Mary that she had worked as a lawyer in the City, lived in Marylebone and moved to the country.

'I'm like EK, only better,' said Sarah. She felt sick saying it. But she couldn't pretend that she didn't feel proud, too.

'Listen,' said Mary needlessly, just as Catherine had, before offering to lend us thousands of pounds. 'When I see something or someone I want, I go for it.' This was like – these are Sarah's words, not mine – my big hard cock. That when-I-see-something-I-go-for-it stuff was my big hard cock. It was vulgar and obvious. But sometimes you want that. It was as vulgar and as obvious as my big hard cock, though it behoves me to say that Mary's excitement made it, or made it seem, bigger and harder. Sarah and Mary were having business sex, which was different from the sex Sarah and I had, in this crucial respect: in our sex, there was a yin and yang, a male and a female, a penis and a vagina; but in business sex, whoever was having it, there was no vagina. There were only two big hard cocks, head to head, hard to hard, bashing and clubbing and hurting, even as they felt thrilled.

Mary wanted a partner; but Sarah didn't want to invest in the business, she wanted only to be employed. Mary said she couldn't afford to employ her, not full-time. She could afford to employ her three days a week. Sarah didn't believe in three days a week. Some weeks, given the nature of the venture, there would be two days' work, or no days' work; other weeks there would be ten days' work, squeezed into seven. Sarah wanted a monthly consultancy fee, guaranteed for a year, with an option on both sides to extend or terminate the arrangement at the end of that year. She named a figure, Mary named a lesser figure, they agreed a figure in between. Each felt they had won. Each felt still big, still hard. That was it. There was no release or relief, no orgasm, for that would be followed by a softening, whereas business demanded perpetual erection.

Sarah volunteered to get them two more cups of coffee. Mary, whose turn it was to get the coffee, said: 'That would be great.'

Ten minutes later, they were the only people left, apart from the hotel employee clearing up the cups.

'I have a really good feeling about this,' said Mary.

'Me too,' replied Sarah. It was a professional response – even before her first fee, she was swiftly and loyally seconding Mary's feeling. There would be feelings, of course, with which she wouldn't agree, so Mary could never say *I don't pay you to be a yes man*.

Sarah did indeed have a good feeling about Mary. The more time she spent with her, the more familiar she seemed, as if they'd met before, though maybe – embarrassingly – Mary just looked like someone she'd seen on television. Mary, she thought, would be good on television. She was pretty, in a two-dimensional way, and you could see what she was thinking. Sarah admired her but didn't like her, which was fine. She wasn't looking for a friend. Mary's phone beeped. It was a text.

'My husband's stuck behind a tractor, can you believe that? He was meant to be here by now. Why doesn't he overtake?'

'I'm sure he would if he could.'

'You don't know him.'

Yes, thought Sarah, let's keep it like that. Let's never go on holiday, the four of us, with the menfolk playing golf while the women talk business. (Golf? Since when had I become a future golfer?) Then she felt tearful, on account of her luck. She'd met Mary and now we'd been saved. We had a guaranteed income for the next year and the deal was not exclusive, there was nothing to stop Sarah making a similar deal, as a legal consultant, with another client, whose interests didn't conflict with Mary's. What, she then thought, less tearfully, was luck? *In this world, you make your own luck.* Her own thought embarrassed her. She was thinking with her (business) cock.

EK, who'd been waiting and waiting for Mary in the foyer, appeared in the doorway and shouted: 'Mel! Where's your useless husband?'

It was cruel that Mel's name tag – Mary Mason – was a married name tag. It was cruel that Mel called her sister 'Cathy', the name by which she wasn't known, which in turn provoked 'Cathy' to call her 'Mel'. But then all Sarah knew of Catherine's sister was that Catherine's sister was cruel.

A minute later, Mel put her arms round Sarah, having said: 'No wonder she was hiding you from me!'

'I didn't know your name was Mary,' said Sarah.

'She doesn't use Mel in business,' said EK, 'cos she thinks it sounds like a man.'

Finally, Mel let go of Sarah, confident Sarah knew she was hers.

'Sorry I'm late,' said Mel's husband, the unfortunate Gordon. He held the car keys. He looked more sullen than sorry. Mel and EK ignored him. It seemed that if you knew him, you ignored him; so Sarah, who didn't know him, smiled at him, and began to introduce herself, getting no further than the *hello* before Mel overrode her, to say they were coming to stay with Catherine at the weekend so they'd see her then, but Sarah should email Mel as soon as she got home, with her bank details; so saying, she produced a business card, which had a photo, confirming to Sarah that she'd made the right decision in hitching herself to Mel.

'Would you mind not saying anything till I've told my husband?' said Sarah. Mel understood. She mustn't tell Catherine that Sarah was hers till Sarah had told her husband.

Then, after the agony of telling EK it was lovely to see her again, and kissing her on both cold cheeks, to which she didn't respond, Sarah said goodbye to Mel and EK and Gordon, then went to the lavatory and was sick. This sick, she was sure, was nothing to do with her pregnancy. It was Catherine sick. Then she sat down in the hotel reception and called me, while a girl who looked like a school-leaver took the letters off the free-standing board near the entrance, the ones that spelt 'East Anglian Women in Business Conference'.

Sarah told me to go next door and tell Catherine the story, before Mel did. Mel wouldn't wait, she said she would but she wouldn't. I said I couldn't tell the story because it wasn't my story, it was hers.

'I've done everything,' said Sarah. 'You do this. You go round there now and tell her. Please. She has to hear it from us.'

I agreed. Then I delayed. I wanted her to go over the story again.

The crucial detail of the story was this: when Mel offered Sarah the job, Sarah didn't know she was Catherine's sister. The second crucial detail was: Sarah had accepted a job, not a friendship. She didn't seek a friendship with Mel. In fact, she actively sought – she told me to stress the *actively* – she had actively sought and would actively seek to keep friendship at bay, because friendship might compromise her professional integrity and lead her to give the wrong advice or withhold the right advice.

Mel wanted Sarah to start working for her 'NINS'. Sarah knew that must mean 'now if not sooner'. Before she even left the hotel, Sarah rang Roofspace to explain what had happened and ask if she could give two weeks' notice rather than four, in return for which she was prepared to forfeit her final month's pay. She felt bad but that gesture made her feel less so. She didn't want to keep Mel waiting.

The big sky and the whole of outdoors – these are what bring you to the country. How had it happened that our country life, our sky and outdoors, had contracted to the size of a single cottage, which was not even ours but our neighbour's?

I went the long way: up our path, out of our gate, left, through her gate, down her path. I knocked, at first softly, in the hope she wasn't there. It seemed, after a while, that she wasn't. But I couldn't be sure. I had to be sure. So I knocked loudly.

She opened the door. Then her phone rang. Fearing it was her sister calling, a man would have said: 'Don't answer that!' So that's what I said.

She tensed. 'What's happened?' She thought there was an emergency, concerning Sarah, which meant we had no time.

'No, no, nothing, sorry, answer it.'

Catherine went to answer the phone, assuming I'd follow her inside, but I stayed on the doorstep. Then I retreated a pace when I heard her 'Hi'. It sounded like the tense greeting she'd give her sister.

She didn't return and she didn't return. There was time to reflect: if I'd stepped over the wall and knocked loudly, first time, I could have told her the news, with its crucial details, before her phone rang. I retreated further, to just beyond her gate. Keith walked out of his cottage and down The Lane, carrying a toolbox. He carried it like a woman carries a handbag, except a woman's handbag, famously, contains the essential and the inconsequential, whereas Keith's toolbox contained only the essential.

Catherine walked out of the still-open door of her cottage and joined me at the gate where I was, eccentrically, waiting.

'That was my sister.'

'I'm sorry,' I said.

'Did she send you to tell me?'

I nodded. It was sharp of her to call Sarah 'she'. But then her whole question was sharp, belittling me as the sent one, the one who obeyed 'she'. I detached myself and saw how we might look in a nineteenth-century painting, from the time when paintings told stories. The painting would be called *The Neighbours at the Gate*. The tall, pale neighbour is dignified in her suffering. She's remote. Her heart is hardening. But who's the neighbour with the humble and beseeching air, standing a few feet from her? Has he brought the news that's caused her to suffer, or is he himself the cause of her suffering?

'It will end in tears.'

I waited but no more was said. I was ready to defend Sarah against a series of accusations. But there was only this prediction. Catherine didn't accuse Sarah of anything, so I didn't defend her.

'Doesn't the broom look lovely?' said Catherine. I followed her gaze.

'Yes.'

'Do you know what broom is?' This was definitely an accusation – she was accusing me of not knowing what broom was.

'No.'

Broom, I learned, was the shrub with the yellow flowers that I saw everywhere, even if I didn't know what it was. She asked me what I was doing 'here'. 'Here' didn't mean her gate. It meant the country. What was I doing in the country?

She'd noticed, on our first walk, that I didn't know what 'pollarding' was. What was a man who didn't know what 'pollarding' meant doing in the country?

'I don't know,' I said, with the insolence of my adolescent self, the insolence I believed to be smart. All the time she was attacking me, she wasn't attacking Sarah. I was taking blows that might otherwise have been directed at my wife. I was being a good husband.

'Wasn't your girlfriend a model or something? You should be in a nightclub.'

There was no need for me to defend myself. I just had to let her attack me. Then again, I wasn't sure how to defend myself. Even (or especially) when angry, Catherine either spoke the truth or convinced you it was the truth she was speaking.

'Did Sarah tell my sister she's pregnant?'

Sarah was outraged. How dare Catherine ask that! Was she threatening to tell Mel? In the guise of a loyal sibling, protecting her sister's interests – how hypocritical could you get? – was she intending to rat on Sarah, who'd always been her friend? What kind of sister – and now she meant sister as in fellow female – attempts to deprive a pregnant woman of a job opportunity? Didn't she trust that Sarah would tell Mel in her own time about the goings-on in her own body, which were nothing to do with anyone else? She paused. She turned over in bed.

'And, anyway, it's months away. The actual baby.'

It was some time after midnight and the three of us were connected as never before, Catherine in her cottage, Sarah and I in ours. We had no doubt she was thinking of us. It was a mutual haunting by living ghosts, a trans-wall two-way occupation of the darkest, most disturbing places in any country cottage: the owners' heads.

And then she was off again: how dare Catherine sit in judgement on me! It couldn't matter less that I didn't know what pollarding was, or broom. Sarah knew what they were. I didn't have to. That was the essence of a marriage – the one knew and the other didn't, the other knew and the one didn't. I was quiet, wondering what I knew that Sarah didn't.

'I mean, you know all about music.' She didn't know how to characterise the music I loved, which wasn't the music she loved, so she just called it 'music'.

'We have to compromise, she doesn't have to, she doesn't need to earn money to look after a family, so she shouldn't judge people who do. I have to sleep now,' she went on, as if it were my listening to her that was forcing her to stay awake.

I was woken, an hour later, by a scratchy sound I took to be the skitterings of a rat in the attic. Sarah was sitting at a table, writing by candlelight, which no one had done in our bedroom for a hundred years. She apologised. She thought the dim light wouldn't wake me. She was writing a letter to Catherine.

I got out of bed and read the letter. It said Catherine was 'right about everything' – what Sarah had done was disloyal and would end in tears. But these were difficult times. Catherine had to understand that we'd got ourselves in a financial mess. Sarah was obliged to take work wherever she could get it. She should have recognised Mel as soon as she saw her – even though Mel and Catherine didn't look alike. Catherine was the sister with the beauty and the bone structure. (I read this twice: 'You're the sister with the beauty and the bone structure.' I couldn't imagine the situation in which a person would write that to another person: 'You're the sister with the beauty and the bone structure.' But I didn't have to imagine it, I was in it, I was actually standing in that situation, feeling the tiny warmth of the candle near my belly button. I read on.) Sarah regretted doing anything that threatened her friendship with Catherine. She appreciated Catherine's company. She loved her style and intelligence. The relationship with Mel was professional. Nothing Mel could say or do would alter what Sarah felt for Catherine. Sarah understood that, for all their sibling strife, Catherine wanted to protect her sister, so she'd tell Mel about her pregnancy when they met next week to talk further about their working together, once Sarah had served out her notice at Roofspace. If Mel decided to withdraw her offer, Sarah would understand. Richard (here I was, suddenly, at the bottom of the page, just before the end) valued Catherine's friend-ship too. She (Sarah) would be buying him (Richard) a book on the flora & fauna of Great Britain for his birthday!

I admired the exclamation mark. She was ending the letter with a flourish of humour. Not comedy, which is funny, but humour, which draws attention to foibles in a semi-amusing way. Love, Sarah.

'What do you think? Is it all right? We've all got to live together. Come on, let's put it through her letter box now.'

I followed her to the chest of drawers. I opened the top-right, half-width drawer and took out a pair of pants. Sarah told me not to bother with them. We walked out of the cottage and into the September night, her in a nightdress and slippers, me in a dressing gown and slippers.

'Are you sure?' I asked as she stepped over the wall, letter in hand.

'What?'

'Is this the right thing? Let's think about this.'

Instinctively, I walked up our path and out of our gate and stood at the point between our two gates, where I'd spoken to Catherine. Irritated, Sarah joined me there and we stood in The Lane for some time, in our outdoor unsuitables. This was the country at its best. A man and a woman could have an argument in a lane, after midnight, dressed like sleepwalkers, and no one – because there was no one around – would judge them, or call the police, or think them locked out of their house or fearful of the violence that was taking place in their house. Nobody would look at them and say, in that uniquely urban way: *Look at those fuckwits. Let's cross the road to get away from those fuckwits.*

We argued, then Sarah posted the letter and we went back to bed. The candle had burned down to a stub.

I was the first to wake. It was Saturday morning, just after seven. I got out of bed and went to inspect the doormat. It was bare. I returned to our bedroom.

'Anything?'

I shook my head. 'She's probably not up yet.' What time did she get up, then, and how much time would elapse between her getting up and writing a reply? We speculated, trading lengths of time. I said: 'A few hours.' Sarah said: 'Not that long.' Then she revised it to: 'Or maybe longer.'

I took sane control. (The phrase had come to me in the night.) We had nothing to do other than stay indoors and wait for Catherine's letter. We had to stay indoors because Mel and her

192

family were coming to Catherine's cottage for the weekend. When they'd been to the cottage previously, we couldn't come out for fear of Mel ingratiating herself with us, thereby upsetting Catherine. That fear was redundant now. Mel had indeed ingratiated herself, by offering Sarah thousands and thousands of pounds. Mel had rights now. It was no use talking about professional distance. She'd bought the right to knock on our door, come in, meet Sarah's husband, drink wine and see what changes we'd made to her father's rental cottage. Worse, she'd bought the right to tell her sister Catherine how lovely we were and how bright Sarah was. She would boast about her new discovery, Sarah – Catherine's old discovery. Of course she'd boast. And Catherine couldn't say Mel was boasting just to hurt Catherine, though of course Mel would know she was hurting Catherine. In praising Sarah, Mel was praising herself for her own good judgement.

We had to leave our cottage before Mel came and not come back till she'd gone.

The Maison House Hotel, so named because it was run by a French chef and his English wife, was in Norfolk, ten miles from Sandringham. But you didn't go to the Maison to go anywhere else. It was a retreat, not a base. Hattie and Charles, who'd booked in for the weekend, insisted we join them there. (Hattie, to be accurate, insisted on their behalf. Charles didn't lower himself to that kind of insisting.)

Charles was exhausted, having just completed a TV series on the Future or Not of the Planet. He loved the Maison. He loved the food and the house and the snooker room (though he never used it). He loved the walks and the maze and the stream and the fact that he wasn't bothered by members of the public. (Or children, not even his own daughter, billeted with Hattie's parents. The Maison exuded a child-unfriendly air.)

Hattie was my wife's oldest friend. She cared about Sarah and wanted to make sure she had a soothing weekend. But the Maison, for us, was not soothing. It was a hotel that wasn't patronised by the public, those crass Charles-botherers, but their financial and social superiors, the private. Vanessa, *la patronne*, the English wife, told us when we arrived that we were very lucky there'd been a late cancellation, as they only had eight rooms and were fully booked till the end of the year. We were giving this woman an excessive amount of money and she was telling us we were 'lucky'. No shopkeeper selling you string or parsnips – good, cheap, public things – tells you you're 'lucky'. You're not 'lucky' to be giving them your money. They're lucky to be getting it. There are other shops, other parsnips. You could, if you so desired, not buy any parsnips at all.

The glamorous and unstoppable Vanessa, to compound my tension, had something of the Renate, transposed to the body and shameless soul of an English ex-model in her sixties. On the walls of the Maison foyer, where you'd expect to locate watercolours of Sandringham, paintings of Lord Nelson, ancient maps of Norfolk, were black-and-white photos of Vanessa, taken by the holy surnamed trinity of Bailey, Donovan and Duffy. Vanessa, circa 1966, in a crocheted minidress in Carnaby Street and, circa 1970, in a maxidress, somewhere on the seashore.

'The legs are the last thing to go,' she told Hattie, at the coffee stage of our dinner, when she joined us at our table and showed us the legs. Use them, I thought. Stand. Fuck off.

'You better bring us our bill,' said Charles and now, of course, I felt sick at the prospect of Vanessa's departure.

'This is on us,' said Hattie. Sarah tapped my knee twice, telling me not to worry, we'd be all right, she'd known all along this would happen, we only had to pay for our room. I thanked Hattie – not Charles, you couldn't thank Charles, he made a face like a puppet.

And what a dinner it was! Vanessa's husband Jean-Marie was a poet, which is to say his greatest triumphs were on the menu not in the mouth: what you wanted to do with Jean-Marie's food was read it. A Monkfish Parcel in a Curly Kale Tomato Jus. I read this and reread it, as you do in an exam, for the dish was a question: 'A Monkfish Parcel in a Curly Kale Tomato Jus. Discuss.' Oh yes. I can answer this one. I can fill six sides of paper, because it's one of those questions that spawns other questions, and I can answer those too. For example, how does 'A Monkfish Parcel' differ from 'Monkfish Parcel'? If there's 'A Monkfish Parcel', is there 'The Monkfish Parcel'? Is a Monkfish Parcel a parcel of monkfish or is it a parcel sent by monkfish, as an airmail letter is a letter sent by airmail? No. Is 'Curly Kale Tomato' 'Curly Kale and Tomato' with the 'and' removed in the cooking? Yes. That's the chef's art. A chef removes the 'and's. From disparates, chefs make wholes. I missed my friend Sam Davey, with his sneering gift, that artist's gift for holding the menu and seeing yourself holding the menu and wondering what you were doing there, with these people and this menu. When Sam Davey and I drank our four-hundred-pound bottles of wine, with John Smith's prize money, we did it to mock him, him and prizes and money. I was not at the Maison in a spirit of mockery. This was who I was – a husband sitting with his pregnant wife and her best friend and her very important husband in the Maison House, to escape his own home, which could not, in any event, have accommodated the best friend and her husband, because he was not a sofa bed kind of guy. They would stay when we added a third bedroom. Everything would be different then.

I ordered the Chilled Tiger Prawns in Garlic Aoili with Marinated Cucumber Shreds. A bottle of champagne appeared, courtesy of Vanessa, to congratulate Charles on his series, as no champagne would ever appear when my Crackling and Lard book entered, singly, dying bookshops.

'The series! Sarah and Richard's baby!' toasted Hattie.

Two pairs of Tiger Prawns faced each other across the white space of my plate's central reservation. Each pair was like a twinned crescent moon. The left pair formed two C-shapes; the right, two reversed C-shapes. Jean-Marie's Prawns were no longer words. His words were made flesh. No, not flesh, but graphic design. I looked and I looked and this is what I saw: on the left of my plate, there were open inverted commas; on the right, there were closed. Jean-Marie had created two pairs of prawn quotation marks. I wanted to write, between them, in Cucumber Shreds: *Merde!* But there weren't, of course, enough shreds. Only members of the public confuse cucumber-shred quantity with cucumber-shred value.

I drank. I felt better. I felt like a visitor. The Maison, after all, was a retreat for visitors to the country, as opposed to those like Sarah and me, who lived in retreat. Charles and Hattie would take their breath of fresh air, expel it, then return, restored, to the smoke.

They discussed when Charles might go to Brazil, as the president had invited him for informal talks, something of which Charles didn't seem capable. I'd spent most of Saturday in his unspeaking presence, while the women went off to be massaged and hydrotherapised and otherwise made to smell relaxed. I'd sat next to him, inside the Maison and out, in the Lounge and in the Walled Garden, him silently reading papers, me silently (if reluctantly) reading the papers, for there was a simple distinction between those two monkfish parcels: papers were written by academics for academics, while the papers were written by journalists for the public.

I coaxed the last of my cucumber shreds through a jus drop. I felt champagne in my nostrils. Enough. Enough freedom from stress. We'd come to escape our problems. Now it was time to get back to them. There was no escaping them anyway. We could not escape our own heads.

'So what do you think? The sister problem,' I said, looking at Charles. Hattie was embarrassed, Sarah was worried, Charles was surprised. He hadn't expected me to speak to him. He'd regarded me as little more than a man-shaped hole at his table, but now I'd asked him a question, he expected to be able to answer it, brilliantly, with absolute authority, as he always did, usually into a microphone, while his face was filmed and his words were recorded, onto digital tape or humble paper, by fingers writing shorthand.

'What do I think about the sister problem?' he said, giving himself time. It was a problem, I could tell, of which he hadn't heard. I saw him spooling through his brain for references, in papers, summits and presidential addresses, to the sister problem we all faced, which, if we didn't listen to Charles, might destroy us all. Touchingly, he grasped for a definition.

'You mean, the number of female babies born to Third World mothers?'

'No,' I said. I felt privileged. Few got to say no to Charles; and fewer heard him bullshit in the manner of a first-year student. You wouldn't call the number of female babies born to Third World mothers a 'sister problem'. You'd call it a 'daughter problem'. Did it even exist, this problematic number of female babies born to Third World mothers?

I had the advantage over Charles, which Hattie couldn't allow: I knew what I was talking about and he didn't. She intervened. She briefed him, with the aid of Sarah: our friendship with Catherine, her loathing of her sister, Sarah's unwitting acceptance of the sister's offer. He concentrated, ferociously. He was as unembarrassed by 'gastropub' as a professor of biology would be unembarrassed by a stool. He listened to the evidence. And then he pronounced.

'You can't impose conditions on a friendship,' he said. 'The first party can't make the friendship dependent on the attitude of the second party to a third. Friends aren't like nation states, which tend to say, as it were: "If you want to be my friend, you must hate the United States. And Israel." Friendship isn't politics or diplomacy. It transcends them. In other words, this woman

Catherine can't say to Sarah, "If you want to be my friend, you mustn't be the friend of my sister," any more than she can say, "If you want to be my friend, you have to be the friend of my sister." Such a friendship is unsustainable. It has to be terminated. Thank you.'

Now he looked embarrassed. He tried to hide it by raising a glass to his lips. But I saw his blushing cheeks. He hadn't meant to say 'thank you'. That's what he said at the end of a press conference, not a dinner-table conversation with the friends of his wife.

'No,' I said. 'Thank *you*.'

There were no delays on our journey home that Sunday evening, no dual carriageways reduced to single lanes, no breakdowns, no crashes, no lines of cones. We were hoping for delays but there were none. Now we were nearly home and it was only six thirty, too early to be sure that Mel and her family had left Catherine's cottage for their journey home.

I motored down The Lane, in first gear, at cow pace, till we saw there were two cars outside her cottage. Mel and her husband evidently drove an Audi.

'Nobody must know we're back,' said Sarah.

I drove past our cottage, still in first, and parked with quiet dignity some fifty yards beyond it. All we had to do was walk back unobtrusively to our front door and hope no one next door heard us unlock it. This we achieved, or thought we did: how could we be certain they didn't know we were back, short of knocking and asking them?

I closed our front door, softly. Sarah, who'd entered before me, stood next to me on the doormat. The doormat was unchanged. It was still devoid of a letter.

Sarah didn't move. She had a sort of nervous paralysis. She told me she couldn't do it: she couldn't park fifty yards away and carry her baby home, hoping it wouldn't cry and alert the people next door to her presence. I pointed out, without much confidence, that she'd only have to do that when 'the people next door' were Catherine and Mel. Usually, it would just be Catherine. Catherine was her friend. She'd only just written a letter to Catherine, saying that. What, she asked, if she was with her friend Catherine, walking the baby in its buggy, and her mobile rang, and it was Mel? I said, with no confidence now, that Mel's number would come up on the screen and Sarah would know not to answer.

We went into our kitchen. Alarmingly, she found a pen and paper. 'We'll have to write to her again. Charles is right. We have to end it.'

'You can't end it with a letter. She'll reply.'

'But she hasn't replied to my first letter.'

'Exactly! If you write another one, we'll be waiting for *two* replies. And then they'll come. And then we'll reply to her replies.'

'What do you suggest, then?'

I suggested we went round and told her. We'd wait till Mel and her family left and we knew Catherine was on her own. Then we'd end the friendship as we'd begun it, by going round and knocking on her door. As I said all this, I played with Sarah's gardening gloves, which were on the sideboard. When Sarah agreed that, yes, we should go round there, I laid the gloves on top of each other, crossed, like hands on an old lady's lap.

Then we heard voices. Two female ones. A male one. Two child ones. Then angry sounds, female remonstration. When the female voices got angry, I overrode them with *Best of Ethiopia*, loud. I prepared the scrambled eggs on toast, stewed apple and custard that I craved now Sarah was pregnant. I wanted mush, bland mush, food that evoked a soft landing, a custard birth, a skinless warm custard birth, a baby you licked as you lifted it out of the yellow. We ate it all, in a hurry, then we turned the music off. Shortly after that, we heard a car depart.

I took Sarah's hand and led her out of the kitchen and back towards our front door. The taking of the hand was forced and unnatural, making us feel we were off to our own execution. There was a letter on the doormat.

'Sarah & Richard' said the envelope. The ampersand was extravagantly tall. It looked like Catherine in profile, sitting on the beach, hugging her knees, before reluctantly entering the sea with Dad.

I picked up the letter. I knew, from experience, that we were about to be bested. Events concerning Catherine were never in our control. It was foolish to pretend they were.

'What if she says she's ending our friendship? How will we feel about that?' I asked.

Sarah snatched the envelope from me, then punished it further by tearing off the top right-hand corner, violating the hole with her thumb and then ripping out the contents which – surprisingly – she handed back to me, expecting me to read them out loud. I didn't do that. I don't read letters, out loud or to myself. I mean, I don't start at the top on the left with the 'Dear' then criss-cross and descend without stopping till I get to the name, any more than, when I look at a painting, I start at the top and work my way down to the bottom. I scan a letter for the stuff that draws the eye – the word or word-clusters that elate or intrigue or depress or repel. I saw 'wonderful', 'Rome', 'everything', then Sarah took it from me.

She thanked us both for our 'thoughtful and wonderful' letter, which was touching, since the letter referred to me but had been written and signed by Sarah. She was going to Italy for a few days, to get away from everything. Would we go in and water her plants? The key was under the pot of chives.

We opened our door. There was the pot. We looked at the stretch of lane in front of our cottages. Both cars, in fact, had gone: Mel and Gordon's as well as Catherine's. (We must have missed the first car leaving. The music must have drowned that out.)

We were light-headed. We didn't have to terminate our friendship with Catherine. She wasn't there. We'd been let off. We'd celebrate immediately, by going round and watering her plants.

'Where do we start?' I asked, deferring to the one of us who knew about plants.

'Catherine's bedroom.'

We went upstairs. Neither of us had ever seen her bedroom.

'Wow!' said Sarah. The bedroom was beautiful and museum-immaculate. *This is just how she left it*: that's what the tour guide would say, before attributing the painting above her bed, of a yellow bird – one of his favourite subjects – to *the famous Scots painter Craigie Aitchison*. I loved Aitchison's work. The man could do colours. (This is the kind of thing you can think, if you're a graduate in history of art and have worked, however briefly, as an illustrator. You know it all. You can therefore afford to be basic, which people aspiring to prove themselves cannot.) What was it about the bird? Was it the singularity? I'd been in enough bedrooms to know – this is vain now, this is arrogant, but it's a fact – I'd been in enough bedrooms to know that the painting a single woman has above her bed is of something with which she identifies.

On the table by the front window was the orchid we had bought her. I fiddled with its leaves, teasing and straightening them, like some botanical hairdresser.

'Well, I suppose I better get some water,' I said. Sarah moved to the window overlooking the garden, just as Catherine had done, and the coincidence made me think of the rear view of

Catherine at that window, the buttocks and the back and the shoulder blades – the rear view which, of course, I hadn't seen. Then I got name blindness, but in a new form. Now it was word blindness. I forgot the word for the thing you water plants with. I reckoned if I pictured it, the word would come. The water-thing had a body like a small squat bin, with a big-eared handle on one side and an arch-shaped handle over the top. There was a hole in the top in the shape of a D, into which you put the water. On the opposite side from the big-eared handle was a long spout, like an elongated snout, a stout spout sticking out at an angle of fifty or sixty degrees. At the end of the stout snout spout was a perforated head, in the shape of a big mince pie, out of which, when you angled the water-thing, little streams of water would jet with a 'whee!'. Where had I heard that sound before? Oh yes, that was the sound of Stone's office chair, as he sent it reeling backwards from his desk to his radiator; and the sound I'd make, in our new extension, when I held the baby up in the air.

'Slut!' said Sarah. She was rarely mischievous. But now she was goblinesque with the stuff. On the floor, by her foot, was a cream-coloured, silky-looking bra. Sarah picked it up and hung it over the back of the chair by the bed. She picked up the evidence of Catherine's body and moved it. I told her to put it back exactly where she'd found it – we were here to water the plants, we weren't here to alter things. This only made her more mischievous.

'It's beautiful. Feel it.' She took it off the chair and brought it to me. I refused.

'Don't tell me you don't think she's got a lovely body. It was the first thing I noticed.'

I said nothing. I couldn't tell from her tone if Sarah thought Catherine our enemy or our friend, her enemy or her friend. At one on Saturday morning, she'd been writing to her, saying how much she valued her friendship and beauty and bone structure; at six thirty this evening, she'd decided their friendship had to end; and now, a few moments ago, she'd read Catherine's description of her as 'thoughtful and wonderful'. I massaged the bra strap, between thumb and forefinger, in the hope that, by doing so, I'd recall the name of the water-thing.

'She thinks you're weaker than you look and I'm harder.'

'Right,' I said, with caution. In what sense was I 'weaker'? I was, it turned out, weaker in the sense that I had a 'weakness' for women.

'She thinks you want the voucher. You know? You don't want to be unfaithful but you want other women to give you the voucher. Which you can exchange for sex with them. But you don't want to exchange it. You just want the voucher.'

My wife was provoking me. So I let myself be provoked. I told her the story of Catherine at the window, which delighted her, especially her (off-screen) cameo, phoning Catherine and thereby ensuring that she moved away from the window. She laughed and was euphoric and now it was open season in our friend's or enemy's or neighbour's bedroom; rummaging through various drawers, Sarah found an eyeliner pencil and a flyer for the Worth Farmers' Market, which was blank on the back, then sat me on the bed and told me to draw Catherine's body. But I didn't draw Catherine's body, any more than Aitchison painted a yellow bird. He painted what he thought about that bird, just as, when I drew an O-shape on that flyer, I wasn't drawing Catherine's right breast but the hold that Catherine had over us. I was drawing the thing that couldn't be drawn.

Sarah sat next to me and put her arm round me. I was excited. I wanted to draw a likeness, at speed, but in my haste I'd made a mark of which I was unsure. Was this O I'd drawn the outline of a nipple or a breast? If a nipple, the paper was too small for me to draw both breasts – I'd only have room for one. If a breast, it was too round, too perfect, too ill-observed and too small. I needed to start again.

'I've messed it up,' I said. This wouldn't surprise Catherine, said Sarah. Catherine had told her I wasn't a great illustrator. I was perfectly competent but I wasn't original. Catherine was concerned, as Sarah's friend, that I'd never earn much money and I'd always be a drain on her. Catherine thought Sarah would prefer a man who was more ambitious and successful, and I'd prefer a woman who was wilder, which Sarah interpreted as 'less dull'.

These were Catherine's thoughts, not ours. But I didn't argue with them. We were on her bed in her cottage, where her thoughts reigned. Sarah didn't argue with them either. We held Catherine's intelligence in high esteem. Her thoughts couldn't hurt or divide us, though, accurate as they were. They brought us together, they had a galvanising effect, which I could feel, because Sarah was now stroking my left nipple with her right hand, which she'd never done before, and soon she was sitting on my belly, surfing my cock, and it was wonderful. It was the thing married sex struggles to be: it was filthy. We felt like two strangers fucking on a third stranger's bed. I banged my head backwards onto the headboard, over and over, leaving a bald head's sweat. I shut my eyes and kept them shut, and when I opened them and looked up at the ceiling, I was thrilled and surprised that the ceiling wasn't ours.

Was this the sex she owed us, for her sex with Dad? Were we drawing her in with this sex? Or were we using this sex – if you can use sex, as opposed to using a person for sex, or each other – to drive her away?

'Stop thinking about her!' said Sarah. By saying that, of course, she showed she was thinking about her too.

'I'm trying!' I said, as if you can try to not think about someone. We reconfigured ourselves. That helped. Now the sex changed its nature. It wasn't filthy and it wasn't a tribute to Catherine or a protest against her. It was a glorious celebration of the baby's contraceptive power. This was what you could do when you couldn't get pregnant because you already were. You could just rip your clothes off and jump in.

'Oh yes!' said Sarah, which she never had before. 'You come

now!' She was shouting, as if I were at the other end of a mobile phone. I loved my wife, I loved my wife, I loved my wife. Now I remembered. Now it came back to me. I wanted to shout it out as I came. So I did: 'Watering can!'

We could do it. Sarah could work for Mel and we could be friends of Catherine. It would test us but a friendship wasn't a friendship till it had been tested. This was what we concluded, in the after-glow. We cared about Catherine, which meant nothing if we didn't care about her with, and despite, her faults.

'Because of her faults,' said Sarah.

'Yes.' This was loving and mature: we loved Catherine because of her faults, which were indivisible from her virtues, as were ours. Her faults and her virtues, our virtues, our faults: these were our humanity.

'Go on then,' said Sarah, shooing me off the bed. 'It's probably in the cupboard under the kitchen sink.' She got off the bed and, naked as Catherine, stood at the window, opening it. I sauntered out of the room and down the stairs, cock-happy, to look for a watering can.

At the bottom of the stairs, I turned to walk down the corridor to her kitchen. I glanced, to my left, through the quarter-open door of the living room, a room I barely knew, since Catherine's guests were always invited to sit in the famous glass extension. We were determined that soon she'd come to our cottage and sit in ours. We'd have matching cottages with matching glass extensions. Previously, I'd thought of them as 'twinned'. But that wasn't right, that gave the wrong impression. We weren't setting out, slavishly, to create a facsimile. It was more that we wanted our cottage to be a friend of her cottage, if that was not too far-fetched.

What I saw through the living-room door was this: the legs, below the knees, and the feet. They were the legs and feet of a woman in a sitting position. She was sitting in her living room.

I moved on, a pace or two, then I turned and stood with my face and arms and torso and crotch and legs pressed nakedly against her corridor wall, so that when she came out of the living room, she'd see only my profile. Had she been there all the time? No. It wasn't possible. She'd have heard us come in. She can't have been there when we came in, because when we came in her car was gone. No, she must have come back when we were upstairs. She must have come in, very quietly – worried to find the door unlocked – heard us upstairs, loud in her attic, and realised what we were doing. Then what? Not wanting to disturb us, or be disturbed herself, she'd decided to wait in her living room. Now what? She'd heard me walk downstairs. What would she do? What did she expect *me* to do? Her letter said she'd gone to Italy, which led us to believe she wouldn't be here. Our sex in her bedroom was her fault. Let her be angry with us. I was angry with her.

Here's what I'll do, I thought: nothing. Let her sort out this situation, with her poise and her clarity and her authority and her languages and her private education and her first-class degree and her money. I'm weaker than I look and I'm an unoriginal illustrator, who belongs in a nightclub. So be it. If she's superior to me, let her walk out of that room into her corridor and exercise her superiority.

Now, face to the wall, I knew – albeit, in retrospect – that the sex was an act of hostility. She'd see it as such. What could I say? That an act of love between two people who love each other could never be an act of hostility? No. I couldn't be so pompous. We'd gone upstairs and used her bedroom for sex. How could she not see that as an act of termination, ending our friendship? We'd literally fucked her off.

Why hadn't she come out? Was she giving me time to go back upstairs and put on my clothes? Yes. She was allowing me, and granting herself, that dignity. I couldn't move though, I had reverted to that man at the end of the garden in the dark. I licked her wall.

'You OK?' This was Sarah. I didn't respond. I couldn't talk to Sarah, who was at the top of the stairs, when I hadn't talked to Catherine. But she was dressed and she was my wife and these two things gave me hope.

I put my finger to my lips and kept it there. She registered her alarm and stayed where she was. I walked up the stairs, past her and, at the top, turned right to Catherine's bathroom. She followed me inside. I shut the door and explained.

'We'll deal with it,' she said. 'It's nothing terrible. Put your clothes on.'

She wasn't afraid of the downstairs. She wouldn't be, would she? She was harder than she looked.

Dressed, I followed her down the stairs: the husband heading for difficulty, two steps behind his wife.

Sarah opened the door of the living room and said, 'Guilty!' then stopped so sharply I cannoned into her. Catherine was sitting with her torso twisted. Her face was down on the arm of the chaise longue. The hair on the crown of her head was matted with blood.

'Jesus Christ!' I shouted. I felt shock and repulsion. But more shocking than the shock or the repulsion was the speed with which those feelings passed. They were sensations, not feelings. I wanted to stick to them but I couldn't. Within seconds, I wasn't thinking what you're supposed to think when you see the corpse of someone you know. Death had shrunk her: that was my first thought. Murder's made Catherine shorter. Then I thought I wanted to do something to help Sarah, who was shaking. I wanted to show I cared about Sarah. Show whom? Show Sarah? No, I felt I was being filmed. I felt I was on camera and the director was waiting for me to do something for Sarah, as was meant to happen in the scene.

On the floor near Catherine's feet was an empty bottle of

Chassagne-Montrachet Rouge. I recognised the label. Catherine and Sarah and I had drunk Chassagne-Montrachet Rouge together. It was one of the burgundy heirlooms she'd inherited from her father's cellar. I decided to pick up the bottle, so Sarah didn't have to. Sarah had picked up that bra in Catherine's bedroom. She'd done that and now I'd do this, to share the chores.

I picked it up. Sarah shouted, 'Put it down!' I cursed myself. I knew she was right. The bedroom was only a bedroom but this living room was a murder scene, which shouldn't be altered. It should be freeze-framed.

I put the bottle back at the angle I had found it. There was a small pool of dried blood on the area of carpet I'd exposed by picking it up. It was the shape of the Isle of Wight.

I hugged Sarah to comfort her and block her view of Catherine. In doing so, of course, I turned my back to Catherine and blocked my own view too. I knew this was the right thing to do. And now, having done a wrong thing then a right thing, I wanted to say a right thing.

'Who'd do that to Catherine?' I asked. That definitely felt like the right thing to say. She was no longer a curiously shrunken corpse, but a person we knew, to whom a terrible thing had happened, which she did not deserve – which no human being deserved. The name was a recognition of her humanity, the basic and simple quality to which Sarah had referred. Just to say that name was extraordinarily potent. It cued a series of images which told the story of our friendship from the first time we'd seen her – a tall, pale woman telling her removal men, with natural command, where in her cottage they should put the chaise longue, upholstered in yellow velvet – to the sight of her dead, on that same chaise longue. I saw our first walk, our first dinner in the glass extension, I saw Catherine entering our kitchen, the night of her introduction to Dad, perfumed and lovely in her black dress, and then I got sexually excited, in a discreet way, I got a kind of mourner's stiffy, of a respectfully small scale, which made me breathe in, to distance myself from Sarah, to keep her from it. I forgave myself for it, immediately. Catherine would not mind my remembering her as she looked that night. It was what she would have wanted.

Sarah was crying. She'd been crying ever since I spoke. I wanted to cry too. So I tried. I broke it down into steps, little baby steps of noise. You made a *boo* and then a *hoo* and then you cried. But no sound came out. Why couldn't I do it?

'That's not Catherine!' shouted Sarah. 'That's Mel!'

This was far more stunning than finding Catherine dead. This was a triple jolt: the shock of Catherine coming back to life, the shock of Mel's murder and the shock to my pride. I was an illustrator. How could I claim to be an illustrator, then mis-identify an immobile body? What was I doing, thinking that murder made Catherine 'shorter'? No, it fucking didn't, you visually unaware cunt. (I'd never, in my life, called myself a cunt. But I meant it.)

Now, of course, I didn't even try to do, or think, anything appropriate and mature. I was beyond that. I felt hot with anger. I was angry at this woman Mel, for being dead. She was our designated financial saviour and now she was dead. Catherine was right, as always. It had ended in tears.

Sarah released herself from my embrace. We had to get out.

PART FIVE

PART FIVE

We walked out of Catherine's cottage. All I wanted was to keep walking. In the city, a person can walk, keep walking and soon be lost in a crowd. But I could walk one, two, three, four, five miles from The Lane and still not find a crowd in which I could become a missing person. A lone man, walking in the country, could not be missed.

Sarah shut the door of our cottage and locked it. She was locking it, I thought, to protect us against the body. I understood that. I'd have done that too. The body was more terrifying now, for the knowledge that we'd moved but it hadn't. She was protecting us against the idea of that body, in that room, as we'd left it. That was why it was fatuous of me to want to walk and keep walking. However far we went from it, the body would still be there.

My instinct, though, was to distance ourselves as much as we could. If we couldn't do it geographically, we'd do it historically. We'd go back in time. No one had seen us enter Catherine's cottage or leave it. So we hadn't done so. We would go back to the time before we went into Catherine's cottage to water the plants. We would un-live the previous hour.

Sarah didn't hear me say this or, if she did, it meant nothing to her. She gave me the phone. She was too shocked to make the call herself. She wouldn't be able to get the words out. That was the first thing I had to do: call Catherine. (Many might say the first thing was to call the police. But that's a misunderstanding of what it meant for us to live in Hay Cottage, next to Myrtle Cottage, Worth. That was a tiny world. The police lived outside it. We'd get to them later, when we'd sorted out our world, among ourselves.)

I went to find Catherine's mobile number, which was on our Useful Numbers pad, on the little round table next to the kitchen door, obscured beneath the menu for the Saxmundham Curry House. I found the number but I knew it was irrelevant. Its irrelevancy infuriated me. I tossed our phone onto the floor. Its two little batteries exploded from its base.

'She already knows!'

'Course she doesn't,' said Sarah, but I was utterly convinced of my rightness. Catherine already knew because it was Catherine who'd murdered her sister. She'd hit her over the head with a wine bottle, in a fury, because Mel had their father's love, their father's big house, a husband and two children, and now she'd grabbed the one thing Catherine had which she didn't have: Sarah. (I discounted myself.) It was no use saying we'd known Catherine for six months and Catherine wasn't a murderer. Of course she wasn't a murderer. No one was a murderer until they'd committed a murder. For ninety-nine point nine nine nine per cent of her life, she wasn't a murderer.

'I know she's not a murderer,' said Sarah.

'No you don't. Nobody knows anyone.'

Sarah thought this absurd. She accused me of talking about myself – I was in love with the idea of nobody knowing anyone, because I'd spent most of my life trying not to be known, being cool, eluding commitment, not allowing any woman to know me in case she discovered I was 'ridiculous'.

Shocked as she was, she was still able to dismantle my personality. Nothing, it seems, could stop marital criticism. It can happen after a murder or during an earthquake and it can make a person stronger, as it did here – Sarah was no longer numb now, she brimmed with energy and logic: why would Catherine murder her sister and not dispose of the body? Why would Catherine murder her sister then leave us a note asking us to go in and water her plants, thereby ensuring we'd discover the body?

'So we'd see what we'd made her do,' I replied.

She kept a dignified silence, which was a lawyer's trick, to make me think about what I said, for a long time, till I doubted it, which I duly did. Sarah was right. Catherine hadn't murdered her sister. It was a nonsensical accusation, which I'd invented out of fear. I was afraid of calling Catherine. I didn't want to tell her her sister was dead.

I got down on my knees and put the batteries back into the phone. I studied the number on the pad.

'Don't ring the curry house!' shouted Sarah. She thought I was going to ring the Saxmundham Curry House, pretending it was Catherine's mobile number, then claim her mobile was switched off. This astonished me, since that was exactly what I was intending. That was how well my wife knew me. But that was all right, that was good, I had – as she'd just said – to let myself be known.

I rang Catherine's mobile, which was switched off. She was probably on the plane.

I'd been spared. That which I'd wanted to be true had turned out to be so. I felt blessed.

'Don't say it on her voicemail,' said Sarah.

'Of course not,' I said. 'I would never do that.'

Half an hour later, we still hadn't called the police. I couldn't face them, meaning I didn't want them to see my face. I wasn't guilty, but I felt weak and overwhelmed. Did a weak and over-whelmed expression look different from a guilty one? I doubted it, especially when the face's owner had his fingerprints on the murder weapon. We could explain that, just as we could explain our presence in the cottage. But I asked myself, just as a policeman would: why did it take two of us to water the plants? One to carry the watering can and one to hold down the plants? The policeman would ask us to talk him through our *'watering'* – his sarcastic inverted commas, his cynical italics. We'd say we'd watered the plants upstairs then come down and found the body. But his dogs would say different, wouldn't they? Sniffing around Catherine's bedroom, they'd bark their 'Semen!' bark.

The more fearful I was, the more balanced Sarah became, cleaving to reason.

'Why would we want to murder her? She'd just offered me a job.'

I told her that she couldn't understand, she was a good and decent person, a law-abiding person. But I had, within me, a criminal seed. I was the son of an antiques dealer. I'd worked in advertising. 'We stole nine hundred pounds from John Smith!'

She was upset that I called Sam Davey and myself 'we'. We were the only we and we had to call the police, tell them what we'd seen and clear ourselves of any suspicion. They had to know what we'd seen and done next door. They didn't know or care what I'd done in John Smith's loft. 'They're not interested in you.' To make the point – the point already made, which was that I was drawing attention to myself, building up my part, being vain – she told me our baby wanted its father to call the police. It was an absurd and pretentious thing to say, but I didn't berate her for it.

I dialled 999.

'Fire, police or ambulance?'

I asked the woman to repeat the question, which she did. I saw the things she named. It was not as if her words had no meanings. Ambulance: big and white. Fire: bigger, red, with a ladder. But I didn't know if I wanted them. Was it stupid to wonder if a dead person needed an ambulance? What happened to the body if no ambulance came?

'Not fire,' I said. And then we heard sirens.

We walked to our gate to see the miracles: two police cars and an ambulance, summoned by the power of our thoughts.

I knew, even as we walked – because we walked with a synchronised tread, side by side down the narrow path – that we were good citizens now, with public faces.

The officers got out of their cars. Taking the initiative, I led us to the one who was a woman. As I spoke to her, her colleagues set to work, cordoning off Catherine's cottage, diminishing ours further – Catherine's cottage had the extra bedroom, the extension, and now it had a cordon. It had the attention. In the distance, I could see Margaret come out of her house.

'Good evening, officer,' I said. 'We live next door.'

'We went into the cottage,' Sarah continued. 'We found the body. We were just about to call you.'

'We have a key. You don't,' I added, 'have to break the door down.'

The officer thanked us then asked when we'd found the body. It was a straightforward question with a complicated answer.

As Sarah gave a straightforward answer – 'About an hour ago' – I overlapped her with 'Ten minutes ago.'

We gave her the key then we were driven off, in separate cars, to the station.

'Do you know Margaret?' I asked, as we went past Keith and Margaret's house. They were standing outside it. 'She owns the beauty parlour in Leiston.'

'Everyone knows Margaret,' said the policewoman. Her male colleague nodded.

'Can't make *me* beautiful,' he said. She laughed.

'Nor me,' I volunteered. 'Hard to be beautiful when you've got no hair.' I paused. 'We live here all the time.'

They didn't say anything. They weren't interested in information they hadn't sought. Nevertheless, I wanted to let them know we weren't outsiders or weekenders. We were local. We could be trusted.

I wasn't under arrest. I was a 'material witness'. I didn't know why I wasn't under arrest or who'd killed Catherine's sister, if not us, or how the police knew there was a dead body in the cottage, or whether I could graduate from material witness to suspect. All I knew was that I had to tell them exactly what Sarah told them, whatever that was – they'd interviewed her separately. My interview was therefore a test of my love, given that knowledge was love. Did I know Sarah well enough to know what she'd said?

The policewoman had a wedding ring. Her colleague had a birthmark on his right cheek, shaped like a splatted strawberry.

'Just tell us what happened, in your own words,' said the policewoman, but it was *our* own words that mattered.

'My wife and I went in to water the plants at about seven thirty. But we didn't just water the plants. We went upstairs to the bedroom and had sex on the bed. Do you have neighbours?'

The policewoman told me just to tell them what happened, in my own words, and not ask any questions. I told her that in order to tell them what happened, I had to tell them why it happened, so they'd understand. They wouldn't believe what had happened if they didn't know why it had.

'Sometimes your neighbours can have a hold on you that you have to release.' Having started, I carried on, not caring if they were interested or not, on and on, till: 'And I saw the body and then I saw this wine bottle on the floor and I picked it up. Are you married?' I knew from the ring that the woman was married but I didn't know about the man. He indicated, not for the first time, the digital recording machine, reminding me that neither of them would answer any questions but then, simply to get me to carry on, he nodded. 'Then you know,' I said. 'One of you picks things up and the other doesn't. I'm the one who doesn't. So I decided, just to help her, I'd be the one who does. It was stupid and it was wrong but it was done out of love. Then we left.'

They sprang to their feet, like filmgoers who don't want to stay for the end credits. The man turned the tape off. The woman said: 'Next time, please report a crime immediately.'

'Of course,' I said, as the woman led me to the door. 'But there'll never be a next time. I mean, you only find a body once in your life. Unless you're, I don't know, a policewoman. Are you a policewoman? Is that what you're called? A female policeman?' It seemed to me I was disintegrating. I'd never wittered, but now I couldn't stop. She didn't reply.

'Do you mind my asking, do you know who did it?'

'An arrest has been made.'

'I don't suppose you can tell me the name,' I said. She shook her head.

There was no sleep that night, only a weightless dozing. We agreed, tacitly, that either of us could talk about it any time and the other would do their best to listen. The worst of it was the detective work, which was based on ignorance and fit only for passing the time. But that was good enough. We lay there fearing the time wouldn't pass.

It must have been Mel's husband. He found the body, drove the kids away, called the police. Or he murdered her and someone else found the body, after we did.

'Maybe,' said Sarah. Trained, as a lawyer, to assume nothing, she wasn't interested in speculation. She only wanted to talk about what she knew. She'd known from the first that Catherine was obsessed with her sister Mel. All Sarah had ever done – until, that is, she'd met Mel – was agree with Catherine that her sister was a monster, instead of trying to help Catherine deal with that anger.

It was 03.29. The digits on the clock were the only source of light in the room.

She cried, this time at the callousness of anyone who could kill a mother.

At 04.55, Sarah said I was right. Catherine could have killed Mel, then put a note through our letter box inviting us to see the body, then driven off without disposing of that body. It was irrational, which murder was and murderers were. Sarah herself had a sister who had, since infancy, the power to make her feel angry and inadequate and irrational, a power she'd always chosen to exercise. Sarah could imagine killing Jane. She'd been lying there, imagining it. She'd imagined hitting her sister over the head with a wine bottle and then – which was worse – she'd imagined trying to make it all right for her sister, afterwards, so her sister couldn't say Sarah was useless and inadequate, unable to put things right, as if it were possible to reassemble a sister from her ashes. Catherine would imagine this too. She would feel she had to prove something to her sister, even in death.

'We have to do what we can for her.'

'How do you mean? Visit her in prison?'

'Yes. Once a week. At least.'

I hadn't visited anyone once a week since I'd been a schoolboy. To teach us that life was shit but we had the power to do something about it, the school made us visit an old person every Tuesday afternoon. I went with a boy called Norman Coates, who was six foot five and stupid. We did tasks in the basement flat of an old woman. I had nothing to say to Coates and I couldn't say anything to the old woman, because she was deaf, though I did do some drawings of her bone-china dogs and a sketch, based on her photographs, of a man in an RAF uniform, whom I took to be her husband.

Coates found the old woman's deafness funny. Every Tuesday afternoon, at the same time, he found it funny when she showed us a list of the tasks she wanted done. She would point to 'Clean floor' and Coates would ask, in his big friendly way, the question he always asked, because to him it was perfect and needed no change: 'Can I shit in your wank fuck bollocks?' And she'd always smile and say he could.

Sarah fell asleep. I smothered the face of the clock with a T-shirt.

I found myself in the kitchen, with no memory of my journey from our bed to the bread bin. I stood with my right hand on the bread and my left on the bread knife, unwilling to go on till I could recall an image of myself putting on my pants, brushing my teeth, or walking, via the rug and the floorboards, from our bed to the bedroom door.

'Just cut it!' Sarah shouted from the table.

'OK!' I shouted back and she didn't complain or question as I sawed the entire loaf into twelve slices, trying and failing to make the slices of equal width, a failure that made me want to cry, though still I couldn't cry. Then I asked her if she wanted toast.

'You know I don't have toast,' she said. But it was not an accusation. It was to let me know who I was, to ground me. I was the man who knew his pregnant wife did not have toast. If I knew that, I would soon know everything else.

I brought her a grapefruit and told her I blamed the country. The country did it. She knew exactly what I meant. A woman had been murdered in a cottage in a lane, on a Sunday evening, after dark, a time and a place utterly conducive to death, by one's own hand or another's. The country made murders happen. It was depressing and depressed, isolated and isolating, and it didn't provide distractions from a murderous impulse. In the city, you raised the bottle above your victim's head, the better to bring it down, then a car passed, playing hip hop distractingly loud and you were – what else? – distracted. (Possibly, you felt a murderous impulse towards the driver. That was fine, you couldn't act on that, the driver wasn't sitting beneath your bottle.) You were distracted and, just as important, your victim was too. Your victim got up to go to the window and look at the car that was making the noise. You lowered your bottle. Your victim said something banal – 'Why do they have to play their music so loud?' – which wasn't right, not for a murderous moment, which was meant to be special. The moment had passed.

She finished her grapefruit and said: 'We have to change the subject.' But I couldn't. I wanted to know if she agreed with me that it wasn't just the country that was to blame, it was Catherine's single state. Sarah tensed.

'Are you saying that a woman's more likely to be a murderer if she's single?'

I said I was.

'Where's your evidence? I find that offensive.'

I said my evidence was next door and then I told her not to try so hard to think and behave correctly; she should stop being so earnest. I set about dismantling her personality, which I'd never done, because I admired her so much for having married me and never wanted to think she was anything other than a magnificent person. (This was vanity, of course. I was telling myself I'd been chosen by a magnificent person.)

'So women go mad and murder people unless they get married.'

'I'm not saying that, I'm just saying they're more likely to. You're going to get more extreme, if you stay single. The whole point of getting married is to stop yourself going mad. It's the same for men.'

'Oh. Right. So you're less likely to murder someone now you're married to me.'

'Yes.'

'What about me? You're more likely to murder me now you're married to me.'

Moments later, she was thanking me for my attack on her and saying I should attack her more, it showed that I noticed her and understood her. And then, moments after that, we were upstairs having sex. We knew it was death-related. For every person he reaped, the Grim Reaper made two others have sex. That's how it seemed.

At 09.20 on Monday morning, we changed the subject. But the time is misleading, being a standard time, by which we were not now living. This was Day One, about thirteen hours after we'd found the body. It was 14.00 on Day One.

Sarah went to our country pine dresser and took, from below the cups on hooks, a yellow box file named Pension/Investments which sat next to her laptop. The pine dresser was 'country' but there was nothing 'country' about the box file and the laptop. Five years earlier, Mark had taken out an ISA in Sarah's name, a tax-free investment in ethical companies that cared about the environment. Mark didn't care about the environment, or claim to, but he cared about money and he cared about Sarah and believed the ISA, which he paid for, would flourish. He was right. It had doubled in value in five years. Sarah rang the number of the head office in Blackburn and arranged to cash it. Blackburn would send her a cheque, which would reach us in three days. And that was that.

Mel was gone. We had a new saviour. Mark, who'd cared about Sarah, was now, by default, caring about both of us. He owed me nothing but he was looking after me.

I gave thanks for the man's potency, even as I felt emasculated by it.

I asked what we did now. Sarah didn't know, so we did the thing you do in the country when you don't know what to do, which is go for a walk. We walked down The Lane, then along the footpath which led through the marshes. All the time we were walking, we knew we'd have to walk back.

We were two hundred yards from our cottage when we saw her sitting on our wall. That was enough. She was sitting there, without policemen, wearing dark glasses, though the sky was overcast.

Sarah ran, so I ran too, though I was worried that her running might agitate the baby. When Catherine saw us, she stood up and opened her arms wide, wide enough to encompass us both. The two of us ran into her arms, which was curious, since you might have thought she would run into ours, she being the one whose sister had been murdered.

Sarah wept into the right-hand side of her neck, from our point of view, while I just closed my eyes into the left. Then Catherine released us and asked us to forgive her for wearing the dark glasses.

We couldn't ask her to forgive us for thinking she'd murdered her sister with a blow or blows to the head from a wine bottle. Those were private thoughts. They didn't concern her.

We knew, because she'd been sitting on our wall, that she wanted to be in our cottage, not hers. So we led her inside. Did she want to eat? Could she eat? She nodded. She wanted scrambled eggs on toast. We seized on the same slice of bread, from my collection of twelve slices, and inadvertently tore it in two.

This is the story she told us: Mel and her husband Gordon and her children Phoebe and Jack arrived at her cottage at midday on Saturday. Within seconds, Mel said what a shame it was that Sarah and her husband had gone away for the weekend, since Mel had never met him (me) and was looking forward to a chance to get us (Sarah, me, Catherine, Mel, Gordon, Phoebe, Jack) together.

Catherine understood, soon as Mel said it, that we'd gone away solely to prevent this. Wasn't that right? (We agreed it was right, completely right. It was absolutely right.) She thought this was very loyal of us. We didn't want her to have to endure our being friendly to her sister in front of her. (Sarah agreed. I kept quiet. I didn't want to speak unless to answer a question.) We hadn't wanted to go away for the weekend but we'd done it. We'd put ourselves out, we'd literally put ourselves out for Catherine's sake. So she'd decided, with neighbourly symmetry, that she too would go away. She went online and booked herself on the first available cheap flight to Rome, which was not till the Sunday night. She wished it had been earlier. (I appreciated that 'cheap'. She was bereaved, yet she remembered we were worried about money, more than ever now. Out of fellow feeling, she'd booked a cheap flight, the kind we'd have booked. She didn't know that, for our getaway, we'd booked an expensive room at the Maison House.)

Saturday afternoon and night and Sunday morning and afternoon had been tense. She and Mel had got on unbearably badly. (Here, Catherine cried, briefly. By the time Sarah joined her on the sofa and took her hand, Catherine had stopped, leaving Sarah unsure if she should withdraw the hand. She kept it there.) Catherine said she didn't want to go over the arguments she'd had with her sister. We understood: the last ever arguments she'd had with her sister were about Sarah.

Catherine left her cottage to drive to the airport, shortly after we arrived home from the Maison.

'You parked further down and sneaked back home, so she wouldn't see you. Didn't you?'

Sarah nodded and looked to me to nod too.

'That's when I told Mel I was off. I said I thought it would be better if she didn't come to my cottage for a while.' Before she drove off, she put a note through our letter box, thanking us for our wonderful and thoughtful letter; a lovely little blast of Ethiopian music came through our letter-box flap.

The flight landed in Rome in the early hours of Monday morning. She was paged at the airport and asked to contact the Suffolk police. She spoke to them and then made arrangements to fly home, never having left the airport.

While Jack played football in Catherine's garden and Phoebe lay on the lawn, reading, Gordon and Mel Mason argued in the front room, as they had throughout the weekend, about the wisdom of Mel's new business venture, which Mel didn't want Gordon to have anything to do with, which was fine by Gordon, who didn't want have anything to do with it either.

Mel belittled him and said he had no business acumen. He then went down to the cellar. (Did we know Catherine's cottage had a cellar? No, we didn't know; and now, inevitably, we wanted our cottage to have a cellar too.) He came back up with a bottle of burgundy. Mel, sitting on the chaise longue, reading the papers, asked him what he was going to do with the wine. He said he was going to drink it. A further argument ensued. (That was what the police had told her: 'A further argument ensued.') Mel said she'd driven from Norfolk to Suffolk the previous day and was damned if she was going to drive home as well, so he'd better not drink that bottle. He said OK. But he refused to let go of the bottle. He walked round the room holding the bottle. She'd told him not to drink the bottle but she hadn't told him not to hold it, so he was going to carry on holding it. Then 'something snapped' and he hit her on the back of the head with the bottle. He wasn't sure he wanted to kill her. But then when he saw what he'd done, he was worried that she'd be permanently brain-damaged, so he thought it would be kinder to hit her again, which he did.

Then he shut the door of the living room. (Not so, I thought. He left it a little bit open.) He went out into the garden and told the children that they were leaving now, that their mother was upstairs having a nap as she had a headache, and she was going to spend the night there, but they weren't, and they shouldn't disturb her. Then he packed up all their stuff and led them out of the cottage.

He drove them, to their bafflement, not to their home in Norfolk but his parents' house in Leicester, where he told his mother to put them to bed. Then he drove off to the nearest police station and told the whole story to the police, informing them his wife's next of kin was Catherine and she'd be landing at Rome airport soon.

Sarah signalled to me to join them. I sat down on the other side of Catherine but didn't take her hand. Catherine slumped. Her head lolled. She was concave.

Sarah put her arm round her and kissed her gently on the cheek, like a mother. I don't mean it was an antenatal exercise. She wasn't practising comforting her child, she was expressing maternal feelings for Catherine, while I sat there with my hands on my knees. It wasn't right that Sarah should mother Catherine without my fathering her. But what would that involve?

I put my arm round Catherine, which led to my hand coming to rest on Sarah's shoulder, then I tried to kiss Catherine tenderly on the cheek. Given that tenderness was not, and never was, what I felt for her – unlike admiration, respect, wariness, pity, exasperation, resentment and a sporadic but intense craving for her voucher – I was sure that the tender kiss was fated, and so it was, for as I moved my mouth to plant the kiss on her cheek, she turned her head to rest it on Sarah's cheek and I kissed her earlobe. But I didn't allow myself to feel angry, for that would be about me, my anger, my embarrassment, all of which were unimportant. What was important was comforting Catherine. So I sat there. I was present. I hoped that was enough.

I thought of Gordon Mason, the man who'd murdered his wife

on the other side of our wall. What kind of man was Gordon? He'd hit his wife with a bottle. I'd never had a strong sense of right and wrong – that was one of the reasons I'd married Sarah, to have access to hers – but hitting your wife with a bottle, hitting anyone with a bottle, was wrong. Then he hit her again, believing it was better to kill her than let her live with the consequences of his first blow. I wasn't sure the second blow was wrong. It seemed to me that the second blow was a country blow. Keith, when we fished all night on the beach at Aldeburgh, told me he'd hit a muntjac the previous night, on the road from Snape to Orford. He'd got out of his car, looked at the muntjac, then got back in his car and driven into the muntjac again, to save it from further suffering. Then he'd put it in the back of his car, with the seat down, so that he could get it butchered for his freezer. Mel was not a muntjac, whatever a muntjac was. But the logic was similar: there was life and there was death, and you were better off dead than more dead than alive.

Gordon had murdered his wife and then what? He'd driven to Leicester. How could anyone not be awed by a man who, after killing his wife, which must affect your driving, drives his kids from Suffolk to Leicester, which was a two- or three-hour drive, surely. How did he do it? Did he drive to the end of the A14 then ask, or did they have satnav? Yes, Mel was a woman whose car would have satnav; how good it must have been to hear the satnav voice, a female telling Gordon what to do without judging or belittling him, providing him with a service, like an aural prostitute who understood and didn't complain that Leicester was the orgasm. What did he tell his kids when they asked him why he was driving them a hundred miles from their home, on a Sunday night, with school in the morning, to see their grandparents?

The thing about Gordon, as I sat on that sofa, not earning, living off the proceeds of the green ISA that my wife's ex-boyfriend had bought her, was that Gordon was a man who did what had to be done. The murder didn't have to be done. I'm referring to what came after, the series of actions he'd taken, having murdered the mother of his children, that made me think he was the kind of man I had, in some sense, to be. Gordon was a golf pro, that was all I knew about him, so I thought of what he'd done as a course. He'd completed the course, in a professional manner, never losing his focus or his discipline. And then he'd gone to the police station – the clubhouse – because that was what you did. You went to the clubhouse and you talked about what you'd done, on the course. That was the nineteenth hole, was it not? That was the end.

'What would you like us to do?' asked Sarah. It wasn't the *Is there anything we can do?* of someone who wants the answer *Nothing*.

Something simple was now revealed. Catherine wasn't just reluctant to enter her cottage but unable. She was off to spend a few days with her best friend Victoria and her husband Duncan, the brother of John Smith. (With uncharacteristic girlishness, Catherine actually called her 'my best friend Victoria', deriving strength from that. We knew we weren't her best friends; we understood that new friends can never be best. But I hoped we weren't her 'new best friends', which was a status Renate conferred on almost anyone exciting, whom she'd just met.) Could Sarah go into her cottage and get her some warmer clothes? She'd packed for a trip to Rome but now it was a trip to England. Sarah said of course, and we'd carry on watering her plants for as long as she was away. This was a coded message to me: Catherine didn't know we'd discovered the dead body, or she'd have referred to it. The police hadn't told her. Why would they? They had a confession from the man who'd discovered she was dead because he'd killed her.

'I hope you don't mind,' said Sarah, 'but when we went into

your bedroom this morning, we saw a bra on the floor, so I picked it up.' The lie – 'this morning' – was a lie only I would appreciate.

'That's so kind,' said Catherine, and then she wept again, far more copiously than before, on account, she said, of our kindness. Then, when she composed herself, she gave us Victoria and Duncan's number in Norfolk and told us she was going to arrange for some local firm to remove the carpet in her living room and sand and polish the floorboards, and would we let them in? I said she mustn't upset herself with this: we'd find the firm and we'd arrange everything.

She thanked us again and, now she was thinking of her living room, told us she was going to get her chaise longue reupholstered. What did we think? Neither of us was sure what her question meant. Did she want advice on fabrics? Was she asking us to recommend an upholsterer? (No – Catherine had known this area of the country, its artisans and craftspeople, far longer than we had.) Or was she asking if we thought it a good idea to get the chaise longue reupholstered, given it might have bloodstains?

'Because, you know,' said Catherine. 'I mean, you might like to get it reupholstered yourselves.' Seeing we were still baffled, she added: 'I mean you might like to have it.'

Catherine was offering us the chaise longue on which her sister had been murdered. We couldn't say no and we didn't want to say yes. So we said nothing.

'Sorry, no. It's not the right time to discuss it,' said Catherine. And then she was gone.

One road leads out of Worth but on that day – Day One – all roads led into it. Something had happened in Worth. Within an hour of Catherine leaving, we were wanted on television.

The news reporter who knocked on our door – her cameraman hanging back, weapon ready – smiled at me, seeking information, wanting to draw me out. She had heroic faith in her regional charm. Her job was to speak to, and for, the people of the countryside. That required a woman of regional intelligence, a woman of regional height with a regional face. She had to be ordinary and she was. You couldn't say what she looked like. I had to keep staring at her, for fear that if I looked away and looked back, I wouldn't remember who she was.

She wanted to gain access to the cottage next door but the owner was out. Did we have a number for the owner? Or a key to the cottage? All she wanted was a shot of the room in which the murder had taken place. Sarah, who was behind me, at a disrespectful distance, much as the cameraman in front of me was at a bored one, said we didn't have a key and had been instructed by the owner not to let anyone trespass on her front or back gardens. With that, Sarah, fierce in her loyalty, withdrew.

The reporter remained there, to give us both time to get over Sarah's departure, before forging a relationship of our own. We were alone now, she and I. The force that was denying me my freedom of speech had gone. I could do what I wanted now. Didn't I want to see myself on television?

'Is there any chance you could just make a comment, now we're here?'

Yes, there was a chance, now she was here, now she'd come to the place where I lived, to get the news of that place. I *was* the news of that place. Why shouldn't I be nice to this woman, after my wife had been sharp? Tomorrow, I might be sharp to someone and Sarah might be nice.

'I'd be so grateful,' said the woman, lowering her head and looking up at me, in the manner of a luscious courtesan, or a regional dog. Why not enjoy her gratitude for my niceness, while I could?

I told her, unsolicited, that I'd found the body. She was delighted. Could I describe that for her? She signalled to her cameraman, who advanced. 'We went into the cottage to water

231

the plants,' I began. (I could not, in the telling, be anything other than 'we'.) The woman nodded at me. She seemed so interested. I concluded: 'She was sitting there. Slumped on the sofa. Dead. It was terrible.' As I said it, I congratulated myself. I sounded – and was sure I looked – like a man in a murder item on the TV news. She nodded again. She seemed grateful.

As she got in the cameraman's car, the crowd that had gathered on account of her presence – a boy, two girls, a man, an old woman – dispersed, except the man. I stayed on our doorstep. I knew Sarah would be upset by what I'd done but I knew she'd understand. I was drawn to crowds. The crowd watching from The Lane and the crowd who'd watch on television.

'TV star!' shouted Keith.

Murder engenders kindness. How else to explain the presence in our cottage, at the end of Day One, of Keith and Margaret and a cake Margaret had baked? The cake was a cream sponge. Sarah thanked her but declined, so I ate two pieces. The cream was horrendous. It made me feel sick, not the taste of it but the idea of it, the idea of ooze and squishiness, as if I were eating Mel's creamed brains.

We hadn't been in a room with Keith and Margaret since we'd met Catherine. Keith's outburst, which had terminated our friendship, was not forgotten – on the contrary, his presence at our kitchen table reminded us of every detail – but it was overridden by the cake and the occasion.

All Margaret wanted, in exchange for her cake, was gossip. But kindness came first. It must, she said, have been terrible for us to go next door and find the body. She felt for us, she wouldn't have wanted to do that. It must have been a shock. It wasn't what you expect, not when you go into someone's cottage to water their plants. You don't expect to find a dead body next door. On a

232

Sunday evening. That's the sort of thing that happens to other people, not you.

Margaret didn't know what she was supposed to say, nor did we know what to reply. Had we been related to the victim, she could have said she was sorry for our loss. But we hadn't lost someone. On the contrary, we'd found someone. From the discovery of a body, no phrases flowed: there was no *sorry for your find*. So Margaret asked if there was anything she could do. We liked Margaret. It would be a gesture of friendship, a reciprocal kindness, if we gave her what she wanted, which was something to do.

We told her we were looking for a local firm to remove the living-room carpet next door and sand the floorboards. Margaret said it was good of us to do that for Catherine, the first time she'd mentioned Catherine's name. She didn't really know Catherine but admired her, thought she was a woman of great style and elegance, who'd never been too friendly but – quickly qualified – had never been unfriendly. Then she turned and asked Keith who could do the carpet. Keith said: 'I can.' He said he'd do it the following day, after he'd done his round. We asked him if he was sure.

'Seen worse,' said Keith. What did he mean? What had he seen that was worse than a carpet stained with blood from the head of a murdered woman? No, he hadn't seen worse. He was expressing an attitude, was all. These things – murders, rapes, floods, earthquakes, stabbings, punches, hitting your thumb with a hammer, knocking your knee against the leg of the table – happened. They happened. Then you got on with it.

It was 19.15, the end of Day One. I apologised. I'd offered them nothing to drink. We had no drink in the house. Margaret asked Sarah if she wasn't drinking. Sarah nodded.

'You're pregnant, aren't you? I knew as soon as you turned down my sponge cake.' Sarah smiled, so glad to have a retrospective reason for turning down the cake. Margaret went over to her

233

and kissed her, then kissed me and, wanting to supply some salty and restorative post-murder humour, said, 'Well done, John Thomas!' to my crotch. We laughed, in recognition of, and thanks for, her effort.

She sent Keith home to get a bottle of Spanish cava. Keith, it was obvious, loved that – he loved Margaret, he loved Margaret telling him what to do, he loved Spanish cava, he loved that he could leave and come back, getting four or five minutes on his own.

For the next hour, Margaret and Keith made us happy. We'd missed them, though we hadn't known it. Margaret planned the life of our baby, from nought to ten, which she could do with authority, being the mother of nineteen-year-old twins who'd lived in Worth all their lives; what's more, though she was only a few years older than Sarah, Margaret was a grandmother. She knew all about childminders, day-care centres, bouncy castles, swimming pools, farm parks, paedophiles – she knew them by name and where they lived, she knew how much time they'd spent in what prison, and she recommended one of them as a painter and decorator, though you wouldn't want him to do the nursery. She told us of schools for thick kids and clever kids and rich kids. (This was the local intelligence that Catherine, not being a mother, couldn't provide.) Margaret thought that private schools were essentially schools for parents; for ten or twelve thousand pounds a year, you could drive your four-by-four into a private-school car park and get the chance to run over a rich mum, which wouldn't matter, they liked being flattened, anything to be skinny. Sarah giggled and I clapped, I actually clapped, like a seal. This was village life, we were part of it, and it was good. This was our life to come. Keith, meanwhile, was at our sink. He'd noticed that some of our glasses were cloudy and was cleaning them with water and vinegar.

I'd been Keith's friend and I could be his friend again. He hated black people because he didn't know any. I'd introduce him. He'd be fine with them, he'd do the things with them he did with anyone else, and in no time Keith would see that black people were just people that happened. I'd introduce him to all the black people I knew: there was Dad's dental nurse Sharon; there was Grace who worked in Sam Davey's gallery; there were the Two Tonys (Iwulemo and Dunn) who worked, if they hadn't left by now, at Hammond Law Stone Fisk; there was Carmel, the receptionist at the Where House; and Expensive, the mechanic who fixed Renate's cars, whose proper name I'd never learned. There. I knew six black people, or five and a half, given that Carmel was mixed race. I'd get them all together and invite them up to Worth, to meet Keith the racist and change him. It would be a nice day out.

I felt woozy with all this, uncertain how much I was mocking Keith or myself. It was the furthest I'd travelled in twenty-four hours, mentally, from next door. Then Margaret stood up, saying they must go, because we must be exhausted. We agreed. (That was what happened, wasn't it? You found a body and were exhausted.)

What cued her departure, more than our exhaustion, was the phone. The phone rang and Margaret thought, as we did, that it must be something to do with the murder. The murder was the subject to which we must return. We didn't answer the phone. We saw them out, then returned to listen to the just-left message.

Catherine was at Victoria and Duncan's house in Norfolk. She was feeling all right. She'd just seen me on the local news. She hadn't known we'd found Mel. She was so sorry. She'd talk to us about it, if we'd like that. She knew we hadn't wanted to bother her with it, which was why we hadn't told her. 'We should have told her!' said Sarah. 'I know!' I said and, as if she could hear us, Catherine said she'd prefer it if we told her everything, because she wanted to know, and was strong enough to hear it; but we weren't to ring back now as she was having an early night. Duncan's brother Angus – John Smith – was staying at the house. He sent me his love.

The message ended. We agreed that she sounded like herself. But that was one of Catherine's strengths. She could only be herself.

Moth Fraser's letter, sent before the murder, was archaeological. It might as well have been written to our ancestors and dug up. She'd invited three firms, one from Saxmundham, one from Ipswich and one from Cratfield, to tender for our work. She believed we could have our attic bedroom and ground-floor extension for less than (here she named a figure which of course we didn't believe).

'It's not going to happen, is it? You're just going to have to work here.' Sarah gestured to our kitchen table. That was where I'd work, when I had work.

'Let's try and get everything back to normal,' she said.

I went quiet, the married quiet, the screaming quiet that only your spouse can hear. What was she talking about, 'back to normal'? She'd quit her job, voluntarily, and I'd quit mine, by default. We were jobless. Was that the 'normal' to which she wanted everything back?

She told me to draw the mulberry tree in our garden. I hadn't done any drawing for weeks, which wasn't right. She, meanwhile, would go through the local directory, call every firm of solicitors within a fifty-mile radius and ask if they had any vacancies. Then Keith, a postman, already at the end of his day's work, knocked. He needed the key to Catherine's cottage. Sarah suggested I go next door with Keith and draw the mulberry tree in Catherine's garden, bought the same time as ours. Keith and I could keep each other company. Heroically, she made that sound normal: our being together, my drawing the tree, his uprooting the blood-stained carpet.

I did as she suggested. We went next door then Keith went into the living room. To keep us close, I drew the tree from a chair in the glass extension, the glass extension we'd never have. That made the drawing more time-consuming, because I struggled to draw the glass between the viewer and the object. I completed my drawing of the mulberry tree in the time it took Keith to remove the carpet and sand the floorboards. Then I helped him load the carpet into the back of his car, dead-muntjac-style. I offered to accompany him to the dump with it. But he said, no, that's fine, I should get some rest. I could tell Margaret had told him to say this.

We weren't sure how to get through Day Three, till Catherine's friend Duncan called on her behalf, to say she'd really appreciate it if we came to Mel's funeral, which was to take place on Friday. Sarah promised we'd be there.

'Right,' she said to me. 'Today we go out and get you a suit.' I was puzzled. I already had a suit. I had two suits, a cream linen and a turquoise. She told me – which was true – that I didn't have a dark suit. At funerals, men wore dark suits. I told her I couldn't afford to buy a dark suit, so I'd wear the cream linen or the turquoise, no, I'd wear the cream, because the turquoise was unfashionable but the cream (which I'd worn for our wedding) was a classic. She said I couldn't afford a dark suit but *we* could, because the cheque from Blackburn would arrive tomorrow. I told her that Blackburn was a euphemism for Mark and I refused to have a dark suit bought for me by her ex-boyfriend Mark. She found this juvenile. She said the money was hers, not her ex-boyfriend's, and that the dark suit was an investment in my future. I was thirty-seven; more and more people I knew would die. I had to be mature about it.

That's when I started walking from side to side, from sink to dresser and back again, like an inmate in a cell, maddening himself, building up the momentum to hurl himself at the door. What was I doing, going to the funeral of a woman I'd never met? I hated it when Sarah explained, too patiently, so patiently as to belittle me, that I was going to the funeral to support Catherine, not Mel. I asked her if my entire life was devoted to Catherine, and she said, yes, at this point it was. Why would it not be? Catherine's sister had been murdered. Wasn't that a reason to devote your life to a person?

'Then fuck off and marry Catherine!' I said.

She ran upstairs and slammed the door of our bedroom. A few minutes later, I went upstairs and talked to her through the door. I told her I was sorry for what I'd said but I couldn't come to the funeral anyway, suit or no suit, because I'd just called Stone in the hope of getting some illustration work for his Blue Catalogue. Friday was the only day he could do. So I had to see him Friday. She'd go to the funeral and I'd seek work. That was balanced. I told her I loved her and I kissed the door, much as I'd licked Catherine's wall.

It wasn't true that I'd called Stone. But I'd make it true. I'd call him and ask if I could see him and say that the only day I could do was Friday.

When you travel by train from the east, it's the Romford greyhound racing stadium which welcomes you to London. It doesn't matter that it's still in Essex, or that at ten in the morning there are no punters or dogs. It speaks to you of the city. The stadium is where dogs do not, as in the country, run free, chasing the finch that's alighted on the hay bale. The stadium is the doggy harbinger of the metropolitan rat race. Shortly afterwards, you go through Forest Gate, capital of London's nowhere, so ungreen and unpleasant it would be better named Garage Door. There, on an industrial estate, I found the sky-blue warehouse from which Stone ran the Blue Catalogue. I rang the buzzer and shouted my name into the grille; someone I didn't know didn't hear me, then let me in.

The Blue Catalogue was not like Hammond Law Stone Fisk, where you found yourself at first in a big and underpopulated shock-and-awe reception, beyond which were too many people. Here, the too many people came first, in an ugly office, all PCs and phones and wall charts and polystyrene cups and noise, beyond which was the big and underpopulated warehouse.

I had imagined that everyone would be dressed in blue, but not the same blue – there wouldn't be a uniform, not as such, just an insistence that everyone wore the hero colour, which would make Stone feel he was controlling his staff, at the same time as giving them freedom. I was right, which made me feel lucky. I had, whether I liked it or not, an affinity with the man. I knew how he thought.

I saw him before he saw me. He was staring into a blue plastic washing-up bowl, with creative intent, running both hands through his hair. He was a middle-aged man, ten years older than me, neither as thin nor as black and white as when I'd last seen him. His hair was grey now, though the colour looked calculated rather than natural, as if he'd dyed it from a bottle marked Gravitas. He filled his chair. Previously, his sides hadn't touched the armrests.

'Richard, hi, thanks for coming in, find yourself a chair.' His eyes, too, had changed. They had an alcoholic's devil-haunted expression. But Stone's essential quality – his transparency – was intact. *Find yourself a chair.* He was already painting an obvious picture for me: this was a world in which you found your own chair, there weren't chairs lying around waiting for you, nothing lay around here, not the people, not the chairs, everyone and everything worked, all the time, was loose, spontaneous, reactive: a chair, vacated, saw an un-chaired person and decided to give them seat.

'This is my son Casper. Richard, old friend of mine, used to work for me.' Stone glad-handed a man of about thirty, a son, I assumed, from Stone's first marriage. Casper grinned without looking away from his screen, as I walked over and took the chair next to him then returned, via two women in their twenties whose faces were already upturned, grin-ready.

'That's Daisy, that's Pol, my stepdaughters. Everyone's family here.' This was another broad stroke. Stone was telling me he'd made his workforce into a family, who pulled together and worked for each other, which would have been more impressive if they hadn't, in fact, been members of his family.

Daisy and Pol didn't look like sisters or like Stone. I supposed they were stepdaughters from different marriages, and therefore unrelated, except by a knowledge of Stone and a common desire to get a job from him.

'And this is my new wife and baby.' His baby was still inside his new wife, a great smiling vessel of a woman, with glasses of a loyal blue, who looked about nineteen months pregnant, but still wore an East Anglian Women in Business-style suit.

'Hiya, handsome. Going to kiss me or what?'

'Congratulations,' I said. I got to my feet and kissed her on both cheeks knowing, by the second cheek, who she was.

'Didn't recognise me with my tits like this, did you? I think they'll do the job.'

She was right. I hadn't recognised her, on account of the glasses and the breasts, which were near the end of their journey from sexual appendages to fruits of motherhood. But there was something else I hadn't recognised: her contentedness. She wasn't desperate any more. She'd got Stone.

'Ros and I got married in Mauritius,' said Stone, not just for the sake of the 'Mauritius', but to tell me that now she was his third wife, I should no longer think of her as Oz.

I looked at them – the grey Stone and his ballooning wife – and knew I too was a changed man.

'To what do I owe the pleasure of this visit?' asked Stone, only for his wife to correct him: 'To what do we owe the pleasure!'

'Can we go somewhere and talk?' I asked. I was nervous and anxious. But that was true to my new, changed self.

'Sure,' said Stone. 'Let's go outside.'

'I'll see you out there,' said Oz. 'Must just go for a wee.'

She went. But Stone didn't move. He told me he wanted to thank me. (I had no idea what for.) Then he thanked me for all I'd done for Ros.

'She was addicted to musicals,' he said humourlessly, with the addict's need to detect addiction in others. 'She was low. And you were there for her. Thank you.' He continued like this, for a wee's length, thanking me as if he were the God of his wife, and when she returned I thanked him for the letter he'd sent me. I said I didn't want the awards. It was enough to receive the letter.

Stone looked blank, till Oz reminded him that he'd written me a letter, apologising for all the wrongs he'd done me, which she'd typed.

'He wrote about a hundred of those letters,' she told me. 'The longest one was to me. I made him type that himself.'

'Let's go outside,' said Stone.

'So. How are you? You look shit,' said Oz, when we got outside.

She lived a hundred miles from Worth and was ignorant of the murder. She and Stone were the first people I'd spoken to, since it happened, who didn't know it had happened. I had to tell them, surely. But I didn't. Stone was addicted to drink, so he couldn't drink a drop. I was addicted to Catherine, so I couldn't say her name. I couldn't mention the body, because a sentence later I'd have to mention her. Even to say 'our neighbour', without saying her name, would be to open the Catherine bottle and put it to the lips.

'My wife has just lost her job,' I said. There, I'd said it without saying *my wife got a job with the sister of our neighbour Catherine, but she lost that job when the sister was murdered and I'm here because I'm sorry about that loss.* 'She's expecting a baby in April.'

'Fantastic!' said Oz. 'We love babies!'

'We do,' said Stone. 'It'll be my fifth.'

I knew then they'd help me. I felt I was Catherine and they were Sarah and me. Couples help people on their own.

'You know I'm an illustrator now. I think your website and your catalogue could use some of my illustrations.'

This did not go well. It had an arrogant, cool edge. That was no longer what was wanted.

'What sort of illustrations?' asked Stone. It wasn't an unreasonable or unforeseeable question. I'd had three days to prepare an answer but I had none.

'Lately, I've been drawing a lot of animals.'

'What animals are blue?'

Stone was no longer an alcoholic, thankful for his dryness, thankful for his wife, thankful to me, bizarrely, for helping his wife by having sex with her on the eighth of August, years earlier. No, this was Stone the blue fundamentalist. What animals were blue? I couldn't say that was the wrong question. It didn't matter what animals were naturally blue. If I drew a blue dog next to a blue dog bowl, that was not a blue dog but a representation of a generic dog, drawn in blue for the Blue Catalogue. It wasn't a dog but an illustration.

Oz stepped in. She was my saviour. It's the woman who is the saviour.

'He can do *my* job. I've only got another month.'

'He doesn't want your job,' said Stone. 'He lives in the country. He's an illustrator. You don't want her job, do you?

'What's your job?' I asked Oz. She told me she wrote the copy for the women's blue stuff and did some admin and dealt with the letters of complaint. She told me that Stone didn't pay her much, but she was his wife. And then Stone grew quieter, in that husbandly way, as his wife grew louder and louder, telling me what Stone planned to do, which was branch out into other catalogues – a Grey Catalogue, a Purple Catalogue – though he really only wanted to do classic colours, not ones that went in and out of fashion.

'Like turquoise,' I said, but she didn't acknowledge my interruption. Instead she added, as a tribute to our past, that as well as the copy and the admin and the letters, she sometimes gave Stone a handjob, because it improved his temper, and it was better than giving him a drink.

'You could do all that, no prob,' Oz said. 'If you want to. Are you desperate? You don't have to do the handjobs. I'll do those. Or Stoney can do them for himself.'

I was no more amused by the sexual banter than Stone because, yes, I was desperate. There was no shame in that, or was there? If there was, I ought to express it. That's what Stone did, in his AA meetings: he shared his shame.

I looked him in the eye as, when sharing your shame, you're supposed to.

'When I left Hammond Stone, you told me I was too old to do what I wanted to do. You were right.' Stone nodded, pleased to be right, though I could tell he didn't remember the conversation. 'I was self-indulgent. That was wrong. Now I have to support my wife and family so I'd like the job if you'll have me.'

'This is happening too fast,' said Stone to Oz, not feeling in control.

'I know what you're thinking,' I said. 'How much do I want this? So I'll tell you. We'll move back to London. We'll sell our cottage and come back to the smoke. Do you know anyone who wants to buy a two-bedroom cottage? It's beautiful. Very private. We've loved it. But it's over.'

Stone liked this. He liked the *it's over*. He identified with that. He'd said *it's over* to alcohol. He liked the passion and commitment and intensity. These were what I'd always lacked.

'Go on, Stoney,' said Oz. I felt like a handbag she wanted him to buy her.

'Well. My wife thinks it's a good idea.'

'Fan-fucking-tastic,' said Oz.

'I always do what my wives tell me,' he added, as if his wives had told him to be alcoholic or adulterous or run both his hands through his hair.

'Me too,' I said. We were two husbands in love, in love with our wives and each other.

'I'm sure we'll find someone for your cottage,' said Oz. 'What are the neighbours like?'

'There's no one there at the moment,' I said. Then we heard a chorus of drills: ten, twelve, twenty drills. Drills to the north, south, east and west. It seemed they were drilling every bit of London, apart from the bit where we stood. They were drilling, as always, to find wealth. They were drilling for money.

The smallness of our cottage was a shock, after the blue warehouse. I carried the bigness of London with me.

I asked Sarah to tell me about the funeral before I told her about London: 'You first!'

Catherine, she said, was magnificent. She stood at that pulpit and spoke about her sister's life and achievements, praising her energy and dynamism and all she'd given the world, especially her two children. From the awfulness and horror, what would follow was 'love'.

She said nothing she didn't mean. Sarah could tell she genuinely admired Mel's energy and dynamism. (She just didn't like the way Mel used them.) Yes, she meant what she said and everything else she omitted. She didn't, for example, say she 'loved' her sister.

After the service, everyone went back to Duncan and Victoria's house, in a village called Norton St Andrew. Her best friend Victoria was lovely, as was Duncan. She was a mosaicist and he was a second-hand book dealer, a thoughtful and modest man with a wry humour. He was also a very good pianist. After the lunch, when nobody felt like talking, he played for an hour

– nothing funereal, it was all beautifully judged. Their boys were six and eight and were lovely too, proper country kids who loved to be outdoors. Victoria and the older boy, Magnus, were members of the Norfolk Nature Trust and were involved in a local scheme to track the movement of the water voles that had just been reintroduced into the river, now the mink that ate them had been removed. I would like Magnus. I would like them all. Catherine was going to stay with them a few more days and we'd been invited to join them for Sunday lunch.

It was the voles that did it. I couldn't listen to this tale of vole-loving people, given what I had to say. Sarah asked what the matter was. I wanted her to forgive me for doing what I'd done without consulting her, so I told her everything, however tedious, from seeing the dog track to hearing the drills to the time when Oz had had sex with me while talking to her mother – I was including her, retrospectively, I was making Sarah feel she was there with me, even when, as with the phone sex, she couldn't have been there, because the incident occurred before we met. I was including her in my past, as well as our present and our future, which was scheduled to begin on the first of December, the day I started work at the Blue Catalogue.

I thought she'd be angry so I said: 'We've got weeks to sort ourselves out.' In my nervousness, I made those weeks sound like seconds.

She wasn't angry, though. She congratulated me on my initiative, though she damned me too, by pointing out it was uncharacteristic: 'Well done. That's not like you.' Then she looked sad and just sat there, resigning herself to leaving.

I had a speech ready for when she was angry, so I gave it anyway. I'd worked it out and memorised it, roughly, on the journey from Ipswich to our local station. As it might be the last time I ever did the journey, I made a point of memorising, along with my speech, the order of the stations: Westerfield, Woodbridge, Melton, Wickham Market, Saxmundham.

The theme of my speech was: we had to leave, because nothing could save us now. We couldn't live the life we wanted, in the Catherine-sized cottage we wanted, with the money we wanted. Maybe Sarah could find a job with a local law firm. Maybe I could find a job with a local advertising agency. What would be the point? We'd come here to lead a better life, not go back to our old one, at lower wages, while living next door to a murder. Catherine would come back but the murder would never go away. The third party, Mel, was dead. But her ghost would live on and curse us for ever. Our friendship with Catherine was cursed.

With Sarah sitting there silently, my speech turned into an address, which was unfortunate, because it made our cottage seem like a church and our marriage like a funeral. After I finished, all she wanted to know was whether my job involved any illustration. I told her it didn't, but that was all right, because drawing was my hobby. Catherine was right. I could never make a living at it.

Kenny Gold was Pol's dad. He'd been married to Pol's mother before Pol's mother married Stone. She was Stone's first wife and Oz was his third. The numbers were important, Oz told me, in an email which had no capital letters or punctuation. A third wife couldn't talk to a second wife, who in turn couldn't talk to a first. But a third wife could talk to a first, no problem, so Oz had called Pol's mother as soon as I left the warehouse, because Pol's mother was an interior decorator who lived in Chelsea and knew 'everyone in London'. But in this case she only needed to know her ex-husband – her first ex-husband – Kenny Gold, who now stood in our cottage, now being eleven on Saturday morning, less than twenty-four hours after Oz told me she'd think of someone for our cottage.

Kenny Gold had driven from his flat in Highgate to our cottage in Worth in what he claimed was 'one hour twenty'. He was delighted by this time, so I was too. It was in my interest to share in his delight, even though I didn't think the time was plausible without running people over. Kenny was a squat, bull-chested man, with long hair the texture and colour of thatch, which looks good on a roof but bad on the head of a man in his early sixties. I could tell that Sarah found him repellent, on account of his purpose as much as his appearance. He'd come to see if he wanted to buy our cottage. Still shocked that we were selling it, she couldn't take his looking at her mulberry tree and wondering whether he wanted it to be his.

'What sort of tree's that?' he asked. He was only making a friendly noise but his ignorance upset her so much that she told him, then made an excuse and went upstairs.

Kenny, now he was alone with me, said he could tell I wasn't a gardener. Then he asked if I was 'in the advertising game' like Stone, the man who linked us, his ex-wife's ex-husband; to speed things up, I said yes, though neither Stone nor I was still in that game. I wanted to get on to what Kenny did. I only wanted to talk about Kenny. Kenny, I learned, had been a manager, he'd managed bands, metal bands. I asked what bands he'd managed and he told me I didn't look like a metal fan. I agreed. In that case, said Kenny, I probably wouldn't have heard of the bands he'd managed, who were big in what he called 'the metal community'. But I was very keen to have heard of them, of course I was, I wanted and needed to ingratiate myself, so I decided I'd claim to have heard of one. One was a believable number of his bands for a man like me to have heard of. I asked him to tell me the names.

'Axe?' I shook my head. 'Manslaughter?' I shook my head. 'Nine of Spades?' I paused, as if deciding whether I'd heard of them or not. I felt tense now. How many bands had he managed? I didn't want to recognise the last name on his list. He'd see through that.

'Black Rose? Rat Skull?'

'I've heard of Black Rose,' I said.

'Don't lie,' said Kenny Gold, with an ego and a humourlessness that reminded me of Stone, which made sense, given that Pol's mother had been attracted to both of them.

'I'm sorry,' I said.

'Don't be,' he said. 'I hate them all. Every last ungrateful bastard.'

I asked what drew him to Suffolk. Nothing, I learned, drew him to Suffolk. He just wanted a country retreat. He'd done the marriage thing, he'd done the kids thing, he'd done the city thing, he'd done the management thing, he'd amassed enough air miles for a free trip to the moon. Now he wanted somewhere he could be on his own and write. I asked him what he wanted to write.

'Best-selling thrillers,' said Kenny. I didn't advise him to start with good-sellers, then proceed via better-sellers to best, thereby reassuring his readers that he'd struggled en route to the top. No, I said our cottage was a perfect place to write best-selling thrillers, because a murder had been committed next door.

Kenny looked alarmed. 'When?'

'Don't worry,' I said. 'It was days ago.'

Kenny blinked. He didn't understand – and I couldn't explain – how elongated a day was, when it was after a murder.

I tried to put him at his ease, by being chatty. 'Yes, it was extraordinary, my wife and I found the body, as a matter of fact. That's something you don't want to do too often. But it wasn't so bad for me, because I didn't know the body, the woman whose body it was, but it's fine now. There's no trace. And the killer confessed. Keith the postman took the carpet up,' I added, not exactly changing the subject but massaging the subject, warming it up. 'He lives a few doors down. He's very into cars, you'll like him.'

Kenny resented this *you'll like him*. He, not I, would decide whether he liked Keith. In fact, he might decide he was never coming to our cottage again, in which case he'd never even meet the man.

He asked how much we wanted. I told him to wait there. I knew not to say any more without talking to Sarah. I didn't want to make any more unilateral decisions, because Sarah, having thought about it overnight, was hurt that I hadn't called her from the blue warehouse, so we could make the leaving decision together. She believed I could only be true to myself if I did things on my own, which was damning. I'd gone against the spirit of our marriage – we were meant to be one flesh. She said we had to make a rule, from now on, that we'd make big decisions together. Had she already breached that rule by leaving me alone with Kenny? I wasn't sure I'd made any 'big decisions' while I'd been alone with Kenny. Nevertheless, when I went upstairs and shut the door behind me, I told her she shouldn't have left me alone with him. We had to deal with these things together. She agreed. So the rule evolved from *We make big decisions together* to *We deal with things together*. It was a simple, easily remembered rule, which we broke instantly. I told her that, from now on, I wanted her to deal with Kenny Gold. She agreed.

Sarah told me he was horrible and she didn't want him to live in our cottage. Then we went downstairs together and she told him, on our behalf, that the price was two hundred thousand, cash. Kenny kept his head still. Kenny's head, as you'd expect from the manager of Black Rose, Nine of Spades, Rat Skull, Manslaughter and Axe – those twenty-strong bastards or more – was a weapon. You didn't want to be near Kenny when he was using his head. He said he'd think about it.

When he called from his car, half an hour later, I put him on speaker and stood back from the phone, close to Sarah. He boomed at us, in his hands-free, open-road voice.

'When's your baby due?' (He must have heard from Pol's mother, who heard from Oz.)

Sarah stared at the phone with contempt, as if the phone were Kenny. She didn't want to tell him. I gave her hand a little squeeze, to cue her.

'April,' she said.

'Your first?'

'That's right!' I said, with an enthusiasm that could only help our cause.

'First year's the worst,' boomed Kenny. 'After that, it gets easier. You got to stop going to it when it cries. That's the trick. It cries, you don't go, it stops. Yeah? Promise?'

Sarah shook her head. She didn't want Kenny Gold's tips on managing our baby.

I shouted: 'We promise!' (You see? I was dealing with him now, despite her having agreed to be the Kenny dealer.)

'OK, listen. I like you and I like your cottage. It's the only one I'm going to look at. But the thing about it is this.'

'I'm sorry, we have to go out now,' said Sarah, releasing my hand, not interested in the thing about it. 'Quick sale. Two hundred thousand. Cash. Yes or no?'

'Fair enough,' he said, 'we don't have to be friends. Friends is good, but if that's how you like to do business, fine – I'll give you one eighty, take it or leave it. It's next door to a murder. That's twenty grand off.' He stated this as a fact which everybody knows: a murder next door takes twenty thousand pounds off the value of your house.

Sarah walked out of the cottage. I didn't know whether to follow her or stay with the voice of Kenny. He asked if we were still there. I told him we'd call him back and ran after Sarah, who'd got as far as our gate. I said I was sorry, I shouldn't have told him, that was foolish. But she wasn't angry at me so much as angry at the murder.

'That's who we are now, isn't it? We're the people who found a body next door.'

I told her it wouldn't be next door for long. We'd move away and forget it. She walked back with me into our cottage and agreed we should accept the one eighty, because it was quick and cash.

Tomorrow, at lunch, we'd tell Catherine we were selling up and leaving.

While I drove, Sarah talked. She said we could stay with Hattie and Charles, or her sister Jane, if we couldn't find a place in time. She hadn't spoken to any of them yet. She didn't want to. She felt it was private. I drove on, saying nothing. I couldn't understand what was 'private' about it. Did she mean it was a murder between a husband and a wife? Or was it private in the sense of private to East Anglia – not a murder they'd know about in London.

I took advantage of the silence to turn on the radio. A woman was presenting a programme about eighteenth-century garden designers. Within seconds, I was no longer absorbing the information, only her intelligence, her balance, her Englishness, her radio presenter-ness. Through the speakers of the car came an aural vapour, a perfume of sound. I let the perfume suffuse my brain. To describe it was no simpler than describing a wine. There was grass, obviously there was grass, what with its being a gardening programme, and then there was dignity, and toast, cricket bats, linen, strawberries, sugar tongs, parasols, library books, Western democracy, window boxes, uncles and aunts, bicycles and boredom – oh yes, there was much boredom, she was filling an hour of time, but the boredom was of the most reassuring Sunday-ish kind. And then Sarah jabbed the on/off button with her forefinger. In place of the programme, I knew, would come some kind of reckoning.

'Would you want to live in the country if we didn't live next door to Catherine?'

I turned into the lane that led to Duncan and Victoria's village.

251

A wall began and showed no sign of ending. Sarah told me to turn right at the gatehouse.

'Hello, come in, there's just me, Cats has taken everyone for a walk.' So saying, Catherine's best friend Victoria kissed Sarah, whom she'd met at the funeral, then me, either because she thought she'd met me, or because I was with Sarah, or because she kissed everyone as an expression of her warmth towards her fellow creatures, be they people or voles.

I did sort of know this Victoria, though. I knew, without knowing her, the sort of life she'd led, which wasn't hard to detect, given her clothes – soft, expensive, discreet furnishings – and the way she said *Caaaats*. She was tall and skinny with a face, in aristocratic style, somewhere between the beautiful and the bonkers. I followed her into the kitchen and predicted her past. I guessed she was a model at eighteen (it turned out to be sixteen), had lived in Paris (Los Angeles), had got herself addicted to heroin and/or booze (coke and booze) and had lived with a musician (the son of a musician, in fact, the lighting designer son of a member of the Byrds). Now she was teetotal, married to a nice man, made mosaics and looked after her kids. I understood. What she wanted from the country – mental health – was what I'd wanted, too, except she'd grown up here. She was born to country life and entitled to it. She was a Linnett, living in a cottage on the Linnett estate, a mile from the Hall where her brother Johnny, the Earl, lived with his family and their old ma.

In the kitchen, Victoria told us to help ourselves to a drink, as she had to make a salad dressing, which she did with great splashings of soya oil and cider vinegar, as if she were trying to get the lettuce leaves pissed. Sarah asked how Catherine and the children were doing. Victoria said they were doing 'wonderfully', everyone had just got on with things: Jack had made a big bonfire, Phoebe had done a thousand-piece jigsaw puzzle, she and Catherine had cooked lots of meals. It had been lovely having them all to stay. Catherine had been 'a brick' to Victoria all her life and she was glad of the chance to give something in return. She didn't feel she'd ever cared for Catherine the way Catherine had cared for her. She spoke, as Catherine had done in the church, as if the murder were an opportunity for goodness, which was humbling and inspiring but unsettling too; her veneer of goodness was too shiny, too polished.

'They're back.'

We looked out the window. Catherine was leading a line of people up the garden, which wasn't really a garden, this being an estate – it was land. Behind her were Duncan, his two sons, her niece Phoebe and nephew Jack, and Skimper the Labrador. She was leading them up the land from the stream to the house. Jack was throwing sticks for the dog to fetch, or so I thought, till I realised he was throwing sticks at the dog.

There had always been two of us and one of Catherine. (Briefly, in the Dad interlude, there'd been two of her.) Now, including the dog, she was eight. She outnumbered us and outmassed us, what with the great weight of her sister's murder and coffin and memory. We in turn were weighed down with a burden of guilt that had got no lighter in the days since we'd last seen her sitting on our wall. How could we have thought our friend was a murderer? What did that say about us?

She came into the house, kissed us both and asked us how we were. We said we were fine, which wasn't true, so I knew we'd pay for it. But what else could we have said? Her sister had just been murdered. We were fine, compared to her.

Phoebe sat on her Aunt Catherine's knee. Jack didn't eat his food but played with it hard, mashing his chicken, potato and broccoli into an edible waste-ground with the odd patch of green. Catherine told him I drew for a living: did he want me to do a drawing of

253

Skimper? It was a question expecting the answer 'yes', which Jack didn't give, but he didn't say no either. Catherine said I'd do the drawing if Jack ate his food.

'That's right,' I said. I wanted to help her.

Jack scooped a spoonful of food into his mouth. I asked for a pencil and a sheet of paper. Catherine and Sarah told me I shouldn't hurry – in my eagerness to help Catherine, it seemed I was spoiling Jack – but the dog was nicely positioned in its basket, so I left the table and sat nearby and got on with my work. Duncan, gentle and modest as advertised, brought me a glass of red wine, unsolicited, and found me an atlas on which to rest my paper. We talked, awkwardly, about my knowing his brother. (I was talking to the brother of a pseudonym, which was awkward in itself – 'John Smith' was a made-up person, but Duncan here was real.) I denied I knew John Smith well, which was a way of saying I didn't like him. I said I'd only met him through my ex-girlfriend Renate, his manager; and then, to distance myself further, I insisted I wasn't a 'serious artist' like John Smith. I relished the phrase. I was damning John Smith with (apparently) strong praise. Anyone could be 'serious'. An artist could be 'seriously' bad.

Duncan, wanting only to be nice, said Catherine had been magnificent. She'd been gracious and restrained. He didn't think he'd be that restrained if someone murdered his brother. And then the poor man rehearsed the face he'd make if someone murdered his brother. He tried to look vengeful but he couldn't do it. He was too nice. Niceness was his defence against, and gulf from, his brother. But then he couldn't bear his own niceness any longer. It was plain I didn't like his brother, which allowed him to say: 'My brother's more of a murderer than a victim.'

When the drawing was complete, an hour later, only the adults remained. Phoebe and Jack had left the table first, followed by

Duncan and Victoria's boys – as they left the room, they said to their mother, in turn: 'Love you, Mum.'

Victoria said Jack would love the drawing. Duncan thought I had a very nice 'line'.

'My pleasure,' I kept saying. 'My pleasure.'

'I told you he was good,' Catherine said to Victoria, though I knew she thought I was competent.

'He's better than he thinks he is,' said Sarah. The other two women ignored her. Catherine and Victoria had the senior friend-ship, going back to their childhood. Sarah would never call Catherine 'Cats'.

Then it happened: Victoria offered me a job. She offered me, in fact, eight jobs. Her brother Johnny, in the big house, was looking for someone to draw each of his five kids and all their three dogs as a fortieth birthday present for his wife. Could I do that? Would I do that? It would be so lovely if I did.

I could tell there was nothing spontaneous about this offer. Catherine, aware of our difficulties – though ignorant of my new job – had urged her oldest friend to help us in any way she could. This was touching. I liked being the object of Victoria and Catherine's attention. Of course I did.

'You should definitely do it,' said Sarah.

A small girl, new to me, rushed into the kitchen and buried her head in Victoria's skirt, at thigh level. Evidently, this was a previously unmentioned daughter, a beautiful little thing that had been lying around the house, somewhere, while her mother and father and brother got on with their lives. An au pair, silent, unintroduced, came no further than the doorway.

'What would you charge?' asked Victoria. (It came out as *chaaaarge*.)

This was sexy. She was treating me as a guy who knew what he charged to draw five children and three dogs. I had no idea. But I wanted the job. I'd drive up from London to do the work and charge the Earl for the petrol. No, I'd come by train, which was greener, and taxi, which was sexier. But what was I thinking? We still had a few weeks left in the country. I'd do the drawings before we moved. They'd be my earnings before I started working for Stone.

'I'd better meet the children and the dogs first,' I said. Victoria nodded, as if this was how it worked – your illustrator, like your builder, came round and judged the scale and difficulty of the work, tutting and shaking his head as he looked at the children and dogs, before he gave you a quote.

Catherine, brighter than her friend, laughed.

'You mean, you have to see how big they all are. You charge by the inch.'

'It's so wonderful to see you laugh, Cats,' said Victoria, taking the attention away from me. The little girl turned her head and studied Sarah and me.

'You're little!' she shouted at Sarah. Her mother told her not to be rude. (She could have said there was nothing wrong with being little but she didn't. Victoria was an ex-model. She knew it was wrong to be short.) Then she invited me to come over in the next few days to meet Johnny and his wife Cassie and their brood. They were, predictably, 'all lovely'.

'You three should go out for your walk,' she said to Catherine and Sarah and me. Sarah and I hadn't known till she said it that we three were due a walk.

'Grazyna will look after all the kids.' The au pair, hearing her name, smiled at us.

Catherine stood up. 'Come on. We won't let a little rain put us off.'

Sarah and I shook our heads and the three of us trooped off to the boot room. It was the first time we'd been on our own with Catherine since we'd got to the house. She gave us various pairs to try, for which we were excessively grateful, not wanting her to expend energy on us. We both tried on several pairs till we found ones that fitted or 'fitted' – Sarah's were too big, mine too small, but we couldn't keep asking for more. We didn't care about the discomfort. The discomfort was nothing compared with her bereavement. I'd say we sought some discomfort; we didn't want her to suffer alone. And so we set off into the rain with feet that didn't fit Duncan and Victoria's footwear. That's how it felt: it was our feet that were wrong.

We walked to the church, which had been built by the Linnetts in the eighteenth century for the use of the family and the estate workers. There were four churches in the diocese, Catherine told us, with one vicar looking after the needs of a congregation of two hundred or so, of whom no more than twenty attended this church. (We nodded and nodded.) Catherine had been to the service that morning. Did we think that was slovenly or hypocritical, since she wasn't a believer? Sarah said Catherine should find comfort wherever she could; and I said she was the least slovenly person I'd ever met, which was true. I had fired a truth into the air, as if shooting at a grouse. I wasn't frightened of truths, not now, convinced as I was that, after today, we wouldn't see Catherine again. Geography had brought us together and it would break us apart. We couldn't see Catherine once or twice or three times a year, when she was in London or we were in Suffolk. Our friendship was all or nothing, so it would be nothing, having been all.

Catherine, though, thought the day a beginning: our introduction to Norfolk society and my launch as a society portraitist. I couldn't be a society painter because I didn't paint, but that would be to my advantage – I would do society drawings, which were cheaper. Victoria would introduce me to her brother Johnny, who'd introduce me to other patrons. If I could draw likenesses and be amusing, I'd do well.

'You can be amusing, can't you?' asked Catherine. I wasn't sure if she was teasing or not and looked to Sarah for a cue but

I could tell she didn't know either. We were too self-conscious to risk any kind of humorous response. Catherine was a bereaved person. We didn't know if the decent interval had passed, after which humour was permitted, or whether there was any such interval.

Catherine took Sarah's arm, putting down her own umbrella and sheltering under Sarah's. Then she gestured to me and we walked with Catherine in the middle, our inner arms joined to hers, our outer arms holding two umbrellas to protect the three of us from the rain. It was tricky, given the disparity in heights – Sarah had to extend her arm like a child wanting a teacher's attention.

Catherine told us Victoria and Duncan were lovely; I told her Duncan said *she* was lovely, and so began a sort of lovely tennis, with Catherine hitting the lovely ball back at us, for all our support and friendship, and our returning it with thanks for all her loveliness in promoting me to Victoria.

And then she let go of our arms, we put down our umbrellas and we entered the church, that place of eternal shelter from the rain.

We thought we ought to walk round, making little awestruck grunts at the vaulted ceiling, the stained-glass windows, the tomb of the first Earl (which he shared with his wife, out of love, or to save money). Mercifully, Catherine told us the church was 'functional', which allowed us to cut the tour short.

There were seats, fifty or sixty of them, but how do three people in a church arrange themselves for a heart-to-heart-to-heart? I sat in the middle of the back row, but they didn't join me, so I got up again and we stood by the door, which seemed tentative. We were in God's house, in the hall.

We waited for Catherine to begin, which she did by remarking that I'd never met her sister. I agreed and apologised that I'd been

258

unable to come to her funeral. Then I paused and left a gap for the reason, which I was too ashamed to fill with the reason itself. I didn't know if Sarah had told her I had to go London for work. In any event, I wasn't going to say that or repeat it here. I knew there was no excuse for missing that funeral, short of my own death, so I gave a hearsay eulogy of Mel, based on Catherine's funeral address and Sarah's first-hand knowledge of Mel. Mel's energy, Mel's vivacity, Mel's liveliness – my eulogy turned into a thesaurus, so I shut up.

Catherine then asked if it had been all right for me to be in her cottage since the murder. I was shocked to hear her say the word. It was like hearing a cancer patient say 'cancer'. We didn't want Catherine's life to be defined by the murder, so we'd conspired with her to avoid the word, as if by not saying it we'd reduce its power.

I only wanted to tell Catherine what she wanted to hear, as long as that wasn't a lie. It was clear she wanted to hear it was all right for me to be in her cottage, which it was – I'd spent hours there, drawing, while Keith cleared up. So I told her, yes, it was all right. Then she asked Sarah whether she'd be all right there and Sarah said she didn't know, she hadn't been there since it happened, but if there was anything Catherine wanted done, of course she'd be all right to do it. The two of us would do it together.

She now digressed, or so we thought, not sure where she was heading. She understood how difficult this was for us: we'd spent too many hours hearing how much she hated Mel, so how were we supposed to feel now? Did the awfulness of Mel's death make Mel a better person? Catherine had thought hard about this and the answer was: 'No. Course not. It's a terrible thing. But it doesn't cancel her faults. Her faults live on. I'm still entitled to resent everything she did to me. The murder doesn't mean she's won. Does it?'

I didn't know what to say. Surely, the murder meant Mel had

lost. She'd been hit on the head by a wine bottle, twice, which couldn't be seen as any kind of victory. I was glad when Sarah simply said: 'Go on.'

She went on to say she now appreciated the difference between liking and loving. She hadn't liked her sister but she'd loved her, which meant she had a duty to devote herself to her sister's children. Their mother had been murdered and their father would receive a life sentence. In effect, they'd been orphaned. She'd consulted with their godparents and all had agreed with her plan: Catherine would live in her sister's house with her sister's children. They already thought of her as the closest thing to their mum, so their mum she would be. Jack was angry but he'd calm down; Phoebe, who often seemed brattish, was a lovely girl, with academic potential, who had to be encouraged to think about books not possessions. (Catherine, the so-called 'closest thing to their mum', was already positioning herself as a better influence.)

They had the rest of their lives to understand and forgive their father, a process Catherine would initiate by taking them to visit him in prison, when they (and he) were ready. (At this point, Sarah cried and I put my arm round her.)

Catherine would do everything she could to give them stability. In doing so, she'd stabilise herself too. In the time we'd known her, she'd lacked purpose. She'd indulged herself, she'd travelled, she'd had affairs with unsatisfactory men. She was going to rent out the flat in Rome, the flat she'd shared with her sister, which would now pass to Phoebe and Jack, since their father couldn't benefit from the estate of a wife he'd murdered. She'd live off the income from the flat, supplemented by jobs in Norwich teaching English as a Foreign Language.

'Mel and Gordon promised the children a dog but could never agree on the breed,' she said, referring fearlessly to the time when Mel and Gordon were Mel and Gordon, not Victim and Murderer. 'Gordon and the kids wanted a West Highland terrier but she didn't like them.'

She was proving her own point. Mel's faults lived on, in her children's doglessness, her refusal to allow her husband and children to have the dog they wanted. There we were, by the church door, instinctively siding with Gordon, that West Highland terrier-loving murderer, against his victim Mel. Yes, he murdered her. But he murdered her once, whereas she bullied and controlled him and made him unhappy ten thousand times.

'I'm going to get them a Westie and you're going to draw it.'

I waved my hand, hoping she'd understand that to mean: thank you, I'll draw the dog, for nothing. She wanted us to visit her and the children, often. We were very important to her. We were her links to her life in Worth. (This wasn't the end, then. I was wrong about that. We'd definitely see her again. It was just a question of defining that 'often'.)

'It's wonderful what you're doing,' said Sarah. 'That's a family. In a house. With a dog.' She couldn't stop herself sounding inappropriately envious. We didn't quite have a family, not yet, nor a house nor a dog. Here was Catherine, racing ahead of us, somehow acquiring all these things, albeit in a terrible way, not that the dog would care about that.

Catherine appeared sensitive to this, wanting to know how we were getting on with our plans for expanding our home. 'Moth tells me you haven't started on the building work yet.'

We shook our heads.

'There's a reason for that,' said Sarah, taking my hand. If this was meant to give me strength, it didn't. In fact, it seemed to give Catherine strength.

'You don't have to say any more,' she said. 'I understand.'

She thought we hadn't started the building work because we couldn't afford it. That had been true but it wasn't now. There was no need for building work. We were selling up and moving.

'This is what I'd like to happen.'

Sarah took her hand away, because it was sweating. *This is what I'd like to happen.* For Sarah, it was akin to hearing Mel

say: 'When I see something or someone I want, I go for it.'
There was nothing paranormal about this – Catherine wasn't
channelling the voice of her dead sister – on the contrary, it
was normal. They were sisters, so there'd be times when they'd
both sound like their father or their mother or, as here, each
other.

'I can never go in my cottage again. You understand that.'

'Of course,' said Sarah, and now she was back with me again,
putting her arm round my waist, so her palm could rest on the
fabric of my shirt, where I wouldn't register her sweat.

'I've got my sister's house now. I could sell my cottage to a
stranger, for profit, but that would be wrong. I don't want to
make a profit out of the place where my sister was murdered.
You understand that.' Once again, we understood.

'I want you two to live there. You'll have the extra bedroom,
the extension, everything you want, then the baby will come and
it won't be the place where my sister was murdered, there'll be
new life in it, which is perfect. You can move in, soon as you
like. Meanwhile you can put your cottage on the market. Whatever
you get for your cottage, you can pay me for mine.' Sarah
started to speak. I heard the smack of a consonant, then Catherine
silenced her.

'Let me finish. I know your cottage isn't worth as much as
mine. The difference is my gift to you. I'm giving you my bedroom
and my extension. That's how I see it. You wanted to have a
cottage like mine. And you will.'

As she said this, Sarah, through my shirt, found a fold of flesh
I didn't know I had, somewhere just north of my hip, and
squeezed it till it hurt. She was urging me to fight, inflicting pain
on me to make me unafraid of inflicting it on someone else. And
so I replied, without hesitation, that things had changed. I told
her about the job with Stone starting on the first of December,
the consequent move to London, the quick sale of the cottage
to an aggressive man with a bull chest called Kenny Gold, who'd

managed Axe, Manslaughter, Nine of Spades, Black Rose and Rat Skull. The names, of course, weren't relevant, except in the sense that I wanted her to believe me and details make a story true. No, the names, like much else I said, were there to delay her reply, which I feared. So I didn't stop, I just kept on talking, adding, finally, that we'd had to reduce the price by twenty thousand pounds on account of the murder next door. It was a terrible way to end, tactless and tasteless. Catherine had offered us her cottage for the price of ours, which was generous, magnanimous and noble, and here I was complaining that her sister's murder had cost us twenty thousand pounds. So I started up again, saying how grateful we were for her offer, but my gratitude was disjointed and repetitive, it had no momentum, and, worst of all, it seemed false. How could we be 'grateful' for an offer we were rejecting?

When I shut up, she didn't speak. Instead, she looked at me for a long time.

'Is that what you want to do?' she asked me, with exaggerated calm. 'Work for your old boss?'

I didn't want to tell her it wasn't what I wanted to do. She turned on Sarah.

'Don't make him do that,' she said, making it clear that Sarah controlled me, as Mel had controlled Gordon. 'Buy my cottage. Your lives will get better.'

Sarah stiffened, then she pounced, which was thrilling, because Catherine was huge, in hurt and righteousness. A cat was pouncing on a lioness.

'Don't tell us what to do with our lives. They're our lives.'

'Just accept my help.'

'We don't want your help.'

'Why not? You were happy to take my sister's.'

'That was different,' said Sarah, but I could tell she didn't know why, and even if she did, she couldn't debate it, not now. She could only attack.

'I'm not living in your bloodstained cottage to make you feel better. And I'm not going to exploit your sister's murder to get a free bedroom and conservatory.'

'It's an extension.'

'I don't care what it is!' Having shouted, she tried to compensate with a soft: 'I'm sorry. I know you mean well.'

And now Catherine out-softed her, her voice tiny, as if she'd been wounded. 'I've thought about you so much. I've cared about you and I've been generous and I find your ingratitude monstrous.'

'Do you?' said Sarah. 'Well, I find your generosity monstrous.'

It was over, in that Sarah wanted it to be over, now she'd said what she hoped was the last word. So she stormed out of the church, which wasn't easy, given the size of the door, which she wanted and needed to slam, however much effort that took.

It was Sarah's last word but not mine. I couldn't leave without saying something.

'I'm sorry,' I said.

'Don't let her ruin your life,' she said.

'I'm sorry,' I said again, then I walked out, shutting the door with delicacy.

Sarah was standing by the gravestones, with the rain falling on her. She'd forgotten her umbrella. But, having stormed out, she couldn't storm back in; nor did she ask me to go in and get it for her.

We told Duncan and Victoria we had to go. We'd left Catherine in the church. We agreed that the church was a comforting place to be. I gave them my number, so they could call me to fix a time to see those children and dogs. Then we thanked them, said goodbye to the children, and got in the car.

I drove towards the gatehouse, too fast, running over a rabbit.

As it died, it made a muffled bam-bam-bam sound, not with its mouth but its body, against the underside of the car.

'Shit, sorry,' I said, 'it came from nowhere. Shall we go back and get it? That's what Keith would do. We should have at least one roadkill meal while we're still in the country.'

I was euphoric. I thought we'd escaped. I thought I could change the subject. But a dead body, even a rabbit's, could not be a new subject.

'I had to be the cruel one,' said Sarah. 'You couldn't do it because you fancy her or worship her or something. I was too cruel. Wasn't I?'

I told her she'd been as cruel as she had to be, no more, but she thought I was saying it in order to move on, much as a husband tells his wife she looks good in that dress, not because he believes it but so they can leave the house.

We went to bed. It was the first time we'd gone to bed in Hay Cottage since she'd offered us the chance to go to bed in Myrtle Cottage, as owners, not neighbours using the bed for sex.

'We wouldn't need a removal van,' offered Sarah, but I didn't receive it as humour. By now, I knew the rhythm: we fell out with Catherine, then we fell back in, fell out, fell in, fell out, fell in; it was friendship as love affair, every end preceding a beginning, every death a rebirth; this removal-van remark was the first cuckoo of yet another spring. So I told her, in passion-killing detail, that of course we'd need a removal van. We couldn't carry this bed out of our bedroom, down the stairs, out of our door, over the wall and up the stairs of Myrtle Cottage. Sarah admitted we'd need removal men. But that wasn't the same as needing a removal van. I said there was no difference. The removal men came in a removal van.

She was silent. I knew that didn't mean I had 'won'. I kept my eyes open, in the dark, for her eventual reply.

'We couldn't live next door to Kenny Gold,' she said. That, surely, was a victory, for both of us. No, we couldn't live next door to Kenny Gold, nor introduce him – a single divorced man who worked at home, writing best-selling thrillers – to our friend Catherine. This was goodbye.

PART SIX

We looked out of the window of the twenty-ninth floor of Centre Point. It was intoxicating. Then we went through the automatic double doors into the club reception. As is traditional, there was one receptionist on the phone and another, even more delicious and even less friendly, doing a poised kind of nothing. Immediately, I did what I did when I was cool: I ignored them, letting my companion do the talking.

'We're here to see John Smith,' said Sarah.

'He's waiting for you, at the back on the left, go on through,' said the do-nothing woman, who wore glasses, as did her partner. I'd been absent from clubland for years. I'd missed the arrival of fashion glasses which flattered your cheekbones, framed your eyes and gave you a three-dimensional glow of intelligence. Glasses, which had once enhanced the world, now looked inwards and enhanced the purchaser.

'Try not to run,' said Sarah, as I led her, too fast – she was now eight months – to the back of the clubroom. But hers was a teasing remark, nothing more. She didn't want to control me, knowing what happened to controlling women, though of course I was happy to be controlled by her and had volunteered for it, by marrying her: with this ring, control me. Tonight was an exception, though. I'd insisted we accept John Smith's invitation to meet him at his club, against her wishes. She argued that he didn't like me and he didn't know her, so he must want something. I thought that an argument for accepting. I was excited to discover what he wanted.

'Richard! I hear you're back in London,' said his message, though we were merely on the edge of John Smith's London, where the people who mattered made the things that mattered happen. I was toiling in Stone's warehouse, writing about blue tea cosies, blue staplers, blue pedal-bin liners, despairing at his insistence that every item in the Blue Catalogue had to be described as 'blue'.

John Smith stood up, shook our hands, then pulled back a chair to allow Sarah to sit down, a gesture more suited to his nice brother Duncan. Then he poured champagne, saying to Sarah: 'Just a splash for you, darling, eh?' There was nothing camp about his 'darling'. It was tough and Scots.

'I hear' – he must have heard from Duncan and Victoria – 'you're giving birth next month.'

He made the giving birth sound truly gynaecological, all flesh and slime. That's what artists did, though. Even an artist like John Smith, whose work didn't make his hands dirty, was drawn to viscera and earth. I knew this because I was somehow related to Art, a remote cousin, a fraudster even, someone who claims kinship to Art so he can use the name. I'd studied history of art and, for eight months in the country, I'd been an Artist, of sorts, an illustrator of children's book: book, singular, for there'd be no more Crackling and Lard, Kinski refusing to do as the editor suggested and turn his animal detectives into meerkats, meerkats being the animals of the moment, as glasses were the accessory. Kinski, bless him and curse him, loved pigs and their porcine heritage and their piggy associations. No one, he told her, not without contempt, sat down to a Sunday roast of meerkat.

John Smith, reaching down beside his chair, told Sarah he had a present for her, at which she baulked.

'You don't know me,' she said. 'You can't give me a present.'

He said he wasn't giving her a present, he was giving her unborn baby a present. Then he handed it over and told her to open it: a baby's woollen shawl.

'That's lovely,' she said. 'Thank you.' But John Smith wasn't finished.

'Then there's this.' On the *this*, he produced from behind his chair a ceramic clockwork sheep. When he wound it up, it played 'Baa Baa Black Sheep', even though it was white.

'You've got wool and you've got sheep,' he said to Sarah, turning the presents into a conceptual work of Art.

'Take *that* home on the tube!' he said to me, with venom, indicating the sheep, which was the size and weight of a small – there's no other word for it – sheep. 'You mustn't carry it, darling.'

An hour later, having got what he wanted, from me if not from Sarah, John Smith followed me into the Gents. We stood side by side at the white bowls that were waiting to receive our urine.

'Did you and your friend take that money from my coat?'

I waited till our parallel penises were shaken and withdrawn.

'Yeah. Sorry.' I made a point of sounding not sorry.

'That's OK,' he said, 'it's a long time ago.' He extended his hand which, offensively, he'd not yet washed. I shook it.

'What did you do with my money?'

I explained that we'd gone to a restaurant and bought a meal with it. I regretted that we hadn't filmed the meal, which was an Arty thing to say – I was implying that if we'd filmed the meal, the meal and the film would have been Art.

'You should have filmed yourself eating the money,' he said, which was both an insult and a better Art idea than mine.

'Did Renate buy our presents?' I asked. The question discombobulated him. (It was a pleasure to discombobulate a discombobulator.) He couldn't lie, given that I knew what Renate did for her clients. It was Renate's genius to make her clients feel important. The time that the rest of us spent shopping: important John Smith had to spend that time on his art.

'Renate bought them,' he admitted. 'But they were my idea.'

When the baby was born, Sam Davey told us how great it was to see two people so wrong for each other so happy.

I stopped working for the Blue Catalogue soon afterwards. I was only a substitute for Stone's wife and, like Stone's first two wives, I left. Within weeks, Geoff and I were working as a copywriter/art director team again, for an advertising agency in Holborn that specialised in pharmaceutical work. It was a Happy Ending, given that the money was better, but the key word is Ending: pharmaceutical work is what people do at the end of their advertising careers, when they're getting older and slower and have no ambition, other than to keep going. We were like advertising donkeys. I didn't care. I was a father doing it for the money.

Sarah, when Bobby was weaned, got a job with an East End law firm, most of whose clients did not have English as their first language. It was badly paid, but not as badly paid as a part-time job at a homeless charity; and it was honourable.

Sarah wanted nothing to do with *Finding the Body*, which she thought offensive to Catherine and the children. Charles, a trustee of Tate Modern, where the exhibition was held, argued that John Smith's right to free expression encompassed 'the right to offend'. I argued that the exhibition, as its title suggested, didn't concern the victim's family. It told the story of those who found the body.

'That's absolutely correct,' said Charles, bestowing on my remark the highest order of correctness known to man.

Finding the Body consisted of eight black-and-white photos, blown up to the size of cinema screens. Each depicted the finding of a twenty-first-century murder victim: two in houses, one in a backyard, one in a wood, one in a river, one on a beach, one in a street and one in the living room of a Suffolk cottage. The photos were staged in studio sets, which gave them a strange and alienating artificiality. John Smith used models to play the victims and the people who found them. (By 'models', I mean people who model, not articulated people made of wood.) He based his compositions on the testimonies of people in India, Brazil, the United States, Zimbabwe, New Zealand, Russia, Spain and England. *Bodyfinders* was the term he coined. He recorded the bodyfinders' testimonies and played extracts from them on an audio loop, so when you stood in front of the Suffolk cottage murder screen, you heard me saying: 'We went in to water the plants' . . . 'I thought murder had made her shorter' . . . 'We went in to water the plants.'

Two weeks before the exhibition opened, Sam Davey sent me an email with a JPEG, which I opened at work. It was a photo, taken at Archway tube station, of a poster for *Finding the Body*: *Here's a man who looks a bit like you holding a woman who looks a bit like Sarah, so she doesn't have to look at the body on the sofa, which looks a bit like a sofa. What a load of pretentious wank. Can I come to the private view?*

I replied immediately – *Yes* – delighted to find someone to go with, since Sarah didn't want to come. When she said it was offensive to Catherine and the children, she meant it was offensive to her. John Smith's private view was tonight's entertainment. Could I not understand that this is what Mel's murder had become? (I could understand it; it just didn't upset me.) Sarah wasn't even sure I should take the baby. She thought it might corrupt him.

I wore the baby in a sling. He was my son and my accessory and I knew he made me look good. I stopped every canapé that passed, whether rectangular, triangular, circular or tubular, and gobbled it, not knowing what it was before or during or after I ate it. Then I saw the man who was the giant on-screen me in the *Murder in the Cottage* photo. I went up to him and introduced myself. Jason was a bald plasterer, registered with a model agency called Characters. He was a man of my age with five children. The last thing he said to me, as our conversation floundered, was: 'Thanks for the work.'

'My pleasure,' I said, which it was, not to find the body but to furnish a fellow father, indirectly, with the opportunity to earn a few extra pounds.

Bobby cried. I took him out of the sling, put him over my shoulder and jiggled him around; and then he felt a hand on his head, just as I'd felt two hands on my head, nine years earlier, at Sam Davey's private view. The hand that touched my head now touched his, the baby's head being almost but not quite as bald as mine.

'She's beautiful!' said Renate. 'What's her name?' I didn't argue. I denied her the knowledge. I was glad she found my son beautiful, as she'd once found me pretty.

'Bobby,' I said, which – happily – sounded like a shortening of Roberta.

'Oh, he's gorgeous,' said Ingrid, joining us.

'It's a girl, you silly bitch,' said Renate. It was clear, instantly, that she and Ingrid were a couple, but I felt none of the shrivelling a man's meant to feel when he finds his ex-girlfriend's a lesbian, because I wasn't convinced that Renate would define herself as such. She was a woman who was currently with a woman.

'Is her mother here?' she asked. 'Never mind. She looks like you. Girls always look like their daddies.' I nodded my agreement. Renate was powerful. She'd created a world in which my son was my daughter and, for as long as I was in that world, I'd enjoy it. Why not? Renate took my boy – her girl – in her arms and shouted: 'I want her!'

Ingrid explained that she and Renate were trying to adopt a

Guatemalan baby, but the process, in the borough of Hammersmith where they lived, took forever. There were endless security checks, forms to fill in, personal statements to write. They had thought they were near the end of the process, but then their social worker discovered that John Smith had moved into their house, so he too had to undergo checks, even though the baby would not be 'his'.

As she was talking, my brain was windscreen-wiping her, the better to see the blonde woman behind her, making her way to the drinks table. Ingrid, aware I was distracted, turned to talk to Renate, who was now with John Smith. I approached the blonde woman, convinced that by the time I got to her, I'd remember who she was, which I duly did: she was John Smith's sister-in-law and Catherine's best friend, Victoria.

I'd arrived at her now. It was too late to do anything other than say hello.

'Hello,' she said, offering nothing further.

I asked her if she remembered me.

'Of course,' she said. 'But I don't remember this little fellow.' I apologised that I'd never got back to her, with a view to drawing her brother's dogs and children. She blanked my apology and kept her eyes on the baby. I asked her how Catherine was. She said Catherine was fine. *Fiiine*. Then she said 'Excuse me' and moved on. Sam Davey, who'd been watching, came up to me.

'Wow,' he said. 'That woman really likes you.'

Bobby wasn't christened. I knew I was godless and Sarah wasn't sure, though she was sure there was something beyond us which gave us purpose and meaning. In any event, we decided we would teach Bobby to 'love thy neighbour as thyself'. If we taught him that, we would not have brought him up in vain. I thought about this, for a long time, on the tube train journey home from *Finding the Body*. What was meant by loving thy

275

neighbour 'as thyself'? What if you hated yourself? And what, exactly, was the geographical definition of a neighbour? How far did you have to go from your house before you got to a non-neighbour? A hundred yards? A mile? Or did your neighbours never end, the word simply denoting a fellow human being?

Had she lived a mile away, had we met her once, when our trolley hit hers at the T-junction at the top of a supermarket aisle, had we apologised profusely, lovingly even, though the fault wasn't ours: well, then we'd have succeeded in loving our neighbour. But our neighbour had a problem we could never overcome: she lived next door.

At three the next morning, we ate some beans. When the baby was born, 'beans' was code for food that took minimal effort to cook – poached, boiled, fried or scrambled eggs, mushrooms on toast, grilled tomatoes. Now it was code for 'beans'. Beans was our Dish of the Day and our Dish of the Darkest Hour because, like the baby, the beans had no concept of time; they were a midnight breakfast or a seven-in-the evening lunch. I made beans from our bean-can and cooked them in our bean-pan, over a bean-warming flame for a hundred and twenty seconds, measured by counting thus: one bean, two beans, three beans, four beans – to amuse the baby and ourselves, even though, at this point, the baby was asleep in another room – then I poured the beans onto plates and ate them with imaginary toast, because I'd forgotten to buy some bread on the way home from Tate Modern, even though the city, gloriously, had so many bread-buying outlets.

Bobby began to cry. We listened to him crying, together, on the other side of the kitchen wall. He sounded as if he were twenty feet long. He cried like a shark who didn't understand why it had to live in a flat.

'It's OK, I'll go,' I said.

'No, I'll go,' said Sarah.

'No, no, it's OK.'

'No, really, I'll go.'

'Yes, no.'

In this way, neither of us went. But that was all right. We'd resolved to let him cry till he fell asleep, all cried out. That was the next stage in his life and ours.

I picked up my plate, concealing my face, and licked off the juice, which had coagulated nicely, like bean blood.

By the time I'd finished, Bobby had stopped, so we sneaked into his bedroom. We stood over his cot and watched him sleep, illuminated by the light from the corridor through the half-open door. His fists were clenched, either side of his head, at ear level, palm-side up. I bent and sniffed his scalp, with its poppadom aroma. Despite the beans, that made me crave a Chicken Jalfrezi with Sag Aloo and Cucumber Raita from the Indian takeaway next to Whitechapel station, even though the Chicken Jalfrezi never failed to disappoint. Like a frog does, or one's knee, the Jalfrezi tasted a bit like chicken. I didn't care. I craved routine and took it where I found it. I always had the Jalfrezi, because I always had it.

We left Bobby's bedroom and headed for our own. I sat on the bed and thought about taking off my clothes. But what was the point? I'd only have to put them on again when Bobby woke up. I was dressed in a vest and boxer shorts, like a character in an American sitcom, who can't go to bed naked because of the advertisers. Outside, in the middle of the road, the drug dealer from the second-floor flat opposite our own was having a loud argument with a woman, as he did most nights. The woman varied but the argument was always the same – he'd let her down.

I crossed to the window to watch the show.

'It ain't all about you!' tonight's woman shouted, with the phenomenal lung power of a woman aggrieved. The fact that we knew he was a drug dealer, the fact that he drew attention to himself so crudely that the back of his jacket might as well have said Police Aware: all this should have made us fearful that he lived in the same street. But I simply gave thanks, as I always did. We lived in a street. Look, another street! Street upon street, a city of streets! All those months living down a country lane. Who came up with that name, 'The Lane'? No one. 'The Lane' named itself. There were no other lanes in Worth. In the beginning was The Lane. And that was it.

I looked over my shoulder. Sarah was seated on the edge of our bed, with her laptop. I perched next to her. She typed 'Myrtle Cottage Worth' into Google, to see if Catherine's cottage was for sale through an estate agent, which it wasn't. That made her sad. Had it been for sale, she said, she'd have felt some connection with Catherine, in search of which she then typed 'Ethiopian music' into YouTube and clicked on something called Paradise of Ethiopia, which then served as the soundtrack to our argument. Sarah wanted to send Catherine a CD of Amadou and Mariam, the Malian duo. She loved their music and knew Catherine would love it too. I said that probably meant Catherine owned it already, which angered her. It didn't matter whether Catherine owned it already, she could give it to a charity shop for all Sarah cared, the point was to get in touch with her. She wanted Catherine to know she was thinking of her.

'What do you want, though?'

'I told you. I want her to know I'm thinking of her.'

'Yeah. But then what?'

Sarah told me she thought Catherine would make a good godmother for Bobby, given that she had knowledge and languages and many interests and lived in the country. After all, we'd thought Bobby would be a country child.

'But he hasn't got any godparents.'

'Then we'll call her something else. Aunt. She can be his Aunt Catherine. You don't have to be related to someone to call them Aunt.'

I didn't argue with this. I didn't know where to start or where to end.

'Sorry, I'm exhausted,' said Sarah, trying to un-say all she'd just said. She shut up the Ethiopians then shut down her laptop.

'Let's get some sleep.'

Six months later, I was prone in Dad's chair, in my surgery sunglasses, looking up into his light, listening to Schumann's Fantasy in C.

He leaned over me.

'Have you heard from our mutual friend?' he asked.

He didn't want to say her name in front of his nurse. He'd had an affair with this mutual friend, before reuniting with his wife. I could tell he was proud of Catherine's place in his past.

Dad was wielding a sharp-pointed object in my mouth, so I kept my head still and my mouth open, in a silent scream.

www.vintage-books.co.uk